PENGUIN ⊕ CLASSICS

THE LUCK OF ROARING CAMP
AND OTHER WRITINGS

Bret Harte (1836–1902) was born in Albany, New York, which he left for California when he was seventeen. There he mined gold and taught school before he became a journalist and helped found (1868) and edited the *Overland Monthly*. During the late 1860s, he published a collection of his poetry, *The Lost Galleon and Other Tales* (1867), and his satirical *Condensed Novels* (1867). It was during this period that he wrote his best-remembered pieces: *The Luck of Roaring Camp*, *The Outcasts of Poker Flat*, and *Plain Language from Truthful James*. He returned to the East in 1871 and from 1878 to 1885 he served as U.S. consul in Germany and Scotland and was a favorite in European literary circles. He then settled in England.

Gary Scharnhorst is editor of *American Literary Realism* and editor in alternating years of the research annual *American Literary Scholarship*. He has held three Fulbright fellowships to Germany and at present is Professor of English at the University of New Mexico. He has published books on Mark Twain, Charlotte Perkins Gilman, W. D. Howells, Bret Harte, Horatio Alger, Jr., Nathaniel Hawthorne, and Henry David Thoreau.

THE LUCK OF ROARING CAMP
AND OTHER WRITINGS

BRET HARTE

WITH AN INTRODUCTION AND
NOTES BY GARY SCHARNHORST

PENGUIN BOOKS

PENGUIN BOOKS
Published by the Penguin Group
Penguin Putnam Inc., 375 Hudson Street,
New York, New York 10014, U.S.A.
Penguin Books Ltd, 27 Wrights Lane,
London W8 5TZ, England
Penguin Books Australia Ltd, Ringwood,
Victoria, Australia
Penguin Books Canada Ltd, 10 Alcorn Avenue,
Toronto, Ontario, Canada M4V 3B2
Penguin Books (N. Z.) Ltd, 182–190 Wairau Road,
Auckland 10, New Zealand

Penguin Books Ltd, Registered Offices:
Harmondsworth, Middlesex, England

First published in Penguin Books 2001

3 5 7 9 10 8 6 4 2

Selection and introduction copyright © Gary Scharnhorst, 2001
All rights reserved

CIP data available

Printed in the United States of America
Set in Stemple Garamond

CONTENTS

INTRODUCTION

"Though I am generally placed at the head of my breed of scribblers in this part of the country," Mark Twain wrote his family from California in January 1866, "the place properly belongs to Bret Harte." Twain later allowed that Harte, his mentor, editor, and occasional friend, had "trimmed and trained and schooled me patiently until he changed me from an awkward utterer of coarse grotesquenesses to a writer of paragraphs and chapters that have found a certain favor."[1] To be sure, Harte was not the first California author to write about the Gold Rush—"Dame Shirley" (aka Louise A.K. Smith Clappe) published *The Shirley Letters* from the mines in 1854. Nor was he the first California humorist to win a national reputation—that honor belongs to "John Phoenix" (aka John H. Derby). But with the founding of the *Overland Monthly* under Harte's editorial direction in 1868 and especially with the publication of his own stories and poems in the first five semiannual volumes of the magazine, western American literature began to come of age. "The Luck of Roaring Camp" was "the first resounding note" in the development of an indigenous western literature, as Kate Chopin remarked in 1900. "It reached across the continent and startled the Academists on the Atlantic Coast, that is to say, in Boston. They opened their eyes and ears at the sound and awoke to the fact that there might some day be a literary West."[2] Harte figuratively blazed a trail into parlors and reading rooms in the East. As Carl Van Doren declared in 1926, his "discovery that California was full of fiction made almost as much a stir as Marshall's discovery that the State was full of gold."[3] More than any other writer, Harte opened the pages of the *Atlantic Monthly* and other magazines to the contributions of such western writers as Twain, Joaquin Miller, Ina Coolbrith, Prentice Mulford, and Charles Warren Stoddard.

Harte was also one of the first important professional writers in

America, typifying what W.D. Howells later termed "the man of letters as a man of business." He changed American literary history by challenging genteel assumptions about literary production, particularly that the best writers lived in the East and that with rare exceptions they wrote for artistic rather than for commercial reasons. Lured east by the promise of literary success and a lucrative salary, Harte was arguably both the best-known and the highest-paid writer in the country in 1871–1872. His professional life over the next few years consisted largely of negotiations with literary middlemen (editors, producers, and agents) whose interests rarely coincided with his own. Unfortunately, too, his career spiraled steadily downward after he left California and wore out his welcome in the East. His revival as a writer occurred only after he hired A.P. Watt, one of the first literary agents, in England in 1884 to negotiate with publishers in his stead, and he adjusted his method of writing to meet the increased demands of the market. Harte wrote plays, poems, and dozens of stories over the final twenty years of his career, a collection of them every year between 1883 and 1902. Though his modern reputation is based almost entirely on the stories and poems he contributed to the *Overland Monthly* from 1868–1870, he mined the same profitable vein his entire life, as this representative selection of his writings may suggest.

*   *   *

Francis Brett Harte (1836–1902) was born in Albany, New York, to an improvident schoolteacher and his wife Elizabeth, a descendant of old Knickerbocker families and Revolutionary War heroes. His paternal grandfather, Bernard Hart, was an Orthodox Jew and a founder of the New York Stock Exchange, a family secret Bret Harte (as he began to sign his work in 1860) never publicly acknowledged. Harte's formal schooling ended when he was thirteen. Among his most formative influences were the novels of Charles Dickens: He was introduced to Dickens's fiction at the age of seven, or so he claimed, and read *Dombey and Son* in monthly parts in 1846. Twain once averred that Harte's "pathetics" were "imitated from Dickens,"[4] and one of his most popular poems, "Dickens in Camp," was written on the occasion of Dickens's death. "It was very hastily but very honestly written," Harte remembered. In fact, Dickens read some of Harte's early stories shortly before his death in 1870 and reportedly remarked that "Mr. Harte can do the best things."[5]

In 1853 Harte's widowed mother married an Oakland lawyer and moved to California, and Harte and his younger sister Maggie soon followed. In 1856, at the tender age of twenty, he became a schoolteacher like his father, though like Thoreau he seems never to have been a very good one. By the spring of 1857 he had surfaced in Tuolumne County, where he spent a few weeks placer mining "but met with indifferent success," as he recalled in his semiautobiographical essay "How I Went to the Mines" (1899). He lived for nearly three years around Humboldt Bay, near his sister, where he first began to write for publication in the *Humboldt Times*, the Uniontown *Northern Californian*, and the San Francisco *Golden Era*. As the acting editor of the *Northern Californian*, he outraged the local citizenry by condemning a massacre of Indians in February 1860 and barely escaped with his life back to San Francisco. Forty years later, in "Bohemian Days in San Francisco" (1900) he reminisced about his first week in the city amid the gambling saloons, waterfront warehouses, and the Spanish Quarter.

He also began his literary career in earnest. He became a typesetter for the *Golden Era*, much as Twain and Walt Whitman, among others, learned their craft at the typestick. He often contributed to the pages of the paper, and he was paid a dollar per column in addition to his salary. As Harte later remembered, "I was very young when I first began to write for the press. I learned to combine the composition of the editorial with the setting of its type" and so "to save my fingers mechanical drudgery somewhat condensed my style." His stories and sketches in the *Golden Era* soon caught the eye of Jessie Benton Frémont, wife of the Republican candidate for President in 1856, who became his patron and invited him to join her salon. "I had to insist this very shy young man should come to see me," Frémont remembered, "but soon he settled into a regular visit on Sunday, his only time of leisure, and for more than a year dined with us that day, bringing his manuscripts." Through her patronage, Harte soon met Thomas Starr King, the minister of the First Unitarian Church of San Francisco and a recent Boston émigré, best known today as the man who saved California for the Union. Through Frémont's patronage, too, Harte was awarded a series of government jobs, first with the office of the U.S. Surveyor General, then with the U.S. Marshal in San Francisco, finally as Secretary to the Superintendent of the U.S. Mint. "If I were to be cast away on a desert island," he later wrote Frémont, "I should expect a savage to come forward with a three-cornered note from you to tell me that, at your request, I had been appointed governor of the island at a salary of two thousand four hundred dollars." As a result of these government sinecures, Harte was able to devote more of his time to writing.

Both King and Frémont were instrumental in first bringing Harte to the attention of James T. Fields, the editor of the *Atlantic Monthly*. King sent a note to the editor in January 1862 recommending the manuscript of "The Legend of Monte del Diablo" by "Mr. F.B. Harte, a very bright young man who has been in literary ways for a few years" and "a particular friend of Mrs. Jessie Frémont. . . . I hope the editors will accept it if it is worthy, for I am sure there is a great deal in Harte, & an acceptance of his piece would inspirit him, & help literature on this coast where we raise bigger trees & squashes than literati & brains." Frémont also praised the story in a letter to Fields. She presumed Harte would impress him "as he does Mr. King and myself. But of that there can be no doubt for his is a fresh mind filled with unworn pictures." She hoped Fields would admire the story as much as she had, and indeed the editor accepted the tale for publication in the October 1863 issue of the *Atlantic*. It immediately preceded Thoreau's essay "Life Without Principle." The tale exhibits Harte's interest in local history and his ambivalence over Spanish and Anglo colonialism in California. However, Fields eventually wrote Frémont to discourage her from sending him more submissions from Harte's pen. "Your young friend fails to interest," he explained. "He is not piquant enough for the readers of the *Atlantic*." Not until Harte had earned his spurs in the pages of the *Overland* would Fields repent his words.

Though his "Condensed Novels," parodies of such novels as Cooper's *Leatherstocking Tales* and Dickens's *A Christmas Carol*, attracted an eastern audience in the mid-1860s, Harte had reached

an impasse in his literary career by early 1868. He earned a generous salary at the Mint—$270 a month—and directed a staff of
twelve. In contrast, he earned a paltry $10 for each article he con-
tributed to the *Californian* or the San Francisco *Evening Bulletin*.
He had also begun to resent "these spoiled and pampered San
Franciscans" and what he considered the subtle restraints on intellectual life in the West. "The curse of California," he wrote a
friend in February 1868, "has been its degrading, materialistic influences." Neither of his options—stay the course at the Mint or
quit his job, move back east, and risk failure—was very attractive.
Then he struck gold, as it were: Anton Roman, a San Francisco
publisher, decided to found a slick monthly magazine modeled on
the *Atlantic Monthly* and he asked Harte to edit it.

Harte early acquired the habit of quarreling with his publishers,
and his vexed relations with Roman and his successor John Car-
many were no exception. Harte wanted the magazine to be a
purely literary publication, while the publisher wanted it to hew
the Chamber of Commerce line, to promote "the material development of this Coast." In the end, Harte's vision of the magazine prevailed. He contributed "The Luck of Roaring Camp" to
the second issue of the magazine and the rest is literary history. As
he remembered in his essay "The Rise of the 'Short Story'"
(1899), "The Luck" reached print, despite the objections of the
printer and proofreader about its vulgarity, only after Harte insisted upon its publication as a matter of editorial prerogative. Local reviews of the tale were equivocal if not hostile—the *Alta
California* judged it merely "a pleasant little sketch"—but the tide
turned in Harte's favor when it was hailed in the East as one of the
best magazine stories of the year. In Boston, one of the sub-
editors of the *Atlantic* passed it along to James Fields, who then
wrote the anonymous author of "The Luck" to solicit "anything
he chose to write, upon his own terms."

Harte was vindicated, not only among local critics who had
panned his story, but by the editor who had spurned his contributions five years before. "I'll try to find time to send you something," he replied to Fields. "The *Overland* is still an experiment,"
and "should it fail . . . why I dare say I may be able to do more."
In fact, the experiment was a resounding success. By the end of its

first year, the magazine enjoyed total sales of about 3,000 copies per number. It sold as many copies in the eastern U.S. as in the states of California, Nevada, and Oregon combined.

The popularity of "The Luck of Roaring Camp" persuaded Harte "to follow it with other stories of a like character." All the tales he published in the *Overland* over the next two and half years were designed to appeal to eastern readers intrigued by the romance of the Gold Rush. Or as he asserted in the introduction to his collection of early tales, he wished to collect "the materials for the Iliad that is yet to be sung" about the '49ers. His next *Overland* story, "The Outcasts of Poker Flat," both evokes the pathos of the Donner Pass tragedy in the winter of 1846–47 and burlesques the myth of the hardy pioneers. Trapped by an early winter blizzard, the outcasts suffer their deaths honorably, though Harte offers no moral to their story. In his stock character of John Oakhurst, too, Harte introduced the rougish but charming gambler typified by Bret Maverick in the 1950s television series.

Briefly put, Harte's humor challenged social norms and conventional values. His gamblers may be libertines, but they are also chivalrous; his miners may be coarse, but they share their grubstakes with the poor and friendless; and his fallen women may have "easy virtue," but in their breasts beat proverbial hearts of gold. Read according to the conventions of western humor— that is, as a hoax that traps the unwary reader—"Tennessee's Partner" is a model or "paradigm text" for the way to read Harte. Though it has been vilified for its apparent sentimentality, for example, "Tennessee's Partner" is less a tale of two miners' undying affection than it is a subtle story of deceit and revenge. As William F. Conner remarks, the author "tricks his readers all the while he seems to be trying to satisfy their pious presuppositions."[6]

In fact, though he disclaimed any didactic purpose in his fiction, several of Harte's early stories parody biblical text in order to challenge narrow, parochial belief. While these stories defy overtly didactic readings, they also subvert religious orthodoxy and ridicule sham and hypocrisy. Put another way, Harte wrote such tales as "The Luck of Roaring Camp," "Miggles," and "Mr. Thompson's Prodigal" from a Unitarian or liberal Christian perspective. Though the first of these stories may seem at first blush to be a modern retelling of the Nativity with the Christ child renamed "the Luck" and the dissolute mining camp a "city of refuge" redeemed through his influence, I believe it evokes the Gospel account of the birth of Christ to make a very different point. Harte cautions the reader in the opening paragraph to beware of appearances: The "greatest scamp" in the camp "had a Raphael face." As a "dissolute, abandoned, and irreclaimable" prostitute, a "very sinful woman," Cherokee Sal is an ironic Madonna. Little Tommy Luck's father is unknown, but not because he is born of a virgin. The miners are ironic Magi whose gifts to the child include stolen silverware, a tobacco box, and a revolver. They christen the child in a "ludicrous" ceremony that is a "burlesque of the church service." Rather than an incarnation of Christ on the frontier, Tommy Luck is a false Messiah. His first name recalls the Doubting Apostle and an apocryphal gospel, and his surname evokes blind Chance. To be sure, that "golden summer" the mines "yield enormously" and in these "flush times" the "Luck was with them." The town soon launches a program of civic improvement, but to what effect? Merely that the saloon is refurbished and the men begin to bathe. The narrator concedes that tales of Tommy Luck's ability to talk with animals "rest upon the statements of prejudiced friends." Such statements are as spurious and unreliable as similar reports about Jesus recorded in the apocryphal Gospel of Thomas. In the final paragraphs, Roaring Camp washes away in a flood of biblical proportions, as though by a judgment of God. In the last sentence of the story, Kentuck clings to the "frail" body of the child who "drift[s] away into the shadowy river that flows forever to the unknown seas." These adjectives hardly suggest his martyrdom or vicarious sacrifice; on the contrary, they indicate his death is relatively insignificant. The luck of Roaring Camp is, in the end, all bad. In all, the story is a subtle parody, a nineteenth-century version of Monty Python's *The Life of Brian* that suggests the consequences of worshipping Mammon or a false god.

Similarly, "Mr. Thompson's Prodigal" inverts or reverses the parable of the prodigal son. Whereas in the parable the son repents his rebellion and returns home, the elder Thompson in Harte's story comes to the West—represented as a far country that corrupts the young and innocent—to seek his son. Whereas the father in Christ's parable rejoices in their reunion, Mr. Thompson is a religious hypocrite, fond of quoting Scripture. He finds his son (or so he thinks) but he "did not seem to be happy," mostly because "he had little love for the son he had regained." The tale ends on a pathetic note, with the true prodigal son still steeped in iniquity, and Thompson estranged "forever" from the man he had thought his son.

Harte's tale "Miggles" also takes off from a biblical source: the character of Mary Magdalene. The narrator of this story, in company with several others aboard a stagecoach, is forced by inclement weather to spend a night in the cabin where Miggles lives with an "imbecile paralytic" named Jim or James, according to legend the name of Jesus's brother, and her pet bear. (Harte also evokes the memory of the actress Lola Montez, who had performed in San Francisco in 1853 and retired to Grass Valley with her third husband and a pet bear.) Formerly the proprietor of the Polka Saloon in Marysville—that is, a brothel—Miggles sold her business when Jim fell ill and bought a ranch where she could nurse him until he died. She has atoned for her sins by a life of selfless devotion. The next morning, the narrator awakens to see the light of a full moon "baptize with a shining flood the lowly head of the woman whose hair, as in the sweet old story, bathed the feet of him she loved." Harte here makes explicit the association of Miggles with Mary Magdalene. The tale ends as the passengers, arrived at their destination, raise a toast to her: "Here's to *Miggles*—GOD BLESS HER!" "Perhaps he had," concludes the narrator. "Who knows?"

Several of Harte's other *Overland* tales are written according to the same formula. "Brown of Calaveras" revises Christ's parable of the Good Samaritan. In "The Idyl of Red Gulch" Harte compares the dissolute miner Sandy Morton to Samson and the schoolmarm Miss Mary to Delilah, though in this version Samson remains untamed and Delilah flees the vulgar and uncouth West for the genteel society of Boston. Not only does this tale foreshadow Harte's own departure for the East a few months later, but in Miss Mary he invented the stock character of the eastern schoolmarm epitomized by Molly Stark Wood in Owen Wister's *The Virginian* and Amy Kane, played by Grace Kelly, in the movie *High Noon*.

To be sure, the satirical formula Harte followed in his fiction was not universally acclaimed. It was, in fact, condemned in such religious journals as *Zion's Herald*, a Methodist weekly published in Boston, which complained that Harte "gilded vice" and "abolished moral distinctions." At the close of "The Outcasts of Poker Flat," for example, "nobody can tell" which of the women "is pure and which corrupt" and so "they are buried in the same grave," which is of course Harte's point. Moreover, the reviewer complained, Harte's "heaven is free love and good humor. Gamblers, harlots, thieves, murderers . . . are sent by him to heaven." He apparently subscribed to "Universalism and free religion." Ironically, this was precisely the brand of dogma Harte satirized in these stories. His fiction was occasionally denigrated in such prudish terms well into the next century.

Harte's poem "Plain Language from Truthful James," published in the September 1870 issue of the *Overland*, was arguably his greatest literary triumph. By any objective measure—the frequency with which it was reprinted, the number of parodies it inspired, the times it was set to music—"The Heathen Chinee," as the poem was commonly called, was one of the most popular poems ever published. Mark Twain later remembered that Harte had "written [it] for his own amusement" and "threw it aside, but being one day suddenly called upon for copy he sent that very piece in. It put a trademark on him at once."[7] Ambrose Bierce recalled that Harte had offered the poem to him for publication in the *San Francisco News-Letter*, but that he persuaded Harte it belonged in the more upscale *Overland*. In any event, the verse struck a nerve. It was an overnight sensation and made Harte a household name in the East. Twain allowed in March 1871 that he was "the most celebrated man in America to-day," "the man whose name is on every single tongue from one end of the continent to the other," and this poem "did it for him." While it was undeniably popular, however, there was (and is) no critical consensus about exactly what it *means*.

The question is not one of authorial intention. Harte clearly intended the poem to satirize anti-Chinese prejudices common among Irish day-laborers with whom Chinese immigrants competed for jobs. To the end of his life, Harte insisted he wrote it "with a satirical political purpose." Of course, what Harte intended has nothing to do with how readers actually read the poem. Like the poem of Mr. Milton Chubbuck in Harte's story "The Poet of Sierra Flat," "Some unhappy ambiguities of expression gave rise to many new readings, notes, and commentaries, which, I regret to state, were more often marked by ingenuity than delicacy of thought or expression." In fact, to many xenophobic readers, "Plain Language from Truthful James" seemed to lampoon not the Irish cardsharks but the "yellow peril." Only when read ironically does it subvert the racial stereotype. Opponents of Chinese immigration publicly recited the poem, at least once on the floor of Congress. Put another way, "The Heathen Chinee" became a culture-text that was appropriated for a variety of purposes, few of them intended by the poet.

By the close of 1870, Harte was at the height of his popularity. He was offered the editorship of *Putnam's Magazine* and the *Lakeside Monthly* in Chicago, and the editors of the *New York Tribune*, the *Galaxy*, *Scribner's*, *Harper's Weekly*, and the *Atlantic Monthly* all solicited contributions from him. He left San Francisco with his family in tow on February 2, 1871, never to return. Howells later compared his trip across the continent to "the progress of a prince" in the attention it attracted from the press, and Twain also remembered that Harte "crossed the continent through such a prodigious blaze of national interest and excitement that one might have supposed he was the Viceroy of India." The Hartes finally arrived in Boston on February 24, and after a memorable week among the literary gentry he contracted with the firm of James R. Osgood & Co. to contribute exclusively to their family of magazines for a year for a salary of $10,000, an unprecedented sum at the time. Harte wrote Ambrose Bierce that "of the commercial value of my own stuff I really had no conception whatever."

Though according to literary legend Harte's contract with Osgood & Co. led to his ruination, in fact he probably should be credited with saving the *Atlantic*. Subscriptions to the magazine had plummeted the year before, in the wake of the controversy over Harriet Beecher Stowe's essay "Lady Byron Vindicated" in the September 1869 issue. Harte was the marquee name the publisher needed to shore up subscriptions and raise advertising revenue. And, for the record, Harte fulfilled the terms of the contract by contributing more than the twelve articles it required during the year, though to be sure, these poems and stories were mostly undistinguished. For example, Henry James thought the Christmas story "How Santa Claus Came to Simpson's Bar," published three months late in the March 1872 *Atlantic*, "better than anything" in Harte's "second manner—though not quite as good as his first." This tale still proved popular among polite readers—the young hero of W.D. Howells' novel *The Minister's Charge* reads it aloud to an elderly Boston Brahmin. But to no one's surprise, except perhaps Harte's, his contract with Osgood & Co. was not renewed in the spring of 1872. Between July 1872 and June 1873, when he should have been in the prime of his career, he published exactly one story and four poems. The joke made the rounds that Harte's career had reversed the path of the sun, rising brightly in the west and setting in darkness in the east.

Barely a year after his departure from San Francisco at the height of his fame, Harte tried to salvage his fortunes by capitalizing on his celebrity and trading on his name. He was still bankable, even if he was no longer a rising literary star. He earned most of his income between 1872 and 1874 by delivering his lecture "The Argonauts of '49" by his own estimate some 150 times, from Boston and New York to Omaha in the west, Toronto in the north, and Macon, Montgomery, and Atlanta in the south. The lecture was crafted to exploit his reputation as a historian of the Gold Rush, though he often disappointed his audiences. "What the people expected in me I do not know, possibly a six-foot mountaineer, with a voice and lecture in proportion," he later admitted. "Whenever I walked out before a strange audience there was a general sense of disappointment, a gasp of astonishment that I could feel, and it always took at least fifteen minutes before they recovered from their surprise sufficiently to listen to what I had to say." Harte eventually published the lecture in German translation under the title "Aus Kaliforniens frühen Tagen" in *Deutsche Rundschau* in 1880 and as the introduction to the British edition of his collected works in 1882.

To his credit, Harte continued to protest racial discrimination in several of his writings over the years. He drew the premise for "Wan Lee, the Pagan" from personal experience. In the late 1860s he had deplored the "late riots and outrages on the Chinese," how "the youth" of San Francisco threw stones at the Chinese in the streets, and he returned to the issue in this story. Unlike "Plain Language from Truthful James," "Wan Lee" was unambiguous in its condemnation of violence and race hatred. Similarly, in his topical poem "That Ebrew Jew," Harte alluded to a recent, blatant act of anti-Semitism: In June 1877, the New York banker Joseph Seligman (1819–1880) and his family were refused accommodations at the Grand Union Hotel in Saratoga Springs, New York, by Judge Henry Hilton, who distinguished in the press between respectable "Hebrews" and rapacious "Jews." Seligman belonged, Hilton asserted, "to a class not of Hebrews, but Jews" in the "trade sense of the word."[8] Harte, who had occasionally stayed at the Grand Union, realized that were his Jewish heritage known he would have been liable to the same discriminatory treatment. As the poet asks: "Now, how shall we know? Prophet, tell us, pray do, / Where the line of the Hebrew fades into the Jew?" Harte did not afterwards collect this poem, it was so topical; but like "Wan Lee" it exhibits his sympathy for the victims of racial prejudice.

As the result of his profligate ways, Harte was broke and, with his family, living hand-to-mouth during the winter of 1877–78. *Ah Sin,* a play on which he collaborated with Mark Twain, had been a critical and financial disaster and led to the end of their friendship. Desperately Harte sold a jingle, a parody of Longfellow's "Excelsior," to the Sapolio soap company for fifty dollars. The New York *World* noted at the time that "it is an open question as to what improvement in Mr. Harte's style would be wrought by his reduction to a state of abject penury; but the experiment of ruining him is worth trying." He begged William Waldorf Astor for a job to no avail. To the end of his life he remembered that hardscrabble winter. "I could not, and *would not under any circumstances,* again go through what I did in New York the last two years and particularly the last winter I passed there," he later wrote. Finally, in April 1878, he was appointed U.S. Consul to the small commercial town of Crefeld, Germany. After a free fall of many months, he at last landed on his feet. On June 27, from his hotel room in Heidelberg, Twain fumed in a letter to Howells that "Harte is a liar, a thief, a swindler, a snob, a sot, a sponge, a coward, a Jeremy Diddler. . . . To send this nasty creature to puke upon the American name in a foreign land is too much." The same day Harte sailed for Europe, never to return to the U.S.

The next several years were a fallow period in Harte's literary career. He remained in Crefeld for two years before the State Department transferred him to Glasgow, where he served as U.S. Consul until 1885. He sent his family $200 to $250 a month, his consular salary, and largely lived on the income from a few western potboilers and German and French translation rights to his earlier works. As his popularity in the U.S. waned, in fact, his sales in Europe steadily grew, and Harte, ever attuned to the nuances of the market, adjusted his style accordingly. Whereas in 1879 he admitted that "I grind out the old tunes on the old organ and gather up the coppers," over the years he revised his formula by pandering to European readers' ideas about "the Wild West" and experimenting with more sensational plots punctuated by violence and more transgressive sexuality. The strategy worked. In 1884, the year Harte hired the pioneering literary agent, A.P. Watt, to market his writings, the British publisher Andrew Chatto ranked him fourth, after Ouida, Charles Reade, and Mark Twain, among the most popular writers in his stable; and the next year Lewis Rosenthal reported in the *Critic* that Harte "is of all living Americans the best known and most read" in Germany. As late as 1914 his books had appeared in more German editions than had Twain's.[9] By the early 1890s, moreover, he annually earned from all sources more than the $10,000 he had been paid by Osgood & Co. in 1871–72—as much as $16,000 per year by one contemporary estimate.[10] He also increased his literary productivity so that by 1889–90, for example, he published twelve stories totaling some 230,000 words.

Though he has often been hailed as one of the first American literary realists, Harte always depicted the West through a soft lens and in muted light. His ideal tale, as he explains in "The Rise of the 'Short Story,'" was "concise and condensed, yet suggestive. It was delightfully extravagant—or a miracle of understatement. It voiced not only the dialect, but the habits of a people or locality. It gave a new interest to slang" and it "was often irreverent." Over time, his skill at rendering western local color ebbed; after all, he was a writer who normally set his stories in the American West but who had left the region in 1871 and never returned. That is, his fiction became increasingly *less* realistic toward the end of his career. Like Buffalo Bill Cody, he reinforced a popular if sensational

mythology about the American West. To compensate for his fading memories, Harte constructed a fictional California with a romantic past that appealed to his middlebrow European audience.
Little wonder that Wallace Stegner once joked that his popularity
"was always greatest in direct proportion to the reader's distance
from and ignorance of the mines."

As his friend Henry Adams noted in his *Education,* moreover,
Harte insisted on the "power of sex" in his late stories "as far as
the magazines would let him venture." While such early tales as
"The Luck of Roaring Camp" and "Miggles" skirted all direct
mention of sexuality, "The Pupil of Chestnut Ridge" eroticizes the
figure of an eleven-year-old *mestiza* named Concepcion or "Concha." (The Spanish nickname suggests the sexually symbolic
conch shell.) Her teacher broods upon "the precocious maturity
of the mixed races" and recalls having seen "brides of twelve and
mothers of fourteen among the native villagers." Though Harte
ostensibly satirized anti-Hispanic prejudices, he compromised the
satire, even referring twice to Concha's "languid indifference" to
study, which is a trait allegedly specific "to her race." The teacher's
worst fears are realized one day when he spies Concha in the
woods at the center of a circle of children as she dances "that most
extravagant feat of the fandango—the audacious sembicuaca" with
its seductive moves. The tale ends abruptly when Concha elopes
with a vaquero. Her white adoptive mother explains that she "was
a grown woman—accordin' to these folks' ways and ages." Rather
than offer a solution to the prejudice against mixed-bloods, Harte
surrenders to pessimism and to the belief that heredity is destiny.
If the children in Harte's *Overland* stories, such as little Tommy
Luck, seem impressionable to the imprint of Nature, the girls
in his late fiction, like Concha, seem fated to become "fallen
women." Whereas he wrote his early fiction in the "Dickensian
mode," his later fiction betrays the influence of Émile Zola and
Thomas Hardy and anticipates the naturalism of Stephen Crane
and Theodore Dreiser. Little wonder that such editors as Robert
Underwood Johnson and Richard Watson Gilder of *Century* re-
peatedly cautioned Harte to consider "very carefully the limitations under which a writer [must labor] who contributes to a
family magazine" and to omit whatever would "too greatly 'shock
the properties.' "

Harte sometimes still injected a political subtext into his writing. For example, in his poem "Free Silver at Angel's," narrated by Truthful James and again featuring Ah Sin, he ridiculed the advocates of bimetallism and the silver plank in the 1896 Democratic Party platform. He forcefully denounced the doctrine of Manifest Destiny and the policy of racial extermination in the overtly anti-imperialist satire "Three Vagabonds of Trinidad," written in oblique response to the Spanish-American and Boer Wars. Set in a fictional settlement whose name Harte apparently selected for its Caribbean associations, the story illustrates how the presumption of racial superiority and race hatred preached by the xenophobic town father Parkin Skinner abetted American and British imperialism at the close of the turn of the last century. Though the citizens of Trinidad little "dream of Expansion and Empire," Skinner (whose surname suggests his racist ideology) declares that "this is a white man's country" and the "nigger of every description . . . hez to clar off of God's footstool when the Anglo-Saxon get started! . . . It's our manifest destiny to clar them out." Infected by this virulent strain of racism, his young son becomes a "little white tyrant" who brutalizes his Chinese and Indian playmates. Ironically, Harte expressed surprise in 1901 that Mark Twain had shifted or drifted into political commentary. "He's a very nervous man—a man of strong prejudices—but he is sincere."[11] It was his final public comment about Twain. Ironically, the two old antagonists shared similar doubts about imperialist policies.

Not that they ever reconciled. Their earliest dispute, which Harte dramatized in "The Iliad of Sandy Bar" in 1869, had ended amicably. This story recounts the bitter and "inexplicable" quarrel of two former partners, Matthew Scott (Harte) and Henry York (Twain). Even though their common claim seems played out and worthless, it becomes the bone of their contention. After York returns from a trip abroad, much as Twain returned from his tour of Europe and the Holy Land aboard the *Quaker City* in 1867, the two antagonists finally patch up their differences. The rupture in their relations in 1878, however, was permanent. Harte again touched on their feud in his late story "An Ingénue of the Sierras," which alludes to an embarrassing episode in Twain's career. In December 1870, soon after the publication of "Plain Language from Truthful James," a dialect poem in transparent imitation of Harte's style entitled "Three Aces" appeared in the *Buffalo Express,* co-owned at the time by Twain, over the signature "Carl Byng." Twain denied its authorship, though it was widely attributed to him, and Harte believed the poet was Twain, too. Years later, in any event, he encoded the incident in "An Ingénue." The high-wayman Ramon Martinez (the surname contains six letters—Mar*t**in—in the same sequence that they appear in "Mark Twain") poses as a bill collector named Charley (or Charles, the English equivalent of Carl) Byng. That is, Harte rips Twain in this tale as a thief and impostor whose reign of terror is "about played out." Twain's recent potboilers *Merry Tales* and *The American Claimant* were commercial failures and he was sliding into bankruptcy. Although Margaret Duckett contended that their feud was largely one-sided, with Twain heaping both private and public scorn on Harte, it seems Harte reciprocated Twain's abuse, though he expressed it more subtly.

Harte continued to write literally to the end of his life. After his health began to fail in 1899, he tried desperately to provide a nest egg for his family. He published twenty-seven stories and earned about $17,000 during the two years preceding his death. As late as February 1902, he accepted a commission from a British newspaper syndicate for three stories of 5,000 words each. The next month a London physician diagnosed his throat cancer, too late to operate. On April 17, he began a new story, "A Friend of Colonel Starbottle's," one of the tales he had agreed to write in February. Three weeks later he died from a hemorrhage of the throat in the country home near London of Mme Van de Velde, his longtime companion. His estate was valued at about $1,800, less than he owed his creditors and less than half what he had spent for a summer rental in Newport in 1871.

* * *

The family fortunes were rebuilt early in the twentieth century by several successful theatrical and motion-picture adaptations of his stories. The play *Salomy Jane,* based on his story "Salomy Jane's Kiss," was a hit on Broadway in 1907. This horse opera was followed by no fewer than twenty-four feature films released between 1909 and 1955, including a silent version of "The Outcasts of Poker Flat" (1919) directed by John Ford, another version of "Outcasts" (1952) starring Dale Robertson and Anne Baxter, and a loose adaptation of "Tennessee's Partner" (1955) starring Ronald Reagan and Rhonda Fleming.

Like wing tips and wide ties, the "Bret Harte" brand of western fiction falls in and out of fashion every few years. His standing in the canonical pecking order may be inferred from the comments about his writings in textbooks over the years. Julian Hawthorne and Leonard Lemmon in *American Literature: An Elementary Text-book* (1891) praised Harte as "a brilliant innovator" who spoke in "a new voice." Fred Lewis Pattee echoed the point in his *History of American Literature* (1903): Harte's *Overland* stories "were works of literary art worthy to be compared with the rarest product of American genius." Brander Matthews asserted in 1907 that Harte "had a finer sense of form" than Dickens, and John Erskine argued in 1910 that Harte was one of six American writers of fiction whom "time has sifted . . . for special remembrance." Howells reprinted "The Outcasts" in his edition of *Best American Short Stories* in 1920.

Harte was clearly at the height of his modern popularity during the second quarter of the century. The gold regions of central California became known as "Bret Harte country," and with the construction of State Highway 108 in Tuolumne Country, the small town of Twain-Harte, near Sonora and Angels Camp, became a popular tourist destination with an annual Bret Harte Pageant. Travel writer Mildred Adams declared in 1930 that "Of all the Californias that men have invented for their delight or their profit, Bret Harte's is the most charming." As late as 1940, he was still considered a major American author whose work was routinely represented in all anthologies.

Ironically, Harte has been shuffled aside over the past generation during a canon debate that has served to rehabilitate dozens of other writers. The critical case against Harte, moreover, mirrors exactly the old argument for ignoring such writers as Harriet Beecher Stowe and Louisa May Alcott. Bernard De Voto made this case, such as it was, as long ago as 1932: "The syrupy tales that he spun out . . . drifted opportunely before a public relieved of war and facing westward. They were prettily written, between laughter and kind tears. They informed readers enamored of sentiment that even in the Sierras the simpler virtues were imperishable and that humanity remained capable of sweetness on the Pacific slope."[12] Neither the new *Heath* nor the recent *Harper* anthologies of American literature contains a single word Harte wrote.

Yet he deserves to be resurrected from the footnote. He was a literary pioneer who helped develop a formula, including an ensemble of characters, to which western writers have subscribed ever since. While he founded no literary school, he set a standard for such twentieth-century local colorists as Damon Runyon and O. Henry, the so-called "Bret Harte of the City." No less than the roguish gamblers and colorful miners who people his stories, he deserves our admiration even if he does not inspire our affection.

NOTES

1. *Mark Twain's Letters*, ed. Edgar Marquess Branch et al. (Berkeley: U of California P, 1988), I, 328; *Mark Twain's Letters*, ed. A.B. Paine (New York and London: Harper & Bros., 1917), I, 182–83.

2. Heather Kirk Thomas, " 'Development of the Literary West': An Undiscovered Kate Chopin Essay," *American Literary Realism*, 22 (Winter 1990), p. 70.

3. Carl Van Doren, New York *World*, 28 February 1926, p. 6.

4. *Mark Twain in Eruption*, ed. Bernard DeVoto (New York and London: Harper & Bros., 1940), p. 265.

5. *Cincinnati Commercial*, 9 February 1871, 4:5; T. Edgar Pemberton, *The Life of Bret Harte* (New York: Dodd, Mead, 1903), pp. 163–64.

6. William F. Conner, "The Euchring of Tennessee: A Reexamination of Bret Harte's 'Tennessee's Partner,' " *Studies in Short Fiction*, 17 (Spring 1980), p. 115.

7. "Mark Twain on Humor," New York *World*, semi-weekly edition, 2 June 1891, 6:7.

8. "A Sensation at Saratoga/New Rules for the Grand Union," *New York Times*, 19 June 1877, 1:5–6.

9. Grace Isabel Colbron, "The American Novel in Germany," *Bookman*, 39 (March 1914), 47–48.

10. "Notes," *Critic*, 30 May 1891, p. 293.

11. "Kate Carew's 12-Minute Interview on 12 Subjects with Bret Harte," New York *World*, 22 December 1901, p. 5.

12. De Voto, *Mark Twain's America* (Boston: Little, Brown, 1932), p. 162.

SUGGESTIONS FOR FURTHER READING

WORKS BY BRET HARTE

The standard editions are the 19-volume Standard Library Edition of *The Writings of Bret Harte* published by Houghton Mifflin (c. 1897–1906), largely reproduced in the 25-volume "Argonaut" edition of *The Works of Bret Harte* issued by P. F. Collier & Son of New York (1907). These editions should be supplemented by *Stories and Poems and Other Uncollected Writings*, ed. Charles Meeker Kozlay (Boston and New York: Houghton Mifflin, 1914); *Ah Sin: A Dramatic Work*, by Harte and Mark Twain, ed. Frederick Anderson (San Francisco: Book Club of California, 1961); and *Bret Harte's California: Letters to the Springfield Republican and Christian Register 1866–1867*, ed. Gary Scharnhorst (Albuquerque: University of New Mexico Press, 1990).

Scharnhorst has edited the most recent edition of Harte's letters: *Selected Letters of Bret Harte* (Norman and London: University of Oklahoma Press, 1997). However, Geoffrey Bret Harte's *Letters of Bret Harte* (Boston: Houghton Mifflin, 1926) contains texts of additional correspondence. See also Bradford A. Booth's "Unpublished Letters of Bret Harte," *American Literature*, 16 (May 1944), 131–142; "Bret Harte Goes East: Some Unpublished Letters," *American Literature*, 19 (January 1948), 318–335; and Brenda Murphy and George Monteiro's "The Unpublished Letters of Bret Harte to John Hay," *American Literary Realism*, 12 (Spring 1979), 77–110.

The most comprehensive listing of Harte's writings is Scharnhorst's *Bret Harte: A Bibliography* (Metuchen, N.J.: Lanham, MD: Scarecrow Press, 1995).

WORKS ABOUT BRET HARTE

While dated, the standard list of criticism and scholarship is Linda Diz Barrett's *Bret Harte: A Reference Guide* (Boston: G. K. Hall, 1980).

Harte has been fortunate in his biographers, among them George R. Stewart, Jr.'s *Bret Harte: Argonaut and Exile* (Boston: Houghton Mifflin, 1931); Axel Nissen's *Bret Harte: Prince and Pauper* (Jackson: University Press of Mississippi, 2000); and Scharnhorst's *Bret Harte: Opening the American Literary West* (Norman and London: University of Oklahoma Press, 2000).

Duckett, Margaret. *Mark Twain and Bret Harte.*
Norman: University of Oklahoma Press, 1964. May, Ernest R. "Bret Harte and the *Overland Monthly*," *American Literature*, 22 (November 1950), 260–271.
Scharnhorst, Gary. *Bret Harte.* New York: Twayne, 1992.
———. "Browning and Bret Harte," *ANQ*, ns 12 (Summer 1999), 41–43.
Williams, Stanley T. "Ambrose Bierce and Bret Harte," *American Literature*, 17 (May 1945), 179–180.

ESSAYS ON HARTE'S STORIES AND POEMS

Boggan, J.R. "The Regeneration of Roaring Camp," *Nineteenth Century Fiction*, 22 (December 1967), 271–280.
Connor, William F. "The Euchring of Tennessee: A Reexamination of Bret Harte's 'Tennessee's Partner,' " *Studies in Short Fiction*, 17 (Spring 1980), 113–120.
Duckett, Margaret. "Bret Harte's Portrayal of Half-Breeds," *American Literature*, 25 (May 1953), 193–212.
———. "Plain Language from Bret Harte," *Nineteenth Century Fiction*, 11 (March 1957), 241–260.
Gardner, Joseph H. "Bret Harte and the Dickensian Mode in America," *Canadian Review of American Studies*, 2 (Fall 1971), 89–101.
Glover, Donald E. "A Reconsideration of Bret Harte's Later Works." *Western American Literature*, 8 (Fall 1973), 143–151.
Kolb, Harold H., Jr. "The Outcasts of Literary Flat: Bret Harte

as Humorist," *American Literary Realism*, 23 (Winter 1991), 52–63.

May, Charles E. "Bret Harte's 'Tennessee's Partner': The Reader Euchred," *South Dakota Review*, 15 (Spring 1977), 109–117.

Scharnhorst, Gary. " 'Ways That Are Dark': Appropriations of Bret Harte's 'Plain Language from Truthful James,' " *Nineteenth-Century Literature*, 51 (December 1996), 377–399.

Thomas, Jeffrey F. "Bret Harte and the Power of Sex," *Western American Literature*, 8 (Fall 1973), 91–109.

GENERAL STUDIES OF WESTERN LITERATURE

Bold, Christine. *Selling the Wild West: Popular Western Fiction, 1860–1960*. Bloomington: Indiana University Press, 1987.

Bredahl, A. Carl. *New Ground: Western American Narrative and the Literary Canon*, Chapel Hill: University of North Carolina Press, 1989.

Etulain, Richard W. *Telling Western Stories: From Buffalo Bill to Larry McMurtry*. Albuquerque: University of New Mexico Press, 1999.

Gale, Robert L., ed. *Nineteenth-Century American Western Writers*, Dictionary of American Biography volume 186. Detroit: Gale Research, 1997.

Kowalewski, Michael, ed. *Reading the West: New Essays on the Literature of the American West*. Cambridge and New York: Cambridge University Press, 1996.

Lyon, Thomas J., ed. *A Literary History of the American West*. Fort Worth: Texas Christian University Press, 1987.

Mitchell, Lee Clark. *Westerns: Making the Man in Fiction and Film*. Chicago: University of Chicago Press, 1996.

A NOTE ON THE TEXTS

All of the texts in this edition, with four exceptions, are reproduced from the Standard Library Edition of Harte's *Works* (Boston and New York: Houghton Mifflin, c. 1897–1906). Two of the exceptions are the poems "That Ebrew Jew" and "Free Silver at Angel's," here reprinted from Harte's *Stories and Poems and Other Uncollected Writings*, ed. Charles Meeker Kozlay (Boston and New York: Houghton Mifflin, 1914). Harte's "The Rise of the 'Short Story' " is here reprinted for the first time since its original publication in *Cornhill Magazine,* ns 7 (July 1899), 1–8. In addition, "The Argonauts of '49" was first published as the "General Introduction" to the second volume of *The Works of Bret Harte* (London: Chatto & Windus, 1882) and reprinted in the Standard Library Edition as the "Introduction" to volume 2, pp. ix–xxxv. As Harte remarked in a footnote to that edition, "This Introduction, in its original use, was a lecture to English and American audiences, and is now, with some trifling alterations, printed for the first time."

TEXTUAL EMENDATIONS

Page	Line	
3	17	"Serro": "Serra"
16	30	"dismissed": "dismissed from"
221	29	"Morissey": "Morrisey"
246	6	"deseños: "diseños"
246	12	"semicuaca": "sembicuaca"
151	12	*"Grey"*: *"Gray"*
253	6	"Bigelow": "Biglow"
255	26	"Condemned": "Condensed"

STORIES

The Legend of Monte del Diablo

THE CAUTIOUS READER will detect a lack of authenticity in the following pages. I am not a cautious reader myself, yet I confess with some concern to the absence of much documentary evidence in support of the singular incident I am about to relate. Disjointed memoranda, the proceedings of *ayuntamientos* and early departmental *juntas*,[1] with other records of a primitive and superstitious people, have been my inadequate authorities. It is but just to state, however, that though this particular story lacks corroboration, in ransacking the Spanish archives of Upper California I have met with many more surprising and incredible stories, attested and supported to a degree that would have placed this legend beyond a cavil or doubt. I have, also, never lost faith in the legend myself, and in so doing have profited much from the examples of divers grant-claimants, who have often jostled me in their more practical researches, and who have my sincere sympathy at the scepticism of a modern hard-headed and practical world.

For many years after Father Junipero Serra[2] first rang his bell in the wilderness of Upper California, the spirit which animated that adventurous priest did not wane. The conversion of the heathen went on rapidly in the establishment of Missions throughout the land. So sedulously did the good Fathers set about their work, that around their isolated chapels there presently arose *adobe* huts, whose mud-plastered and savage tenants partook regularly of the provisions, and occasionally of the Sacrament, of their pious hosts. Nay, so great was their progress, that one zealous Padre[3] is reported to have administered the Lord's Supper one Sabbath morning to "over three hundred heathen Salvages." It was not to be wondered that the Enemy of Souls, being greatly incensed thereat, and alarmed at his decreasing popularity, should have grievously tempted and embarrassed these Holy Fathers, as we shall presently see.

Yet they were happy, peaceful days for California. The vagrant keels of prying Commerce had not as yet ruffled the lordly gravity of her bays. No torn and ragged gulch betrayed the suspicion of golden treasure. The wild oats drooped idly in the morning heat, or wrestled with the afternoon breezes. Deer and antelope dotted the plain. The watercourses brawled in their familiar channels, nor dreamed of ever shifting their regular tide. The wonders of the Yosemite and Calaveras were as yet unrecorded. The Holy Fathers noted little of the landscape beyond the barbaric prodigality with which the quick soil repaid the sowing. A new conversion, the advent of a Saint's day, or the baptism of an Indian baby, was at once the chronicle and marvel of their day.

At this blissful epoch there lived at the Mission of San Pablo Father José Antonio Haro, a worthy brother of the Society of Jesus. He was of tall and cadaverous aspect. A somewhat romantic history had given a poetic interest to his lugubrious visage. While a youth, pursuing his studies at famous Salamanca,[4] he had become enamored of the charms of Doña Cármen de Torrencevara, as that lady passed to her matutinal devotions. Untoward circumstances, hastened, perhaps, by a wealthier suitor, brought this amour to a disastrous issue; and Father José entered a monastery, taking upon himself the vows of celibacy. It was here that his natural fervor and poetic enthusiasm conceived expression as a missionary. A longing to convert the uncivilized heathen succeeded his frivolous earthly passion, and a desire to explore and develop unknown fastnesses continually possessed him. In his flashing eye and sombre exterior was detected a singular commingling of the discreet Las Casas and the impetuous Balboa.[5]

Fired by this pious zeal, Father José went forward in the van of Christian pioneers. On reaching Mexico, he obtained authority to establish the Mission of San Pablo. Like the good Junipero, accompanied only by an acolyte and muleteer, he unsaddled his mules in a dusky *cañon,* and rang his bell in the wilderness. The savages—a peaceful, inoffensive, and inferior race—presently flocked around him. The nearest military post was far away, which contributed much to the security of these pious pilgrims, who found their open trustfulness and amiability better fitted to repress hostility than the presence of an armed, suspicious, and brawling soldiery. So the good Father José said matins and prime, mass and vespers, in the heart of Sin and Heathenism, taking no heed to himself, but looking only to the welfare of the Holy Church. Conversions soon followed, and, on the 7th of July, 1760, the first Indian baby was baptized,—an event which, as Father José piously records, "exceeds the richnesse of gold or precious jewels or the chancing upon the Ophir of Solomon."[6] I quote this incident as best suited to show the ingenious blending of poetry and piety which distinguished Father José's record.

The Mission of San Pablo progressed and prospered until the pious founder thereof, like the infidel Alexander, might have wept that there were no more heathen worlds to conquer. But his ardent and enthusiastic spirit could not long brook an idleness that seemed begotten of sin; and one pleasant August morning, in the year of grace 1770, Father José issued from the outer court of the Mission building, equipped to explore the field for new missionary labors.

Nothing could exceed the quiet gravity and unpretentiousness of the little cavalcade. First rode a stout muleteer, leading a pack-mule laden with the provisions of the party, together with a few cheap crucifixes and hawks' bells. After him came the devout Padre José, bearing his breviary and cross, with a black *serapa* thrown around his shoulders; while on either side trotted a dusky convert, anxious to show a proper sense of their regeneration by acting as guides into the wilds of their heathen brethren. Their new condition was agreeably shown by the absence of the usual mud-plaster, which in their unconverted state they assumed to keep away vermin and cold. The morning was bright and propitious. Before their departure, mass had been said in the chapel, and the protection of St. Ignatius[7] invoked against all contingent evils, but especially against bears, which, like the fiery dragons of old, seemed to cherish unconquerable hostility to the Holy Church.

As they wound through the *cañon,* charming birds disported upon boughs and sprays, and sober quails piped from the alders; the willowy water-courses gave a musical utterance, and the long grass whispered on the hillside. On entering the deeper defiles, above them towered dark green masses of pine, and occasionally the *madroño*[8] shook its bright scarlet berries. As they toiled up many a steep ascent, Father José sometimes picked up fragments of scoria, which spake to his imagination of direful volcanoes and impending earthquakes. To the less scientific mind of the muleteer Ignacio they had even a more terrifying significance; and he once or twice snuffed the air suspiciously, and declared that it smelt of sulphur. So the first day of their journey wore away, and at night they encamped without having met a single heathen face.

It was on this night that the Enemy of Souls appeared to Ignacio in an appalling form. He had retired to a secluded part of the camp and had sunk upon his knees in prayerful meditation, when he looked up and perceived the Arch-Fiend in the likeness of a monstrous bear. The Evil One was seated on his hind legs immediately before him, with his fore paws joined together just below his black muzzle. Wisely conceiving this remarkable attitude to be in mockery and derision of his devotions, the worthy muleteer was transported with fury. Seizing an arquebuse,[9] he instantly closed his eyes and fired. When he had recovered from the effects of the terrific discharge, the apparition had disappeared. Father José, awakened by the report, reached the spot only in time to chide the muleteer for wasting powder and ball in a contest with one whom a single *ave*[10] would have been sufficient to utterly discomfit. What further reliance he placed on Ignacio's story is not known; but, in commemoration of a worthy Californian custom, the place was called *La Cañada de la Tentacion del Pio Muletero,* or "The Glen of the Temptation of the Pious Muleteer," a name which it retains to this day.

The next morning the party, issuing from a narrow gorge, came upon a long valley, sear and burnt with the shadeless heat. Its lower extremity was lost in a fading line of low hills, which, gathering might and volume toward the upper end of the valley, upheaved a stupendous bulwark against the breezy North. The peak of this awful spur was just touched by a fleecy cloud that shifted to and fro like a banneret. Father José gazed at it with mingled awe and admiration. By a singular coincidence, the muleteer Ignacio uttered the simple ejaculation "*Diablo!*"[11]

As they penetrated the valley, they soon began to miss the agreeable life and companionable echoes of the *cañon* they had quitted. Huge fissures in the parched soil seemed to gape as with thirsty mouths. A few squirrels darted from the earth, and disappeared as mysteriously before the jingling mules. A gray wolf trotted leisurely along just ahead. But whichever way Father José turned, the mountain always asserted itself and arrested his wandering eye. Out of the dry and arid valley, it seemed to spring into cooler and bracing life. Deep cavernous shadows dwelt along its base; rocky fastnesses appeared midway of its elevation; and on either side huge black hills diverged like massy roots from a central trunk. His lively fancy pictured these hills peopled with a majestic and intelligent race of savages; and looking into futurity, he already saw a monstrous cross crowning the dome-like summit. Far different were the sensations of the muleteer, who saw in those awful solitudes only fiery dragons, colossal bears, and break-neck trails. The converts, Concepcion and Incarnacion, trotting modestly beside the Padre, recognized, perhaps, some manifestation of their former weird mythology.

At nightfall they reached the base of the mountain. Here Father José unpacked his mules, said vespers, and, formally ringing his bell, called upon the Gentiles within hearing to come and accept the Holy Faith. The echoes of the black frowning hills around him caught up the pious invitation, and repeated it at intervals; but no Gentiles appeared that night. Nor were the devotions of the muleteer again disturbed, although he afterward asserted that, when the Father's exhortation was ended, a mocking peal of laughter came from the mountain. Nothing daunted by these intimations of the near hostility of the Evil One, Father José declared his intention to ascend the mountain at early dawn; and before the sun rose the next morning he was leading the way.

The ascent was in many places difficult and dangerous. Huge fragments of rock often lay across the trail, and after a few hours' climbing they were forced to leave their mules in a little gully, and continue the ascent afoot. Unaccustomed to such exertion, Father José often stopped to wipe the perspiration from his thin cheeks. As the day wore on, a strange silence oppressed them. Except the occasional pattering of a squirrel, or a rustling in the *chimisal* bushes,[12] there were no signs of life. The half-human print of a bear's foot sometimes appeared before them, at which Ignacio always crossed himself piously. The eye was sometimes cheated by a dripping from the rocks, which on closer inspection proved to be a resinous oily liquid with an abominable sulphurous smell. When they were within a short distance of the summit, the discreet Ignacio, selecting a sheltered nook for the camp, slipped aside and

busied himself in preparations for the evening, leaving the Holy
Father to continue the ascent alone. Never was there a more
thoughtless act of prudence, never a more imprudent piece of caution. Without noticing the desertion, buried in pious reflection,
Father José pushed mechanically on, and, reaching the summit,
cast himself down and gazed upon the prospect.

Below him lay a succession of valleys opening into each other
like gentle lakes, until they were lost to the southward. Westerly
the distant range hid the bosky *cañada*[13] which sheltered the mission of San Pablo. In the farther distance the Pacific Ocean
stretched away, bearing a cloud of fog upon its bosom, which
crept through the entrance of the bay, and rolled thickly between
him and the northeastward; the same fog hid the base of mountain
and the view beyond. Still, from time to time the fleecy veil
parted, and timidly disclosed charming glimpses of mighty rivers,
mountain defiles, and rolling plains, sear with ripened oats, and
bathed in the glow of the setting sun. As Father José gazed, he was
penetrated with a pious longing. Already his imagination, filled
with enthusiastic conceptions, beheld all that vast expanse gathered under the mild sway of the Holy Faith, and peopled with
zealous converts. Each little knoll in fancy became crowned with a
chapel; from each dark *cañon* gleamed the white walls of a mission
building. Growing bolder in his enthusiasm, and looking farther
into futurity, he beheld a new Spain rising on these savage shores.
He already saw the spires of stately cathedrals, the domes of
palaces, vineyards, gardens, and groves. Convents, half hid among
the hills, peeping from plantations of branching limes; and long
processions of chanting nuns wound through the defiles. So completely was the good Father's conception of the future confounded
with the past, that even in their choral strain the well-remembered
accents of Cármen struck his ear. He was busied in these fanciful
imaginings, when suddenly over that extended prospect the faint,
distant tolling of a bell rang sadly out and died. It was the *Angelus*.[14] Father José listened with superstitious exaltation. The mission of San Pablo was far away, and the sound must have been
some miraculous omen. But never before, to his enthusiastic sense,
did the sweet seriousness of this angelic symbol come with such
strange significance. With the last faint peal, his glowing fancy
seemed to cool; the fog closed in below him, and the good Father

remembered he had not had his supper. He had risen and was wrapping his *serapa* around him, when he perceived for the first time that he was not alone.

Nearly opposite, and where should have been the faithless Ignacio, a grave and decorous figure was seated. His appearance was that of an elderly *hidalgo*,[15] dressed in mourning, with mustaches of iron-gray carefully waxed and twisted around a pair of lantern-jaws. The monstrous hat and prodigious feather, the enormous ruff and exaggerated trunk-hose, contrasted with a frame shrivelled and wizened, all belonged to a century previous. Yet Father José was not astonished. His adventurous life and poetic imagination, continually on the lookout for the marvellous, gave him a certain advantage over the practical and material minded. He instantly detected the diabolical quality of his visitant, and was prepared. With equal coolness and courtesy he met the cavalier's obeisance.

"I ask your pardon, Sir Priest," said the stranger, "for disturbing your meditations. Pleasant they must have been, and right fanciful, I imagine, when occasioned by so fair a prospect."

"Worldly, perhaps, Sir Devil,—for such I take you to be," said the Holy Father, as the stranger bowed his black plumes to the ground; "worldly, perhaps; for it hath pleased Heaven to retain even in our regenerated state much that pertaineth to the flesh, yet still, I trust, not without some speculation for the welfare of the Holy Church. In dwelling upon yon fair expanse, mine eyes have been graciously opened with prophetic inspiration, and the promise of the heathen as an inheritance hath marvellously recurred to me. For there can be none lack such diligence in the True Faith, but may see that even the conversion of these pitiful salvages hath a meaning. As the blessed St. Ignatius discreetly observes," continued Father José, clearing his throat and slightly elevating his voice, " 'the heathen is given to the warriors of Christ, even as the pearls of rare discovery which gladden the hearts of shipmen.'[16] Nay, I might say—"

But here the stranger, who had been wrinkling his brows and twisting his mustaches with well-bred patience, took advantage of an oratorical pause:—

"It grieves me, Sir Priest, to interrupt the current of your eloquence as discourteously as I have already broken your medita-

tions; but the day already waneth to night. I have a matter of
serious import to make with you, could I entreat your cautious
consideration a few moments."

Father José hesitated. The temptation was great, and the
prospect of acquiring some knowledge of the Great Enemy's plans
not the least trifling object. And if the truth must be told, there
was a certain decorum about the stranger that interested the Padre.
Though well aware of the Protean shapes the Arch-Fiend could
assume, and though free from the weaknesses of the flesh, Father
José was not above the temptations of the spirit. Had the Devil appeared, as in the case of the pious St. Anthony, in the likeness of a
comely damsel,[17] the good Father, with his certain experience of
the deceitful sex, would have whisked her away in the saying of a
paternoster.[18] But there was, added to the security of age, a grave
sadness about the stranger,—a thoughtful consciousness as of being at a great moral disadvantage,—which at once decided him on
a magnanimous course of conduct.

The stranger then proceeded to inform him, that he had been
diligently observing the Holy Father's triumphs in the valley.
That, far from being greatly exercised thereat, he had been only
grieved to see so enthusiastic and chivalrous an antagonist wasting
his zeal in a hopeless work. For, he observed, the issue of the great
battle of Good and Evil had been otherwise settled, as he would
presently show him. "It wants but a few moments of night," he
continued, "and over this interval of twilight, as you know, I have
been given complete control. Look to the West."

As the Padre turned, the stranger took his enormous hat from
his head, and waved it three times before him. At each sweep of
the prodigious feather, the fog grew thinner, until it melted impal-
pably away, and the former landscape returned, yet warm with the
glowing sun. As Father José gazed, a strain of martial music arose
from the valley, and issuing from a deep *cañon*, the good Father
beheld a long cavalcade of gallant cavaliers, habited like his companion. As they swept down the plain, they were joined by like
processions, that slowly defiled from every ravine and *cañon* of
the mysterious mountain. From time to time the peal of a trumpet
swelled fitfully upon the breeze; the cross of Santiago[19] glittered,
and the royal banners of Castile and Aragon[20] waved over the
moving column. So they moved on solemnly toward the sea,

where, in the distance, Father José saw stately caravels, bearing the same familiar banner, awaiting them. The good Padre gazed with conflicting emotions, and the serious voice of the stranger broke the silence.

"Thou hast beheld, Sir Priest, the fading footprints of adventurous Castile. Thou hast seen the declining glory of old Spain,—declining as yonder brilliant sun. The sceptre she hath wrested from the heathen is fast dropping from her decrepit and fleshless grasp. The children she hath fostered shall know her no longer. The soil she hath acquired shall be lost to her as irrevocably as she herself hath thrust the Moor from her own Granada."[21]

The stranger paused, and his voice seemed broken by emotion; at the same time, Father José, whose sympathizing heart yearned toward the departing banners, cried in poignant accents,—

"Farewell, ye gallant cavaliers and Christian soldiers! Farewell, thou, Nuñes de Balboa! thou, Alonzo de Ojeda![22] and thou, most venerable Las Casas! Farewell, and may Heaven prosper still the seed ye left behind!"

Then turning to the stranger, Father José beheld him gravely draw his pocket-handkerchief from the basket-hilt of his rapier, and apply it decorously to his eyes.

"Pardon this weakness, Sir Priest," said the cavalier, apologetically; "but these worthy gentlemen were ancient friends of mine, and have done me many a delicate service,—much more, perchance, than these poor sables may signify," he added, with a grim gesture toward the mourning suit he wore.

Father José was too much preoccupied in reflection to notice the equivocal nature of this tribute, and, after a few moments' silence, said, as if continuing his thought,—

"But the seed they have planted shall thrive and prosper on this fruitful soil."

As if answering the interrogatory, the stranger turned to the opposite direction, and, again waving his hat, said, in the same serious tone,—

"Look to the East!"

The Father turned, and, as the fog broke away before the waving plume, he saw that the sun was rising. Issuing with its bright beams through the passes of the snowy mountains beyond, appeared a strange and motley crew. Instead of the dark and romantic visages of his last phantom train, the Father beheld with strange concern the blue eyes and flaxen hair of a Saxon race. In place of martial airs and musical utterance, there rose upon the ear a strange din of harsh gutturals and singular sibilation. Instead of the decorous tread and stately mien of the cavaliers of the former vision, they came pushing, bustling, panting, and swaggering. And as they passed, the good Father noticed that giant trees were prostrated as with the breath of a tornado, and the bowels of the earth were torn and rent as with a convulsion. And Father José looked in vain for holy cross or Christian symbol; there was but one that seemed an ensign, and he crossed himself with holy horror as he perceived it bore the effigy of a bear.

"Who are these swaggering Ishmaelites?"[23] he asked, with something of asperity in his tone.

The stranger was gravely silent.

"What do they here, with neither cross nor holy symbol?" he again demanded.

"Have you the courage to see, Sir Priest?" responded the stranger, quietly.

Father José felt his crucifix, as a lonely traveller might his rapier, and assented.

"Step under the shadow of my plume," said the stranger.

Father José stepped beside him, and they instantly sank through the earth.

When he opened his eyes, which had remained closed in prayerful meditation during his rapid descent, he found himself in a vast vault, bespangled overhead with luminous points like the starred firmament. It was also lighted by a yellow glow that seemed to proceed from a mighty sea or lake that occupied the center of the chamber. Around this subterranean sea dusky figures flitted, bearing ladles filled with the yellow fluid, which they had replenished from its depths. From this lake diverging streams of the same mysterious flood penetrated like mighty rivers the cavernous distance. As they walked by the banks of this glittering Styx,[24] Father José perceived how the liquid stream at certain places became solid. The ground was strewn with glittering flakes. One of these the Padre picked up and curiously examined. It was virgin gold.

An expression of discomfiture overcast the good Father's face at this discovery; but there was trace neither of malice nor satisfaction in the stranger's air, which was still of serious and fateful contemplation. When Father José recovered his equanimity, he said, bitterly,—

"This, then, Sir Devil, is your work! This is your deceitful lure for the weak souls of sinful nations! So would you replace the Christian grace of holy Spain!"

"This is what must be," returned the stranger, gloomily. "But listen, Sir Priest. It lies with you to avert the issue for a time. Leave me here in peace. Go back to Castile, and take with you your bells, your images, and your missions. Continue here, and you only precipitate results. Stay! Promise me you will do this, and you shall not lack that which will render your old age an ornament and a blessing"; and the stranger motioned significantly to the lake.

It was here, the legend discreetly relates, that the Devil showed—as he always shows sooner or later—his cloven hoof. The worthy Padre, sorely perplexed by his threefold vision, and, if the truth must be told, a little nettled at this wresting away of the glory of holy Spanish discovery, had shown some hesitation. But the unlucky bribe of the Enemy of Souls touched his Castilian spirit. Starting back in deep disgust, he brandished his crucifix in the face of the unmasked Fiend, and in a voice that made the dusky vault resound, cried,—

"Avaunt thee, Sathanas!²⁵ Diabolus, I defy thee! What! wouldst thou bribe me,—me, a brother of the Sacred Society of the Holy Jesus, Licentiate of Cordova and Inquisitor of Guadalaxara? Thinkest thou to buy me with thy sordid treasure? Avaunt!"

What might have been the issue of this rupture, and how complete might have been the triumph of the Holy Father over the Arch-Fiend, who was recoiling aghast at these sacred titles and the flourishing symbol, we can never know, for at that moment the crucifix slipped through his fingers.

Scarcely had it touched the ground before Devil and Holy Father simultaneously cast themselves toward it. In the struggle they clinched, and the pious José, who was as much the superior of his antagonist in bodily as in spiritual strength, was about to treat the Great Adversary to a back somersault, when he suddenly felt the

long nails of the stranger piercing his flesh. A new fear seized his
heart, a numbing chillness crept through his body, and he struggled to free himself, but in vain. A strange roaring was in his ears;
the lake and cavern danced before his eyes and vanished; and with
a loud cry he sank senseless to the ground.

When he recovered his consciousness he was aware of a gentle
swaying motion of his body. He opened his eyes, and saw it was
high noon, and that he was being carried in a litter through the
valley. He felt stiff, and, looking down, perceived that his arm was
tightly bandaged to his side.

He closed his eyes and after a few words of thankful prayer,
thought how miraculously he had been preserved, and made a
vow of candlesticks to the blessed Saint José. He then called in a
faint voice, and presently the penitent Ignacio stood beside him.

The joy the poor fellow felt at his patron's returning consciousness for some time choked his utterance. He could only ejaculate,
"A miracle! Blessed Saint José, he lives!" and kiss the Padre's
bandaged hand. Father José more intent on his last night's experience, waited for his emotion to subside, and asked where he had
been found.

"On the mountain, your Reverence, but a few *varas*[26] from
where he attacked you."

"How?—you saw him then?" asked the Padre, in unfeigned astonishment.

"Saw him, your Reverence! Mother of God, I should think I
did! And your Reverence shall see him too, if he ever comes again
within range of Ignacio's arquebuse."

"What mean you, Ignacio?" said the Padre, sitting bolt-upright
in his litter.

"Why, the bear, your Reverence,—the bear, Holy Father, who
attacked your worshipful person while you were meditating on
the top of yonder mountain."

"Ah!" said the Holy Father, lying down again. "Chut, child! I
would be at peace."

When he reached the Mission, he was tenderly cared for, and in
a few weeks was enabled to resume those duties from which, as
will be seen, not even the machinations of the Evil One could
divert him. The news of his physical disaster spread over the
country; and a letter to the Bishop of Guadalaxara contained a

confidential and detailed account of the good Father's spiritual temptation. But in some way the story leaked out; and long after José was gathered to his fathers, his mysterious encounter formed the theme of thrilling and whispered narrative. The mountain was generally shunned. It is true that Señor Joaquin Pedrillo afterward located a grant near the base of the mountain; but as Señoro, Pedrillo was known to be a termagant half-breed, the Señor was not supposed to be over-fastidious.

Such is the Legend of Monte del Diablo. As I said before, it may seem to lack essential corroboration. The discrepancy between the Father's narrative and the actual climax has given rise to some scepticism on the part of ingenious quibblers. All such I would simply refer to that part of the report of Señor Julio Serro, Sub-Prefect of San Pablo, before whom attest of the above was made. Touching this matter, the worthy Prefect observes, "That although the body of Father José doth show evidence of grievous conflict in the flesh, yet that is no proof that the Enemy of Souls, who could assume the figure of a decorous elderly *caballero*,[27] could not at the same time transform himself into a bear for his own vile purposes."

Oct. 1863

The Luck of Roaring Camp

THERE WAS COMMOTION in Roaring Camp. It could not have been a fight, for in 1850 that was not novel enough to have called together the entire settlement. The ditches and claims were not only deserted, but "Tuttle's grocery" had contributed its gamblers, who, it will be remembered, calmly continued their game the day that French Pete and Kanaka Joe shot each other to death over the bar in the front room. The whole camp was collected before a rude cabin on the outer edge of the clearing. Conversation was carried on in a low tone, but the name of a woman was frequently repeated. It was a name familiar enough in the camp,—"Cherokee Sal."

Perhaps the less said of her the better. She was a coarse, and, it is to be feared, a very sinful woman. But at that time she was the only woman in Roaring Camp, and was just then lying in sore extremity, when she most needed the ministration of her own sex. Dissolute, abandoned, and irreclaimable, she was yet suffering a martyrdom hard enough to bear even when veiled by sympathizing womanhood, but now terrible in her loneliness. The primal curse had come to her in that original isolation which must have made the punishment of the first transgression so dreadful. It was, perhaps, part of the expiation of her sin, that, at a moment when she most lacked her sex's intuitive tenderness and care, she met only the half-contemptuous faces of her masculine associates. Yet a few of the spectators were, I think, touched by her sufferings. Sandy Tipton thought it was "rough on Sal," and, in the contemplation of her condition, for a moment rose superior to the fact that he had an ace and two bowers in his sleeve.

It will be seen, also, that the situation was novel. Deaths were by no means uncommon in Roaring Camp, but a birth was a new thing. People had been dismissed from the camp effectively, finally, and with no possibility of return; but this was the first time that anybody had been introduced *ab initio*.[1] Hence the excitement.

"You go in there, Stumpy," said a prominent citizen known as "Kentuck," addressing one of the loungers. "Go in there, and see what you kin do. You've had experience in them things."

Perhaps there was a fitness in the selection. Stumpy, in other climes, had been the putative head of two families; in fact, it was owing to some legal informality in these proceedings that Roaring Camp—a city of refuge[2]—was indebted to his company. The crowd approved the choice, and Stumpy was wise enough to bow to the majority. The door closed on the extempore surgeon and midwife, and Roaring Camp sat down outside, smoked its pipe, and awaited the issue.

The assemblage numbered about a hundred men. One or two of these were actual fugitives from justice, some were criminal, and all were reckless. Physically, they exhibited no indication of their past lives and character. The greatest scamp had a Raphael[3] face, with a profusion of blond hair; Oakhurst, a gambler, had the melancholy air and intellectual abstraction of a Hamlet;[4] the coolest and most courageous man was scarcely over five feet in height, with a soft voice and an embarrassed, timid manner. The term "roughs" applied to them was a distinction rather than a definition. Perhaps in the minor details of fingers, toes, ears, etc., the camp may have been deficient, but these slight omissions did not detract from their aggregate force. The strongest man had but three fingers on his right hand; the best shot had but one eye.

Such was the physical aspect of the men that were dispersed around the cabin. The camp lay in a triangular valley, between two hills and a river. The only outlet was a steep trail over the summit of a hill that faced the cabin, now illuminated by the rising moon. The suffering woman might have seen it from the rude bunk whereon she lay,—seen it winding like a silver thread until it was lost in the stars above.

A fire of withered pine-boughs added sociability to the gathering. By degrees the natural levity of Roaring Camp returned. Bets were freely offered and taken regarding the result. Three to five that "Sal would get through with it"; even, that the child would survive; side bets as to the sex and complexion of the coming stranger. In the midst of an excited discussion an exclamation came from those nearest the door, and the camp stopped to listen. Above the swaying and moaning of the pines, the swift rush of the river, and the crackling of the fire, rose a sharp, querulous cry,—a cry unlike anything heard before in the camp. The pines stopped moaning, the river ceased to rush, and the fire to crackle. It seemed as if Nature had stopped to listen too.

The camp rose to its feet as one man! It was proposed to explode a barrel of gunpowder, but, in consideration of the situation of the mother, better counsels prevailed, and only a few revolvers were discharged; for, whether owing to the rude surgery of the camp, or some other reason, Cherokee Sal was sinking fast. Within an hour she had climbed, as it were, that rugged road that led to the stars, and so passed out of Roaring Camp, its sin and shame forever. I do not think that the announcement disturbed them much, except in speculation as to the fate of the child. "Can he live now?" was asked of Stumpy. The answer was doubtful. The only other being of Cherokee Sal's sex and maternal condition in the settlement was an ass. There was some conjecture as to fitness, but the experiment was tried. It was less problematical than the ancient treatment of Romulus and Remus,[5] and apparently as successful.

When these details were completed, which exhausted another hour, the door was opened, and the anxious crowd of men who had already formed themselves into a queue, entered in single file. Beside the low bunk or shelf, on which the figure of the mother was starkly outlined below the blankets, stood a pine table. On this a candle-box was placed, and within it, swathed in staring red flannel, lay the last arrival at Roaring Camp. Beside the candle-box was placed a hat. Its use was soon indicated. "Gentlemen," said Stumpy, with a singular mixture of authority and *ex officio*[6] complacency,—"Gentlemen will please pass in at the front door, round the table, and out at the back door. Them as wishes to contribute anything toward the orphan will find a hat handy." The first man entered with his hat on; he uncovered, however, as he looked about him, and so, unconsciously, set an example to the next. In such communities good and bad actions are catching. As the procession filed in, comments were audible,—criticisms addressed, perhaps, rather to Stumpy, in the character of showman,—"Is that him?" "mighty small specimen"; "hasn't mor'n got the color"; "ain't bigger nor a derringer."[7] The contributions were as characteristic: A silver tobacco-box; a doubloon; a navy revolver, silver mounted; a gold specimen; a very beautifully embroidered lady's handkerchief (from Oakhurst the gambler); a diamond breastpin; a diamond ring (suggested by the pin, with the remark from the giver that he "saw that pin and went two diamonds better"); a slung shot; a Bible (contributor not detected); a golden spur; a silver teaspoon (the initials, I regret to say, were not the giver's); a pair of surgeon's shears; a lancet; a Bank of England note for £5; and about $200 in loose gold and silver coin. During these proceedings Stumpy maintained a silence as impassive as the dead on his left, a gravity as inscrutable as that of the newly born on his right. Only one incident occurred to break the monotony of the curious procession. As Kentuck bent over the candle-box half curiously, the child turned, and, in a spasm of pain, caught at his groping finger, and held it fast for a moment. Kentuck looked foolish and embarrassed. Something like a blush tried to assert itself in his weather-beaten cheek. "The d—d little cuss!" he said, as he extricated his finger, with, perhaps, more tenderness and care than he might have been deemed capable of showing. He held that finger a little apart from its fellows as he went out, and examined it curiously. The examination provoked the same original remark in regard to the child. In fact, he seemed to enjoy repeating it. "He rastled with my finger," he remarked to Tipton, holding up the member, "the d—d little cuss!"

It was four o'clock before the camp sought repose. A light burnt in the cabin where the watchers sat, for Stumpy did not go to bed that night. Nor did Kentuck. He drank quite freely, and related with great gusto his experience, invariably ending with his characteristic condemnation of the new-comer. It seemed to relieve him of any unjust implication of sentiment, and Kentuck had the weaknesses of the nobler sex. When everybody else had gone to bed, he walked down to the river, and whistled reflectingly. Then he walked up the gulch, past the cabin, still whistling with demonstrative unconcern. At a large red-wood tree he paused and retraced his steps, and again passed the cabin. Half-way down to the river's bank he again paused, and then returned and knocked at the door. It was opened by Stumpy. "How goes it?" said Kentuck, looking past Stumpy toward the candle-box. "All serene," replied

Stumpy. "Anything up?" "Nothing." There was a pause—an embarrassing one—Stumpy still holding the door. Then Kentuck had recourse to his finger, which he held up to Stumpy. "Rastled with it,—the d—d little cuss," he said, and retired.

The next day Cherokee Sal had such rude sepulture as Roaring Camp afforded. After her body had been committed to the hillside, there was a formal meeting of the camp to discuss what should be done with her infant. A resolution to adopt it was unanimous and enthusiastic. But an animated discussion in regard to the manner and feasibility of providing for its wants at once sprung up. It was remarkable that the argument partook of none of those fierce personalities with which discussions were usually conducted at Roaring Camp. Tipton proposed that they should send the child to Red Dog,—a distance of forty miles,—where female attention could be procured. But the unlucky suggestion met with fierce and unanimous opposition. It was evident that no plan which entailed parting from their new acquisition would for a moment be entertained. "Besides," said Tom Ryder, "them fellows at Red Dog would swap it, and ring in somebody else on us." A disbelief in the honesty of other camps prevailed at Roaring Camp as in other places.

The introduction of a female nurse in the camp also met with objection. It was argued that no decent woman could be prevailed to accept Roaring Camp as her home, and the speaker urged that "they didn't want any more of the other kind." This unkind allusion to the defunct mother, harsh as it may seem, was the first spasm of propriety,—the first symptom of the camp's regeneration. Stumpy advanced nothing. Perhaps he felt a certain delicacy in interfering with the selection of a possible successor in office. But when questioned, he averred stoutly that he and "Jinny"—the mammal before alluded to—could manage to rear the child. There was something original, independent, and heroic about the plan that pleased the camp. Stumpy was retained. Certain articles were sent for to Sacramento. "Mind," said the treasurer, as he pressed a bag of gold-dust into the expressman's hand, "the best that can be got,—lace, you know, and filigree-work and frills,—d—m the cost!"

Strange to say, the child thrived. Perhaps the invigorating climate of the mountain camp was compensation for material deficiencies. Nature took the foundling to her broader breast. In that rare atmosphere of the Sierra foothills,—that air pungent with balsamic odor, that ethereal cordial at once bracing and exhilarating,—he may have found food and nourishment, or a subtle chemistry that transmuted asses' milk to lime and phosphorus. Stumpy inclined to the belief that it was the latter and good nursing. "Me and that ass," he would say, "has been father and mother to him! Don't you," he would add, apostrophizing the helpless bundle before him, "never go back on us."

By the time he was a month old, the necessity of giving him a name became apparent. He had generally been known as "the Kid," "Stumpy's boy," "the Cayote" (an allusion to his vocal powers), and even by Kentuck's endearing diminutive of "the d—d little cuss." But these were felt to be vague and unsatisfactory, and were at last dismissed under another influence. Gamblers and adventurers are generally superstitious, and Oakhurst one day declared that the baby had brought "the luck" to Roaring Camp. It was certain that of late they had been successful. "Luck" was the name agreed upon, with the prefix of Tommy for greater convenience. No allusion was made to the mother, and the father was unknown. "It's better," said the philosophical Oakhurst, "to take a fresh deal all round. Call him Luck, and start him fair." A day was accordingly set apart for the christening. What was meant by this ceremony the reader may imagine, who has already gathered some idea of the reckless irreverence of Roaring Camp. The master of ceremonies was one "Boston," a noted wag, and the occasion seemed to promise the greatest facetiousness. This ingenious satirist had spent two days in preparing a burlesque of the church service, with pointed local allusions. The choir was properly trained, and Sandy Tipton was to stand godfather. But after the procession had marched to the grove with music and banners, and the child had been deposited before a mock altar, Stumpy stepped before the expectant crowd. "It ain't my style to spoil fun, boys," said the little man, stoutly, eying the faces around him, "but it strikes me that this thing ain't exactly on the squar. It's playing it pretty low down on this yer baby to ring in fun on him that he ain't going to understand. And ef there's going to be any godfathers round, I'd like to see who's got any better rights than me." A silence followed Stumpy's speech. To the credit of all humorists be it said, that the first man to acknowledge its justice was the satirist, thus stopped of his fun. "But," said Stumpy, quickly, following up his advantage, "we're here for a christening, and we'll have it. I proclaim you Thomas Luck, according to the laws of the United States and the State of California, so help me God." It was the first time that the name of the Deity had been uttered otherwise than profanely in the camp. The form of christening was perhaps even more ludicrous than the satirist had conceived; but, strangely enough, nobody saw it and nobody laughed. "Tommy" was christened as seriously as he would have been under a Christian roof, and cried and was comforted in as orthodox fashion.

And so the work of regeneration began in Roaring Camp. Almost imperceptibly a change came over the settlement. The cabin assigned to "Tommy Luck"—or "The Luck," as he was more frequently called—first showed signs of improvement. It was kept scrupulously clean and white-washed. Then it was boarded, clothed, and papered. The rosewood cradle—packed eighty miles by mule—had, in Stumpy's way of putting it, "sorter killed the rest of the furniture." So the rehabilitation of the cabin became a necessity. The men who were in the habit of lounging in at Stumpy's to see "how The Luck got on" seemed to appreciate the change, and, in self-defense, the rival establishment of "Tuttle's grocery" bestirred itself, and imported a carpet and mirrors. The reflections of the latter on the appearance of Roaring Camp tended to produce stricter habits of personal cleanliness. Again, Stumpy imposed a kind of quarantine upon those who aspired to the honor and privilege of holding "The Luck." It was a cruel mortification to Kentuck—who, in the carelessness of a large nature and the habits of frontier life, had begun to regard all garments as a second cuticle, which, like a snake's, only sloughed off through decay—to be debarred this privilege from certain prudential reasons. Yet such was the subtle influence of innovation that he thereafter appeared regularly every afternoon in a clean shirt, and face still shining from his ablutions. Nor were moral and social sanitary laws neglected. "Tommy," who was supposed to spend his whole existence in a persistent attempt to repose, must not be disturbed by noise. The shouting and yelling which had gained the camp its infelicitous title were not permitted within hearing distance of Stumpy's. The men conversed in whispers, or smoked with Indian gravity. Profanity was tacitly given up in these sacred precincts, and throughout the camp a popular form of expletive, known as "D—n the luck!" and "Curse the luck!" was abandoned, as having a new personal bearing. Vocal music was not interdicted, being supposed to have a soothing, tranquilizing quality, and one song, sung by "Man-o'-War Jack," an English sailor, from her Majesty's Australian colonies, was quite popular as a lullaby. It was a lugubrious recital of the exploits of "the Arethusa, Seventy-four," in a muffled minor, ending with a prolonged dying fall at the burden of each verse, "On b-o-o-o-ard of the Arethusa."[8] It was a fine sight to see Jack holding The Luck, rocking from side to side as if with the motion of a ship, and crooning forth this naval ditty. Either through the peculiar rocking of Jack or the length of his song,—it contained ninety stanzas, and was continued with conscientious deliberation to the bitter end,—the lullaby generally had the desired effect. At such times the men would lie at full length under the trees, in the soft summer twilight, smoking their pipes and drinking in the melodious utterances. An indistinct idea that this was pastoral happiness pervaded the camp. "This 'ere kind o' think," said the Cockney Simmons, meditatively reclining on his elbow, "is 'evingly." It reminded him of Greenwich.

On the long summer days The Luck was usually carried to the gulch, from whence the golden store of Roaring Camp was taken. There, on a blanket spread over pine-boughs, he would lie while the men were working in the ditches below. Latterly, there was a rude attempt to decorate this bower with flowers and sweet-smelling shrubs, and generally someone would bring him a cluster of wild honeysuckles, azaleas, or the painted blossoms of Las Mariposas. The men had suddenly awakened to the fact that there were beauty and significance in these trifles, which they had so long trodden carelessly beneath their feet. A flake of glittering mica, a fragment of variegated quartz, a bright pebble from the bed of the creek, became beautiful to eyes thus cleared and strengthened, and were invariably put aside for "The Luck." It was wonderful how many treasures the woods and hillsides

yielded that "would do for Tommy." Surrounded by playthings
such as never child out of fairy-land had before, it is to be hoped
that Tommy was content. He appeared to be securely happy albeit
there was an infantine gravity about him a contemplative light in
his round gray eyes that sometimes worried Stumpy. He was always tractable and quiet, and it is recorded that once having crept
beyond his "corral,"—a hedge of tessellated pine-boughs, which
surrounded his bed,—he dropped over the bank on his head in the
soft earth, and remained with his mottled legs in the air in that position for at least five minutes with unflinching gravity. He was ex-
tricated without a murmur. I hesitate to record the many other
instances of his sagacity, which rest, unfortunately, upon the statements of prejudiced friends. Some of them were not without a
tinge of superstition. "I crep' up the bank just now," said Kentuck
one day, in a breathless state of excitement, "and dern my skin if
he wasn't a talking to a jaybird as was a sittin' on his lap. There
they was, just as free and sociable as anything you please, a jawin'
at each other just like two cherry-bums." Howbeit, whether creeping over the pine-boughs or lying lazily on his back blinking at the
leaves above him, to him the birds sang, the squirrels chattered,
and the flowers bloomed. Nature was his nurse and playfellow.
For him she would let slip between the leaves golden shafts of
sunlight that fell just within his grasp; she would send wandering
breezes to visit him with the balm of bay and resinous gums;
to him the tall red-woods nodded familiarly and sleepily, the
bumble-bees buzzed, and the rooks cawed a slumbrous accompaniment.

Such was the golden summer of Roaring Camp. They were
"flush times,"—and the Luck was with them. The claims had
yielded enormously. The camp was jealous of its privileges and
looked suspiciously on strangers. No encouragement was given to
immigration, and, to make their seclusion more perfect, the land
on either side of the mountain wall that surrounded the camp they
duly preempted. This, and a reputation for singular proficiency
with the revolver, kept the reserve of Roaring Camp inviolate. The
expressman—their only connecting link with the surrounding
world—sometimes told wonderful stories of the camp. He would
say, "They've a street up there in 'Roaring,' that would lay over

any street in Red Dog. They've got vines and flowers round their houses, and they wash themselves twice a day. But they're mighty rough on strangers, and they worship an Ingin baby."

With the prosperity of the camp came a desire for further improvement. It was proposed to build a hotel in the following spring, and to invite one or two decent families to reside there for the sake of "The Luck,"—who might perhaps profit by female companionship. The sacrifice that this concession to the sex cost these men, who were fiercely sceptical in regard to its general virtue and usefulness, can only be accounted for by their affection for Tommy. A few still held out. But the resolve could not be carried into effect for three months, and the minority meekly yielded in the hope that something might turn up to prevent it. And it did.

The winter of 1851 will long be remembered in the foothills. The snow lay deep on the Sierras, and every mountain creek became a river, and every river a lake. Each gorge and gulch was transformed into a tumultuous watercourse that descended the hillsides, tearing down giant trees and scattering its drift and débris along the plain. Red Dog had been twice under water, and Roaring Camp had been forewarned. "Water put the gold into them gulches," said Stumpy. "It's been here once and will be here again!" And that night the North Fork suddenly leaped over its banks, and swept up the triangular valley of Roaring Camp.

In the confusion of rushing water, crushing trees, and crackling timber, and the darkness which seemed to flow with the water and blot out the fair valley, but little could be done to collect the scattered camp. When the morning broke, the cabin of Stumpy nearest the river-bank was gone. Higher up the gulch they found the body of its unlucky owner; but the pride, the hope, the joy, the Luck, of Roaring Camp had disappeared. They were returning with sad hearts, when a shout from the bank recalled them.

It was a relief-boat from down the river. They had picked up, they said, a man and an infant, nearly exhausted, about two miles below. Did anybody know them, and did they belong here?

It needed but a glance to show them Kentuck lying there, cruelly crushed and bruised, but still holding the Luck of Roaring Camp in his arms. As they bent over the strangely assorted pair, they saw that the child was cold and pulseless. "He is dead," said one. Kentuck opened his eyes. "Dead?" he repeated feebly. "Yes, my man, and you are dying too." A smile lit the eyes of the expiring Kentuck. "Dying," he repeated, "he's a taking me with him,— tell the boys I've got the Luck with me now"; and the strong man, clinging to the frail babe as a drowning man is said to cling to a straw, drifted away into the shadowy river that flows forever to the unknown sea.

Aug. 1868

The Outcasts of Poker Flat

AS MR. JOHN OAKHURST, gambler, stepped into the main street of Poker Flat on the morning of the twenty-third of November, 1850, he was conscious of a change in its moral atmosphere since the preceding night. Two or three men, conversing earnestly together, ceased as he approached, and exchanged significant glances. There was a Sabbath lull in the air, which, in a settlement unused to Sabbath influences, looked ominous.

Mr. Oakhurst's calm, handsome face betrayed small concern in these indications. Whether he was conscious of any predisposing cause was another question. "I reckon they're after somebody," he reflected; "likely it's me." He returned to his pocket the handkerchief with which he had been whipping away the red dust of Poker Flat from his neat boots, and quietly discharged his mind of any further conjecture.

In point of fact, Poker Flat was "after somebody." It had lately suffered the loss of several thousand dollars, two valuable horses, and a prominent citizen. It was experiencing a spasm of virtuous reaction, quite as lawless and ungovernable as any of the acts that had provoked it. A secret committee had determined to rid the town of all improper persons. This was done permanently in regard of two men who were then hanging from the boughs of a sycamore in the gulch, and temporarily in the banishment of certain other objectionable characters. I regret to say that some of these were ladies. It is but due to the sex, however, to state that their impropriety was professional, and it was only in such easily established standards of evil that Poker Flat ventured to sit in judgment.

Mr. Oakhurst was right in supposing that he was included in this category. A few of the committee had urged hanging him as a possible example, and a sure method of reimbursing themselves from his pockets of the sums he had won from them. "It's agin justice," said Jim Wheeler, "to let this yer young man from Roaring Camp—an entire stranger—carry away our money." But a crude sentiment of equity residing in the breasts of those who had been fortunate enough to win from Mr. Oakhurst overruled this narrower local prejudice.

Mr. Oakhurst received his sentence with philosophic calmness, none the less coolly that he was aware of the hesitation of his judges. He was too much of a gambler not to accept Fate. With him life was at best an uncertain game, and he recognized the usual percentage in favor of the dealer.

A body of armed men accompanied the deported wickedness of Poker Flat to the outskirts of the settlement. Besides Mr. Oakhurst, who was known to be a coolly desperate man, and for whose intimidation the armed escort was intended, the expatriated party consisted of a young woman familiarly known as "The Duchess"; another who had won the title of "Mother Shipton";[1] and "Uncle Billy," a suspected sluice-robber and confirmed drunkard. The cavalcade provoked no comments from the spectators, nor was any word uttered by the escort. Only, when the gulch which marked the uttermost limit of Poker Flat was reached, the leader spoke briefly and to the point. The exiles were forbidden to return at the peril of their lives.

As the escort disappeared, their pent-up feelings found vent in a few hysterical tears from the Duchess, some bad language from Mother Shipton, and a Parthian volley[2] of expletives from Uncle Billy. The philosophic Oakhurst alone remained silent. He listened calmly to Mother Shipton's desire to cut somebody's heart out, to the repeated statements of the Duchess that she would die in the road, and to the alarming oaths that seemed to be bumped out of Uncle Billy as he rode forward. With the easy good-humor characteristic of his class, he insisted upon exchanging his own riding-horse, "Five Spot," for the sorry mule which the Duchess rode. But even this act did not draw the party into any closer sympathy. The young woman readjusted her somewhat draggled plumes with a feeble, faded coquetry; Mother Shipton eyed the possessor of "Five Spot" with malevolence, and Uncle Billy included the whole party in one sweeping anathema.

The road to Sandy Bar—a camp that, not having as yet experienced the regenerating influences of Poker Flat, consequently seemed to offer some invitation to the emigrants—lay over a steep mountain range. It was distant a day's severe travel. In that advanced season, the party soon passed out of the moist, temperate regions of the foot-hills into the dry, cold, bracing air of the Sierras. The trail was narrow and difficult. At noon the Duchess, rolling out of her saddle upon the ground, declared her intention of going no farther, and the party halted.

The spot was singularly wild and impressive. A wooded amphitheater surrounded on three sides by precipitous cliffs of naked granite, sloped gently toward the crest of another precipice that overlooked the valley. It was, undoubtedly, the most suitable spot for a camp, had camping been advisable. But Mr. Oakhurst knew that scarcely half the journey to Sandy Bar was accomplished, and the party were not equipped or provisioned for delay. This fact he pointed out to his companions curtly, with a philosophic commentary on the folly of "throwing up their hand before the game was played out." But they were furnished with liquor, which in this emergency stood them in place of food, fuel, rest, and prescience. In spite of his remonstrances, it was not long before they were more or less under its influence. Uncle Billy passed rapidly from a bellicose state into one of stupor, the Duchess became maudlin, and Mother Shipton snored. Mr. Oakhurst alone remained erect, leaning against a rock, calmly surveying them.

Mr. Oakhurst did not drink. It interfered with a profession which required coolness, impassiveness, and presence of mind, and, in his own language, he "couldn't afford it." As he gazed at his recumbent fellow-exiles, the loneliness begotten of his pariah-trade, his habits of life, his very vices, for the first time seriously oppressed him. He bestirred himself in dusting his black clothes, washing his hands and face, and other acts characteristic of his studiously neat habits, and for a moment forgot his annoyance. The thought of deserting his weaker and more pitiable companions never perhaps occurred to him. Yet he could not help feeling the want of that excitement which, singularly enough, was most conducive to that calm equanimity for which he was notorious. He looked at the gloomy walls that rose a thousand feet sheer above the circling pines around him; at the sky, ominously clouded; at the valley below, already deepening into shadow. And, doing so, suddenly he heard his own name called.

A horseman slowly ascended the trail. In the fresh, open face of the new-comer Mr. Oakhurst recognized Tom Simson, otherwise known as "The Innocent" of Sandy Bar. He had met him some months before over a "little game," and had, with perfect equanimity, won the entire fortune—amounting to some forty dollars—of that guileless youth. After the game was finished, Mr. Oakhurst drew the youthful speculator behind the door and thus addressed him: "Tommy, you're a good little man, but you can't gamble worth a cent. Don't try it over again." He then handed him his money back, pushed him gently from the room, and so made a devoted slave of Tom Simson.

There was a remembrance of this in his boyish and enthusiastic greeting of Mr. Oakhurst. He had started, he said, to go to Poker Flat to seek his fortune. "Alone?" No, not exactly alone; in fact (a giggle), he had run away with Piney Woods.[3] Didn't Mr. Oakhurst remember Piney? She that used to wait on the table at the Temperance House? They had been engaged a long time, but old Jake Woods had objected, and so they had run away, and were going to Poker Flat to be married, and here they were. And they were tired out, and how lucky it was they had found a place to camp and company. All this the Innocent delivered rapidly, while Piney, a stout, comely damsel of fifteen, emerged from behind the pine-tree, where she had been blushing unseen, and rode to the side of her lover.

Mr. Oakhurst seldom troubled himself with sentiment, still less with propriety; but he had a vague idea that the situation was not fortunate. He retained, however, his presence of mind sufficiently to kick Uncle Billy, who was about to say something, and Uncle Billy was sober enough to recognize in Mr. Oakhurst's kick a superior power that would not bear trifling. He then endeavored to dissuade Tom Simson from delaying further, but in vain. He even pointed out the fact that there was no provision, nor means of making a camp. But, unluckily, the Innocent met this objection by assuring the party that he was provided with an extra mule loaded with provisions, and by the discovery of a rude attempt at a log-house near the trail. "Piney can stay with Mrs. Oakhurst," said the Innocent, pointing to the Duchess, "and I can shift for myself."

Nothing but Mr. Oakhurst's admonishing foot saved Uncle Billy from bursting into a roar of laughter. As it was, he felt compelled to retire up the cañon until he could recover his gravity. There he confided the joke to the tall pine-trees, with many slaps of his leg, contortions of his face, and the usual profanity. But when he returned to the party, he found them seated by a fire—for the air had grown strangely chill and the sky overcast—in apparently amicable conversation. Piney was actually talking in an impulsive, girlish fashion to the Duchess, who was listening with an interest and animation she had not shown for many days. The Innocent was holding forth, apparently with equal effect, to Mr. Oakhurst and Mother Shipton, who was actually relaxing into amiability. "Is this yer a d—d picnic?" said Uncle Billy, with inward scorn, as he surveyed the sylvan group, the glancing firelight, and the tethered animals in the foreground. Suddenly an idea mingled with the alcoholic fumes that disturbed his brain. It was apparently of a jocular nature, for he felt impelled to slap his leg again and cram his fist into his mouth.

As the shadows crept slowly up the mountain, a slight breeze rocked the tops of the pine-trees, and moaned through their long and gloomy aisles. The ruined cabin, patched and covered with pine-boughs, was set apart for the ladies. As the lovers parted, they unaffectedly exchanged a kiss, so honest and sincere that it might have been heard above the swaying pines. The frail Duchess and the malevolent Mother Shipton were probably too stunned to remark upon this last evidence of simplicity, and so turned without a word to the hut. The fire was replenished, the men lay down before the door, and in a few minutes were asleep.

Mr. Oakhurst was a light sleeper. Toward morning he awoke benumbed and cold. As he stirred the dying fire, the wind, which was now blowing strongly, brought to his cheek that which caused the blood to leave it,—snow!

He started to his feet with the intention of awakening the sleepers, for there was no time to lose. But turning to where Uncle Billy had been lying, he found him gone. A suspicion leaped to his brain and a curse to his lips. He ran to the spot where the mules had been tethered; they were no longer there. The tracks were already rapidly disappearing in the snow.

The momentary excitement brought Mr. Oakhurst back to the fire with his usual calm. He did not waken the sleepers. The Innocent slumbered peacefully, with a smile on his good-humored, freckled face; the virgin Piney slept beside her frailer sisters as sweetly as though attended by celestial guardians, and Mr. Oakhurst, drawing his blanket over his shoulders, stroked his mustaches and waited for the dawn. It came slowly in a whirling mist of snow-flakes, that dazzled and confused the eye. What could be seen of the landscape appeared magically changed. He looked over the valley, and summed up the present and future in two words,—"snowed in!"

A careful inventory of the provisions, which, fortunately for the party, had been stored within the hut, and so escaped the felonious fingers of Uncle Billy, disclosed the fact that with care and prudence they might last ten days longer. "That is," said Mr. Oakhurst, *sotto voce*[4] to the Innocent, "if you're willing to board us. If you ain't—and perhaps you'd better not—you can wait till Uncle Billy gets back with provisions." For some occult reason, Mr. Oakhurst could not bring himself to disclose Uncle Billy's rascality, and so offered the hypothesis that he had wandered from the camp and had accidentally stampeded the animals. He dropped a warning to the Duchess and Mother Shipton, who of course knew the facts of their associate's defection. "They'll find out the truth about us *all* when they find out anything," he added, significantly, "and there's no good frightening them now."

Tom Simson not only put all his worldly store at the disposal of Mr. Oakhurst, but seemed to enjoy the prospect of their enforced seclusion. "We'll have a good camp for a week, and then the snow'll melt, and we'll all go back together." The cheerful gaiety of the young man and Mr. Oakhurst's calm infected the others. The Innocent, with the aid of pine-boughs, extemporized a thatch for the roofless cabin, and the Duchess directed Piney in the re-arrangement of the interior with a taste and tact that opened the blue eyes of that provincial maiden to their fullest extent. "I reckon now you're used to fine things at Poker Flat," said Piney. The Duchess turned away sharply to conceal something that reddened her cheeks through its professional tint, and Mother Shipton requested Piney not to "chatter." But when Mr. Oakhurst returned from a weary search for the trail, he heard the sound of happy laughter echoed from the rocks. He stopped in some alarm, and his thoughts first naturally reverted to the whiskey, which he had prudently *cachéd*.[5] "And yet it don't somehow sound like whiskey," said the gambler. It was not until he caught sight of the blazing fire through the still-blinding storm and the group around it that he settled to the conviction that it was "square fun."

Whether Mr. Oakhurst had *cachéd* his cards with the whiskey as something debarred the free access of the community, I cannot say. It was certain that, in Mother Shipton's words, he "didn't say cards once" during that evening. Haply the time was beguiled by an accordion, produced somewhat ostentatiously by Tom Simson from his pack. Notwithstanding some difficulties attending the manipulation of this instrument, Piney Woods managed to pluck several reluctant melodies from its keys, to an accompaniment by the Innocent on a pair of bone castinets. But the crowning festivity of the evening was reached in a rude camp-meeting hymn, which the lovers, joining hands, sang with great earnestness and vociferation. I fear that a certain defiant tone and Covenanter's swing to its chorus,[6] rather than any devotional quality, caused it speedily to infect the others, who at last joined in the refrain:—

> "I'm proud to live in the service of the Lord,
> And I'm bound to die in His army."[7]

The pines rocked, the storm eddied and whirled above the miserable group, and the flames of their altar leaped heavenward, as if in token of the vow.

At midnight the storm abated, the rolling clouds parted, and the stars glittered keenly above the sleeping camp. Mr. Oakhurst, whose professional habits had enabled him to live on the smallest possible amount of sleep, in dividing the watch with Tom Simson, somehow managed to take upon himself the greater part of that duty. He excused himself to the Innocent, by saying that he had "often been a week without sleep." "Doing what?" asked Tom. "Poker!" replied Oakhurst, sententiously; "when a man gets a streak of luck,—nigger-luck,—he don't get tired. The luck gives in first. Luck," continued the gambler, reflectively, "is a mighty queer thing. All you know about it for certain is that it's bound to change. And it's finding out when it's going to change that makes you. We've had a streak of bad luck since we left Poker Flat,—you come along, and slap you get into it, too. If you can hold your cards right along you're all right. For," added the gambler, with cheerful irrelevance,—

> " 'I'm proud to live in the service of the Lord,
>   And I'm bound to die in His army.' "

The third day came, and the sun, looking through the white-curtained valley, saw the outcasts divide their slowly decreasing store of provisions for the morning meal. It was one of the peculiarities of that mountain climate that its rays diffused a kindly warmth over the wintry landscape, as if in regretful commiseration of the past. But it revealed drift on drift of snow piled high around the hut,—a hopeless, uncharted, trackless sea of white lying below the rocky shores to which the castaways still clung. Through the marvellously clear air the smoke of the pastoral village of Poker Flat rose miles away. Mother Shipton saw it, and from a remote pinnacle of her rocky fastness, hurled in that direction a final malediction. It was her last vituperative attempt, and perhaps for that reason was invested with a certain degree of sublimity. It did her good, she privately informed the Duchess. "Just you go out there and cuss, and see." She then set herself to the task of amusing "the child," as she and the Duchess were pleased to call Piney. Piney was no chicken, but it was a soothing and original theory of the pair thus to account for the fact that she didn't swear and wasn't improper.

When night crept up again through the gorges, the reedy notes of the accordion rose and fell in fitful spasms and long-drawn gasps by the flickering camp-fire. But music failed to fill entirely the aching void left by insufficient food, and a new diversion was proposed by Piney,—story-telling. Neither Mr. Oakhurst nor his female companions caring to relate their personal experiences, this plan would have failed, too, but for the Innocent. Some months before he had chanced upon a stray copy of Mr. Pope's ingenious translation of the Iliad.[8] He now proposed to narrate the principal incidents of that poem—having thoroughly mastered the argument and fairly forgotten the words—in the current vernacular of Sandy Bar. And so for the rest of that night the Homeric demigods again walked the earth. Trojan bully and wily Greek wrestled in the winds, and the great pines in the *cañon* seemed to bow to the wrath of the son of Peleus.[9] Mr. Oakhurst listened with quiet satisfaction. Most especially was he interested in the fate of "Ash-heels," as the Innocent persisted in denominating the "swift-footed Achilles."[10]

So with small food and much of Homer and the accordion, a week passed over the heads of the outcasts. The sun again forsook them, and again from leaden skies the snow-flakes were sifted over the land. Day by day closer around them drew the snowy circle, until at last they looked from their prison over drifted walls of dazzling white, that towered twenty feet above their heads. It became more and more difficult to replenish their fires, even from the fallen trees beside them, now half hidden in the drifts. And yet no one complained. The lovers turned from the dreary prospect and looked into each other's eyes, and were happy. Mr. Oakhurst settled himself coolly to the losing game before him. The Duchess, more cheerful than she had been, assumed the care of Piney. Only Mother Shipton—once the strongest of the party—seemed to sicken and fade. At midnight on the tenth day she called Oakhurst to her side. "I'm going," she said, in a voice of querulous weakness, "but don't say anything about it. Don't waken the kids. Take the bundle from under my head and open it." Mr. Oakhurst did so. It contained Mother Shipton's rations for the last week, untouched. "Give 'em to the child," she said, pointing to the sleeping Piney. "You've starved yourself," said the gambler. "That's what they call it," said the woman, querulously, as she lay down again, and, turning her face to the wall, passed quietly away.

The accordion and the bones were put aside that day, and Homer was forgotten. When the body of Mother Shipton had been committed to the snow, Mr. Oakhurst took the Innocent aside, and showed him a pair of snow-shoes, which he had fashioned from the old pack-saddle. "There's one chance in a hundred to save her yet," he said, pointing to Piney; "but it's there," he added, pointing toward Poker Flat. "If you can reach there in two days she's safe." "And you?" asked Tom Simson. "I'll stay here," was the curt reply.

The lovers parted with a long embrace. "You are not going,

too?" said the Duchess, as she saw Mr. Oakhurst apparently waiting to accompany him. "As far as the *cañon,*" he replied. He
turned suddenly, and kissed the Duchess, leaving her pallid face
aflame, and her trembling limbs rigid with amazement.

Night came, but not Mr. Oakhurst. It brought the storm again
and the whirling snow. Then the Duchess, feeding the fire, found
that some one had quietly piled beside the hut enough fuel to last
a few days longer. The tears rose to her eyes, but she hid them
from Piney.

The women slept but little. In the morning, looking into each
other's faces, they read their fate. Neither spoke; but Piney, accepting the position of the stronger, drew near and placed her arm
around the Duchess's waist. They kept this attitude for the rest of
the day. That night the storm reached its greatest fury, and, rend-
ing asunder the protecting pines, invaded the very hut.

Toward morning they found themselves unable to feed the fire,
which gradually died away. As the embers slowly blackened, the
Duchess crept closer to Piney, and broke the silence of many
hours: "Piney, can you pray?" "No, dear," said Piney, simply. The
Duchess, without knowing exactly why, felt relieved, and, putting
her head upon Piney's shoulder, spoke no more. And so reclining,
the younger and purer pillowing the head of her soiled sister upon
her virgin breast, they fell asleep.

The wind lulled as if it feared to waken them. Feathery drifts of
snow, shaken from the long pine-boughs, flew like white-winged
birds, and settled about them as they slept. The moon through the
rifted clouds looked down upon what had been the camp. But all
human stain, all trace of earthly travail, was hidden beneath the
spotless mantle mercifully flung from above.

They slept all that day and the next, nor did they waken when
voices and footsteps broke the silence of the camp. And when
pitying fingers brushed the snow from their wan faces, you could
scarcely have told from the equal peace that dwelt upon them,
which was she that had sinned. Even the law of Poker Flat recognized this, and turned away, leaving them still locked in each
other's arms.

But at the head of the gulch, on one of the largest pine-trees,
they found the deuce of clubs pinned to the bark with a bowie-
knife. It bore the following, written in pencil, in a firm hand—

†

BENEATH THIS TREE
LIES THE BODY
OF
JOHN OAKHURST,
WHO STRUCK A STREAK OF BAD LUCK
ON THE 23D OF NOVEMBER, 1850,
AND
HANDED IN HIS CHECKS
ON THE 7TH DECEMBER, 1850.

⊥

And pulseless and cold, with a Derringer by his side and a bullet in his heart, though still calm as in life, beneath the snow lay he who was at once the strongest and yet the weakest of the outcasts of Poker Flat.

Jan. 1869

Miggles

WE WERE EIGHT, including the driver. We had not spoken during the passage of the last six miles, since the jolting of the heavy vehicle over the roughening road had spoiled the Judge's last poetical quotation. The tall man beside the Judge was asleep, his arm passed through the swaying strap and his head resting upon it,—altogether a limp, helpless-looking object; as if he had hanged himself and been cut down too late. The French lady on the back seat was asleep, too, yet in a half-conscious propriety of attitude, shown even in the disposition of the handkerchief which she held to her forehead and which partially veiled her face. The lady from Virginia City, travelling with her husband, had long since lost all individuality in a wild confusion of ribbons, veils, furs, and shawls. There was no sound but the rattling of wheels and the dash of rain upon the roof. Suddenly the stage stopped and we became dimly aware of voices. The driver was evidently in the midst of an exciting colloquy with someone in the road,—a colloquy of which such fragments as "bridge gone," "twenty feet of water," "can't pass," were occasionally distinguishable above the storm. Then came a lull, and a mysterious voice from the road shouted the parting adjuration,—

"Try Miggles's."

We caught a glimpse of our leaders as the vehicle slowly turned, of a horseman vanishing through the rain, and we were evidently on our way to Miggles's.

Who and where was Miggles? The Judge, our authority, did not remember the name, and he knew the country thoroughly. The Washoe[1] traveller thought Miggles must keep a hotel. We only knew that we were stopped by high water in front and rear, and that Miggles was our rock of refuge.[2] A ten minutes' splashing through a tangled by-road, scarcely wide enough for the stage, and we drew up before a barred and boarded gate in a wide stone wall or fence about eight feet high. Evidently Miggles's, and evidently Miggles did not keep a hotel.

The driver got down and tried the gate. It was securely locked.

"Miggles! O Miggles!"

No answer.

"Migg-ells! You Miggles!" continued the driver, with rising wrath.

"Migglesy!" joined in the expressman, persuasively. "O Miggy! Mig!"

But no reply came from the apparently insensate Miggles. The Judge, who had finally got the window down, put his head out and propounded a series of questions, which if answered categorically would have undoubtedly elucidated the whole mystery, but which the driver evaded by replying that "if we didn't want to sit in the coach all night, we had better rise up and sing out for Miggles."

So we rose up and called on Miggles in chorus; then separately. And when we had finished, a Hibernian fellow-passenger from the roof called for "Maygells!" whereat we all laughed. While we were laughing, the driver cried "Shoo!"

We listened. To our infinite amazement the chorus of "Miggles" was repeated from the other side of the wall, even to the final and supplemental "Maygells."

"Extraordinary echo," said the Judge.

"Extraordinary d—d skunk!" roared the driver, contemptuously. "Come out of that, Miggles, and show yourself! Be a man, Miggles! Don't hide in the dark; I wouldn't if I were you, Miggles," continued Yuba Bill, now dancing about in an excess of fury.

"Miggles!" continued the voice, "O Miggles!"

"My good man! Mr. Myghail!" said the Judge, softening the asperities of the name as much as possible. "Consider the inhospitality of refusing shelter from the inclemency of the weather to helpless females. Really, my dear sir—" But a succession of "Miggles," ending in a burst of laughter, drowned his voice.

Yuba Bill hesitated no longer. Taking a heavy stone from the road, he battered down the gate, and with the expressman entered the enclosure. We followed. Nobody was to be seen. In the gathering darkness all that we could distinguish was that we were in a garden—from the rosebushes that scattered over us a minute spray from their dripping leaves—and before a long, rambling wooden building.

"Do you know this Miggles?" asked the Judge of Yuba Bill.

"No, nor don't want to," said Bill, shortly, who felt the Pioneer Stage Company insulted in his person by the contumacious Miggles.

"But, my dear sir," expostulated the Judge, as he thought of the barred gate.

"Lookee here," said Yuba Bill, with fine irony, "hadn't you better go back and sit in the coach till yer introduced? I'm going in," and he pushed open the door of the building.

A long room lighted only by the embers of a fire that was dying on the large hearth at its further extremity; the walls curiously papered, and the flickering firelight bringing out its grotesque pattern; somebody sitting in a large arm-chair by the fireplace. All this we saw as we crowded together into the room, after the driver and expressman.

"Hello, be you Miggles?" said Yuba Bill to the solitary occupant.

The figure neither spoke nor stirred. Yuba Bill walked wrathfully toward it, and turned the eye of his coach-lantern upon its face. It was a man's face, prematurely old and wrinkled, with very large eyes, in which there was that expression of perfectly gratuitous solemnity which I had sometimes seen in an owl's. The large eyes wandered from Bill's face to the lantern, and finally fixed their gaze on that luminous object, without further recognition.

Bill restrained himself with an effort.

"Miggles! Be you deaf? You ain't dumb anyhow, you know"; and Yuba Bill shook the insensate figure by the shoulder.

To our great dismay, as Bill removed his hand, the venerable stranger apparently collapsed,—sinking into half his size and an undistinguishable heap of clothing.

"Well, dern my skin," said Bill, looking appealingly at us, and hopelessly retiring from the contest.

The Judge now stepped forward, and we lifted the mysterious invertebrate back into his original position. Bill was dismissed with the lantern to reconnoiter outside, for it was evident that from the helplessness of this solitary man there must be attendants near at hand, and we all drew around the fire. The Judge, who had regained his authority, and had never lost his conversational amiability,—standing before us with his back to the hearth,—charged us, as an imaginary jury, as follows:—

"It is evident that either our distinguished friend here has reached that condition described by Shakespeare as 'the sere and yellow leaf,'[3] or has suffered some premature abatement of his mental and physical faculties. Whether he is really the Miggles—"

Here he was interrupted by "Miggles! O Miggles! Migglesy! Mig!" and, in fact, the whole chorus of Miggles in very much the same key as it had once before been delivered unto us.

We gazed at each other for a moment in some alarm. The Judge, in particular, vacated his position quickly, as the voice seemed to come directly over his shoulder. The cause, however, was soon discovered in a large magpie who was perched upon a shelf over the fireplace, and who immediately relapsed into a sepulchral silence, which contrasted singularly with his previous volubility. It was, undoubtedly, his voice which we had heard in the road, and our friend in the chair was not responsible for the discourtesy. Yuba Bill, who re-entered the room after an unsuccessful search, was loath to accept the explanation, and still eyed the helpless sitter with suspicion. He had found a shed in which he had put up his horses, but he came back dripping and sceptical. "Thar ain't nobody but him within ten mile of the shanty, and that 'ar d—d old skeesicks knows it."

But the faith of the majority proved to be securely based. Bill had scarcely ceased growling before we heard a quick step upon the porch, the trailing of a wet skirt, the door was flung open, and with a flash of white teeth, a sparkle of dark eyes, and an utter absence of ceremony or diffidence, a young woman entered, shut the door, and, panting, leaned back against it.

"O, if you please, I'm Miggles!"

And this was Miggles! this bright-eyed, full-throated young woman, whose wet gown of coarse blue stuff could not hide the beauty of the feminine curves to which it clung; from the chestnut crown of whose head, topped by a man's oil-skin sou'wester, to the little feet and ankles, hidden somewhere in the recesses of her boy's brogans, all was grace;—this was Miggles, laughing at us, too, in the most airy, frank, off-hand manner imaginable.

"You see, boys," said she, quite out of breath, and holding one little hand against her side, quite unheeding the speechless discomfiture of our party, or the complete demoralization of Yuba Bill, whose features had relaxed into an expression of gratuitous and imbecile cheerfulness,—"you see, boys, I was mor'n two miles away when you passed down the road. I thought you might pull up here, and so I ran the whole way, knowing nobody was home but Jim,—and—and—I'm out of breath—and—that lets me out."

And here Miggles caught her dripping oil-skin hat from her head, with a mischievous swirl that scattered a shower of raindrops over us; attempted to put back her hair; dropped two hairpins in the attempt; laughed and sat down beside Yuba Bill, with her hands crossed lightly on her lap.

The Judge recovered himself first, and essayed an extravagant compliment.

"I'll trouble you for that thar har-pin," said Miggles, gravely. Half a dozen hands were eagerly stretched forward; the missing hair-pin was restored to its fair owner; and Miggles, crossing the room, looked keenly in the face of the invalid. The solemn eyes looked back at her with an expression we had never seen before. Life and intelligence seemed to struggle back into the rugged face. Miggles laughed again,—it was a singularly eloquent laugh,—and turned her black eyes and white teeth once more toward us.

"This afflicted person is—" hesitated the Judge.

"Jim," said Miggles.

"Your father?"

"No."

"Brother?"

"No."

"Husband?"

Miggles darted a quick, half-defiant glance at the two lady passengers who I had noticed did not participate in the general masculine admiration of Miggles, and said, gravely, "No; it's Jim."

There was an awkward pause. The lady passengers moved closer to each other; the Washoe husband looked abstractedly at the fire; and the tall man apparently turned his eyes inward for self-support at this emergency. But Miggles's laugh, which was very infectious, broke the silence. "Come," she said briskly, "you must be hungry. Who'll bear a hand to help me get tea?"

She had no lack of volunteers. In a few moments Yuba Bill was engaged like Caliban in bearing logs for this Miranda;[4] the expressman was grinding coffee on the veranda; to myself the arduous duty of slicing bacon was assigned; and the Judge lent each man his good-humored and voluble counsel. And when Miggles, assisted by the Judge and our Hibernian "deck passenger," set the table with all the available crockery, we had become quite joyous, in spite of the rain that beat against windows, the wind that whirled down the chimney, the two ladies who whispered together in the corner, or the magpie who uttered a satirical and croaking commentary on their conversation from his perch above. In the now bright, blazing fire we could see that the walls were papered with illustrated journals, arranged with feminine taste and discrimination. The furniture was extemporized, and adapted from candle-boxes and packing-cases, and covered with gay calico, or the skin of some animal. The arm-chair of the helpless Jim was an ingenious variation of a flour-barrel. There was neatness, and even a taste for the picturesque, to be seen in the few details of the long low room.

The meal was a culinary success. But more, it was a social triumph,—chiefly, I think, owing to the rare tact of Miggles in guiding the conversation, asking all the questions herself, yet bearing throughout a frankness that rejected the idea of any concealment on her own part, so that we talked of ourselves, of our prospects, of the journey, of the weather, of each other,—of everything but our host and hostess. It must be confessed that Miggles's conversation was never elegant, rarely grammatical, and that at times she employed expletives, the use of which had generally been yielded to our sex. But they were delivered with such a lighting up of teeth and eyes, and were usually followed by a laugh—a laugh peculiar to Miggles—so frank and honest that it seemed to clear the moral atmosphere.

Once, during the meal, we heard a noise like the rubbing of a heavy body against the outer walls of the house. This was shortly followed by a scratching and sniffling at the door. "That's Joaquin," said Miggles, in reply to our questioning glances; "would you like to see him?" Before we could answer she had opened the door, and disclosed a half-grown grizzly, who instantly raised himself on his haunches, with his forepaws hanging down in the popular attitude of mendicancy, and looked admiringly at Miggles, with a very singular resemblance in his manner to Yuba Bill. "That's my watch-dog," said Miggles, in explanation. "O, he don't bite," she added, as the two lady passengers fluttered into a corner. "Does he, old Toppy?" (the latter remark being addressed directly to the sagacious Joaquin). "I tell you what, boys," continued Miggles, after she had fed and closed the door on *Ursa Minor*,[5] "you were in big luck that Joaquin wasn't hanging round when you dropped in to-night." "Where was he?" asked the Judge. "With me," said Miggles. "Lord love you; he trots round with me nights like as if he was a man."

We were silent for a few moments, and listened to the wind. Perhaps we all had the same picture before us,—of Miggles walking through the rainy woods, with her savage guardian at her side. The Judge, I remember, said something about Una and her lion;[6] but Miggles received it as she did other compliments, with quiet gravity. Whether she was altogether unconscious of the admiration she excited,—she could hardly have been oblivious of Yuba Bill's adoration,—I know not; but her very frankness suggested a perfect sexual equality that was cruelly humiliating to the younger members of our party.

The incident of the bear did not add anything in Miggles's favor to the opinions of those of her own sex who were present. In fact, the repast over, a chillness radiated from the two lady passengers that no pine-boughs brought in by Yuba Bill and cast as a sacrifice upon the hearth could wholly overcome. Miggles felt it; and, suddenly declaring that it was time to "turn in," offered to show the ladies to their bed in an adjoining room. "You, boys, will have to camp out here by the fire as well as you can," she added, "for thar ain't but the one room."

Our sex—by which, my dear sir, I allude of course to the stronger portion of humanity—has been generally relieved from the imputation of curiosity, or a fondness for gossip. Yet I am constrained to say, that hardly had the door closed on Miggles than we crowded together, whispering, snickering, smiling, and exchanging suspicions, surmises, and a thousand speculations in regard to our pretty hostess and her singular companion. I fear that we even hustled that imbecile paralytic, who sat like a voiceless Memnon[7] in our midst, gazing with the serene indifference of the

Past in his passionless eyes upon our wordy counsels. In the midst of an exciting discussion the door opened again, and Miggles re-entered.

But not, apparently, the same Miggles who a few hours before had flashed upon us. Her eyes were downcast, and as she hesitated for a moment on the threshold, with a blanket on her arm, she seemed to have left behind her the frank fearlessness which had charmed us a moment before. Coming into the room, she drew a low stool beside the paralytic's chair, sat down, drew the blanket over her shoulders, and saying, "If it's all the same to you, boys, as we're rather crowded, I'll stop here to-night," took the invalid's withered hand in her own, and turned her eyes upon the dying fire. An instinctive feeling that this was only premonitory to more confidential relations, and perhaps some shame at our previous curiosity, kept us silent. The rain still beat upon the roof, wander-ing gusts of wind stirred the embers into momentary brightness, until, in a lull of the elements, Miggles suddenly lifted up her head, and, throwing her hair over her shoulder, turned her face upon the group and asked,—

"Is there any of you that knows me?"

There was no reply.

"Think again! I lived at Marysville in '53. Everybody knew me there, and everybody had the right to know me. I kept the Polka Saloon until I came to live with Jim. That's six years ago. Perhaps I've changed some."

The absence of recognition may have disconcerted her. She turned her head to the fire again, and it was some seconds before she again spoke, and then more rapidly:—

"Well, you see, I thought some of you must have known me. There's no great harm done, anyway. What I was going to say was this: Jim here"—she took his hand in both of hers as she spoke—"used to know me, if you didn't, and spent a heap of money upon me. I reckon he spent all he had. And one day—it's six years ago this winter—Jim came into my back room, sat down on my sofy, like as you see him in that chair, and never moved again without help. He was struck all of a heap, and never seemed to know what ailed him. The doctors came and said as how it was caused all along of his way of life,—for Jim was mighty free and wild like,—and that he would never get better, and couldn't last long anyway. They advised me to send him to Frisco to the hospital, for he was no good to any one and would be a baby all his life. Perhaps it was something in Jim's eye, perhaps it was that I never had a baby, but I said 'No.' I was rich then, for I was popular with everybody,—gentlemen like yourself, sir, came to see me,—and I sold out my business and bought this yer place, because it was sort of out of the way of travel, you see, and I brought my baby here."

With a woman's intuitive tact and poetry, she had, as she spoke, slowly shifted her position so as to bring the mute figure of the ruined man between her and her audience, hiding in the shadow behind it, as if she offered it as a tacit apology for her actions. Silent and expressionless, it yet spoke for her; helpless, crushed, and smitten with the Divine thunderbolt, it still stretched an invisible arm around her.

Hidden in the darkness, but still holding his hand, she went on:—

"It was a long time before I could get the hang of things about yer, for I was used to company and excitement. I couldn't get any woman to help me, and a man I dursent trust; but what with the Indians hereabout, who'd do odd jobs for me, and having everything sent from the North Fork, Jim and I managed to worry through. The Doctor would run up from Sacramento once in a while. He'd ask to see 'Miggles's baby,' as he called Jim, and when he'd go away, he'd say, 'Miggles; you're a trump,—God bless you'; and it didn't seem so lonely after that. But the last time he was here he said, as he opened the door to go, 'Do you know, Miggles, your baby will grow up to be a man yet and an honor to his mother; but not here, Miggles, not here!' And I thought he went away sad,—and—and—" and here Miggles's voice and head were somehow both lost completely in the shadow.

"The folks about here are very kind," said Miggles, after a pause, coming a little into the light again. "The men from the fork used to hang around here, until they found they wasn't wanted, and the women are kind,—and don't call. I was pretty lonely until I picked up Joaquin in the woods yonder one day, when he wasn't so high, and taught him to beg for his dinner; and then thar's Polly—that's the magpie—she knows no end of tricks, and makes it quite sociable of evenings with her talk, and so I don't feel like as I was the only living being about the ranch. And Jim here," said

Miggles, with her old laugh again, and coming out quite into the firelight, "Jim—why, boys, you would admire to see how much he knows for a man like him. Sometimes I bring him flowers, and he looks at 'em just as natural as if he knew 'em; and times, when we're sitting alone, I read him those things on the wall. Why, Lord!" said Miggles, with her frank laugh, "I've read him that whole side of the house this winter. There never was such a man for reading as Jim."

"Why," asked the Judge, "do you not marry this man to whom you have devoted your youthful life?"

"Well, you see," said Miggles, "it would be playing it rather low down on Jim, to take advantage of his being so helpless. And then, too, if we were man and wife, now, we'd both know that I was *bound* to do what I do now of my own accord."

"But you are young yet and attractive—"

"It's getting late," said Miggles, gravely, "and you'd better all turn in. Good-night, boys"; and, throwing the blanket over her head, Miggles laid herself down beside Jim's chair, her head pillowed on the low stool that held his feet, and spoke no more. The fire slowly faded from the hearth; we each sought our blankets in silence; and presently there was no sound in the long room but the pattering of the rain upon the roof, and the heavy breathing of the sleepers.

It was nearly morning when I awoke from a troubled dream. The storm had passed, the stars were shining, and through the shutterless window the full moon, lifting itself over the solemn pines without, looked into the room. It touched the lonely figure in the chair with an infinite compassion, and seemed to baptize with a shining flood the lowly head of the woman whose hair, as in the sweet old story, bathed the feet of him she loved.[8] It even lent a kindly poetry to the rugged outline of Yuba Bill, half reclining on his elbow between them and his passengers, with savagely patient eyes keeping watch and ward. And then I fell asleep and only woke at broad day, with Yuba Bill standing over me, and "All aboard" ringing in my ears.

Coffee was waiting for us on the table, but Miggles was gone. We wandered about the house and lingered long after the horses were harnessed, but she did not return. It was evident that she wished to avoid a formal leave-taking, and had so left us to depart as we

had come. After we had helped the ladies into the coach, we returned to the house and solemnly shook hands with the paralytic
Jim, as solemnly settling him back into position after each hand-
shake. Then we looked for the last time around the long low
room, at the stool where Miggles had sat, and slowly took our
seats in the waiting coach. The whip cracked, and we were off!

But as we reached the high-road, Bill's dexterous hand laid the
six horses back on their haunches, and the stage stopped with a
jerk. For there, on a little eminence beside the road, stood Miggles,
her hair flying, her eyes sparkling, her white handkerchief waving,
and her white teeth flashing a last "good-by." We waved our hats
in return. And then Yuba Bill, as if fearful of further fascination,
madly lashed his horses forward, and we sank back in our seats.
We exchanged not a word until we reached the North Fork, and
the stage drew up at the Independence House. Then, the Judge
leading, we walked into the bar-room and took our places gravely
at the bar.

"Are your glasses charged, gentlemen?" said the Judge,
solemnly taking off his white hat.

They were.

"Well, then, here's to *Miggles*. GOD BLESS HER!"

Perhaps He had. Who knows?

June 1869

Tennessee's Partner

I DO NOT THINK that we ever knew his real name. Our ignorance of it certainly never gave us any social inconvenience, for at Sandy Bar in 1854 most men were christened anew. Sometimes these appellatives were derived from some distinctiveness of dress, as in the case of "Dungaree Jack"; or from some peculiarity of habit, as shown in "Saleratus[1] Bill," so called from an undue proportion of that chemical in his daily bread; or from some unlucky slip, as exhibited in "The Iron Pirate," a mild, inoffensive man, who earned that baleful title by his unfortunate mispronunciation of the term "iron pyrites." Perhaps this may have been the beginning of a rude heraldry; but I am constrained to think that it was because a man's real name in that day rested solely upon his own unsupported statement. "Call yourself Clifford, do you?" said Boston, addressing a timid new-comer with infinite scorn; "hell is full of such Cliffords!" He then introduced the unfortunate man, whose name happened to be really Clifford, as "Jay-bird Charley,"—an unhallowed inspiration of the moment, that clung to him ever after.

But to return to Tennessee's Partner, whom we never knew by any other than this relative title; that he had ever existed as a separate and distinct individuality we only learned later. It seems that in 1853 he left Poker Flat to go to San Francisco, ostensibly to procure a wife. He never got any farther than Stockton. At that place he was attracted by a young person who waited upon the table at the hotel where he took his meals. One morning he said something to her which caused her to smile not unkindly, to somewhat coquettishly break a plate of toast over his up-turned, serious, simple face, and to retreat to the kitchen. He followed her, and emerged a few moments later, covered with more toast and victory. That day week they were married by a Justice of the Peace, and returned to Poker Flat. I am aware that something more might be made of this episode, but I prefer to tell it as it was

current at Sandy Bar,—in the gulches and bar-rooms,—where all
sentiment was modified by a strong sense of humor.

Of their married felicity but little is known, perhaps for the
reason that Tennessee, then living with his partner, one day took
occasion to say something to the bride on his own account, at
which, it is said, she smiled not unkindly and chastely retreated,—
this time as far as Marysville, where Tennessee followed her, and
where they went to housekeeping without the aid of a Justice of
the Peace. Tennessee's Partner took the loss of his wife simply and
seriously, as was his fashion. But to everybody's surprise, when
Tennessee one day returned from Marysville, without his partner's
wife,—she having smiled and retreated with somebody else,—
Tennessee's Partner was the first man to shake his hand and greet
him with affection. The boys who had gathered in the *cañon* to see
the shooting were naturally indignant. Their indignation might
have found vent in sarcasm but for a certain look in Tennessee's
Partner's eye that indicated a lack of humorous appreciation. In
fact, he was a grave man, with a steady application to practical detail which was unpleasant in a difficulty.

Meanwhile a popular feeling against Tennessee had grown up
on the Bar. He was known to be a gambler; he was suspected to be
a thief. In these suspicions Tennessee's Partner was equally compromised; his continued intimacy with Tennessee after the affair
above quoted could only be accounted for on the hypothesis of a
copartnership of crime. At last Tennessee's guilt became flagrant.
One day he overtook a stranger on his way to Red Dog. The
stranger afterward related that Tennessee beguiled the time with
interesting anecdote and reminiscence, but illogically concluded
the interview in the following words: "And now, young man, I'll
trouble you for your knife, your pistols, and your money. You see
your weppings might get you into trouble at Red Dog, and your
money's a temptation to the evilly disposed. I think you said your
address was San Francisco. I shall endeavor to call." It may be
stated here that Tennessee had a fine flow of humor, which no
business preoccupation could wholly subdue.

This exploit was his last. Red Dog and Sandy Bar made common cause against the highwayman. Tennessee was hunted in very
much the same fashion as his prototype, the grizzly. As the toils
closed around him, he made a desperate dash through the Bar,

emptying his revolver at the crowd before the Arcade Saloon, and so on up Grizzly Cañon; but at its farther extremity he was stopped by a small man on a gray horse. The men looked at each other a moment in silence. Both were fearless, both self-possessed and independent; and both types of a civilization that in the seventeenth century would have been called heroic, but, in the nineteenth, simply "reckless." "What have you got there?—I call," said Tennessee, quietly. "Two bowers and an ace," said the stranger, as quietly, showing two revolvers and a bowie-knife. "That takes me," returned Tennessee; and with this gamblers' epigram, he threw away his useless pistol, and rode back with his captor.

It was a warm night. The cool breeze which usually sprang up with the going down of the sun behind the *chaparral*[2]-crested mountain was that evening withheld from Sandy Bar. The little *cañon* was stifling with heated resinous odors, and the decaying drift-wood on the Bar sent forth faint, sickening exhalations. The feverishness of day, and its fierce passions, still filled the camp. Lights moved restlessly along the bank of the river, striking no answering reflection from its tawny current. Against the blackness of the pines the windows of the old loft above the express-office stood out staringly bright; and through their curtainless panes the loungers below could see the forms of those who were even then deciding the fate of Tennessee. And above all this, etched on the dark firmament, rose the Sierra, remote and passionless, crowned with remoter passionless stars.

The trial of Tennessee was conducted as fairly as was consistent with a judge and jury who felt themselves to some extent obliged to justify, in their verdict, the previous irregularities of arrest and indictment. The law of Sandy Bar was implacable, but not vengeful. The excitement and personal feeling of the chase were over; with Tennessee safe in their hands they were ready to listen patiently to any defense, which they were already satisfied was insufficient. There being no doubt in their own minds, they were willing to give the prisoner the benefit of any that might exist. Secure in the hypothesis that he ought to be hanged, on general principles, they indulged him with more latitude of defense than his reckless hardihood seemed to ask. The Judge appeared to be more anxious than the prisoner, who, otherwise unconcerned, evidently took a grim pleasure in the responsibility he had created. "I don't take any hand in this yer game," had been his invariable, but good-humored reply to all questions. The Judge—who was also his captor—for a moment vaguely regretted that he had not shot him "on sight," that morning, but presently dismissed this human weakness as unworthy of the judicial mind. Nevertheless, when there was a tap at the door, and it was said that Tennessee's Partner was there on behalf of the prisoner, he was admitted at once without question. Perhaps the younger members of the jury, to whom the proceedings were becoming irksomely thoughtful, hailed him as a relief.

For he was not, certainly, an imposing figure. Short and stout, with a square face, sunburned into a preternatural redness, clad in a loose duck "jumper," and trousers streaked and splashed with red soil, his aspect under any circumstances would have been quaint, and was now even ridiculous. As he stopped to deposit at his feet a heavy carpet-bag he was carrying, it became obvious, from partially developed legends and inscriptions, that the material with which his trousers had been patched had been originally intended for a less ambitious covering. Yet he advanced with great gravity, and after having shaken the hand of each person in the room with labored cordiality, he wiped his serious, perplexed face on a red bandanna handkerchief, a shade lighter than his complexion, laid his powerful hand upon the table to steady himself, and thus addressed the Judge:—

"I was passin' by," he began, by way of apology, "and I thought I'd just step in and see how things was gittin' on with Tennessee thar,—my pardner. It's a hot night. I disremember any sich weather before on the Bar."

He paused a moment, but nobody volunteering any other meteorological recollection, he again had recourse to his pocket-handkerchief, and for some moments mopped his face diligently.

"Have you anything to say in behalf of the prisoner?" said the Judge, finally.

"Thet's it," said Tennessee's Partner, in a tone of relief. "I come yar as Tennessee's pardner,—knowing him nigh on four year, off and on, wet and dry, in luck and out o' luck. His ways ain't allers my ways, but thar ain't any p'ints in that young man, thar ain't any liveliness as he's been up to, as I don't know. And you sez to me, sez you,—confidential-like, and between man and man,—sez you, 'Do you know anything in his behalf?' and I sez to you, sez I,—confidential-like, as between man and man,—'What should a man know of his pardner?' "

"Is this all you have to say?" asked the Judge, impatiently, feeling, perhaps, that a dangerous sympathy of humor was beginning to humanize the Court.

"Thet's so," continued Tennessee's Partner. "It ain't for me to say anything agin' him. And now, what's the case? Here's Tennessee wants money, wants it bad, and doesn't like to ask it of his old pardner. Well, what does Tennessee do? He lays for a stranger, and he fetches that stranger. And you lays for *him,* and you fetches *him;* and the honors is easy. And I put it to you, bein' a far-minded man, and to you, gentlemen, all, as far-minded men, ef this isn't so."

"Prisoner," said the Judge, interrupting, "have you any questions to ask this man?"

"No! no!" continued Tennessee's Partner, hastily. "I play this yer hand alone. To come down to the bed-rock, it's just this: Tennessee, thar, has played it pretty rough and expensive-like on a stranger, and on this yer camp. And now, what's the fair thing? Some would say more; some would say less. Here's seventeen hundred dollars in coarse gold and a watch,—it's about all my pile,—and call it square!" And before a hand could be raised to prevent him, he had emptied the contents of the carpet-bag upon the table.

For a moment his life was in jeopardy. One or two men sprang to their feet, several hands groped for hidden weapons, and a suggestion to "throw him from the window" was only overridden by a gesture from the Judge. Tennessee laughed. And apparently oblivious of the excitement, Tennessee's Partner improved the opportunity to mop his face again with his handkerchief.

When order was restored, and the man was made to understand, by the use of forcible figures and rhetoric, that Tennessee's offense could not be condoned by money, his face took a more serious and sanguinary hue, and those who were nearest to him noticed that his rough hand trembled slightly on the table. He hesitated a moment as he slowly returned the gold to the carpet-bag, as if he had not yet entirely caught the elevated sense of justice which swayed the tribunal, and was perplexed with the belief that he had not offered enough. Then he turned to the Judge, and saying, "This yer is a lone hand, played alone, and without my pardner," he bowed to the jury and was about to withdraw, when the Judge called him back. "If you have anything to say to Tennessee, you had better say it now." For the first time that evening the eyes of the prisoner and his strange advocate met. Tennessee smiled, showed his white teeth, and, saying, "Euchred, old man!" held out his hand. Tennessee's Partner took it in his own, and saying, "I just dropped in as I was passin' to see how things was gettin' on," let the hand passively fall, and adding that "it was a warm night," again mopped his face with his handkerchief, and without another word withdrew.

The two men never again met each other alive. For the unparalleled insult of a bribe offered to Judge Lynch—who, whether bigoted, weak, or narrow, was at least incorruptible—firmly fixed in the mind of that mythical personage any wavering determination of Tennessee's fate; and at the break of day he was marched, closely guarded, to meet it at the top of Marley's Hill.

How he met it, how cool he was, how he refused to say anything, how perfect were the arrangements of the committee, were all duly reported, with the addition of a warning moral and example to all future evil-doers, in the Red Dog Clarion, by its editor, who was present, and to whose vigorous English I cheerfully refer the reader. But the beauty of that midsummer morning, the blessed amity of earth and air and sky, the awakened life of the free woods and hills, the joyous renewal and promise of Nature, and above all, the infinite Serenity that thrilled through each, was not reported, as not being a part of the social lesson. And yet, when the weak and foolish deed was done, and a life, with its possibilities and responsibilities, had passed out of the misshapen thing that dangled between earth and sky, the birds sang, the flowers bloomed, the sun shone, as cheerily as before; and possibly the Red Dog Clarion was right.

Tennessee's Partner was not in the group that surrounded the ominous tree. But as they turned to disperse attention was drawn to the singular appearance of a motionless donkey-cart halted at the side of the road. As they approached, they at once recognized the venerable "Jenny" and the two-wheeled cart as the property of Tennessee's Partner,—used by him in carrying dirt from his claim; and a few paces distant the owner of the equipage himself, sitting under a buckeye-tree, wiping the perspiration from his glowing face. In answer to an inquiry, he said he had come for the body of the "diseased," "if it was all the same to the committee." He didn't wish to "hurry anything"; he could "wait." He was not working that day; and when the gentlemen were done with the "diseased," he would take him. "Ef thar is any present," he added, in his simple, serious way, "as would care to jine in the fun'l, they kin come." Perhaps it was from a sense of humor, which I have already intimated was a feature of Sandy Bar,—perhaps it was from something even better than that; but two thirds of the loungers accepted the invitation at once.

It was noon when the body of Tennessee was delivered into the hands of his partner. As the cart drew up to the fatal tree, we noticed that it contained a rough, oblong box,—apparently made from a section of sluicing,—and half filled with bark and the tassels of pine. The cart was further decorated with slips of willow, and made fragrant with buckeye-blossoms. When the body was deposited in the box, Tennessee's Partner drew over it a piece of tarred canvas, and gravely mounting the narrow seat in front, with his feet upon the shafts, urged the little donkey forward. The equipage moved slowly on, at that decorous pace which was habitual with "Jenny" even under less solemn circumstances. The men—half curiously, half jestingly, but all good-humoredly— strolled along beside the cart; some in advance, some a little in the rear of the homely catafalque. But, whether from the narrowing of the road or some present sense of decorum, as the cart passed on, the company fell to the rear in couples, keeping step, and otherwise assuming the external show of a formal procession. Jack Folinsbee, who had at the outset played a funeral march in dumb show upon an imaginary trombone, desisted, from a lack of sympathy and appreciation,—not having, perhaps, your true humorist's capacity to be content with the enjoyment of his own fun.

The way led through Grizzly Cañon,—by this time clothed in funereal drapery and shadows. The redwoods, burying their moccasined feet in the red soil, stood in Indian-file along the track, trailing an uncouth benediction from their bending boughs upon

the passing bier. A hare, surprised into helpless inactivity, sat upright and pulsating in the ferns by the roadside, as the *cortége*
went by. Squirrels hastened to gain a secure outlook from higher
boughs; and the blue-jays, spreading their wings, fluttered before
them like outriders, until the outskirts of Sandy Bar were reached,
and the solitary cabin of Tennessee's Partner.

Viewed under more favorable circumstances, it would not have
been a cheerful place. The unpicturesque site, the rude and
unlovely outlines, the unsavory details, which distinguish the
nest-building of the California miner, were all here, with the drea-
riness of decay superadded. A few paces from the cabin there was
a rough enclosure, which, in the brief days of Tennessee's Partner's
matrimonial felicity, had been used as a garden, but was now over-
grown with fern. As we approached it we were surprised to find
that what we had taken for a recent attempt at cultivation was the
broken soil about an open grave.

The cart was halted before the enclosure; and rejecting the offers of assistance with the same air of simple self-reliance he had
displayed throughout, Tennessee's Partner lifted the rough coffin
on his back, and deposited it, unaided, within the shallow grave.
He then nailed down the board which served as a lid; and mounting the little mound of earth beside it, took off his hat, and slowly
mopped his fade with his handkerchief. This the crowd felt was a
preliminary to speech; and they disposed themselves variously on
stumps and boulders, and sat expectant.

"When a man," began Tennessee's Partner, slowly, "has been
running free all day, what's the natural thing for him to do? Why,
to come home. And if he ain't in a condition to go home, what can
his best friend do? Why, bring him home! And here's Tennessee
has been running free, and we brings him home from his wandering." He paused, and picked up a fragment of quartz, rubbed it
thoughtfully on his sleeve, and went on: "It ain't the first time that
I've packed him on my back, as you see'd me now. It ain't the first
time that I brought him to this yer cabin when he couldn't help
himself; it ain't the first time that I and 'Jinny' have waited for him
on yon hill, and picked him up and so fetched him home, when he
couldn't speak, and didn't know me. And now that it's the last
time, why—" he paused, and rubbed the quartz gently on his
sleeve—"you see it's sort of rough on his pardner. And now, gen-

tlemen," he added, abruptly, picking up his long-handled shovel, "the fun'ls over; and my thanks, and Tennessee's thanks, to you for your trouble."

Resisting any proffers of assistance, he began to fill in the grave, turning his back upon the crowd, that after a few moments' hesitation gradually withdrew. As they crossed the little ridge that hid Sandy Bar from view, some, looking back, thought they could see Tennessee's Partner, his work done, sitting upon the grave, his shovel between his knees, and his face buried in his red bandanna handkerchief. But it was argued by others that you couldn't tell his face from his handkerchief at that distance; and this point remained undecided.

In the reaction that followed the feverish excitement of that day, Tennessee's Partner was not forgotten. A secret investigation had cleared him of any complicity in Tennessee's guilt, and left only a suspicion of his general sanity. Sandy Bar made a point of calling on him, and proffering various uncouth, but well-meant kindnesses. But from that day his rude health and great strength seemed visibly to decline; and when the rainy season fairly set in, and the tiny grass-blades were beginning to peep from the rocky mound above Tennessee's grave, he took to his bed.

One night, when the pines beside the cabin were swaying in the storm, and trailing their slender fingers over the roof, and the roar and rush of the swollen river were heard below, Tennessee's Partner lifted his head from the pillow, saying, "It is time to go for Tennessee; I must put 'Jinny' in the cart"; and would have risen from his bed but for the restraint of his attendant. Struggling, he still pursued his singular fancy: "There, now, steady, 'Jinny,'— steady, old girl. How dark it is! Look out for the ruts,—and look out for him, too, old gal. Sometimes, you know, when he's blind drunk, he drops down right in the trail. Keep on straight up to the pine on the top of the hill. Thar—I told you so!—thar he is,— coming this way, too,—all by himself, sober, and his face a-shining. Tennessee! Pardner!"

And so they met.

Oct. 1869

The Idyl of Red Gulch

SANDY WAS VERY DRUNK. He was lying under an azalea-bush, in pretty much the same attitude in which he had fallen some hours before. How long he had been lying there he could not tell, and didn't care; how long he should lie there was a matter equally indefinite and unconsidered. A tranquil philosophy, born of his physical condition, suffused and saturated his moral being.

The spectacle of a drunken man, and of this drunken man in particular, was not, I grieve to say, of sufficient novelty in Red Gulch to attract attention. Earlier in the day some local satirist had erected a temporary tombstone at Sandy's head, bearing the inscription, "Effects of McCorkle's whiskey,—kills at forty rods," with a hand pointing to McCorkle's saloon. But this, I imagine, was, like most local satire, personal; and was a reflection upon the unfairness of the process rather than a commentary upon the impropriety of the result. With this facetious exception, Sandy had been undisturbed. A wandering mule, released from his pack, had cropped the scant herbage beside him, and sniffed curiously at the prostrate man; a vagabond dog, with that deep sympathy which the species have for drunken men, had licked his dusty boots, and curled himself up at his feet, and lay there, blinking one eye in the sunlight, with a simulation of dissipation that was ingenious and dog-like in its implied flattery of the unconscious man beside him.

Meanwhile the shadows of the pine-trees had slowly swung around until they crossed the road, and their trunks barred the open meadow with gigantic parallels of black and yellow. Little puffs of red dust, lifted by the plunging hoofs of passing teams, dispersed in a grimy shower upon the recumbent man. The sun sank lower and lower; and still Sandy stirred not. And then the repose of this philosopher was disturbed, as other philosophers have been, by the intrusion of an unphilosophical sex.

"Miss Mary," as she was known to the little flock that she had just dismissed from the log school-house beyond the pines, was taking her afternoon walk. Observing an unusually fine cluster of blossoms on the azalea-bush opposite, she crossed the road to pluck it,—picking her way through the red dust, not without certain fierce little shivers of disgust, and some feline circumlocution. And then she came suddenly upon Sandy!

Of course she tittered the little *staccato* cry of her sex. But when she had paid that tribute to her physical weakness she became overbold, and halted for a moment,—at least six feet from this prostrate monster,—with her white skirts gathered in her hand, ready for flight. But neither sound nor motion came from the bush. With one little foot she then overturned the satirical head-board, and muttered "Beasts!"—an epithet which probably, at that moment, conveniently classified in her mind the entire male population of Red Gulch. For Miss Mary, being possessed of certain rigid notions of her own, had not, perhaps, properly appreciated the demonstrative gallantry for which the Californian has been so justly celebrated by his brother Californians, and had, as a new-comer, perhaps, fairly earned the reputation of being "stuck up."

As she stood there she noticed, also, that the slant sunbeams were heating Sandy's head to what she judged to be an unhealthy temperature, and that his hat was lying uselessly at his side. To pick it up and to place it over his face was a work requiring some courage, particularly as his eyes were open. Yet she did it and made good her retreat. But she was somewhat concerned, on looking back, to see that the hat was removed, and that Sandy was sitting up and saying something.

The truth was, that in the calm depths of Sandy's mind he was satisfied that the rays of the sun were beneficial and healthful; that from childhood he had objected to lying down in a hat; that no people but condemned fools, past redemption, ever wore hats; and that his right to dispense with them when he pleased was inalienable. This was the statement of his inner consciousness. Unfortunately, its outward expression was vague, being limited to a repetition of the following formula,—"Su'shine all ri'! Wasser maär, eh? Wass up, su'shine?"

Miss Mary stopped, and, taking fresh courage from her vantage of distance, asked him if there was anything that he wanted.

"Wass up? Wasser maär?" continued Sandy, in a very high key.

"Get up, you horrid man!" said Miss Mary, now thoroughly incensed; "get up, and go home."

Sandy staggered to his feet. He was six feet high, and Miss Mary trembled. He started forward a few paces and then stopped.

"Wass I go home for?" he suddenly asked, with great gravity.

"Go and take a bath," replied Miss Mary, eying his grimy person with great disfavor.

To her infinite dismay, Sandy suddenly pulled off his coat and vest, threw them on the ground, kicked off his boots, and, plunging wildly forward, darted headlong over the hill, in the direction of the river.

"Goodness Heavens!—the man will be drowned!" said Miss Mary; and then, with feminine inconsistency, she ran back to the school-house, and locked herself in.

That night, while seated at supper with her hostess, the blacksmith's wife, it came to Miss Mary to ask, demurely, if her husband ever got drunk. "Abner," responded Mrs. Stidger, reflectively, "let's see; Abner hasn't been tight since last 'lection." Miss Mary would have liked to ask if he preferred lying in the sun on these occasions, and if a cold bath would have hurt him; but this would have involved an explanation, which she did not then care to give. So she contented herself with opening her gray eyes widely at the red-cheeked Mrs. Stidger,—a fine specimen of Southwestern efflorescence,—and then dismissed the subject altogether. The next day she wrote to her dearest friend, in Boston: "I think I find the intoxicated portion of this community the least objectionable. I refer, my dear, to the men, of course. I do not know anything that could make the women tolerable."

In less than a week Miss Mary had forgotten this episode, except that her afternoon walks took thereafter, almost unconsciously, another direction. She noticed, however, that every morning a fresh cluster of azalea-blossoms appeared among the flowers on her desk. This was not strange, as her little flock were aware of her fondness for flowers, and invariably kept her desk bright with anemones, syringas, and lupines; but, on questioning them, they, one and all, professed ignorance of the azaleas. A few days later, Master Johnny Stidger, whose desk was nearest to the window, was suddenly taken with spasms of apparently gratuitous laughter, that threatened the discipline of the school. All that Miss Mary could get from him was, that some one had been "looking in the winder." Irate and indignant, she sallied from her hive to do battle with the intruder. As she turned the corner of the school-house, she came plump upon the quondam drunkard,—now perfectly sober, and inexpressibly sheepish and guilty looking.

These facts Miss Mary was not slow to take a feminine advantage of, in her present humor. But it was somewhat confusing to observe, also, that the beast, despite some faint signs of past dissipation, was amiable-looking,—in fact, a kind of blond Samson, whose corn-colored, silken beard apparently had never yet known the touch of barber's razor or Delilah's shears.[1] So that the cutting speech which quivered on her ready tongue died upon her lips, and she contented herself with receiving his stammering apology with supercilious eyelids and the gathered skirts of uncontamination. When she re-entered the school-room, her eyes fell upon the azaleas with a new sense of revelation. And then she laughed, and the little people all laughed, and they were all unconsciously very happy.

It was on a hot day—and not long after this—that two short-legged boys came to grief on the threshold of the school with a pail of water, which they had laboriously brought from the spring, and that Miss Mary compassionately seized the pail and started for the spring herself. At the foot of the hill a shadow crossed her path, and a blue-shirted arm dexterously but gently relieved her of her burden. Miss Mary was both embarrassed and angry. "If you carried more of that for yourself," she said, spitefully, to the blue arm, without deigning to raise her lashes to its owner, "you'd do better." In the submissive silence that followed she regretted the speech, and thanked him so sweetly at the door that he stumbled. Which caused the children to laugh again,—a laugh in which Miss Mary joined, until the color came faintly into her pale cheek. The next day a barrel was mysteriously placed beside the door, and as mysteriously filled with fresh spring-water every morning.

Nor was this superior young person without other quiet attentions. "Profane Bill," driver of the Slumgullion Stage, widely known in the newspapers for his "gallantry" in invariably offering the box-seat to the fair sex, had excepted Miss Mary from this attention, on the ground that he had a habit of "cussin' on up grades," and gave her half the coach to herself. Jack Hamlin, a gambler, having once silently ridden with her in the same coach, afterward threw a decanter at the head of a confederate for mentioning her name in a bar-room. The over-dressed mother of a pupil whose paternity was doubtful had often lingered near this astute Vestal's temple, never daring to enter its sacred precincts, but content to worship the priestess from afar.

With such unconscious intervals the monotonous procession of blue skies, glittering sunshine, brief twilights, and starlit nights passed over Red Gulch. Miss Mary grew fond of walking in the sedate and proper woods. Perhaps she believed, with Mrs. Stidger, that the balsamic odors of the firs "did her chest good," for certainly her slight cough was less frequent and her step was firmer; perhaps she had learned the unending lesson which the patient pines are never weary of repeating to heedful or listless ears. And so, one day, she planned a picnic on Buckeye Hill, and took the children with her. Away from the dusty road, the straggling shanties, the yellow ditches, the clamor of restless engines, the cheap finery of shop-windows, the deeper glitter of paint and colored glass, and the thin veneering which barbarism takes upon itself in such localities,—what infinite relief was theirs! The last heap of ragged rock and clay passed, the last unsightly chasm crossed,—how the waiting woods opened their long files to receive them! How the children—perhaps because they had not yet grown quite away from the breast of the bounteous Mother—threw themselves face downward on her brown bosom with uncouth caresses, filling the air with their laughter; and how Miss Mary herself—felinely fastidious and intrenched as she was in the purity of spotless skirts, collar, and cuffs—forgot all, and ran like a crested quail at the head of her brood, until, romping, laughing, and panting, with a loosened braid of brown hair, a hat hanging by a knotted ribbon from her throat, she came suddenly and violently, in the heart of the forest, upon—the luckless Sandy.

The explanations, apologies, and not overwise conversation that ensued, need not be indicated here. It would seem, however, that Miss Mary had already established some acquaintance with this ex-drunkard. Enough that he was soon accepted as one of the party; that the children, with that quick intelligence which

Providence gives the helpless, recognized a friend, and played with his blond beard, and long silken mustache, and took other liberties,—as the helpless are apt to do. And when he had built a fire against a tree, and had shown them other mysteries of wood-craft, their admiration knew no bounds. At the close of two such foolish, idle, happy hours he found himself lying at the feet of the schoolmistress, gazing dreamily in her face, as she sat upon the sloping hillside, weaving wreaths of laurel and syringa, in very much the same attitude as he had lain when first they met. Nor was the similitude greatly forced. The weakness of an easy, sensuous nature, that had found a dreamy exaltation in liquor, it is to be feared was now finding an equal intoxication in love.

I think that Sandy was dimly conscious of this himself. I know that he longed to be doing something,—slaying a grizzly, scalping a savage, or sacrificing himself in some way for the sake of this sallow-faced, gray-eyed schoolmistress. As I should like to present him in a heroic attitude, I stay my hand with great difficulty at this moment, being only withheld from introducing such an episode by a strong conviction that it does not usually occur at such times. And I trust that my fairest reader, who remembers that, in a real crisis, it is always some uninteresting stranger or unromantic policeman, and not Adolphus,[2] who rescues, will forgive the omission.

So they sat there, undisturbed,—the woodpeckers chattering overhead, and the voices of the children coming pleasantly from the hollow below. What they said matters little. What they thought—which might have been interesting—did not transpire. The woodpeckers only learned how Miss Mary was an orphan; how she left her uncle's house, to come to California, for the sake of health and independence; how Sandy was an orphan, too; how he came to California for excitement; how he had lived a wild life, and how he was trying to reform; and other details, which, from a woodpecker's view-point, undoubtedly must have seemed stupid, and a waste of time. But even in such trifles was the afternoon spent; and when the children were again gathered, and Sandy, with a delicacy which the schoolmistress well understood, took leave of them quietly at the outskirts of the settlement, it had seemed the shortest day of her weary life.

As the long, dry summer withered to its roots, the school term of Red Gulch—to use a local euphuism—"dried up" also. In an-other day Miss Mary would be free; and for a season, at least, Red Gulch would know her no more. She was seated alone in the school-house, her cheek resting on her hand, her eyes half closed in one of those day-dreams in which Miss Mary—I fear, to the danger of school discipline—was lately in the habit of indulging. Her lap was full of mosses, ferns, and other woodland memories. She was so preoccupied with these and her own thoughts that a gentle tapping at the door passed unheard, or translated itself into the remembrance of far-off woodpeckers. When at last it asserted itself more distinctly, she started up with a flushed cheek and opened the door. On the threshold stood a woman, the self-assertion and audacity of whose dress were in singular contrast to her timid, irresolute bearing.

Miss Mary recognized at a glance the dubious mother of her anonymous pupil. Perhaps she was disappointed, perhaps she was only fastidious; but as she coldly invited her to enter, she half un-consciously settled her white cuffs and collar, and gathered closer her own chaste skirts. It was, perhaps, for this reason that the em-barrassed stranger, after a moment's hesitation, left her gorgeous parasol open and sticking in the dust beside the door, and then sat down at the farther end of a long bench. Her voice was husky as she began:—

"I heerd tell that you were goin' down to the Bay to-morrow, and I couldn't let you go until I came to thank you for your kind-ness to my Tommy."

Tommy, Miss Mary said, was a good boy, and deserved more than the poor attention she could give him.

"Thank you, miss; thank ye!" cried the stranger, brightening even through the color which Red Gulch knew facetiously as her "war paint," and striving, in her embarrassment, to drag the long bench nearer the schoolmistress. "I thank you, miss, for that! And if I am his mother, there ain't a sweeter, dearer, better boy lives than him. And if I ain't much as says it, thar ain't a sweeter, dearer, angeler teacher lives than he's got."

Miss Mary, sitting primly behind her desk, with a ruler over her shoulder, opened her gray eyes widely at this, but said nothing.

"It ain't for you to be complimented by the like of me, I

know," she went on, hurriedly. "It ain't for me to be comin' here, in broad day, to do it, either; but I come to ask a favor,—not for me, miss,—not for me, but for the darling boy."

Encouraged by a look in the young schoolmistress's eye, and putting her lilac-gloved hands together, the fingers downward, between her knees, she went on, in a low voice:—

"You see, miss, there's no one the boy has any claim on but me, and I ain't the proper person to bring him up. I thought some, last year, of sending him away to 'Frisco to school, but when they talked of bringing a schoolma'am here, I waited till I saw you, and then I knew it was all right, and I could keep my boy a little longer. And O, miss, he loves you so much; and if you could hear him talk about you, in his pretty way, and if he could ask you what I ask you now, you couldn't refuse him.

"It is natural," she went on, rapidly, in a voice that trembled strangely between pride and humility,—"it's natural that he should take to you, miss, for his father, when I first knew him, was a gentleman,—and the boy must forget me, sooner or later,—and so I ain't a goin' to cry about that. For I come to ask you to take my Tommy,—God bless him for the bestest, sweetest boy that lives,—to—to—take him with you."

She had risen and caught the young girl's hand in her own, and had fallen on her knees beside her.

"I've money plenty, and it's all yours and his. Put him in some good school, where you can go and see him, and help him to—to—to forget his mother. Do with him what you like. The worst you can do will be kindness to what he will learn with me. Only take him out of this wicked life, this cruel place, this home of shame and sorrow. You will; I know you will,—won't you? You will,—you must not, you cannot say no! You will make him as pure, as gentle as yourself; and when he has grown up, you will tell him his father's name,—the name that hasn't passed my lips for years,—the name of Alexander Morton, whom they call here Sandy! Miss Mary!—do not take your hand away! Miss Mary, speak to me! You will take my boy? Do not put your face from me. I know it ought not to look on such as me. Miss Mary!—my God, be merciful!—she is leaving me!"

Miss Mary had risen, and, in the gathering twilight, had felt her

way to the open window. She stood there, leaning against the case-
ment, her eyes fixed on the last rosy tints that were fading from
the western sky. There was still some of its light on her pure
young forehead, on her white collar, on her clasped white hands,
but all fading slowly away. The suppliant had dragged herself, still
on her knees, beside her.

"I know it takes time to consider. I will wait here all night; but
I cannot go until you speak. Do not deny me now. You will!—I
see it in your sweet face,—such a face as I have seen in my dreams.
I see it in your eyes, Miss Mary—you will take my boy!"

The last red beam crept higher, suffused Miss Mary's eyes with
something of its glory, flickered, and faded, and went out. The sun
had set on Red Gulch. In the twilight and silence Miss Mary's
voice sounded pleasantly.

"I will take the boy. Send him to me tonight."

The happy mother raised the hem of Miss Mary's skirts to her
lips. She would have buried her hot face in its virgin folds, but she
dared not. She rose to her feet.

"Does—this man—know of your intention?" asked Miss Mary,
suddenly.

"No, nor cares. He has never even seen the child to know it."

"Go to him at once,—to-night,—now! Tell him what you have
done. Tell him I have taken his child, and tell him—he must never
see—see—the child again. Wherever it may be, he must not come;
wherever I may take it, he must not follow! There, go now,
please,—I'm weary, and—have much yet to do!"

They walked together to the door. On the threshold the woman
turned.

"Good night."

She would have fallen at Miss Mary's feet. But at the same moment the young girl reached out her arms, caught the sinful
woman to her own pure breast for one brief moment, and then
closed and locked the door.

It was with a sudden sense of great responsibility that Profane Bill
took the reins of the Slumgullion Stage the next morning, for the
schoolmistress was one of his passengers. As he entered the high-
road, in obedience to a pleasant voice from the "inside," he sud-

denly reined up his horses and respectfully waited, as "Tommy" hopped out at the command of Miss Mary.

"Not that bush, Tommy,—the next."

Tommy whipped out his new pocket-knife, and, cutting a branch from a tall azalea-bush, returned with it to Miss Mary.

"All right now?"

"All right."

And the stage-door closed on the Idyl of Red Gulch.

Dec. 1869

Brown of Calaveras

A SUBDUED TONE of conversation, and the absence of cigar-smoke and boot-heels at the windows of the Wingdam stage-coach, made it evident that one of the inside passengers was a woman. A disposition on the part of loungers at the stations to congregate before the window, and some concern in regard to the appearance of coats, hats, and collars, further indicated that she was lovely. All of which Mr. Jack Hamlin, on the box-seat, noted with the smile of cynical philosophy. Not that he depreciated the sex, but that he recognized therein a deceitful element, the pursuit of which sometimes drew mankind away from the equally uncertain blandishments of poker,—of which it may be remarked that Mr. Hamlin was a professional exponent.

So that, when he placed his narrow boot on the wheel and leaped down, he did not even glance at the window from which a green veil was fluttering, but lounged up and down with that listless and grave indifference of his class, which was, perhaps, the next thing to good-breeding. With his closely buttoned figure and self-contained air he was a marked contrast to the other passengers, with their feverish restlessness, and boisterous emotion; and even Bill Masters, a graduate of Harvard, with his slovenly dress, his overflowing vitality, his intense appreciation of lawlessness and barbarism, and his mouth filled with crackers and cheese, I fear cut but an unromantic figure beside this lonely calculator of chances, with his pale Greek face and Homeric gravity.

The driver called "All aboard!" and Mr. Hamlin returned to the coach. His foot was upon the wheel, and his face raised to the level of the open window, when, at the same moment, what appeared to him to be the finest eyes in the world suddenly met his. He quietly dropped down again, addressed a few words to one of the inside passengers, effected an exchange of seats, and as quietly took his place inside. Mr. Hamlin never allowed his philosophy to interfere with decisive and prompt action.

I fear that this irruption of Jack cast some restraint upon the other passengers,—particularly those who were making themselves most agreeable to the lady. One of them leaned forward, and apparently conveyed to her information regarding Mr. Hamlin's profession in a single epithet. Whether Mr. Hamlin heard it, or whether he recognized in the informant a distinguished jurist, from whom, but a few evenings before, he had won several thousand dollars, I cannot say. His colorless face betrayed no sign; his black eyes, quietly observant, glanced indifferently past the legal gentleman, and rested on the much more pleasing features of his neighbor. An Indian stoicism—said to be an inheritance from his maternal ancestor—stood him in good service, until the rolling wheels rattled upon the river-gravel at Scott's Ferry, and the stage drew up at the International Hotel for dinner. The legal gentleman and a member of Congress leaped out, and stood ready to assist the descending goddess, while Colonel Starbottle, of Siskiyou, took charge of her parasol and shawl. In this multiplicity of attention there was a momentary confusion and delay. Jack Hamlin quietly opened the *opposite* door of the coach, took the lady's hand,—with that decision and positiveness which a hesitating and undecided sex know how to admire,—and in an instant had dexterously and gracefully swung her to the ground, and again lifted her to the platform. An audible chuckle on the box, I fear, came from that other cynic, "Yuba Bill," the driver. "Look keerfully arter that baggage, Kernel," said the expressman, with affected concern, as he looked after Colonel Starbottle, gloomily bringing up the rear of the triumphant procession to the waiting-room.

Mr. Hamlin did not stay for dinner. His horse was already saddled, and awaiting him. He dashed over the ford, up the gravelly hill, and out into the dusty perspective of the Wingdam road, like one leaving an unpleasant fancy behind him. The inmates of dusty cabins by the roadside shaded their eyes with their hands, and looked after him, recognizing the man by his horse, and speculating what "was up with Comanche Jack." Yet much of this interest centered in the horse, in a community where the time made by

"French Pete's" mare, in his run from the Sheriff of Calaveras, eclipsed all concern in the ultimate fate of that worthy.

The sweating flanks of his gray at length recalled him to himself. He checked his speed, and, turning into a by-road, sometimes used as a cut-off, trotted leisurely along, the reins hanging listlessly from his fingers. As he rode on, the character of the landscape changed, and became more pastoral. Openings in groves of pine and sycamore disclosed some rude attempts at cultivation,—a flowering vine trailed over the porch of one cabin, and a woman rocked her cradled babe under the roses of another. A little farther on Mr. Hamlin came upon some barelegged children, wading in the willowy creek, and so wrought upon them with a badinage peculiar to himself, that they were emboldened to climb up his horse's legs and over his saddle, until he was fain to develop an exaggerated ferocity of demeanor, and to escape, leaving behind some kisses and coin. And then, advancing deeper into the woods, where all signs of habitation failed, he began to sing,—uplifting a tenor so singularly sweet, and shaded by a pathos so subduing and tender, that I wot the robins and linnets stopped to listen. Mr. Hamlin's voice was not cultivated; the subject of his song was some sentimental lunacy, borrowed from the Negro minstrels; but there thrilled through all some occult quality of tone and expression that was unspeakably touching. Indeed, it was a wonderful sight to see this sentimental blackleg, with a pack of cards in his pocket and a revolver at his back, sending his voice before him through the dim woods with a plaint about his "Nelly's grave,"[1] in a way that overflowed the eyes of the listener. A sparrow-hawk, fresh from his sixth victim, possibly recognizing in Mr. Hamlin a kindred spirit, stared at him in surprise, and was fain to confess the superiority of man. With a superior predatory capacity, *he* couldn't sing.

But Mr. Hamlin presently found himself again on the highroad, and at his former pace. Ditches and banks of gravel, denuded hillsides, stumps, and decayed trunks of trees, took the place of woodland and ravine, and indicated his approach to civilization. Then a church-steeple came in sight, and he knew that he had reached home. In a few moments he was clattering down the single narrow street, that lost itself in a chaotic ruin of races, ditches, and tailings at the foot of the hill, and dismounted before the gilded windows of the "Magnolia" saloon. Passing through the long bar-room, he pushed open a green-baize door, entered a dark passage, opened another door with a pass-key, and found himself in a dimly lighted room, whose furniture, though elegant and costly for the locality, showed signs of abuse. The inlaid center-table was overlaid with stained disks that were not contemplated in the original design. The embroidered arm-chairs were discolored, and the green velvet lounge, on which Mr. Hamlin threw himself, was soiled at the foot with the red soil of Wingdam.

Mr. Hamlin did not sing in his cage. He lay still, looking at a highly colored painting above him, representing a young creature of opulent charms. It occurred to him then, for the first time, that he had never seen exactly that kind of a woman, and that, if he should, he would not, probably, fall in love with her. Perhaps he was thinking of another style of beauty. But just then some one knocked at the door. Without rising, he pulled a cord that apparently shot back a bolt, for the door swung open, and a man entered.

The new-comer was broad-shouldered and robust,—a vigor not borne out in the face, which, though handsome, was singularly weak, and disfigured by dissipation. He appeared to be also under the influence of liquor, for he started on seeing Mr. Hamlin, and said, "I thought Kate was here"; stammered, and seemed confused and embarrassed.

Mr. Hamlin smiled the smile which he had before worn on the Wingdam coach, and sat up, quite refreshed and ready for business.

"You didn't come up on the stage," continued the new-comer, "did you?"

"No," replied Hamlin; "I left it at Scott's Ferry. It isn't due for half an hour yet. But how's luck, Brown?"

"D— bad," said Brown, his face suddenly assuming an expression of weak despair; "I'm cleaned out again. Jack," he continued, in a whining tone, that formed a pitiable contrast to his bulky figure, "can't you help me with a hundred till tomorrow's clean-up? You see I've got to send money home to the old woman, and—you've won twenty times that amount from me."

The conclusion was, perhaps, not entirely logical, but Jack overlooked it, and handed the sum to his visitor. "The old woman

business is about played out, Brown," he added, by way of commentary; "why don't you say you want to buck agin' faro? You
know you ain't married!"

"Fact, sir," said Brown, with a sudden gravity, as if the mere
contact of the gold with the palm of the hand had imparted some
dignity to his frame. "I've got a wife—a d— good one, too, if I do
say it—in the States. It's three year since I've seen her, and a year
since I've writ to her. When things is about straight, and we get
down to the lead, I'm going to send for her."

"And Kate?" queried Mr. Hamlin, with his previous smile.

Mr. Brown, of Calaveras, essayed an archness of glance, to
cover his confusion, which his weak face and whiskey-muddled
intellect but poorly carried out, and said,—

"D— it, Jack, a man must have a little liberty, you know. But
come, what do you say to a little game? Give us a show to double
this hundred."

Jack Hamlin looked curiously at his fatuous friend. Perhaps he
knew that the man was predestined to lose the money, and preferred that it should flow back into his own coffers rather than
any other. He nodded his head, and drew his chair toward the
table. At the same moment there came a rap upon the door.

"It's Kate," said Mr. Brown.

Mr. Hamlin shot back the bolt, and the door opened. But, for
the first time in his life, he staggered to his feet, utterly unnerved
and abashed, and for the first time in his life the hot blood crim-
soned his colorless cheeks to his forehead. For before him stood
the lady he had lifted from the Wingdam coach, whom Brown—
dropping his cards with a hysterical laugh—greeted as

"My old woman, by thunder!"

They say that Mrs. Brown burst into tears, and reproaches of
her husband. I saw her, in 1857, at Marysville, and disbelieve the
story. And the Wingdam Chronicle, of the next week, under the
head of "Touching Reunion," said: "One of those beautiful and
touching incidents, peculiar to California life, occurred last week
in our city. The wife of one of Wingdam's eminent pioneers, tired
of the effete civilization of the East and its inhospitable climate,
resolved to join her noble husband upon these golden shores.
Without informing him of her intention, she undertook the long
journey, and arrived last week. The joy of the husband may be eas-

ier imagined than described. The meeting is said to have been indescribably affecting. We trust her example may be followed."

Whether owing to Mrs. Brown's influence, or to some more successful speculations, Mr. Brown's financial fortune from that day steadily improved. He bought out his partners in the "Nip and Tuck" lead, with money which was said to have been won at poker, a week or two after his wife's arrival, but which rumor, adopting Mrs. Brown's theory that Brown had forsworn the gaming-table, declared to have been furnished by Mr. Jack Hamlin. He built and furnished the "Wingdam House," which pretty Mrs. Brown's great popularity kept overflowing with guests. He was elected to the Assembly, and gave largess to churches. A street in Wingdam was named in his honor.

Yet it was noted that in proportion as he waxed wealthy and fortunate, he grew pale, thin, and anxious. As his wife's popularity increased, he became fretful and impatient. The most uxorious of husbands, he was absurdly jealous. If he did not interfere with his wife's social liberty, it was because it was maliciously whispered that his first and only attempt was met by an outburst from Mrs. Brown that terrified him into silence. Much of this kind of gossip came from those of her own sex whom she had supplanted in the chivalrous attentions of Wingdam, which, like most popular chivalry, was devoted to an admiration of power, whether of masculine force or feminine beauty. It should be remembered, too, in her extenuation, that, since her arrival, she had been the unconscious priestess of a mythological worship, perhaps not more ennobling to her womanhood than that which distinguished an older Greek democracy. I think that Brown was dimly conscious of this. But his only confidant was Jack Hamlin, whose *infelix* reputation naturally precluded any open intimacy with the family, and whose visits were infrequent.

It was midsummer, and a moonlit night; and Mrs. Brown, very rosy, large-eyed, and pretty, sat upon the piazza, enjoying the fresh incense of the mountain breeze, and, it is to be feared, another incense which was not so fresh, nor quite as innocent. Beside her sat Colonel Starbottle and Judge Boompointer, and a later addition to her court, in the shape of a foreign tourist. She was in good spirits.

"What do you see down the road?" inquired the gallant Colonel, who had been conscious, for the last few minutes, that Mrs. Brown's attention was diverted.

"Dust," said Mrs. Brown, with a sigh. "Only Sister Anne's 'flock of sheep.' "[2]

The Colonel, whose literary recollections did not extend farther back than last week's paper, took a more practical view. "It ain't sheep," he continued; "it's a horseman. Judge, ain't that Jack Hamlin's gray?"

But the Judge didn't know; and, as Mrs. Brown suggested the air was growing too cold for further investigations, they retired to the parlor.

Mr. Brown was in the stable, where he generally retired after dinner. Perhaps it was to show his contempt for his wife's companions; perhaps, like other weak natures, he found pleasure in the exercise of absolute power over inferior animals. He had a certain gratification in the training of a chestnut mare, whom he could beat or caress as pleased him, which he couldn't do with Mrs. Brown. It was here that he recognized a certain gray horse which had just come in, and, looking a little farther on, found his rider. Brown's greeting was cordial and hearty; Mr. Hamlin's somewhat restrained. But at Brown's urgent request, he followed him up the back stairs to a narrow corridor, and thence to a small room looking out upon the stable-yard. It was plainly furnished with a bed, a table, a few chairs, and a rack for guns and whips.

"This yer's my home, Jack," said Brown, with a sigh, as he threw himself upon the bed, and motioned his companion to a chair. "Her room's t'other end of the hall. It's more'n six months since we've lived together, or met, except at meals. It's mighty rough papers on the head of the house, ain't it?" he said, with a forced laugh. "But I'm glad to see you, Jack, d— glad," and he reached from the bed, and again shook the unresponsive hand of Jack Hamlin.

"I brought ye up here, for I didn't want to talk in the stable; though, for the matter of that, it's all round town. Don't strike a light. We can talk here in the moonshine. Put up your feet on that winder, and sit here beside me. Thar's whiskey in that jug."

Mr. Hamlin did not avail himself of the information. Brown, of Calaveras, turned his face to the wall, and continued:—

"If I didn't love the woman, Jack, I wouldn't mind. But it's loving her, and seeing her, day arter day, goin' on at this rate, and no one to put down the brake; that's what gits me! But I'm glad to see ye, Jack, d— glad."

In the darkness he groped about until he had found and wrung his companion's hand again. He would have detained it, but Jack slipped it into the buttoned breast of his coat, and asked, listlessly, "How long has this been going on?"

"Ever since she came here; ever since the day she walked into the Magnolia. I was a fool then; Jack, I'm a fool now; but I didn't know how much I loved her till then. And she hasn't been the same woman since.

"But that ain't all, Jack; and it's what I wanted to see you about, and I'm glad you've come. It ain't that she doesn't love me any more; it ain't that she fools with every chap that comes along, for, perhaps, I staked her love and lost it, as I did everything else at the Magnolia; and, perhaps, foolin' is nateral to some women, and thar ain't no great harm done, 'cept to the fools. But, Jack, I think,—I think she loves somebody else. Don't move, Jack; don't move; if your pistol hurts ye, take it off.

"It's been more'n six months now that she's seemed unhappy and lonesome, and kinder nervous and scared like. And sometimes I've ketched her lookin' at me sort of timid and pitying. And she writes to somebody. And for the last week she's been gathering her own things,—trinkets, and furbelows, and jew'lry,—and, Jack, I think she's goin' off. I could stand all but that. To have her steal away like a thief—" He put his face downward to the pillow, and for a few moments there was no sound but the ticking of a clock on the mantel. Mr. Hamlin lit a cigar and moved to the open window. The moon no longer shone into the room, and the bed and its occupant were in shadow. "What shall I do, Jack?" said the voice from the darkness.

The answer came promptly and clearly from the window-side,—"Spot the man, and kill him on sight."

"But, Jack?"

"He's took the risk!"

"But will that bring *her* back?"

Jack did not reply, but moved from the window towards the door.

"Don't go yet, Jack; light the candle, and sit by the table. It's a comfort to see ye, if nothin' else."

Jack hesitated, and then complied. He drew a pack of cards from his pocket and shuffled them, glancing at the bed. But Brown's face was turned to the wall. When Mr. Hamlin had shuffled the cards, he cut them, and dealt one card on the opposite side of the table and towards the bed, and another on his side of the table for himself. The first was a deuce; his own card, a king. He then shuffled and cut again. This time "dummy" had a queen, and himself a four-spot. Jack brightened up for the third deal. It brought his adversary a deuce, and himself a king again. "Two out of three," said Jack, audibly.

"What's that, Jack?" said Brown.

"Nothing."

Then Jack tried his hand with dice; but he always threw sixes, and his imaginary opponent aces. The force of habit is sometimes confusing.

Meanwhile, some magnetic influence in Mr. Hamlin's presence, or the anodyne of liquor, or both, brought surcease of sorrow, and Brown slept. Mr. Hamlin moved his chair to the window, and looked out on the town of Wingdam, now sleeping peacefully,— its harsh outlines softened and subdued, its glaring colors mellowed and sobered in the moonlight that flowed over all. In the hush he could hear the gurgling of water in the ditches, and the sighing of the pines beyond the hill. Then he looked up at the firmament, and as he did so a star shot across the twinkling field. Presently another, and then another. The phenomenon suggested to Mr. Hamlin a fresh augury. If in another fifteen minutes another star should fall— He sat there, watch in hand, for twice that time, but the phenomenon was not repeated.

The clock struck two, and Brown still slept. Mr. Hamlin approached the table, and took from his pocket a letter, which he read by the flickering candle-light. It contained only a single line, written in pencil, in a woman's hand,—

"Be at the corral, with the buggy, at three."

The sleeper moved uneasily, and then awoke. "Are you there, Jack?"

"Yes."

"Don't go yet. I dreamed just now, Jack,—dreamed of old

times. I thought that Sue and me was being married agin, and that the parson, Jack, was—who do you think?—you!"

The gambler laughed, and seated himself on the bed,—the paper still in his hand.

"It's a good sign, ain't it?" queried Brown.

"I reckon. Say, old man, hadn't you better get up?"

The "old man," thus affectionately appealed to, rose, with the assistance of Hamlin's outstretched hand.

"Smoke?"

Brown mechanically took the proffered cigar.

"Light?"

Jack had twisted the letter into a spiral, lit it, and held it for his companion. He continued to hold it until it was consumed, and dropped the fragment—a fiery star—from the open window. He watched it as it fell, and then returned to his friend.

"Old man," he said, placing his hands upon Brown's shoulders, "in ten minutes I'll be on the road, and gone like that spark. We won't see each other agin; but, before I go, take a fool's advice: sell out all you've got, take your wife with you, and quit the country. It ain't no place for you, nor her. Tell her she must go; make her go, if she won't. Don't whine because you can't be a saint, and she ain't an angel. Be a man,—and treat her like a woman. Don't be a d— fool. Good by."

He tore himself from Brown's grasp and leaped down the stairs like a deer. At the stable-door he collared the half-sleeping hostler, and backed him against the wall. "Saddle my horse in two minutes, or I'll—" The ellipsis was frightfully suggestive.

"The missis said you was to have the buggy," stammered the man.

"D—n the buggy!"

The horse was saddled as fast as the nervous hands of the astounded hostler could manipulate buckle and strap.

"Is anything up, Mr. Hamlin?" said the man, who, like all his class, admired the *élan* of his fiery patron, and was really concerned in his welfare.

"Stand aside!"

The man fell back. With an oath, a bound, and clatter, Jack was into the road. In another moment, to the man's half-awakened eyes, he was but a moving cloud of dust in the distance, towards which a star just loosed from its brethren was trailing a stream of fire.

But early that morning the dwellers by the Wingdam turnpike, miles away, heard a voice, pure as a sky-lark's, singing afield. They who were asleep turned over on their rude couches to dream of youth and love and olden days. Hard-faced men and anxious gold-seekers, already at work, ceased their labors and leaned upon their picks, to listen to a romantic vagabond ambling away against the rosy sunrise.

Mar. 1870

Mr. Thompson's Prodigal

WE ALL KNEW that Mr. Thompson was looking for his son, and a pretty bad one at that. That he was coming to California for this sole object was no secret to his fellow-passengers; and the physical peculiarities, as well as the moral weaknesses, of the missing prodigal were made equally plain to us through the frank volubility of the parent. "You was speaking of a young man which was hung at Red Dog for sluice-robbing," said Mr. Thompson to a steerage passenger, one day; "be you aware of the color of his eyes?" "Black," responded the passenger. "Ah," said Mr. Thompson, referring to some mental memoranda, "Char-les's eyes was blue." He then walked away. Perhaps it was from this unsympathetic mode of inquiry, perhaps it was from that Western predilection to take a humorous view of any principle or sentiment persistently brought before them, that Mr. Thompson's quest was the subject of some satire among the passengers. A gratuitous advertisement of the missing Charles, addressed to "Jailers and Guardians," circulated privately among them; everybody remembered to have met Charles under distressing circumstances. Yet it is but due to my countrymen to state that when it was known that Thompson had embarked some wealth in this visionary project, but little of this satire found its way to his ears, and nothing was uttered in his hearing that might bring a pang to a father's heart, or imperil a possible pecuniary advantage of the satirist. Indeed, Mr. Bracy Tibbets's jocular proposition to form a joint-stock company to "prospect" for the missing youth received at one time quite serious entertainment.

Perhaps to superficial criticism Mr. Thompson's nature was not picturesque nor lovable. His history, as imparted at dinner, one day, by himself, was practical even in its singularity. After a hard and wilful youth and maturity,—in which he had buried a broken-spirited wife, and driven his son to sea,—he suddenly experienced religion. "I got it in New Orleans in '59," said Mr. Thompson, with the general suggestion of referring to an epidemic. "Enter ye the narrer gate.[1] Parse me the beans." Perhaps this practical quality upheld him in his apparently hopeless search. He had no clew to the whereabouts of his runaway son; indeed, scarcely a proof of his present existence. From his indifferent recollection of the boy of twelve, he now expected to identify the man of twenty-five.

It would seem that he was successful. How he succeeded was one of the few things he did not tell. There are, I believe, two versions of the story. One, that Mr. Thompson, visiting a hospital, discovered his son by reason of a peculiar hymn, chanted by the sufferer, in a delirious dream of his boyhood. This version, giving as it did wide range to the finer feelings of the heart, was quite popular; and as told by the Rev. Mr. Gushington, on his return from his California tour, never failed to satisfy an audience. The other was less simple, and, as I shall adopt it here, deserves more elaboration.

It was after Mr. Thompson had given up searching for his son among the living, and had taken to the examination of cemeteries, and a careful inspection of the "cold *hic jacets*[2] of the dead." At this time he was a frequent visitor of "Lone Mountain,"—a dreary hill-top, bleak enough in its original isolation, and bleaker for the white-faced marbles by which San Francisco anchored her departed citizens, and kept them down in a shifting sand that refused to cover them, and against a fierce and persistent wind that strove to blow them utterly away. Against this wind the old man opposed a will quite as persistent,—a grizzled, hard face, and a tall, crape-bound hat drawn tightly over his eyes,—and so spent days in reading the mortuary inscriptions audibly to himself. The frequency of Scriptural quotation pleased him, and he was fond of corroborating them by a pocket Bible. "That's from Psalms," he said, one day, to an adjacent grave-digger. The man made no reply. Not at all rebuffed, Mr. Thompson at once slid down into the open grave, with a more practical inquiry, "Did you ever, in your profession, come across Char-les Thompson?" "Thompson be d—d!" said the grave-digger, with great directness. "Which, if he hadn't religion, I think he is," responded the old man, as he clambered out of the grave.

It was, perhaps, on this occasion that Mr. Thompson stayed

later than usual. As he turned his face toward the city, lights were beginning to twinkle ahead, and a fierce wind, made visible by fog, drove him forward, or, lying in wait, charged him angrily from the corners of deserted suburban streets. It was on one of these corners that something else, quite as indistinct and malevolent, leaped upon him with an oath, a presented pistol, and a demand for money. But it was met by a will of iron and a grip of steel. The assailant and assailed rolled together on the ground. But the next moment the old man was erect; one hand grasping the captured pistol, the other clutching at arm's length the throat of a figure, surly, youthful, and savage.

"Young man," said Mr. Thompson, setting his thin lips together, "what might be your name?"

"Thompson!"

The old man's hand slid from the throat to the arm of his prisoner, without relaxing its firmness.

"Char-les Thompson, come with me," he said, presently, and marched his captive to the hotel. What took place there has not transpired, but it was known the next morning that Mr. Thompson had found his son.

It is proper to add to the above improbable story, that there was nothing in the young man's appearance or manners to justify it. Grave, reticent, and handsome, devoted to his newly found parent, he assumed the emoluments and responsibilities of his new condition with a certain serious ease that more nearly approached that which San Francisco society lacked, and—rejected. Some chose to despise this quality as a tendency to "psalm-singing"; others saw in it the inherited qualities of the parent, and were ready to prophesy for the son the same hard old age. But all agreed that it was not inconsistent with the habits of money-getting, for which father and son were respected.

And yet, the old man did not seem to be happy. Perhaps it was that the consummation of his wishes left him without a practical mission; perhaps—and it is the more probable—he had little love for the son he had regained. The obedience he exacted was freely given, the reform he had set his heart upon was complete; and yet, somehow, it did not seem to please him. In reclaiming his son, he had fulfilled all the requirements that his religious duty required

of him, and yet the act seemed to lack sanctification. In this perplexity, he read again the parable of the Prodigal Son,—which he
had long ago adopted for his guidance,—and found that he had
omitted the final feast of reconciliation. This seemed to offer the
proper quality of ceremoniousness in the sacrament between himself and his son; and so, a year after the appearance of Charles, he
set about giving him a party. "Invite everybody, Char-les," he said,
dryly; "everybody who knows that I brought you out of the
wine-husks of iniquity, and the company of harlots; and bid them
eat, drink, and be merry."[3]

Perhaps the old man had another reason, not yet clearly ana-
lyzed. The fine house he had built on the sand-hills[4] sometimes
seemed lonely and bare. He often found himself trying to recon-
struct, from the grave features of Charles, the little boy whom he
but dimly remembered in the past, and of whom lately he had
been thinking a great deal. He believed this to be a sign of impending old age and childishness; but coming, one day, in his formal drawing-room, upon a child of one of the servants, who had
strayed therein, he would have taken him in his arms, but the child
fled from before his grizzled face. So that it seemed eminently
proper to invite a number of people to his house, and, from the array of San Francisco maidenhood, to select a daughter-in-law. And
then there would be a child—a boy, whom he could "rare up"
from the beginning, and—love—as he did not love Charles.

We were all at the party. The Smiths, Joneses, Browns, and
Robinsons also came, in that fine flow of animal spirits, un-
checked by any respect for the entertainer, which most of us are
apt to find so fascinating. The proceedings would have been somewhat riotous, but for the social position of the actors. In fact, Mr.
Bracy Tibbets, having naturally a fine appreciation of a humorous
situation, but further impelled by the bright eyes of the Jones
girls, conducted himself so remarkably as to attract the serious regard of Mr. Charles Thompson, who approached him, saying quietly: "You look ill, Mr. Tibbets; let me conduct you to your
carriage. Resist, you hound, and I'll throw you through that window. This way, please; the room is close and distressing." It is
hardly necessary to say that but a part of this speech was audible
to the company, and that the rest was not divulged by Mr. Tibbets,
who afterward regretted the sudden illness which kept him from

witnessing a certain amusing incident, which the fastest Miss Jones characterized as the "richest part of the blow-out," and which I hasten to record.

It was at supper. It was evident that Mr. Thompson had over-looked much lawlessness in the conduct of the younger people, in his abstract contemplation of some impending event. When the cloth was removed, he rose to his feet, and grimly tapped upon the table. A titter, that broke out among the Jones girls, became epidemic on one side of the board. Charles Thompson, from the foot of the table, looked up in tender perplexity. "He's going to sing a Doxology,"[5] "He's going to pray," "Silence for a speech," ran round the room.

"It's one year to-day, Christian brothers and sisters," said Mr. Thompson, with grim deliberation,—"one year to-day since my son came home from eating of wine-husks and spending of his substance on harlots." (The tittering suddenly ceased.) "Look at him now. Char-les Thompson, stand up." (Charles Thompson stood up.) "One year ago to-day,—and look at him now."

He was certainly a handsome prodigal, standing there in his cheerful evening-dress,—a repentant prodigal, with sad, obedient eyes turned upon the harsh and unsympathetic glance of his father. The youngest Miss Smith, from the pure depths of her foolish little heart, moved unconsciously toward him.

"It's fifteen years ago since he left my house," said Mr. Thompson, "a rovier and a prodigal. I was myself a man of sin, O Christian friends,—a man of wrath and bitterness" ("Amen," from the eldest Miss Smith),—"but praise be God, I've fled the wrath to come. It's five years ago since I got the peace that passeth understanding.[6] Have you got it, friends?" (A general sub-chorus of "No, no," from the girls, and, "Pass the word for it," from Midshipman Coxe, of the U.S. sloop Wethersfield.) "Knock, and it shall be opened to you."[7]

"And when I found the error of my ways, and the preciousness of grace," continued Mr. Thompson, "I came to give it to my son. By sea and land I sought him far, and fainted not. I did not wait for him to come to me, which the same I might have done, and justified myself by the Book of books, but I sought him out among his husks, and—" (the rest of the sentence was lost in the rustling withdrawal of the ladies). "Works, Christian friends, is my motto. By their works shall ye know them,[8] and there is mine."

The particular and accepted work to which Mr. Thompson was alluding had turned quite pale, and was looking fixedly toward an open door leading to the veranda, lately filled by gaping servants, and now the scene of some vague tumult. As the noise continued, a man, shabbily dressed, and evidently in liquor, broke through the opposing guardians, and staggered into the room. The transition from the fog and darkness without to the glare and heat within evidently dazzled and stupefied him. He removed his battered hat, and passed it once or twice before his eyes, as he steadied himself, but unsuccessfully, by the back of a chair. Suddenly, his wandering glance fell upon the pale face of Charles Thompson; and with a gleam of childlike recognition, and a weak, falsetto laugh, he darted forward, caught at the table, upset the glasses, and literally fell upon the prodigal's breast.

"Sha'ly! yo'd—d ol' scoun'rel, hoo rar ye!"

"Hush!—sit down!—hush!" said Charles Thompson, hurriedly endeavoring to extricate himself from the embrace of his unexpected guest.

"Look at 'm!" continued the stranger, unheeding the admonition, but suddenly holding the unfortunate Charles at arm's length, in loving and undisguised admiration of his festive appearance. "Look at 'm! Ain't he nasty? Sha'ls, I'm prow of yer!"

"Leave the house!" said Mr. Thompson, rising, with a dangerous look in his cold, gray eye. "Char-les, how dare you?"

"Simmer down, ole man! Sha'ls, who's th' ol' bloat? Eh?"

"Hush, man; here, take this!" With nervous hands, Charles Thompson filled a glass with liquor. "Drink it and go—until tomorrow—any time, but—leave us!—go now!" But even then, ere the miserable wretch could drink, the old man, pale with passion, was upon him. Half carrying him in his powerful arms, half dragging him through the circling crowd of frightened guests, he had reached the door, swung open by the waiting servants, when Charles Thompson started from a seeming stupor, crying,—

"Stop!"

The old man stopped. Through the open door the fog and wind drove chilly. "What does this mean?" he asked, turning a baleful face on Charles.

"Nothing—but stop—for God's sake. Wait till tomorrow, but not tonight. Do not—I implore you—do this thing."

There was something in the tone of the young man's voice, something, perhaps, in the contact of the struggling wretch he held in his powerful arms; but a dim, indefinite fear took possession of the old man's heart. "Who," he whispered, hoarsely, "is this man?"

Charles did not answer.

"Stand back, there, all of you," thundered Mr. Thompson, to the crowding guests around him. "Char-les—come here! I command you—I—I—I—beg you—tell me *who* is this man?"

Only two persons heard the answer that came faintly from the lips of Charles Thompson,—

"YOUR SON."

When day broke over the bleak sand-hills, the guests had departed from Mr. Thompson's banquet-halls. The lights still burned dimly and coldly in the deserted rooms,—deserted by all but three figures, that huddled together in the chill drawing-room, as if for warmth. One lay in drunken slumber on a couch; at his feet sat he who had been known as Charles Thompson; and beside them, haggard and shrunken to half his size, bowed the figure of Mr. Thompson, his gray eye fixed, his elbows upon his knees, and his hands clasped over his ears, as if to shut out the sad, entreating voice that seemed to fill the room.

"God knows I did not set about to wilfully deceive. The name I gave that night was the first that came into my thought,—the name of one whom I thought dead,—the dissolute companion of my shame. And when you questioned further, I used the knowledge that I gained from him to touch your heart to set me free; only, I swear, for that! But when you told me who you were, and I first saw the opening of another life before me—then—then—O, sir, if I was hungry, homeless, and reckless, when I would have robbed you of your gold, I was heart-sick, helpless, and desperate, when I would have robbed you of your love!"

The old man stirred not. From his luxurious couch the newly found prodigal snored peacefully.

"I had no father I could claim. I never knew a home but this. I was tempted. I have been happy,—very happy."

He rose and stood before the old man.

"Do not fear that I shall come between your son and his inheritance. To-day I leave this place, never to return. The world is large, sir, and, thanks to your kindness, I now see the way by which an honest livelihood is gained. Good by. You will not take my hand? Well, well. Good by."

He turned to go. But when he had reached the door he suddenly came back, and, raising with both hands the grizzled head, he kissed it once and twice.

"Char-les."

There was no reply.

"Char-les!"

The old man rose with a frightened air, and tottered feebly to the door. It was open. There came to him the awakened tumult of a great city, in which the prodigal's footsteps were lost forever.

July 1870

The Iliad of Sandy Bar

BEFORE NINE O'CLOCK it was pretty well known all along the river that the two partners of the "Amity Claim" had quarrelled and separated at daybreak. At that time the attention of their nearest neighbor had been attracted by the sounds of altercations and two consecutive pistol-shots. Running out, he had seen, dimly, in the gray mist that rose from the river, the tall form of Scott, one of the partners, descending the hill toward the *cañon;* a moment later, York, the other partner, had appeared from the cabin, and walked in an opposite direction toward the river, passing within a few feet of the curious watcher. Later it was discovered that a serious Chinaman, cutting wood before the cabin, had witnessed part of the quarrel. But John was stolid, indifferent, and reticent. "Me choppee wood, me no fightee," was his serene response to all anxious queries. "But what did they *say,* John?" John did not *sabe.*[1] Colonel Starbottle deftly ran over the various popular epithets which a generous public sentiment might accept as reasonable provocation for an assault. But John did not recognize them. "And this yer's the cattle," said the Colonel, with some severity, "that some thinks oughter be allowed to testify ag'in' a White Man! Git—you heathen!"

Still the quarrel remained inexplicable. That two men, whose amiability and grave tact had earned for them the title of "The Peacemakers," in a community not greatly given to the passive virtues,—that these men, singularly devoted to each other, should suddenly and violently quarrel, might well excite the curiosity of the camp. A few of the more inquisitive visited the late scene of conflict, now deserted by its former occupants. There was no trace of disorder or confusion in the neat cabin. The rude table was arranged as if for breakfast; the pan of yellow biscuit still sat upon that hearth whose dead embers might have typified the evil passions that had raged there but an hour before. But Colonel Starbottle's eye—albeit somewhat bloodshot and rheumy—was more intent on practical details. On examination, a bullet-hole was found in the doorpost, and another, nearly opposite, in the casing of the window. The Colonel called attention to the fact that the one "agreed with" the bore of Scott's revolver, and the other with that of York's derringer. "They must hev stood about yer," said the Colonel, taking position; "not mor'n three feet apart, and— missed!" There was a fine touch of pathos in the falling inflection of the Colonel's voice, which was not without effect. A delicate perception of wasted opportunity thrilled his auditors.

But the Bar was destined to experience a greater disappointment. The two antagonists had not met since the quarrel, and it was vaguely rumored that, on the occasion of a second meeting, each had determined to kill the other "on sight." There was, consequently, some excitement—and, it is to be feared, no little gratification—when, at ten o'clock, York stepped from the Magnolia Saloon into the one long straggling street of the camp, at the same moment that Scott left the blacksmith's shop at the forks of the road. It was evident, at a glance, that a meeting could only be avoided by the actual retreat of one or the other.

In an instant the doors and windows of the adjacent saloons were filled with faces. Heads unaccountably appeared above the river-banks and from behind bowlders. An empty wagon at the cross-road was suddenly crowded with people, who seemed to have sprung from the earth. There was much running and confusion on the hillside. On the mountain-road, Mr. Jack Hamlin had reined up his horse, and was standing upright on the seat of his buggy. And the two objects of this absorbing attention approached each other.

"York's got the sun," "Scott'll line him on that tree," "He's waitin' to draw his fire," came from the cart; and then it was silent. But above this human breathlessness the river rushed and sang, and the wind rustled the tree-tops with an indifference that seemed obtrusive. Colonel Starbottle felt it, and in a moment of sublime preoccupation, without looking around, waved his cane behind him, warningly to all nature, and said, "Shu!"

The men were now within a few feet of each other. A hen ran across the road before one of them. A feathery seed-vessel, wafted from a wayside tree, fell at the feet of the other. And, unheeding this irony of nature, the two opponents came nearer, erect and rigid, looked in each other's eyes, and—passed!

Colonel Starbottle had to be lifted from the cart. "This yer camp is played out," he said, gloomily, as he affected to be supported into the Magnolia. With what further expression he might have indicated his feelings it was impossible to say, for at that moment Scott joined the group. "Did you speak to me?" he asked of the Colonel, dropping his hand, as if with accidental familiarity, on that gentleman's shoulder. The Colonel, recognizing some occult quality in the touch, and some unknown quantity in the glance of his questioner, contented himself by replying, "No, sir," with dignity. A few rods away, York's conduct was as characteristic and peculiar. "You had a mighty fine chance; why didn't you plump him?" said Jack Hamlin, as York drew near the buggy. "Because I hate him," was the reply, heard only by Jack. Contrary to popular belief, this reply was not hissed between the lips of the speaker, but was said in an ordinary tone. But Jack Hamlin, who was an observer of mankind, noticed that the speaker's hands were cold, and his lips dry, as he helped him into the buggy, and accepted the seeming paradox with a smile.

When Sandy Bar became convinced that the quarrel between York and Scott could not be settled after the usual local methods, it gave no further concern thereto. But presently it was rumored that the "Amity Claim" was in litigation, and that its possession would be expensively disputed by each of the partners. As it was well known that the claim in question was "worked out" and worthless, and that the partners, whom it had already enriched, had talked of abandoning it but a day or two before the quarrel, this proceeding could only be accounted for as gratuitous spite. Later, two San Francisco lawyers made their appearance in this guileless Arcadia,[2] and were eventually taken into the saloons, and—what was pretty much the same thing—the confidences of the inhabitants. The results of this unhallowed intimacy were many subpoenas; and, indeed, when the "Amity Claim" came to trial, all of Sandy Bar that was not in compulsory attendance at the county seat came there from curiosity. The gulches and ditches for miles around were deserted. I do not propose to describe that already famous trial. Enough that, in the language of the plaintiff's counsel, "it was one of no ordinary significance, involving the inherent rights of that untiring industry which had developed the Pactolian resources[3] of this golden land"; and, in the homelier phrase of Colonel Starbottle, "A fuss that gentlemen might hev settled in ten minutes over a social glass, ef they meant business; or in ten seconds with a revolver, ef they meant fun." Scott got a verdict, from which York instantly appealed. It was said that he had sworn to spend his last dollar in the struggle.

In this way Sandy Bar began to accept the enmity of the former partners as a lifelong feud, and the fact that they had ever been friends was forgotten. The few who expected to learn from the trial the origin of the quarrel were disappointed. Among the various conjectures, that which ascribed some occult feminine influence as the cause was naturally popular, in a camp given to dubious compliment of the sex. "My word for it, gentlemen," said Colonel Starbottle, who had been known in Sacramento as a Gentlemen of the Old School, "there's some lovely creature at the bottom of this." The gallant Colonel then proceeded to illustrate his theory, by divers sprightly stories, such as Gentlemen of the Old School are in the habit of repeating, but which, from deference to the prejudices of gentlemen of a more recent school, I refrain from transcribing here. But it would appear that even the Colonel's theory was fallacious. The only woman who personally might have exercised any influence over the partners was the pretty daughter of "old man Folinsbee," of Poverty Flat, at whose hospitable house—which exhibited some comforts and refinements rare in that crude civilization—both York and Scott were frequent visitors. Yet into this charming retreat York strode one evening, a month after the quarrel, and, beholding Scott sitting there, turned to the fair hostess with the abrupt query, "Do you love this man?" The young woman thus addressed returned that answer—at once spirited and evasive—which would occur to most of my fair readers in such an exigency. Without another word, York left the house. "Miss Jo" heaved the least possible sigh as the door closed on York's curls and square shoulders, and then, like a good girl, turned to her insulted guest. "But would you believe it, dear?" she afterward related to an intimate friend, "the other creature, after glowering at me for a moment, got upon its hind legs, took its hat, and left, too; and that's the last I've seen of either."

The same hard disregard of all other interests or feelings in the gratification of their blind rancor characterized all their actions. When York purchased the land below Scott's new claim, and obliged the latter, at a great expense, to make a long detour to carry a "tail-race" around it, Scott retaliated by building a dam that overflowed York's claim on the river. It was Scott, who, in conjunction with Colonel Starbottle, first organized that active opposition to the Chinamen, which resulted in the driving off of York's Mongolian laborers; it was York who built the wagon-road and established the express which rendered Scott's mules and pack-trains obsolete; it was Scott who called into life the Vigilance Committee which expatriated York's friend, Jack Hamlin; it was York who created the "Sandy Bar Herald," which characterized the act as "a lawless outrage," and Scott as a "Border Ruffian"; it was Scott, at the head of twenty masked men, who, one moonlight night, threw the offending "forms" into the yellow river, and scattered the types in the dusty road. These proceedings were received in the distant and more civilized outlying towns as vague indications of progress and vitality. I have before me a copy of the "Poverty Flat Pioneer," for the week ending August 12, 1856, in which the editor, under the head of "Country Improvements," says: "The new Presbyterian Church on C Street, at Sandy Bar, is completed. It stands upon the lot formerly occupied by the Magnolia Saloon, which was so mysteriously burnt last month. The temple, which now rises like a Phoenix from the ashes of the Magnolia, is virtually the free gift of H.J. York, Esq., of Sandy Bar, who purchased the lot and donated the lumber. Other buildings are going up in the vicinity, but the most noticeable is the 'Sunny South Saloon,' erected by Captain Mat. Scott, nearly opposite the church. Captain Scott has spared no expense in the furnishing of this saloon, which promises to be one of the most agreeable places of resort in old Tuolumne. He has recently imported two new, first-class billiard-tables, with cork cushions. Our old friend, 'Mountain Jimmy,' will dispense liquors at the bar. We refer our readers to the advertisement in another column. Visitors to Sandy Bar cannot do better than give 'Jimmy' a call." Among the local items occurred the following: "H.J. York, Esq., of Sandy Bar, has offered a reward of $100 for the detection of the parties who hauled away the steps of the new Presbyterian Church, C Street,

Sandy Bar, during divine service on Sabbath evening last. Captain Scott adds another hundred for the capture of the miscreants who broke the magnificent plate-glass windows of the new saloon on the following evening. There is some talk of reorganizing the old Vigilance Committee at Sandy Bar."

When, for many months of cloudless weather, the hard, unwinking sun of Sandy Bar had regularly gone down on the unpacified wrath of these men, there was some talk of mediation. In particular, the pastor of the church to which I have just referred—a sincere, fearless, but perhaps not fully enlightened man—seized gladly upon the occasion of York's liberality to attempt to reunite the former partners. He preached an earnest sermon on the abstract sinfulness of discord and rancor. But the excellent sermons of the Rev. Mr. Daws were directed to an ideal congregation that did not exist at Sandy Bar,—a congregation of beings of unmixed vices and virtues, of single impulses, and perfectly logical motives, of preternatural simplicity, of childlike faith, and grown-up responsibilities. As, unfortunately, the people who actually attended Mr. Daws's church were mainly very human, somewhat artful, more self-excusing than self-accusing, rather good-natured, and decidedly weak, they quietly shed that portion of the sermon which referred to themselves, and, accepting York and Scott—who were both in defiant attendance—as curious examples of those ideal beings above referred to, felt a certain satisfaction—which, I fear, was not altogether Christian-like—in their "raking-down." If Mr. Daws expected York and Scott to shake hands after the sermon, he was disappointed. But he did not relax his purpose. With that quiet fearlessness and determination which had won for him the respect of men who were too apt to regard piety as synonymous with effeminacy, he attacked Scott in his own house. What he said has not been recorded, but it is to be feared that it was part of his sermon. When he had concluded, Scott looked at him, not unkindly, over the glasses of his bar, and said, less irreverently than the words might convey, "Young man, I rather like your style; but when you know York and me as well as you do God Almighty, it'll be time to talk."

And so the feud progressed; and so, as in more illustrious examples, the private and personal enmity of two representative men led gradually to the evolution of some crude, half-expressed principle or belief. It was not long before it was made evident that those beliefs were identical with certain broad principles laid down by the founders of the American Constitution, as expounded by the statesmanlike A.; or were the fatal quicksands,[4] on which the ship of state might be wrecked, warningly pointed out by the eloquent B. The practical result of all which was the nomination of York and Scott to represent the opposite factions of Sandy Bar in legislative councils.

For some weeks past, the voters of Sandy Bar and the adjacent camps had been called upon, in large type, to "RALLY!" In vain the great pines at the cross-roads—whose trunks were compelled to bear this and other legends—moaned and protested from their windy watch-towers. But one day, with fife and drum, and flaming transparency, a procession filed into the triangular grove at the head of the gulch. The meeting was called to order by Colonel Starbottle, who, having once enjoyed legislative functions, and being vaguely known as a "war-horse," was considered to be a valuable partisan of York. He concluded an appeal for his friend, with an enunciation of principles, interspersed with one or two anecdotes so gratuitously coarse that the very pines might have been moved to pelt him with their cast-off cones, as he stood there. But he created a laugh, on which his candidate rode into popular notice; and when York rose to speak, he was greeted with cheers. But, to the general astonishment, the new speaker at once launched into bitter denunciation of his rival. He not only dwelt upon Scott's deeds and example, as known to Sandy Bar, but spoke of facts connected with his previous career, hitherto unknown to his auditors. To great precision of epithet and directness of statement, the speaker added the fascination of revelation and exposure. The crowd cheered, yelled, and were delighted, but when this astounding philippic was concluded, there was a unanimous call for "Scott!" Colonel Starbottle would have resisted this manifest impropriety, but in vain. Partly from a crude sense of justice, partly from a meaner craving for excitement, the assemblage was inflexible; and Scott was dragged, pushed, and pulled upon the platform.

As his frowsy head and unkempt beard appeared above the railing, it was evident that he was drunk. But it was also evident, before he opened his lips, that the orator of Sandy Bar—the one man who could touch their vagabond sympathies (perhaps because he was not above appealing to them)—stood before them. A consciousness of this power lent a certain dignity to his figure, and I am not sure but that his very physical condition impressed them as a kind of regal unbending and large condescension. Howbeit, when this unexpected Hector arose from the ditch,[5] York's myrmidons trembled.

"There's naught, gentlemen," said Scott, leaning forward on the railing,—"there's naught as that man hez said as isn't true. I was run outer Cairo; I did belong to the Regulators; I did desert from the army; I did leave a wife in Kansas. But thar's one thing he didn't charge me with, and, maybe, he's forgotten. For three years, gentlemen, I was that man's pardner!—" Whether he intended to say more, I cannot tell; a burst of applause artistically rounded and enforced the climax, and virtually elected the speaker. That fall he went to Sacramento, York went abroad; and for the first time in many years, distance and a new atmosphere isolated the old antagonists.

With little of change in the green wood, gray rock, and yellow river, but with much shifting of human landmarks, and new faces in its habitations, three years passed over Sandy Bar. The two men, once so identified with its character, seemed to have been quite forgotten. "You will never return to Sandy Bar," said Miss Folinsbee, the "Lily of Poverty Flat," on meeting York in Paris, "for Sandy Bar is no more. They call it Riverside now; and the new town is built higher up on the river-bank. By the by, 'Jo' says that Scott has won his suit about the 'Amity Claim,' and that he lives in the old cabin, and is drunk half his time. O, I beg your pardon," added the lively lady, as a flush crossed York's sallow cheek; "but, bless me, I really thought that old grudge was made up. I'm sure it ought to be."

It was three months after this conversation, and a pleasant summer evening, that the Poverty Flat coach drew up before the veranda of the Union Hotel at Sandy Bar. Among its passengers was one, apparently a stranger, in the local distinction of well-fitting clothes and closely shaven face, who demanded a private room and retired early to rest. But before sunrise next morning he arose, and, drawing some clothes from his carpet-bag, proceeded to array himself in a pair of white duck trousers, a white duck over-shirt, and straw hat. When his toilet was completed, he tied a red bandanna handkerchief in a loop and threw it loosely over his shoulders. The transformation was complete. As he crept softly down the stairs and stepped into the road, no one would have detected in him the elegant stranger of the previous night, and but few have recognized the face and figure of Henry York of Sandy Bar.

In the uncertain light of that early hour, and in the change that had come over the settlement, he had to pause for a moment to recall where he stood. The Sandy Bar of his recollection lay below him, nearer the river; the buildings around him were of later date and newer fashion. As he strode toward the river, he noticed here a school-house and there a church. A little farther on, "The Sunny South" came in view, transformed into a restaurant, its gilding faded and its paint rubbed off. He now knew where he was; and, running briskly down a declivity, crossed a ditch, and stood upon the lower boundary of the Amity Claim.

The gray mist was rising slowly from the river, clinging to the tree-tops and drifting up the mountain-side, until it was caught among those rocky altars, and held a sacrifice to the ascending sun. At his feet the earth, cruelly gashed and scarred by his forgotten engines, had, since the old days, put on a show of greenness here and there, and now smiled forgivingly up at him, as if things were not so bad after all. A few birds were bathing in the ditch with a pleasant suggestion of its being a new and special provision of nature, and a hare ran into an inverted sluice-box, as he approached, as if it were put there for that purpose.

He had not yet dared to look in a certain direction. But the sun was now high enough to paint the little eminence on which the cabin stood. In spite of his self-control, his heart beat faster as he raised his eyes toward it. Its window and door were closed, no smoke came from its *adobe* chimney, but it was else unchanged. When within a few yards of it, he picked up a broken shovel, and, shouldering it with a smile, strode toward the door and knocked. There was no sound from within. The smile died upon his lips as he nervously pushed the door open.

A figure started up angrily and came toward him,—a figure whose bloodshot eyes suddenly fixed into a vacant stare, whose arms were at first outstretched and then thrown up in warning gesticulation,—a figure that suddenly gasped, choked, and then fell forward in a fit.

But before he touched the ground, York had him out into the open air and sunshine. In the struggle, both fell and rolled over on the ground. But the next moment York was sitting up, holding the convulsed frame of his former partner on his knee, and wiping the foam from his inarticulate lips. Gradually the tremor became less frequent, and then ceased; and the strong man lay unconscious in his arms.

For some moments York held him quietly thus, looking in his face. Afar, the stroke of a woodman's axe—a mere phantom of sound—was all that broke the stillness. High up the mountain, a wheeling hawk hung breathlessly above them. And then came voices, and two men joined them.

"A fight?" No, a fit; and would they help him bring the sick man to the hotel?

And there, for a week, the stricken partner lay, unconscious of aught but the visions wrought by disease and fear. On the eighth day, at sunrise, he rallied, and, opening his eyes, looked upon York, and pressed his hand; then he spoke:—

"And it's you. I thought it was only whiskey."

York replied by taking both of his hands, boyishly working them backward and forward, as his elbow rested on the bed, with a pleasant smile.

"And you've been abroad. How did you like Paris?"

"So so. How did *you* like Sacramento?"

"Bully."

And that was all they could think to say. Presently Scott opened his eyes again.

"I'm mighty weak."

"You'll get better soon."

"Not much."

A long silence followed, in which they could hear the sounds of wood-chopping, and that Sandy Bar was already astir for the coming day. Then Scott slowly and with difficulty turned his face to York, and said,—

"I might hev killed you once."

"I wish you had."

They pressed each other's hands again, but Scott's grasp was evidently failing. He seemed to summon his energies for a special effort.

"Old man!"

"Old chap."

"Closer!"

York bent his head toward the slowly fading face.

"Do ye mind that morning?"

"Yes."

A gleam of fun slid into the corner of Scott's blue eye, as he whispered,—

"Old man, thar *was* too much saleratus in that bread."

It is said that these were his last words. For when the sun, which had so often gone down upon the idle wrath of these foolish men, looked again upon them reunited, it saw the hand of Scott fall cold and irresponsive from the yearning clasp of his former partner, and it knew that the feud of Sandy Bar was at an end.

Nov. 1870

The Poet of Sierra Flat

AS THE ENTERPRISING EDITOR of the "Sierra Flat Record" stood at his case setting type for his next week's paper, he could not help hearing the woodpeckers who were busy on the roof above his head. It occurred to him that possibly the birds had not yet learned to recognize in the rude structure any improvement on nature, and this idea pleased him so much that he incorporated it in the editorial article which he was then doubly composing. For the editor was also printer of the "Record"; and although that remarkable journal was reputed to exert a power felt through all Calaveras and a greater part of Tuolumne County, strict economy was one of the conditions of its beneficent existence.

Thus preoccupied, he was startled by the sudden irruption of a small roll of manuscript, which was thrown through the open door and fell at his feet. He walked quickly to the threshold and looked down the tangled trail which led to the high-road. But there was nothing to suggest the presence of his mysterious contributor. A hare limped slowly away, a green-and-gold lizard paused upon a pine stump, the woodpeckers ceased their work. So complete had been his sylvan seclusion, that he found it difficult to connect any human agency with the act; rather the hare seemed to have an inexpressibly guilty look, the woodpeckers to maintain a significant silence, and the lizard to be conscience-stricken into stone.

An examination of the manuscript, however, corrected this injustice to defenseless nature. It was evidently of human origin,— being verse, and of exceeding bad quality. The editor laid it aside. As he did so he thought he saw a face at the window. Sallying out in some indignation, he penetrated the surrounding thicket in every direction, but his search was as fruitless as before. The poet, if it were he, was gone.

A few days after this the editorial seclusion was invaded by voices of alternate expostulation and entreaty. Stepping to the door, the editor was amazed at beholding Mr. Morgan McCorkle, a well-known citizen of Angelo, and a subscriber to the "Record," in the act of urging, partly by force and partly by argument, an awkward young man toward the building. When he had finally effected his object, and, as it were, safely landed his prize in a chair, Mr. McCorkle took off his hat, carefully wiped the narrow isthmus of forehead which divided his black brows from his stubby hair, and with an explanatory wave of his hand toward his reluctant companion, said, "A borned poet, and the cussedest fool you ever seed!"

Accepting the editor's smile as a recognition of the introduction, Mr. McCorkle panted and went on: "Didn't want to come! 'Mister Editor don't want to see me, Morg,' sez he. 'Milt,' sez I, 'he do; a borned poet like you and a gifted genius like he oughter come together sociable!' And I fetched him. Ah, will yer?" The born poet had, after exhibiting signs of great distress, started to run. But Mr. McCorkle was down upon him instantly, seizing him by his long linen coat, and settled him back in his chair. " 'Tain't no use stampeding. Yer ye are and yer ye stays. For yer a borned poet,—ef ye are as shy as a jackass rabbit. Look at 'im now!"

He certainly was not an attractive picture. There was hardly a notable feature in his weak face, except his eyes, which were moist and shy and not unlike the animal to which Mr. McCorkle had compared him. It was the face that the editor had seen at the window.

"Knowed him for fower year,—since he war a boy," continued Mr. McCorkle in a loud whisper. "Allers the same, bless you! Can jerk a rhyme as easy as turnin' jack. Never had any eddication; lived out in Missooray all his life. But he's chock full o' poetry. On'y this mornin' sez I to him,—he camps along o' me,—'Milt!' sez I, 'are breakfast ready?' and he up and answers back quite peart and chipper, 'The breakfast it is ready, and the birds is singing free, and it's risin' in the dawnin' light is happiness to me!' When a man," said Mr. McCorkle, dropping his voice with deep solemnity, "gets off things like them, without any call to do it, and handlin' flapjacks over a cookstove at the same time,—that man's a borned poet."

There was an awkward pause. Mr. McCorkle beamed patronizingly on his *protégé*.[1] The born poet looked as if he were meditating another flight,—not a metaphorical one. The editor asked if he could do anything for them.

"In course you can," responded Mr. McCorkle, "that's jest it. Milt, where's that poetry?"

The editor's countenance fell as the poet produced from his pocket a roll of manuscript. He, however, took it mechanically and glanced over it. It was evidently a duplicate of the former mysterious contribution.

The editor then spoke briefly but earnestly. I regret that I cannot recall his exact words, but it appeared that never before, in the history of the "Record," had the pressure been so great upon its columns. Matters of paramount importance, deeply affecting the material progress of Sierra, questions touching the absolute integrity of Calaveras and Tuolumne as social communities, were even now waiting expression. Weeks, nay, months, must elapse before that pressure would be removed, and the "Record" could grapple with any but the sternest of topics. Again, the editor had noticed with pain the absolute decline of poetry in the foothills of the Sierras. Even the works of Byron and Moore attracted no attention in Dutch Flat, and a prejudice seemed to exist against Tennyson in Grass Valley.[2] But the editor was not without hope for the future. In the course of four or five years, when the country was settled,—

"What would be the cost to print this yer?" interrupted Mr. McCorkle, quietly.

"About fifty dollars, as an advertisement," responded the editor with cheerful alacrity.

Mr. McCorkle placed the sum in the editor's hand. "Yer see thet's what I sez to Milt, 'Milt,' sez I, 'pay as you go, for you are a borned poet. Hevin no call to write, but doin' it free and spontaneous like, in course you pays. Thet's why Mr. Editor never printed your poetry.' "

"What name shall I put to it?" asked the editor.

"Milton."

It was the first word that the born poet had spoken during the interview, and his voice was so very sweet and musical that the editor looked at him curiously, and wondered if he had a sister.

"Milton; is that all?"

"Thet's his furst name," exclaimed Mr. McCorkle.

The editor here suggested that as there had been another poet of that name—[3]

"Milt might be took for him! Thet's bad," reflected Mr. McCorkle with simple gravity. "Well, put down his hull name,—Milton Chubbuck."

The editor made a note of the fact. "I'll set it up now," he said. This was also a hint that the interview was ended. The poet and patron, arm in arm, drew towards the door. "In next week's paper," said the editor, smilingly, in answer to the childlike look of inquiry in the eyes of the poet, and in another moment they were gone.

The editor was as good as his word. He straight-way betook himself to his case, and, unrolling the manuscript, began his task. The woodpeckers on the roof recommenced theirs, and in a few moments the former sylvan seclusion was restored. There was no sound in the barren, barn-like room but the birds above, and below the click of the composing-rule as the editor marshalled the types into lines in his stick, and arrayed them in solid column on the galley. Whatever might have been his opinion of the copy before him, there was no indication of it in his face, which wore the stolid indifference of his craft. Perhaps this was unfortunate, for as the day wore on and the level rays of the sun began to pierce the adjacent thicket, they sought out and discovered an anxious ambushed figure drawn up beside the editor's window,—a figure that had sat there motionless for hours. Within, the editor worked on as steadily and impassively as Fate. And without, the born poet of Sierra Flat sat and watched him as waiting its decree.

The effect of the poem on Sierra Flat was remarkable and unprecedented. The absolute vileness of its doggerel, the gratuitous imbecility of its thought, and above all the crowning audacity of the fact that it was the work of a citizen and published in the county paper, brought it instantly into popularity. For many months Calaveras had languished for a sensation; since the last vigilance committee nothing had transpired to dispel the listless *ennui*[4] begotten of stagnant business and growing civilization. In more prosperous moments the office of the "Record" would have been simply gutted and the editor deported; at present the paper was in such demand that the edition was speedily exhausted. In brief, the poem of Mr. Milton Chubbuck came like a special providence to Sierra Flat. It was read by camp-fires, in lonely cabins, in flaring bar-rooms and noisy saloons, and declaimed from the boxes of stagecoaches. It was sung in Poker Flat with the addition of a local chorus, and danced as an unhallowed rhythmic dance by the Pyrrhic phalanx of One Horse Gulch, known as "The Festive Stags of Calaveras." Some unhappy ambiguities of expression gave rise to many new readings, notes, and commentaries, which, I regret to state, were more often marked by ingenuity than delicacy of thought or expression.

Never before did poet acquire such sudden local reputation. From the seclusion of McCorkle's cabin and the obscurity of culinary labors, he was haled forth into the glowing sunshine of Fame. The name of Chubbuck was written in letters of chalk on unpainted walls, and carved with a pick on the sides of tunnels. A drink known variously as "The Chubbuck Tranquillizer," or "The Chubbuck Exalter," was dispensed at the bars. For some weeks a rude design for a Chubbuck statue, made up of illustrations from circus and melodeon posters, representing the genius of Calaveras in brief skirts on a flying steed in the act of crowning the poet Chubbuck, was visible at Keeler's Ferry. The poet himself was overborne with invitations to drink and extravagant congratulations. The meeting between Colonel Starbottle of Siskyion and Chubbuck, as previously arranged by our "Boston," late of Roaring Camp, is said to have been indescribably affecting. The Colonel embraced him unsteadily. "I could not return to my constituents at Siskyion, sir, if this hand, which has grasped that of the gifted Prentice and the lamented Poe, should not have been honored by the touch of the godlike Chubbuck. Gentlemen, American literature is looking up. Thank you, I will take sugar in mine." It was "Boston" who indited letters of congratulations from H. W. Longfellow,[5] Tennyson, and Browning,[6] to Mr. Chubbuck, deposited them in the Sierra Flat post-office, and obligingly consented to dictate the replies.

The simple faith and unaffected delight with which these manifestations were received by the poet and his patron might have touched the hearts of these grim masters of irony, but for the sudden and equal development in both of the variety of weak natures. Mr. McCorkle basked in the popularity of his *protégé*, and became alternately supercilious or patronizing toward the dwellers of Sierra Flat; while the poet, with hair carefully oiled and curled, and bedecked with cheap jewelry and flaunting neck-handkerchief, paraded himself before the single hotel. As may be imagined, this new disclosure of weakness afforded intense satisfaction to Sierra Flat, gave another lease of popularity to the poet, and suggested another idea to the facetious "Boston."

At that time a young lady popularly and professionally known as the "California Pet" was performing to enthusiastic audiences in the interior. Her specialty lay in the personation of youthful masculine character; as a *gamin*[7] of the street she was irresistible, as a Negro-dancer she carried the honest miner's heart by storm. A saucy, pretty brunette, she had preserved a wonderful moral reputation even under the Jove-like advances of showers of gold that greeted her appearance on the stage at Sierra Flat. A prominent and delighted member of that audience was Milton Chubbuck. He attended every night. Every day he lingered at the door of the Union Hotel for a glimpse of the "California Pet." It was not long before he received a note from her,—in "Boston's" most popular and approved female hand,—acknowledging his admiration. It was not long before "Boston" was called upon to indite a suitable reply. At last, in furtherance of his facetious design, it became necessary for "Boston" to call upon the young actress herself and secure her personal participation. To her he unfolded a plan, the successful carrying out of which he felt would secure his fame to posterity as a practical humorist. The "California Pet's" black eyes sparkled approvingly and mischievously. She only stipulated that she should see the man first,—a concession to her feminine weakness which years of dancing Juba and wearing trousers and boots had not wholly eradicated from her wilful breast. By all means, it should be done. And the interview was arranged for the next week.

It must not be supposed that during this interval of popularity Mr. Chubbuck had been unmindful of his poetic qualities. A certain portion of each day he was absent from town,—"a communin' with natur'," as Mr. McCorkle expressed it,—and actually wandering in the mountain trails, or lying on his back under the trees, or gathering fragrant herbs and the bright-colored berries of the Marzanita. These and his company he generally brought to the editor's office, late in the afternoon, often to that enterprising journalist's infinite weariness. Quiet and uncommunicative, he would sit there patiently watching him at his work until the hour for closing the office arrived, when he would as quietly depart. There was something so humble and unobtrusive in these visits that the editor could not find it in his heart to deny them, and accepting them, like the woodpeckers, as a part of his sylvan surroundings, often forgot even his presence. Once or twice, moved by some beauty of expression in the moist, shy eyes, he felt like seriously admonishing his visitor of his idle folly; but his glance falling upon the oiled hair and the gorgeous necktie, he invariably thought better of it. The case was evidently hopeless.

The interview between Mr. Chubbuck and the "California Pet" took place in a private room of the Union Hotel; propriety being respected by the presence of that arch-humorist, "Boston." To this gentleman we are indebted for the only true account of the meeting. However reticent Mr. Chubbuck might have been in the presence of his own sex, toward the fairer portion of humanity he was, like most poets, exceedingly voluble. Accustomed as the "California Pet" had been to excessive compliment, she was fairly embarrassed by the extravagant praises of her visitor. Her personation of boy characters, her dancing of the "champion jig," were particularly dwelt upon with fervid but unmistakable admiration. At last, recovering her audacity and emboldened by the presence of "Boston," the "California Pet" electrified her hearers by demanding, half jestingly, half viciously, if it were as a boy or a girl that she was the subject of his flattering admiration.

"That knocked him out o' time," said the delighted "Boston," in his subsequent account of the interview. "But do you believe the d—d fool actually asked her to take him with her; wanted to engage in the company."

The plan, as briefly unfolded by "Boston," was to prevail upon Mr. Chubbuck to make his appearance in costume (already designed and prepared by the inventor) before a Sierra Flat audience, and recite an original poem at the Hall immediately on the conclusion of the "California Pet's" performance. At a given signal the audience were to rise and deliver a volley of unsavory articles (previously provided by the originator of the scheme); then a se-

lect few were to rush on the stage, seize the poet, and, after marching him in triumphal procession through town, were to deposit
him beyond its uttermost limits, with strict injunctions never to
enter it again. To the first part of the plan the poet was committed,
for the latter portion it was easy enough to find participants.

The eventful night came, and with it an audience that packed
the long narrow room with one dense mass of human beings. The
"California Pet" never had been so joyous, so reckless, so fascinating and audacious before. But the applause was tame and weak
compared to the ironical outburst that greeted the second rising of
the curtain and the entrance of the born poet of Sierra Flat. Then
there was a hush of expectancy, and the poet stepped to the foot-
lights and stood with his manuscript in his hand.

His face was deadly pale. Either there was some suggestion of
his fate in the faces of his audience, or some mysterious instinct
told him of his danger. He attempted to speak, but faltered, tottered, and staggered to the wings.

Fearful of losing his prey, "Boston" gave the signal and leaped
upon the stage. But at the same moment a light figure darted from
behind the scenes, and delivering a kick that sent the discomfited
humorist back among the musicians, cut a pigeon-wing, executed
a double-shuffle, and then advancing to the foot-lights with that
inimitable look, that audacious swagger and utter *abandon* which
had so thrilled and fascinated them a moment before, uttered the
characteristic speech: "Wot are you goin' to hit a man fur, when
he's down, s-a-a-y?"

The look, the drawl, the action, the readiness, and above all the
downright courage of the little woman had its effect. A roar of
sympathetic applause followed the act. "Cut and run while you
can," she whispered hurriedly over her one shoulder, without al-
tering the other's attitude of pert and saucy defiance toward the
audience. But even as she spoke the poet tottered and sank fainting
upon the stage. Then she threw a despairing whisper behind the
scenes, "Ring down the curtain."

There was a slight movement of opposition in the audience, but
among them rose the burly shoulders of Yuba Bill, the tall, erect
figure of Henry York of Sandy Bar, and the colorless, determined
face of John Oakhurst. The curtain came down.

Behind it knelt the "California Pet" beside the prostrate poet.

"Bring me some water. Run for a doctor. Stop!! CLEAR OUT, ALL OF YOU!"

She had unloosed the gaudy cravat and opened the shirt-collar of the insensible figure before her. Then she burst into an hysterical laugh.

"Manuela!"

Her tiring-woman, a Mexican half-breed, came toward her.

"Help me with him to my dressing-room, quick; then stand outside and wait. If any one questions you, tell them he's gone. Do you hear? He's gone."

The old woman did as she was bade. In a few moments the audience had departed. Before morning so also had the "California Pet," Manuela, and—the poet of Sierra Flat.

But, alas! with them also had departed the fair fame of the "California Pet." Only a few, and these it is to be feared of not the best moral character themselves, still had faith in the stainless honor of their favorite actress. "It was a mighty foolish thing to do, but it'll all come out right yet." On the other hand, a majority gave her full credit and approbation for her undoubted pluck and gallantry, but deplored that she should have thrown it away upon a worthless object. To elect for a lover the despised and ridiculed vagrant of Sierra Flat, who had not even the manliness to stand up in his own defense was not only evidence of inherent moral depravity, but was an insult to the community. Colonel Starbottle saw in it only another instance of the extreme frailty of the sex; he had known similar cases; and remembered distinctly, sir, how a well-known Philadelphia heiress, one of the finest women that ever rode in her kerridge, that, gad, sir! had thrown over a Southern member of Congress to consort with a d—d nigger. The Colonel had also noticed a singular look in the dog's eye which he did not entirely fancy. He would not say anything against the lady, sir, but he had noticed—And here haply the Colonel became so mysterious and darkly confidential as to be unintelligible and inaudible to the bystanders.

A few days after the disappearance of Mr. Chubbuck a singular report reached Sierra Flat, and it was noticed that "Boston," who since the failure of his elaborate joke had been even more depressed in spirits than is habitual with great humorists, suddenly found that his presence was required in San Francisco. But as yet nothing but the vaguest surmises were afloat, and nothing definite was known.

It was a pleasant afternoon when the editor of the "Sierra Flat Record" looked up from his case and beheld the figure of Mr. Morgan McCorkle standing in the doorway. There was a distressed look on the face of that worthy gentleman that at once enlisted the editor's sympathizing attention. He held an open letter in his hand, as he advanced toward the middle of the room.

"As a man as has allers borne a fair reputation," began Mr. McCorkle slowly, "I should like, if so be as I could, Mister Editor, to make a correction in the columns of your valooable paper."

Mr. Editor begged him to proceed.

"Ye may not disremember that about a month ago I fetched here what so be as we'll call a young man whose name might be as it were Milton—Milton Chubbuck."

Mr. Editor remembered perfectly.

"Thet same party I'd knowed better nor fower year, two on 'em campin' out together. Not that I'd known him all the time, fur he war shy and strange at spells and had odd ways that I took war nat'ral to a borned poet. Ye may remember that I said he was a borned poet?"

The editor distinctly did.

"I picked this same party up in St. Jo., takin' a fancy to his face, and kinder calklating he'd runn'd away from home,—for I'm a married man, Mr. Editor, and hev children of my own,—and thinkin' belike he was a borned poet."

"Well?" said the editor.

"And as I said before, I should like now to make a correction in the columns of your valooable paper."

"What correction?" asked the editor.

"I said, ef you remember my words, as how he was a borned poet."

"Yes."

"From statements in this yer letter it seems as how I war wrong."

"Well?"

"She war a woman."

July 1871

How Santa Claus Came to Simpson's Bar

IT HAD BEEN RAINING in the valley of the Sacramento. The North Fork had overflowed its banks and Rattlesnake Creek was impassable. The few boulders that had marked the summer ford at Simpson's Crossing were obliterated by a vast sheet of water stretching to the foothills. The up stage was stopped at Grangers; the last mail had been abandoned in the *tules*,[1] the rider swimming for his life. "An area," remarked the "Sierra Avalanche," with pensive local pride, "as large as the State of Massachusetts is now under water."

Nor was the weather any better in the foothills. The mud lay deep on the mountain road; wagons that neither physical force nor moral objurgation could move from the evil ways into which they had fallen, encumbered the track, and the way to Simpson's Bar was indicated by broken-down teams and hard swearing. And farther on, cut off and inaccessible, rained upon and bedraggled, smitten by high winds and threatened by high water, Simpson's Bar, on the eve of Christmas day, 1862, clung like a swallow's nest to the rocky entablature and splintered capitals of Table Mountain, and shook in the blast.

As night shut down on the settlement, a few lights gleamed through the mist from the windows of cabins on either side of the highway now crossed and gullied by lawless streams and swept by marauding winds. Happily most of the population were gathered at Thompson's store, clustered around a red-hot stove, at which they silently spat in some accepted sense of social communion that perhaps rendered conversation unnecessary. Indeed, most methods of diversion had long since been exhausted on Simpson's Bar; high water had suspended the regular occupations on gulch and on river, and a consequent lack of money and whiskey had taken the zest from most illegitimate recreation. Even Mr. Hamlin was fain to leave the Bar with fifty dollars in his pocket,—the only amount actually realized of the large sums won by him in the successful exercise of his arduous profession. "Ef I was asked," he remarked somewhat later,—"ef I was asked to pint out a purty little village where a retired sport as didn't care for money could exercise hisself, frequent and lively, I'd say Simpson's Bar; but for a young man with a large family depending on his exertions, it don't pay." As Mr. Hamlin's family consisted mainly of female adults, this remark is quoted rather to show the breadth of his humor than the exact extent of his responsibilities.

Howbeit, the unconscious objects of this satire sat that evening in the listless apathy begotten of idleness and lack of excitement. Even the sudden splashing of hoofs before the door did not arouse them. Dick Bullen alone paused in the act of scraping out his pipe, and lifted his head, but no other one of the group indicated any interest in, or recognition of, the man who entered.

It was a figure familiar enough to the company, and known in Simpson's Bar as "The Old Man." A man of perhaps fifty years; grizzled and scant of hair, but still fresh and youthful of complexion. A face full of ready, but not very powerful sympathy, with a chameleon-like aptitude for taking on the shade and color of contiguous moods and feelings. He had evidently just left some hilarious companions, and did not at first notice the gravity of the group, but clapped the shoulder of the nearest man jocularly, and threw himself into a vacant chair.

"Jest heard the best thing out, boys! Ye know Smiley, over yar,—Jim Smiley,—funniest man in the Bar?[2] Well, Jim was jest telling the richest yarn about—"

"Smiley's a — fool," interrupted a gloomy voice.

"A particular — skunk," added another in sepulchral accents.

A silence followed these positive statements. The Old Man glanced quickly around the group. Then his face slowly changed. "That's so," he said reflectively, after a pause, "certingly a sort of a skunk and suthin of a fool. In course." He was silent for a moment as in painful contemplation of the unsavoriness and folly of the unpopular Smiley. "Dismal weather, ain't it?" he added, now fully embarked on the current of prevailing sentiment. "Mighty rough papers on the boys, and no show for money this season. And tomorrow's Christmas."

There was a movement among the men at this announcement,

but whether of satisfaction or disgust was not plain. "Yes," continued the Old Man in the lugubrious tone he had, within the last few moments, unconsciously adopted,—"yes, Christmas, and to-night's Christmas eve. Ye see, boys, I kinder thought—that is, I sorter had an idee, jest passin' like, you know—that may be ye'd all like to come over to my house to-night and have a sort of tear round. But I suppose, now, you wouldn't? Don't feel like it, may be?" he added with anxious sympathy, peering into the faces of his companions.

"Well, I don't know," responded Tom Flynn with some cheerfulness. "P'r'aps we may. But how about your wife, Old Man? What does *she* say to it?"

The Old Man hesitated. His conjugal experience had not been a happy one, and the fact was known to Simpson's Bar. His first wife, a delicate, pretty little woman, had suffered keenly and secretly from the jealous suspicions of her husband, until one day he invited the whole Bar to his house to expose her infidelity. On arriving, the party found the shy, *petite* creature quietly engaged in her household duties, and retired abashed and discomfited. But the sensitive woman did not easily recover from the shock of this extraordinary outrage. It was with difficulty she regained her equanimity sufficiently to release her lover from the closet in which he was concealed and escape with him. She left a boy of three years to comfort her bereaved husband. The Old Man's present wife had been his cook. She was large, loyal, and aggressive.

Before he could reply, Joe Dimmick suggested with great directness that it was the "Old Man's house," and that, invoking the Divine Power, if the case were his own, he would invite whom he pleased, even if in so doing he imperilled his salvation. The Powers of Evil, he further remarked, should contend against him vainly. All this delivered with a terseness and vigor lost in this necessary translation.

"In course. Certainly. Thet's it," said the Old Man with a sympathetic frown. "Thar's no trouble about *thet*. It's my own house, built every stick on it myself. Don't you be afeard o' her, boys. She *may* cut up a trifle rough,—ez wimmin do,—but she'll come round." Secretly the Old Man trusted to the exaltation of liquor and the power of courageous example to sustain him in such an emergency.

As yet, Dick Bullen, the oracle and leader of Simpson's Bar, had not spoken. He now took his pipe from his lips. "Old Man, how's that yer Johnny gettin' on? Seems to me he didn't look so peart last time I seed him on the bluff heavin' rocks at Chinamen. Didn't seem to take much interest in it. Thar was a gang of 'em by yar yesterday,—drownded out up the river,—and I kinder thought o' Johnny, and how he'd miss 'em! May be now, we'd be in the way ef he wus sick?"

The father, evidently touched not only by this pathetic picture of Johnny's deprivation, but by the considerate delicacy of the speaker, hastened to assure him that Johnny was better and that a "little fun might liven him up." Whereupon Dick arose, shook himself, and saying, "I'm ready. Lead the way, Old Man: here goes," himself led the way with a leap, a characteristic howl, and darted out into the night. As he passed through the outer room he caught up a blazing brand from the hearth. The action was repeated by the rest of the party, closely following and elbowing each other, and before the astonished proprietor of Thompson's grocery was aware of the intention of his guests, the room was deserted.

The night was pitchy dark. In the first gust of wind their temporary torches were extinguished, and only the red brands dancing and flitting in the gloom like drunken will-o'-the-wisps indicated their whereabouts. Their way led up Pine-Tree Cañon, at the head of which a broad, low, bark-thatched cabin burrowed in the mountain-side. It was the home of the Old Man, and the entrance to the tunnel in which he worked when he worked at all. Here the crowd paused for a moment, out of delicate deference to their host, who came up panting in the rear.

"P'r'aps ye'd better hold on a second out yer, whilst I go in and see thet things is all right," said the Old Man, with an indifference he was far from feeling. The suggestion was graciously accepted, the door opened and closed on the host, and the crowd, leaning their backs against the wall and cowering under the eaves, waited and listened.

For a few moments there was no sound but the dripping of water from the eaves, and the stir and rustle of wrestling boughs above them. Then the men became uneasy, and whispered suggestion and suspicion passed from the one to the other. "Reckon she's caved in his head the first lick!" "Decoyed him inter the tunnel and barred him up, likely." "Got him down and sittin' on him." "Prob'ly bilin suthin to heave on us: stand clear the door, boys!" For just then the latch clicked, the door slowly opened, and a voice said, "Come in out o' the wet."

The voice was neither that of the Old Man nor of his wife. It was the voice of a small boy, its weak treble broken by that preternatural hoarseness which only vagabondage and the habit of premature self-assertion can give. It was the face of a small boy that looked up at theirs,—a face that might have been pretty and even refined but that it was darkened by evil knowledge from within, and dirt and hard experience from without. He had a blanket around his shoulders and had evidently just risen from his bed. "Come in," he repeated, "and don't make no noise. The Old Man's in there talking to mar," he continued, pointing to an adjacent room which seemed to be a kitchen, from which the Old Man's voice came in deprecating accents. "Let me be," he added, querulously, to Dick Bullen, who had caught him up, blanket and all, and was affecting to toss him into the fire, "let go o' me, you d—d old fool, d'ye hear?"

Thus adjured, Dick Bullen lowered Johnny to the ground with a smothered laugh, while the men, entering quietly, ranged themselves around a long table of rough boards which occupied the center of the room. Johnny then gravely proceeded to a cupboard and brought out several articles which he deposited on the table. "Thar's whiskey. And crackers. And red herons.³ And cheese." He took a bite of the latter on his way to the table. "And sugar." He scooped up a mouthful *en route* with a small and very dirty hand. "And terbacker. Thar's dried appils too on the shelf, but I don't admire 'em. Appils is swellin'. Thar," he concluded, "now wade in, and don't be afeard. *I* don't mind the old woman. She don't b'long to *me*. S'long."

He had stepped to the threshold of a small room, scarcely larger than a closet, partitioned off from the main apartment, and holding in its dim recess a small bed. He stood there a moment looking at the company, his bare feet peeping from the blanket, and nodded.

"Hello, Johnny! You ain't goin' to turn in agin, are ye?" said Dick.

"Yes, I are," responded Johnny, decidedly.

"Why, wot's up, old fellow?"

"I'm sick."

"How sick?"

"I've got a fevier. And childblains.[4] And roomatiz," returned Johnny, and vanished within. After a moment's pause, he added in the dark, apparently from under the bedclothes,—"And biles!"

There was an embarrasing silence. The men looked at each other, and at the fire. Even with the appetizing banquet before them, it seemed as if they might again fall into the despondency of Thompson's grocery, when the voice of the Old Man, incautiously lifted, came deprecatingly from the kitchen.

"Certainly! Thet's so. In course they is. A gang o' lazy drunken loafers, and that ar Dick Bullen's the ornariest of all. Didn't hev no more *sabe* than to come round yar with sickness in the house and no provision. Thet's what I said: 'Bullen,' sez I, 'it's crazy drunk you are, or a fool,' sez I, 'to think o' such a thing.' 'Staples,' I sez, 'be you a man, Staples, and 'spect to raise h—ll under my roof and invalids lyin' round?' But they would come,—they would. Thet's wot you must 'spect o' such trash as lays round the Bar."

A burst of laughter from the men followed this unfortunate exposure. Whether it was overheard in the kitchen, or whether the Old Man's irate companion had just then exhausted all other modes of expressing her contemptuous indignation, I cannot say, but a back door was suddenly slammed with great violence. A moment later and the Old Man reappeared, haply unconscious of the cause of the late hilarious outburst, and smiled blandly.

"The old woman thought she'd jest run over to Mrs. McFadden's for a sociable call," he explained, with jaunty indifference, as he took a seat at the board.

Oddly enough it needed this untoward incident to relieve the embarrassment that was beginning to be felt by the party, and their natural audacity returned with their host. I do not propose to record the convivialities of that evening. The inquisitive reader

will accept the statement that the conversation was characterized
by the same intellectual exaltation, the same cautious reverence,
the same fastidious delicacy, the same rhetorical precision, and
the same logical and coherent discourse somewhat later in the
evening, which distinguish similar gatherings of the masculine sex
in more civilized localities and under more favorable auspices. No
glasses were broken in the absence of any; no liquor was uselessly
spilt on floor or table in the scarcity of that article.

It was nearly midnight when the festivities were interrupted.
"Hush," said Dick Bullen, holding up his hand. It was the querulous voice of Johnny from his adjacent closet: "O dad!"

The Old Man arose hurriedly and disappeared in the closet.
Presently he reappeared. "His rheumatiz is coming on agin bad,"
he explained, "and he wants rubbin'." He lifted the demijohn of
whiskey from the table and shook it. It was empty. Dick Bullen
put down his tin cup with an embarrassed laugh. So did the others.
The Old Man examined their contents and said hopefully, "I
reckon that's enough; he don't need much. You hold on all o' you
for a spell, and I'll be back"; and vanished in the closet with an old
flannel shirt and the whiskey. The door closed but imperfectly,
and the following dialogue was distinctly audible:—

"Now, sonny, whar does she ache worst?"

"Sometimes over yar and sometimes under yer; but it's most
powerful from yer to yer. Rub yer, dad."

A silence seemed to indicate a brisk rubbing. Then Johnny:

"Hevin' a good time out yer, dad?"

"Yes, sonny."

"To-morrer's Chrismiss,—ain't it?"

"Yes, sonny. How does she feel now?"

"Better. Rub a little furder down. Wot's Chrismiss, anyway?
Wot's it all about?"

"O, it's a day."

This exhaustive definition was apparently satisfactory, for there
was a silent interval of rubbing. Presently Johnny again:

"Mar sez that everywhere else but yer everybody gives things
to everybody Chrismiss, and then she jist waded inter you. She
sez thar's a man they call Sandy Claws, not a white man, you
know, but a kind o' Chinemin, comes down the chimbley night
afore Chrismiss and gives things to chillern,—boys like me. Puts

'em in their butes! Thet's what she tried to play upon me. Easy
now, pop, whar are you rubbin' to,—thet's a mile from the place.
She jest made that up, didn't she, jest to aggrewate me and you?
Don't rub thar. . . . . Why, dad!"

In the great quiet that seemed to have fallen upon the house the
sigh of the near pines and the drip of leaves without was very
distinct. Johnny's voice, too, was lowered as he went on, "Don't
you take on now, fur I'm gettin' all right fast. Wot's the boys doin'
out thar?"

The Old Man partly opened the door and peered through. His
guests were sitting there sociably enough, and there were a few silver coins and a lean buckskin purse on the table. "Bettin' on
suthin,—some little game or 'nother. They're all right," he replied
to Johnny, and recommenced his rubbing.

"I'd like to take a hand and win some money," said Johnny, reflectively, after a pause.

The Old Man glibly repeated what was evidently a familiar formula, that if Johnny would wait until he struck it rich in the tunnel he'd have lots of money, etc., etc.

"Yes," said Johnny, "but you don't. And whether you strike it
or I win it, it's about the same. It's all luck. But it's mighty cur'o's
about Chrismiss,—ain't it? Why do they call it Chrismiss?"

Perhaps from some instinctive deference to the overhearing of
his guests, or from some vague sense of incongruity, the Old
Man's reply was so low as to be inaudible beyond the room.

"Yes," said Johnny, with some slight abatement of interest,
"I've heerd o' *him* before. Thar, that'll do, dad. I don't ache near
so bad as I did. Now wrap me tight in this yer blanket. So. Now,"
he added in a muffled whisper, "sit down yer by me till I go
asleep." To assure himself of obedience, he disengaged one hand
from the blanket and, grasping his father's sleeve, again composed
himself to rest.

For some moments the Old Man waited patiently. Then the unwonted stillness of the house excited his curiosity, and without
moving from the bed, he cautiously opened the door with his disengaged hand, and looked into the main room. To his infinite surprise it was dark and deserted. But even then a smouldering log on
the hearth broke, and by the upspringing blaze he saw the figure
of Dick Bullen sitting by the dying embers.

"Hello!"

Dick started, rose, and came somewhat unsteadily toward him.

"Whar's the boys?" said the Old Man.

"Gone up the *cañon* on a little *pasear.*[5] They're coming back for me in a minit. I'm waitin' round for 'em. What are you starin' at, Old Man?" he added with a forced laugh; "do you think I'm drunk?"

The Old Man might have been pardoned the supposition, for Dick's eyes were humid and his face flushed. He loitered and lounged back to the chimney, yawned, shook himself, buttoned up his coat and laughed. "Liquor ain't so plenty as that, Old Man. Now don't you git up," he continued, as the Old Man made a movement to release his sleeve from Johnny's hand. "Don't you mind manners. Sit jest whar you be; I'm goin' in a jiffy. Thar, that's them now."

There was a low tap at the door. Dick Bullen opened it quickly, nodded "Good night" to his host, and disappeared. The Old Man would have followed him but for the hand that still unconsciously grasped his sleeve. He could have easily disengaged it: it was small, weak, and emaciated. But perhaps because it *was* small, weak, and emaciated, he changed his mind, and, drawing his chair closer to the bed, rested his head upon it. In this defenseless attitude the potency of his earlier potations surprised him. The room flickered and faded before his eyes, reappeared, faded again, went out, and left him—asleep.

Meantime Dick Bullen, closing the door, confronted his companions. "Are you ready?" said Staples. "Ready," said Dick; "what's the time?" "Past twelve," was the reply; "can you make it?—it's nigh on fifty miles, the round trip hither and yon." "I reckon," returned Dick, shortly. "Whar's the mare?" "Bill and Jack's holdin' her at the crossin'." "Let 'em hold on a minit longer," said Dick.

He turned and re-entered the house softly. By the light of the guttering candle and dying fire he saw that the door of the little room was open. He stepped toward it on tiptoe and looked in. The Old Man had fallen back in his chair, snoring, his helpless feet thrust out in a line with his collapsed shoulders, and his hat pulled over his eyes. Beside him, on a narrow wooden bedstead, lay Johnny, muffled tightly in a blanket that hid all save a strip of forehead and a few curls damp with perspiration. Dick Bullen made a step forward, hesitated, and glanced over his shoulder into the deserted room. Everything was quiet. With a sudden resolution he parted his huge mustaches with both hands and stooped over the sleeping boy. But even as he did so a mischievous blast, lying in wait, swooped down the chimney, rekindled the hearth, and lit up the room with a shameless glow from which Dick fled in bashful terror.

His companions were already waiting for him at the crossing. Two of them were struggling in the darkness with some strange misshapen bulk, which as Dick came nearer took the semblance of a great yellow horse.

It was the mare. She was not a pretty picture. From her Roman nose to her rising haunches, from her arched spine hidden by the stiff *machillas* of a Mexican saddle, to her thick, straight, bony legs, there was not a line of equine grace. In her half-blind but wholly vicious white eyes, in her protruding under lip, in her monstrous color, there was nothing but ugliness and vice.

"Now then," said Staples, "stand cl'ar of her heels, boys, and up with you. Don't miss your first holt of her mane, and mind ye get your off stirrup *quick*. Ready!"

There was a leap, a scrambling struggle, a bound, a wild retreat of the crowd, a circle of flying hoofs, two springless leaps that jarred the earth, a rapid play and jingle of spurs, a plunge, and then the voice of Dick somewhere in the darkness, "All right!"

"Don't take the lower road back onless you're hard pushed for time! Don't hold her in down hill! We'll be at the ford at five. G'lang! Hoopa! Mula! GO!"

A splash, a spark struck from the ledge in the road, a clatter in the rocky cut beyond, and Dick was gone.

*   *   *

Sing, O Muse, the ride of Richard Bullen! Sing, O Muse of chivalrous men! the sacred quest, the doughty deeds, the battery of low churls, the fearsome ride and grewsome perils of the Flower of Simpson's Bar! Alack! she is dainty, this Muse! She will have none of this bucking brute and swaggering, ragged rider, and I must fain follow him in prose, afoot!

It was one o'clock, and yet he had only gained Rattlesnake Hill. For in that time Jovita had rehearsed to him all her imperfections and practiced all her vices. Thrice had she stumbled. Twice had she thrown up her Roman nose in a straight line with the reins, and, resisting bit and spur, struck out madly across country. Twice had she reared, and, rearing, fallen backward; and twice had the agile Dick, unharmed, regained his seat before she found her vicious legs again. And a mile beyond them, at the foot of a long hill, was Rattlesnake Creek. Dick knew that here was the crucial test of his ability to perform his enterprise, set his teeth grimly, put his knees well into her flanks, and changed his defensive tactics to brisk aggression. Bullied and maddened, Jovita began the descent of the hill. Here the artful Richard pretended to hold her in with ostentatious objurgation and well-feigned cries of alarm. It is unnecessary to add that Jovita instantly ran away. Nor need I state the time made in the descent; it is written in the chronicles of Simpson's Bar. Enough that in another moment, as it seemed to Dick, she was splashing on the overflowed banks of Rattlesnake Creek. As Dick expected, the momentum she had acquired carried her beyond the point of balking, and, holding her well together for a mighty leap, they dashed into the middle of the swiftly flowing current. A few moments of kicking, wading, and swimming, and Dick drew a long breath on the opposite bank.

The road from Rattlesnake Creek to Red Mountain was tolerably level. Either the plunge in Rattlesnake Creek had dampened her baleful fire, or the art which led to it had shown her the superior wickedness of her rider, for Jovita no longer wasted her surplus energy in wanton conceits. Once she bucked, but it was from force of habit; once she shied, but it was from a new freshly painted meeting-house at the crossing of the county road. Hollows, ditches, gravelly deposits, patches of freshly springing grasses, flew from beneath her rattling hoofs. She began to smell unpleasantly, once or twice she coughed slightly, but there was no abatement of her strength or speed. By two o'clock he had passed Red Mountain and begun the descent to the plain. Ten minutes later the driver of the fast Pioneer coach was overtaken and passed by a "man on a Pinto hoss,"—an event sufficiently notable for remark. At half past two Dick rose in his stirrups with a great shout. Stars were glittering through the rifted clouds, and beyond him, out of the plain, rose two spires, a flagstaff, and a straggling line of black objects. Dick jingled his spurs and swung his *riata*,[6] Jovita bounded forward, and in another moment they swept into Tuttleville and drew up before the wooden piazza of "The Hotel of All Nations."

What transpired that night at Tuttleville is not strictly a part of this record. Briefly I may state, however, that after Jovita had been handed over to a sleepy ostler, whom she at once kicked into unpleasant consciousness, Dick sallied out with the bar-keeper for a tour of the sleeping town. Lights still gleamed from a few saloons and gambling-houses; but, avoiding these, they stopped before several closed shops, and by persistent tapping and judicious outcry roused the proprietors from their beds, and made them unbar the doors of their magazines and expose their wares. Sometimes they were met by curses, but oftener by interest and some concern in their needs, and the interview was invariably concluded by a drink. It was three o'clock before this pleasantry was given over, and with a small waterproof bag of india-rubber strapped on his shoulders Dick returned to the hotel. But here he was waylaid by Beauty,—Beauty opulent in charms, affluent in dress, persuasive in speech, and Spanish in accent! In vain she repeated the invitation in "Excelsior," happily scorned by all Alpine-climbing youth,[7] and rejected by this child of the Sierras,—a rejection softened in this instance by a laugh and his last gold coin. And then he sprang to the saddle and dashed down the lonely street and out into the lonelier plain, where presently the lights, the black line of houses, the spires, and the flagstaff sank into the earth behind him again and were lost in the distance.

The storm had cleared away, the air was brisk and cold, the outlines of adjacent landmarks were distinct, but it was half past four before Dick reached the meeting-house and the crossing of the county road. To avoid the rising grade he had taken a longer and more circuitous road, in whose viscid mud Jovita sank fetlock deep at every bound. It was a poor preparation for a steady ascent of five miles more; but Jovita, gathering her legs under her, took it with her usual blind, unreasoning fury, and a half-hour later reached the long level that led to Rattlesnake Creek. Another half-hour would bring him to the creek. He threw the reins lightly upon the neck of the mare, chirruped to her, and began to sing.

Suddenly Jovita shied with a bound that would have unseated a less practiced rider. Hanging to her rein was a figure that had leaped from the bank, and at the same time from the road before her arose a shadowy horse and rider. "Throw up your hands," commanded this second apparition, with an oath.

Dick felt the mare tremble, quiver, and apparently sink under him. He knew what it meant and was prepared.

"Stand aside, Jack Simpson, I know you, you d—d thief. Let me pass or—"

He did not finish the sentence. Jovita rose straight in the air with a terrific bound, throwing the figure from her bit with a single shake of her vicious head, and charged with deadly malevolence down on the impediment before her. An oath, a pistol-shot, horse and highwayman rolled over in the road, and the next moment Jovita was a hundred yards away. But the good right arm of her rider, shattered by a bullet, dropped helplessly at his side.

Without slacking his speed he shifted the reins to his left hand. But a few moments later he was obliged to halt and tighten the saddle-girths that had slipped in the onset. This in his crippled condition took some time. He had no fear of pursuit, but looking up he saw that the eastern stars were already paling, and that the distant peaks had lost their ghostly whiteness, and now stood out blackly against a lighter sky. Day was upon him. Then completely absorbed in a single idea, he forgot the pain of his wound, and mounting again dashed on toward Rattlesnake Creek. But now Jovita's breath came broken by gasps, Dick reeled in his saddle, and brighter and brighter grew the sky.

Ride, Richard; run, Jovita; linger, O day!

For the last few rods there was a roaring in his ears. Was it exhaustion from loss of blood, or what? He was dazed and giddy as he swept down the hill, and did not recognize his surroundings. Had he taken the wrong road, or was this Rattlesnake Creek?

It was. But the brawling creek he had swam a few hours before had risen, more than doubled its volume, and now rolled a swift and resistless river between him and Rattlesnake Hill. For the first time that night Richard's heart sank within him. The river, the mountain, the quickening east, swam before his eyes. He shut them to recover his self-control. In that brief interval, by some fantastic mental process, the little room at Simpson's Bar and the figures of the sleeping father and son rose upon him. He opened his eyes wildly, cast off his coat, pistol, boots, and saddle, bound his precious pack tightly to his shoulders, grasped the bare flanks of Jovita with his bared knees, and with a shout dashed into the yellow water. A cry rose from the opposite bank as the head of a man and horse struggled for a few moments against the battling current, and then were swept away amidst uprooted trees and whirling drift-wood.

* * *

The Old Man started and woke. The fire on the hearth was dead, the candle in the outer room flickering in its socket, and somebody was rapping at the door. He opened it, but fell back with a cry before the dripping, half-naked figure that reeled against the doorpost.

"Dick?"

"Hush! Is he awake yet?"

"No,—but, Dick?—"

"Dry up, you old fool! Get me some whiskey *quick!*" The Old Man flew and returned with—an empty bottle! Dick would have sworn, but his strength was not equal to the occasion. He staggered, caught at the handle of the door, and motioned to the Old Man.

"Thar's suthin' in my pack yer for Johnny. Take it off. I can't."

The Old Man unstrapped the pack and laid it before the exhausted man.

"Open it, quick!"

He did so with trembling fingers. It contained only a few poor toys,—cheap and barbaric enough, goodness knows, but bright with paint and tinsel. One of them was broken; another, I fear, was irretrievably ruined by water; and on the third—ah me! there was a cruel spot.

"It don't look like much, that's a fact," said Dick, ruefully. . . . . "But it's the best we could do. . . . . Take 'em, Old Man, and put 'em in his stocking, and tell him—tell him, you know—hold me, Old Man—" The Old Man caught at his sinking figure. "Tell him," said Dick, with a weak little laugh,—"tell him Sandy Claus has come."

—

And even so, bedraggled, ragged, unshaven, and unshorn, with one arm hanging helplessly at his side, Santa Claus came to Simpson's Bar and fell fainting on the first threshold. The Christmas dawn came slowly after, touching the remoter peaks with the rosy warmth of ineffable love. And it looked so tenderly on Simpson's Bar that the whole mountain, as if caught in a generous action, blushed to the skies.

Mar. 1872

Wan Lee, the Pagan

AS I OPENED HOP SING'S LETTER, there fluttered to the ground a square strip of yellow paper covered with hieroglyphics, which, at first glance, I innocently took to be the label from a pack of Chinese fire-crackers. But the same envelope also contained a smaller strip of rice-paper, with two Chinese characters traced in India ink, that I at once knew to be Hop Sing's visiting-card. The whole, as afterwards literally translated, ran as follows:—

"To the stranger the gates of my house are not closed: the rice-jar is on the left, and the sweetmeats on the right, as you enter.
Two sayings of the Master:—
  Hospitality is the virtue of the son and the wisdom of the ancestor.
  The Superior man is light hearted after the crop-gathering: he makes a festival.
When the stranger is in your melon-patch, observe him not too closely: inattention is often the highest form of civility.
              Happiness, Peace, and Prosperity.
                                        HOP SING."

Admirable, certainly, as was this morality and proverbial wisdom, and although this last axiom was very characteristic of my friend Hop Sing, who was that most somber of all humorists, a Chinese philosopher, I must confess, that, even after a very free translation, I was at a loss to make any immediate application of the message. Luckily I discovered a third enclosure in the shape of a little note in English, and Hop Sing's own commercial hand. It ran thus:—

"The pleasure of your company is requested at No. — Sacramento Street, on Friday evening at eight o'clock. A cup of tea at nine, — sharp.
                                        HOP SING."

This explained all. It meant a visit to Hop Sing's warehouse, the opening and exhibition of some rare Chinese novelties and *curios,* a chat in the back office, a cup of tea of a perfection unknown beyond these sacred precincts, cigars, and a visit to the Chinese theater or temple. This was, in fact, the favorite program of Hop Sing when he exercised his functions of hospitality as the chief factor or superintendent of the Ning Foo Company.

At eight o'clock on Friday evening, I entered the warehouse of Hop Sing. There was that deliciously commingled mysterious foreign odor that I had so often noticed; there was the old array of uncouth-looking objects, the long procession of jars and crockery, the same singular blending of the grotesque and the mathematically neat and exact, the same endless suggestions of frivolity and fragility, the same want of harmony in colors, that were each, in themselves, beautiful and rare. Kites in the shape of enormous dragons and gigantic butterflies; kites so ingeniously arranged as to utter at intervals, when facing the wind, the cry of a hawk; kites so large as to be beyond any boy's power of restraint,—so large that you understood why kite-flying in China was an amusement for adults; gods of china and bronze so gratuitously ugly as to be beyond any human interest or sympathy from their very impossibility; jars of sweetmeats covered all over with moral sentiments from Confucius; hats that looked like baskets, and baskets that looked like hats; silks so light that I hesitate to record the incredible number of square yards that you might pass through the ring on your little finger,—these, and a great many other indescribable objects, were all familiar to me. I pushed my way through the dimly lighted warehouse until I reached the back office, or parlor, where I found Hop Sing waiting to receive me.

Before I describe him, I want the average reader to discharge from his mind any idea of a Chinaman that he may have gathered from the pantomime. He did not wear beautifully scalloped drawers fringed with little bells (I never met a Chinaman who did); he did not habitually carry his forefinger extended before him at right angles with his body; nor did I ever hear him utter the mysterious sentence, "Ching a ring a ring chaw;" nor dance under any provocation. He was, on the whole, a rather grave, decorous, handsome gentleman. His complexion, which extended all over his head, except where his long pig-tail grew, was like a very nice piece of glazed brown paper-muslin. His eyes were black and bright, and his eyelids set at an angle of fifteen degrees; his nose straight, and delicately formed; his mouth small; and his teeth white and clean. He wore a dark blue silk blouse; and in the streets, on cold days, a short jacket of astrachan fur. He wore, also, a pair of drawers of blue brocade gathered tightly over his calves and ankles, offering a general sort of suggestion, that he had forgotten his trousers that morning, but that, so gentlemanly were his manners, his friends had forborne to mention the fact to him. His manner was urbane, although quite serious. He spoke French and English fluently. In brief, I doubt if you could have found the equal of this Pagan shopkeeper among the Christian traders of San Francisco.

There were a few others present,—a judge of the Federal Court, an editor, a high government official, and a prominent merchant. After we had drunk our tea, and tasted a few sweetmeats from a mysterious jar, that looked as if it might contain a preserved mouse among its other non-descript treasures, Hop Sing arose, and, gravely beckoning us to follow him, began to descend to the basement. When we got there, we were amazed at finding it brilliantly lighted, and that a number of chairs were arranged in a half-circle on the asphalt pavement. When he had courteously seated us, he said,—

"I have invited you to witness a performance which I can at least promise you no other foreigners but yourselves have ever seen. Wang, the court-juggler, arrived here yesterday morning. He has never given a performance outside of the palace before. I have asked him to entertain my friends this evening. He requires no theater, stage accessories, or any confederate,—nothing more than you see here. Will you be pleased to examine the ground yourselves, gentlemen."

Of course we examined the premises. It was the ordinary basement or cellar of the San-Francisco storehouse, cemented to keep out the damp. We poked our sticks into the pavement, and rapped on the walls, to satisfy our polite host—but for no other purpose. We were quite content to be the victims of any clever deception. For myself, I knew I was ready to be deluded to any extent, and, if I had been offered an explanation of what followed, I should have probably declined it.

Although I am satisfied that Wang's general performance was the first of that kind ever given on American soil, it has, probably, since become so familiar to many of my readers, that I shall not bore them with it here. He began by setting to flight, with the aid of his fan, the usual number of butterflies, made before our eyes of little bits of tissue-paper, and kept them in the air during the remainder of the performance. I have a vivid recollection of the judge trying to catch one that had lit on his knee, and of its evading him with the pertinacity of a living insect. And, even at this time, Wang, still plying his fan, was taking chickens out of hats, making oranges disappear, pulling endless yards of silk from his sleeve, apparently filling the whole area of the basement with goods that appeared mysteriously from the ground, from his own sleeves, from nowhere! He swallowed knives to the ruin of his digestion for years to come; he dislocated every limb of his body; he reclined in the air, apparently upon nothing. But his crowning performance, which I have never yet seen repeated, was the most weird, mysterious, and astounding. It is my apology for this long introduction, my sole excuse for writing this article, and the genesis of this veracious history.

He cleared the ground of its encumbering articles for a space of about fifteen feet square, and then invited us all to walk forward, and again examine it. We did so gravely. There was nothing but the cemented pavement below to be seen or felt. He then asked for the loan of a handkerchief; and, as I chanced to be nearest him, I offered mine. He took it, and spread it open upon the floor. Over this he spread a large square of silk, and over this, again, a large shawl nearly covering the space he had cleared. He then took a position at one of the points of this rectangle, and began a monotonous chant, rocking his body to and fro in time with the somewhat lugubrious air.

We sat still and waited. Above the chant we could hear the striking of the city clocks, and the occasional rattle of a cart in the street overhead. The absolute watchfulness and expectation, the dim, mysterious half-light of the cellar falling in a grewsome way upon the misshapen bulk of a Chinese deity in the background, a faint smell of opium-smoke mingling with spice, and the dreadful uncertainty of what we were really waiting for, sent an uncomfortable thrill down our backs, and made us look at each other with a forced and unnatural smile. This feeling was heightened when Hop Sing slowly rose, and, without a word, pointed with his finger to the center of the shawl.

There was something beneath the shawl. Surely—and something that was not there before; at first a mere suggestion in relief, a faint outline, but growing more and more distinct and visible every moment. The chant still continued; the perspiration began to roll from the singer's face; gradually the hidden object took upon itself a shape and bulk that raised the shawl in its center some five or six inches. It was now unmistakably the outline of a small but perfect human figure, with extended arms and legs. One or two of us turned pale. There was a feeling of general uneasiness, until the editor broke the silence by a gibe, that, poor as it was, was received with spontaneous enthusiasm. Then the chant suddenly ceased. Wang arose, and with a quick, dexterous movement, stripped both shawl and silk away, and discovered, sleeping peacefully upon my handkerchief, a tiny Chinese baby.

The applause and uproar which followed this revelation ought to have satisfied Wang, even if his audience was a small one: it was loud enough to awaken the baby,—a pretty little boy about a year old, looking like a Cupid cut out of sandal-wood. He was whisked away almost as mysteriously as he appeared. When Hop Sing returned my handkerchief to me with a bow, I asked if the juggler was the father of the baby. "No sabe!" said the imperturbable Hop Sing, taking refuge in that Spanish form of non-committalism so common in California.

"But does he have a new baby for every performance?" I asked. "Perhaps: who knows?"—"But what will become of this one?"— "Whatever you choose, gentlemen," replied Hop Sing with a courteous inclination. "It was born here: you are its godfathers."

There were two characteristic peculiarities of any Californian assemblage in 1856,—it was quick to take a hint, and generous to the point of prodigality in its response to any charitable appeal. No matter how sordid or avaricious the individual, he could not resist the infection of sympathy. I doubled the points of my handkerchief into a bag, dropped a coin into it, and, without a word, passed it to the judge. He quietly added a twenty-dollar gold-piece, and passed it to the next. When it was returned to me, it contained over a hundred dollars. I knotted the money in the handkerchief, and gave it to Hop Sing.

"For the baby, from its godfathers."

"But what name?" said the judge. There was a running fire of "Erebus," "Nox," "Plutus," "Terra Cotta," "Antaeus," &c. Finally the question was referred to our host.

"Why not keep his own name?" he said quietly,—"Wan Lee." And he did.

And thus was Wan Lee, on the night of Friday, the 5th of March, 1856, born into this veracious chronicle.

The last form of "The Northern Star" for the 19th of July, 1865,—the only daily paper published in Klamath County,—had just gone to press; and at three A.M., I was putting aside my proofs and manuscripts, preparatory to going home, when I discovered a letter lying under some sheets of paper, which I must have overlooked. The envelope was considerably soiled: it had no post-mark; but I had no difficulty in recognizing the hand of my friend Hop Sing. I opened it hurriedly, and read as follows:—

"MY DEAR SIR,—I do not know whether the bearer will suit you; but, unless the office of 'devil'[1] in your newspaper is a purely technical one, I think he has all the qualities required. He is very quick, active, and intelligent; understands English better than he speaks it; and makes up for any defect by his habits of observation and imitation. You have only to show him how to do a thing once, and he will repeat it, whether it is an offence or a virtue. But you certainly know him already. You are one of his godfathers; for is he not Wan Lee, the reputed son of Wang the conjurer, to whose performances I had the honor to introduce you? But perhaps you have forgotten it.

"I shall send him with a gang of coolies to Stockton, thence by express to your town. If you can use him there, you will do me a favor, and probably save his life, which is at present in great peril from the hands of the younger members of your Christian and highly civilized race who attend the enlightened schools in San Francisco.

"He has acquired some singular habits and customs from his experience of Wang's profession, which he followed for some years,—until he became too large to go in a hat, or be produced from his father's sleeve. The money you left with me has been expended on his education. He has gone through the Tri-literal Classics, but, I think, without much benefit. He knows but little of Confucius, and absolutely nothing of Mencius.[2] Owing to the negligence of his father, he associated, perhaps, too much with American children.

"I should have answered your letter before, by post; but I thought that Wan Lee himself would be a better messenger for this.

"Yours respectfully,

"HOP SING."

And this was the long-delayed answer to my letter to Hop Sing. But where was "the bearer"? How was the letter delivered? I summoned hastily the foreman, printers, and office-boy, but without eliciting anything. No one had seen the letter delivered, nor knew any thing of the bearer. A few days later, I had a visit from my laundry-man, Ah Ri.

"You wantee debbil? All lightee: me catchee him."

He returned in a few moments with a bright-looking Chinese boy, about ten years old, with whose appearance and general intelligence I was so greatly impressed, that I engaged him on the spot. When the business was concluded, I asked his name.

"Wan Lee," said the boy.

"What! Are you the boy sent out by Hop Sing? What the devil do you mean by not coming here before? And how did you deliver that letter?"

Wan Lee looked at me, and laughed. "Me pitchee in top side window."

I did not understand. He looked for a moment perplexed, and then, snatching the letter out of my hand, ran down the stairs. After a moment's pause, to my great astonishment, the letter came flying in the window, circled twice around the room, and then dropped gently, like a bird upon my table. Before I had got over my surprise, Wan Lee re-appeared, smiled, looked at the letter and then at me, said, "So, John," and then remained gravely silent. I said nothing further; but it was understood that this was his first official act.

His next performance, I grieve to say, was not attended with equal success. One of our regular paper-carriers fell sick, and, at a pinch, Wan Lee was ordered to fill his place. To prevent mistakes, he was shown over the route the previous evening, and supplied at about daylight with the usual number of subscribers' copies. He returned, after an hour, in good spirits, and without the papers. He had delivered them all, he said.

Unfortunately for Wan Lee, at about eight o'clock, indignant subscribers began to arrive at the office. They had received their copies; but how? In the form of hard-pressed cannon-balls, delivered by a single shot, and a mere *tour de force*,[3] through the glass of bedroom-windows. They had received them full in the face, like a base ball, if they happened to be up and stirring; they had received them in quarter-sheets, tucked in at separate windows; they had found them in the chimney, pinned against the door, shot through attic-windows, delivered in long slips through convenient keyholes, stuffed into ventilators, and occupying the same can with the morning's milk. One subscriber, who waited for some time at the office-door to have a personal interview with Wan Lee (then comfortably locked in my bedroom), told me, with tears of rage in his eyes, that he had been awakened at five o'clock by a most hideous yelling below his windows; that, on rising in great agitation, he was startled by the sudden appearance of "The Northern Star," rolled hard, and bent into the form of a boomerang, or East-Indian club, that sailed into the window, described a number of fiendish circles in the room, knocked over the light, slapped the baby's face, "took" him (the subscriber) "in the jaw," and then returned out of the window, and dropped helplessly in the area. During the rest of the day, wads and strips of soiled paper, purporting to be copies of "The Northern Star" of that morning's issue, were brought indignantly to the office. An admirable editorial on "The Resources of Humboldt County," which I had constructed the evening before, and which, I had reason to believe, might have changed the whole balance of trade during the ensuing year, and left San Francisco bankrupt at her wharves, was in this way lost to the public.

It was deemed advisable for the next three weeks to keep Wan Lee closely confined to the printing-office, and the purely mechanical part of the business. Here he developed a surprising quickness and adaptability, winning even the favor and good will of the printers and foreman, who at first looked upon his introduction into the secrets of their trade as fraught with the gravest political significance. He learned to set type readily and neatly, his wonderful skill in manipulation aiding him in the mere mechanical act, and his ignorance of the language confining him simply to the mechanical effort, confirming the printer's axiom, that the printer who considers or follows the ideas of his copy makes a poor compositor. He would set up deliberately long diatribes against himself, composed by his fellow-printers, and hung on his hook as copy, and even such short sentences as "Wan Lee is the devil's own imp," "Wan Lee is a Mongolian rascal," and bring the proof to me with happiness beaming from every tooth, and satisfaction shining in his huckleberry eyes.

It was not long, however, before he learned to retaliate on his mischievous persecutors. I remember one instance in which his reprisal came very near involving me in a serious misunderstanding. Our foreman's name was Webster; and Wan Lee presently learned to know and recognize the individual and combined letters of his name. It was during a political campaign; and the eloquent and fiery Col. Starbottle of Siskyou had delivered an effective speech, which was reported especially for "The Northern Star." In a very sublime peroration, Col. Starbottle had said, "In the language of the godlike Webster,[4] I repeat"—and here followed the quotation, which I have forgotten. Now, it chanced that Wan Lee, looking over the galley after it had been revised, saw the name of his chief persecutor, and, of course, imagined the quotation his. After the form was locked up, Wan Lee took advantage of Webster's absence to remove the quotation, and substitute a thin piece of lead, of the same size as the type, engraved with Chinese characters, making a sentence, which, I had reason to believe, was an utter and abject confession of the incapacity and offensiveness of the Webster family generally, and exceedingly eulogistic of Wan Lee himself personally.

The next morning's paper contained Col. Starbottle's speech in full, in which it appeared that the "godlike" Webster had, on one occasion, uttered his thoughts in excellent but perfectly enigmatical Chinese. The rage of Col. Starbottle knew no bounds. I have a vivid recollection of that admirable man walking into my office, and demanding a retraction of the statement.

"But my dear sir," I asked, "are you willing to deny, over your own signature, that Webster ever uttered such a sentence? Dare you deny, that, with Mr. Webster's well-known attainments, a knowledge of Chinese might not have been among the number? Are you willing to submit a translation suitable to the capacity of our readers, and deny, upon your honor as a gentleman, that the late Mr. Webster ever uttered such a sentiment? If you are, sir, I am willing to publish your denial."

The colonel was not, and left, highly indignant.

Webster, the foreman, took it more coolly. Happily, he was unaware, that, for two days after, Chinamen from the laundries, from the gulches, from the kitchens, looked in the front office-door, with faces beaming with sardonic delight; that three hundred extra copies of the "Star" were ordered for the wash-houses on the river. He only knew, that, during the day, Wan Lee occasionally went off into convulsive spasms, and that he was obliged to kick him into consciousness again. A week after the occurrence, I called Wan Lee into my office.

"Wan," I said gravely, "I should like you to give me, for my own personal satisfaction, a translation of that Chinese sentence which my gifted countryman, the late godlike Webster, uttered upon a public occasion." Wan Lee looked at me intently, and then the slightest possible twinkle crept into his black eyes. Then he replied with equal gravity,—

"Mishtel Webstel, he say, 'China boy makee me belly much foolee. China boy makee me heap sick.'" Which I have reason to think was true.

But I fear I am giving but one side, and not the best, of Wan Lee's character. As he imparted it to me, his had been a hard life. He had known scarcely any childhood: he had no recollection of a father or mother. The conjurer Wang had brought him up. He had spent the first seven years of his life in appearing from baskets, in dropping out of hats, in climbing ladders, in putting his little limbs out of joint in posturing. He had lived in an atmosphere of trickery and deception. He had learned to look upon mankind as dupes of their senses: in fine, if he had thought at all, he would have been a sceptic; if he had been a little older, he would have been a cynic; if he had been older still, he would have been a philosopher. As it was, he was a little imp. A good-natured imp it was, too,—an imp whose moral nature had never been awakened,—an imp up for a holiday, and willing to try virtue as a diversion. I don't know that he had any spiritual nature. He was very superstitious. He carried about with him a hideous little porcelain god, which he was in the habit of alternately reviling and propitiating. He was too intelligent for the commoner Chinese vices of stealing or gratuitous lying. Whatever discipline he practiced was taught by his intellect.

I am inclined to think that his feelings were not altogether unimpressible, although it was almost impossible to extract an expression from him; and I conscientiously believe he became attached to those that were good to him. What he might have become under more favorable conditions than the bondsman of an overworked, under-paid literary man, I don't know: I only know that the scant, irregular, impulsive kindnesses that I showed him were gratefully received. He was very loyal and patient, two qualities rare in the average American servant. He was like Malvolio, "sad and civil" with me.[5] Only once, and then under great provocation, do I remember of his exhibiting any impatience. It was my habit, after leaving the office at night, to take him with me to my rooms, as the bearer of any supplemental or happy after-thought, in the editorial way, that might occur to me before the paper went to press. One night I had been scribbling away past the usual hour of dismissing Wan Lee, and had become quite oblivious of his presence in a chair near my door, when suddenly I became aware of a voice saying in plaintive accents, something that sounded like "Chy Lee."

I faced around sternly.

"What did you say?"

"Me say, 'Chy Lee.' "

"Well?" I said impatiently.

"You sabe, 'How do, John?' "

"Yes."

"You sabe, 'So long, John'?"

"Yes."

"Well, 'Chy Lee' allee same!"

I understood him quite plainly. It appeared that "Chy Lee" was a form of "good-night," and that Wan Lee was anxious to go home. But an instinct of mischief, which, I fear, I possessed in common with him, impelled me to act as if oblivious of the hint. I muttered something about not understanding him, and again bent

over my work. In a few minutes I heard his wooden shoes pattering pathetically over the floor. I looked up. He was standing near
the door.

"You no sabe, 'Chy Lee'?"

"No," I said sternly.

"You sabe muchee big foolee! allee same!"

And, with this audacity upon his lips, he fled. The next morning, however, he was as meek and patient as before, and I did not
recall his offense. As a probable peace-offering, he blacked all my
boots,—a duty never required of him,—including a pair of buff
deer-skin slippers and an immense pair of horseman's jack-boots,
on which he indulged his remorse for two hours.

I have spoken of his honesty as being a quality of his intellect
rather than his principle, but I recall about this time two exceptions to the rule. I was anxious to get some fresh eggs as a change
to the heavy diet of a mining-town; and, knowing that Wan Lee's
countrymen were great poultry-raisers, I applied to him. He furnished me with them regularly every morning, but refused to take
any pay, saying that the man did not sell them,—a remarkable instance of self-abnegation, as eggs were then worth half a dollar
apiece. One morning my neighbor Forster dropped in upon me at
breakfast, and took occasion to bewail his own ill fortune, as his
hens had lately stopped laying, or wandered off in the bush. Wan
Lee, who was present during our colloquy, preserved his characteristic sad taciturnity. When my neighbor had gone, he turned to
me with a slight chuckle: "Flostel's hens—Wan Lee's hens allee
same!" His other offense was more serious and ambitious. It was a
season of great irregularities in the mails, and Wan Lee had heard
me deplore the delay in the delivery of my letters and newspapers.
On arriving at my office one day, I was amazed to find my table
covered with letters, evidently just from the post-office, but, unfortunately, not one addressed to me. I turned to Wan Lee, who
was surveying them with a calm satisfaction, and demanded an explanation. To my horror he pointed to an empty mail-bag in the
corner, and said, "Postman he say, 'No lettee, John; no lettee,
John.' Postman plentee lie! Postman no good. Me catchee lettee
last night allee same!" Luckily it was still early: the mails had not
been distributed. I had a hurried interview with the postmaster;
and Wan Lee's bold attempt at robbing the United States mail was

finally condoned by the purchase of a new mail-bag, and the whole affair thus kept a secret.

If my liking for my little Pagan page had not been sufficient, my duty to Hop Sing was enough to cause me to take Wan Lee with me when I returned to San Francisco after my two years' experience with "The Northern Star." I do not think he contemplated the change with pleasure. I attributed his feelings to a nervous dread of crowded public streets (when he had to go across town for me on an errand, he always made a circuit of the outskirts), to his dislike for the discipline of the Chinese and English school to which I proposed to send him, to his fondness for the free, vagrant life of the mines, to sheer wilfulness. That it might have been a superstitious premonition did not occur to me until long after.

Nevertheless it really seemed as if the opportunity I had long looked for and confidently expected had come,—the opportunity of placing Wan Lee under gently restraining influences, of subjecting him to a life and experience that would draw out of him what good my superficial care and ill-regulated kindness could not reach. Wan Lee was placed at the school of a Chinese missionary,—an intelligent and kind-hearted clergyman, who had shown great interest in the boy, and who, better than all, had a wonderful faith in him. A home was found for him in the family of a widow, who had a bright and interesting daughter about two years younger than Wan Lee. It was this bright, cheery, innocent, and artless child that touched and reached a depth in the boy's nature that hitherto had been unsuspected; that awakened a moral susceptibility which had lain for years insensible alike to the teachings of society, or the ethics of the theologian.

These few brief months—bright with a promise that we never saw fulfilled—must have been happy ones to Wan Lee. He worshipped his little friend with something of the same superstition, but without any of the caprice, that he bestowed upon his porcelain Pagan god. It was his delight to walk behind her to school, carrying her books—a service always fraught with danger to him from the little hands of his Caucasian Christian brothers. He made her the most marvellous toys; he would cut out of carrots and turnips the most astonishing roses and tulips; he made life-like chickens out of melon-seeds; he constructed fans and kites, and was singularly proficient in the making of dolls' paper dresses. On the other hand, she played and sang to him, taught him a thousand little prettinesses and refinements only known to girls, gave him a yellow ribbon for his pig-tail, as best suiting his complexion, read to him, showed him wherein he was original and valuable, took him to Sunday school with her, against the precedents of the school, and, small-woman-like, triumphed. I wish I could add here that she effected his conversion, and made him give up his porcelain idol. But I am telling a true story; and this little girl was quite content to fill him with her own Christian goodness, without letting him know that he was changed. So they got along very well together,—this little Christian girl with her shining cross hanging around her plump, white little neck; and this dark little Pagan, with his hideous porcelain god hidden away in his blouse.

There were two days of that eventful year which will long be remembered in San Francisco,—two days when a mob of her citizens set upon and killed unarmed, defenseless foreigners because they were foreigners, and of another race, religion, and color, and worked for what wages they could get. There were some public men so timid, that, seeing this, they thought that the end of the world had come. There were some eminent statesmen,[6] whose names I am ashamed to write here, who began to think that the passage in the Constitution which guarantees civil and religious liberty to every citizen or foreigner was a mistake. But there were, also, some men who were not so easily frightened; and in twenty-four hours we had things so arranged, that the timid men could wring their hands in safety, and the eminent statesmen utter their doubts without hurting any body or any thing. And in the midst of this I got a note from Hop Sing, asking me to come to him immediately.

I found his warehouse closed, and strongly guarded by the police against any possible attack of the rioters. Hop Sing admitted me through a barred grating with his usual imperturbable calm, but, as it seemed to me, with more than his usual seriousness. Without a word, he took my hand, and led me to the rear of the room, and thence down stairs into the basement. It was dimly lighted; but there was something lying on the floor covered by a shawl. As I approached he drew the shawl away with a sudden gesture, and revealed Wan Lee, the Pagan, lying there dead.

Dead, my reverend friends, dead,—stoned to death[7] in the streets of San Francisco, in the year of grace 1869, by a mob of half-grown boys and Christian school-children!

As I put my hand reverently upon his breast, I felt something crumbling beneath his blouse. I looked inquiringly at Hop Sing. He put his hand between the folds of silk, and drew out something with the first bitter smile I had ever seen on the face of that Pagan gentleman.

It was Wan Lee's porcelain god, crushed by a stone from the hands of those Christian iconoclasts!

Sept. 1874

An Ingénue of the Sierras

I.

WE ALL HELD OUR BREATH as the coach rushed through the semi-darkness of Galloper's Ridge. The vehicle itself was only a huge lumbering shadow; its side-lights were carefully extinguished, and Yuba Bill had just politely removed from the lips of an outside passenger even the cigar with which he had been ostentatiously exhibiting his coolness. For it had been rumored that the Ramon Martinez gang of "road agents" were "laying" for us on the second grade, and would time the passage of our lights across Galloper's in order to intercept us in the "brush" beyond. If we could cross the ridge without being seen, and so get through the brush before they reached it, we were safe. If they followed, it would only be a stern chase with the odds in our favor.

The huge vehicle swayed from side to side, rolled, dipped, and plunged, but Bill kept the track, as if, in the whispered words of the Expressman, he could "feel and smell" the road he could no longer see. We knew that at times we hung perilously over the edge of slopes that eventually dropped a thousand feet sheer to the tops of the sugar-pines below, but we knew that Bill knew it also. The half visible heads of the horses, drawn wedge-wise together by the tightened reins, appeared to cleave the darkness like a ploughshare, held between his rigid hands. Even the hoofbeats of the six horses had fallen into a vague, monotonous, distant roll. Then the ridge was crossed, and we plunged into the still blacker obscurity of the brush. Rather we no longer seemed to move—it was only the phantom night that rushed by us. The horses might have been submerged in some swift Lethean stream;[1] nothing but the top of the coach and the rigid bulk of Yuba Bill arose above them. Yet even in that awful moment our speed was unslackened;

it was as if Bill cared no longer to *guide* but only to drive, or as if
the direction of his huge machine was determined by other hands
than his. An incautious whisperer hazarded the paralyzing suggestion of our "meeting another team." To our great astonishment
Bill overheard it; to our greater astonishment he replied. "It' ud be
only a neck and neck race which would get to h—ll first," he said
quietly. But we were relieved—for he had *spoken!* Almost simultaneously the wider turnpike began to glimmer faintly as a visible
track before us; the wayside trees fell out of line, opened up, and
dropped off one after another; we were on the broader table-land,
out of danger, and apparently unperceived and unpursued.

Nevertheless in the conversation that broke out again with the
relighting of the lamps, and the comments, congratulations, and
reminiscences that were freely exchanged, Yuba Bill preserved a
dissatisfied and even resentful silence. The most generous praise of
his skill and courage awoke no response. "I reckon the old man
waz just spilin' for a fight, and is feelin' disappointed," said a passenger. But those who knew that Bill had the true fighter's scorn
for any purely purposeless conflict were more or less concerned
and watchful of him. He would drive steadily for four or five
minutes with thoughtfully knitted brows, but eyes still keenly
observant under his slouched hat, and then, relaxing his strained
attitude, would give way to a movement of impatience. "You ain't
uneasy about anything, Bill, are you?" asked the Expressman con-
fidentially. Bill lifted his eyes with a slightly contemptuous surprise. "Not about anything ter *come*. It's what *hez* happened that I
don't exackly *sabe*. I don't see no signs of Ramon's gang ever
havin' been out at all, and ef they were out I don't see why they
didn't go for us."

"The simple fact is that our ruse was successful," said an outside passenger. "They waited to see our lights on the ridge,
and, not seeing them, missed us until we had passed. That's my
opinion."

"You ain't puttin' any price on that opinion, air ye?" inquired
Bill politely.

"No."

" 'Cos thar's a comic paper in 'Frisco pays for them things, and
I've seen worse things in it."

"Come off, Bill," retorted the passenger, slightly nettled by the tittering of his companions. "Then what did you put out the lights for?"

"Well," returned Bill grimly, "it mout have been because I didn't keer to hev you chaps blazin' away at the first bush you *thought* you saw move in your skeer, and bringin' down their fire on us."

The explanation, though unsatisfactory, was by no means an improbable one, and we thought it better to accept it with a laugh. Bill, however, resumed his abstracted manner.

"Who got in at the Summit?" he at last asked abruptly of the Expressman.

"Derrick and Simpson of Cold Spring, and one of the 'Excelsior' boys," responded the Expressman.

"And that Pike County girl[2] from Dow's Flat, with her bundles. Don't forget her," added the outside passenger ironically.

"Does anybody here know her?" continued Bill, ignoring the irony.

"You'd better ask Judge Thompson; he was mighty attentive to her; gettin' her a seat by the off window, and lookin' after her bundles and things."

"Gettin' her a seat by the *window?*" repeated Bill.

"Yes, she wanted to see everything, and wasn't afraid of the shooting."

"Yes," broke in a third passenger, "and he was so d—d civil that when she dropped her ring in the straw, he struck a match agin all your rules, you know, and held it for her to find it. And it was just as we were crossin' through the brush, too. I saw the hull thing through the window, for I was hanging over the wheels with my gun ready for action. And it wasn't no fault of Judge Thompson's if his d—d foolishness hadn't shown us up, and got us a shot from the gang."

Bill gave a short grunt, but drove steadily on without further comment or even turning his eyes to the speaker.

We were now not more than a mile from the station at the crossroads where we were to change horses. The lights already glimmered in the distance, and there was a faint suggestion of the coming dawn on the summits of the ridge to the west. We had plunged into a belt of timber, when suddenly a horseman emerged at a sharp canter from a trail that seemed to be parallel with our own. We were all slightly startled; Yuba Bill alone preserving his moody calm.

"Hullo!" he said.

The stranger wheeled to our side as Bill slackened his speed. He seemed to be a "packer" or freight muleteer.

"Ye didn't get 'held up' on the Divide?" continued Bill cheerfully.

"No," returned the packer, with a laugh; "*I* don't carry treasure. But I see you're all right, too. I saw you crossin' over Galloper's."

"*Saw* us?" said Bill sharply. "We had our lights out."

"Yes, but there was suthin' white—a handkerchief or woman's veil, I reckon—hangin' from the window. It was only a movin' spot agin the hillside, but ez I was lookin' out for ye I knew it was you by that. Good-night!"

He cantered away. We tried to look at each other's faces, and at Bill's expression in the darkness, but he neither spoke nor stirred until he threw down the reins when we stopped before the station. The passengers quickly descended from the roof; the Expressman was about to follow, but Bill plucked his sleeve.

"I'm goin' to take a look over this yer stage and these yer passengers with ye, afore we start."

"Why, what's up?"

"Well," said Bill, slowly disengaging himself from one of his enormous gloves, "when we waltzed down into the brush up there I saw a man, ez plain ez I see you, rise up from it. I thought our time had come and the band was goin' to play, when he sorter drew back, made a sign, and we just scooted past him."

"Well?"

"Well," said Bill, "it means that this yer coach was *passed through free* to-night."

"You don't object to *that*—surely? I think we were deucedly lucky."

Bill slowly drew off his other glove. "I've been riskin' my everlastin' life on this d—d line three times a week," he said with mock humility, "and I'm allus thankful for small mercies. *But*," he added grimly, "when it comes down to being passed free by some pal of a hoss thief, and thet called a speshal Providence, *I ain't in it*! No, sir, I ain't in it!"

II.

It was with mixed emotions that the passengers heard that a delay of fifteen minutes to tighten certain screw-bolts had been ordered by the autocratic Bill. Some were anxious to get their breakfast at Sugar Pine, but others were not averse to linger for the daylight that promised greater safety on the road. The Expressman, knowing the real cause of Bill's delay, was nevertheless at a loss to understand the object of it. The passengers were all well known; any idea of complicity with the road agents was wild and impossible, and, even if there was a confederate of the gang among them, he would have been more likely to precipitate a robbery than to check it. Again, the discovery of such a confederate—to whom they clearly owed their safety—and his arrest would have been quite against the Californian sense of justice, if not actually illegal. It seemed evident that Bill's quixotic sense of honor was leading him astray.

The station consisted of a stable, a wagon shed, and a building containing three rooms. The first was fitted up with "bunks" or sleeping berths for the employees; the second was the kitchen; and the third and larger apartment was dining-room or sitting-room, and was used as general waiting-room for the passengers. It was not a refreshment station, and there was no "bar." But a mysterious command from the omnipotent Bill produced a demijohn of whiskey, with which he hospitably treated the company. The seductive influence of the liquor loosened the tongue of the gallant Judge Thompson. He admitted to having struck a match to enable the fair Pike Countian to find her ring, which, however, proved to have fallen in her lap. She was "a fine, healthy young woman—a type of the Far West, sir; in fact, quite a prairie blossom! yet simple and guileless as a child." She was on her way to Marysville, he believed, "although she expected to meet friends—a friend, in fact—later on." It was her first visit to a large town—in fact, any civilized center—since she crossed the plains three years ago. Her girlish curiosity was quite touching, and her innocence irresistible. In fact, in a country whose tendency was to produce "frivolity and forwardness in young girls, he found her a most interesting young person." She was even then out in the stable-yard watching the horses being harnessed, "preferring to indulge a pardonable healthy young curiosity than to listen to the empty compliments of the younger passengers."

The figure which Bill saw thus engaged, without being otherwise distinguished, certainly seemed to justify the Judge's opinion. She appeared to be a well-matured country girl, whose frank gray eyes and large laughing mouth expressed a wholesome and abiding gratification in her life and surroundings. She was watching the replacing of luggage in the boot. A little feminine start, as one of her own parcels was thrown somewhat roughly on the roof, gave Bill his opportunity. "Now there," he growled to the helper, "ye ain't carting stone! Look out, will yer! Some of your things, miss?" he added, with gruff courtesy, turning to her. "These yer trunks, for instance?"

She smiled a pleasant assent, and Bill, pushing aside the helper, seized a large square trunk in his arms. But from excess of zeal, or some other mischance, his foot slipped, and he came down heavily, striking the corner of the trunk on the ground and loosening its hinges and fastenings. It was a cheap, common-looking affair, but the accident discovered in its yawning lid a quantity of white, lace-edged feminine apparel of an apparently superior quality. The young lady uttered another cry and came quickly forward, but Bill was profuse in his apologies, himself girded the broken box with a strap, and declared his intention of having the company "make it good" to her with a new one. Then he casually accompanied her to the door of the waiting-room, entered, made a place for her before the fire by simply lifting the nearest and most youthful passenger by the coat collar from the stool that he was occupying, and, having installed the lady in it, displaced another man who was standing before the chimney, and, drawing himself up to his full six feet of height in front of her, glanced down upon his fair passenger as he took his waybill from his pocket.

"Your name is down here as Miss Mullins?" he said.

She looked up, became suddenly aware that she and her questioner were the center of interest to the whole circle of passengers, and, with a slight rise of color, returned, "Yes."

"Well, Miss Mullins, I've got a question or two to ask ye. I ask it straight out afore this crowd. It's in my rights to take ye aside and ask it—but that ain't my style; I'm no detective. I needn't ask it at all, but act as ef I knowed the answer, or I might leave it to be asked by others. Ye needn't answer it ef ye don't like; ye've got a friend over ther—Judge Thompson—who is a friend to ye, right or wrong, jest as any other man here is—as though ye'd packed your own jury. Well, the simple question I've got to ask ye is *this:* Did you signal to anybody from the coach when we passed Galloper's an hour ago?"

We all thought that Bill's courage and audacity had reached its climax here. To openly and publicly accuse a "lady" before a group of chivalrous Californians, and that lady possessing the further attractions of youth, good looks, and innocence, was little short of desperation. There was an evident movement of adhesion towards the fair stranger, a slight muttering broke out on the right, but the very boldness of the act held them in stupefied surprise. Judge Thompson, with a bland propitiatory smile began: "Really, Bill, I must protest on behalf of this young lady"—when the fair accused, raising her eyes to her accuser, to the consternation of everybody answered with the slight but convincing hesitation of conscientious truthfulness:—

"*I did.*"

"Ahem!" interposed the Judge hastily, "er—that is—er—you allowed your handkerchief to flutter from the window,—I noticed it myself,—casually—one might say even playfully—but without any particular significance."

The girl, regarding her apologist with a singular mingling of pride and impatience, returned briefly:—

"I signaled."

"Who did you signal to?" asked Bill gravely.

"The young gentleman I'm going to marry."

A start, followed by a slight titter from the younger passengers, was instantly suppressed by a savage glance from Bill.

"What did you signal to him for?" he continued.

"To tell him I was here, and that it was all right," returned the young girl, with a steadily rising pride and color.

"Wot was all right?" demanded Bill.

"That I wasn't followed, and that he could meet me on the road beyond Cass's Ridge Station." She hesitated a moment, and then, with a still greater pride, in which a youthful defiance was still mingled, said: "I've run away from home to marry him. And I mean to! No one can stop me. Dad didn't like him just because he was poor, and dad's got money. Dad wanted me to marry a man I hate, and got a lot of dresses and things to bribe me."

"And you're taking them in your trunk to the other feller?" said Bill grimly.

"Yes, he's poor," returned the girl defiantly.

"Then your father's name is Mullins?" asked Bill.

"It's not Mullins. I—I—took that name," she hesitated, with her first exhibition of self-consciousness.

"Wot *is* his name?"

"Eli Hemmings."

A smile of relief and significance went round the circle. The fame of Eli or "Skinner" Hemmings, as a notorious miser and usurer, had passed even beyond Galloper's Ridge.

"The step that you're taking, Miss Mullins, I need not tell you, is one of great gravity," said Judge Thompson, with a certain paternal seriousness of manner, in which, however, we were glad to detect a glaring affectation; "and I trust that you and your affianced have fully weighed it. Far be it from me to interfere with or question the natural affections of two young people, but may I ask you what you know of the—er—young gentleman for whom you are sacrificing so much, and, perhaps, imperiling your whole future? For instance, have you known him long?"

The slightly troubled air of trying to understand,—not unlike the vague wonderment of childhood,—with which Miss Mullins had received the beginning of this exordium, changed to a relieved smile of comprehension as she said quickly, "Oh yes, nearly a whole year."

"And," said the Judge, smiling, "has he a vocation—is he in business?"

"Oh yes," she returned; "he's a collector."

"A collector?"

"Yes; he collects bills, you know,—money," she went on, with childish eagerness, "not for himself,—*he* never has any money, poor Charley,—but for his firm. It's dreadful hard work, too; keeps him out for days and nights, over bad roads and baddest weather. Sometimes, when he's stole over to the ranch just to see me, he's been so bad he could scarcely keep his seat in the saddle, much less stand. And he's got to take mighty big risks, too. Times the folks are cross with him and won't pay; once they shot him in the arm, and he came to me, and I helped do it up for him. But he don't mind. He's real brave,—jest as brave as he's good." There was such a wholesome ring of truth in this pretty praise that we were touched in sympathy with the speaker.

"What firm does he collect for?" asked the Judge gently.

"I don't know exactly—he won't tell me; but I think it's a Spanish firm. You see"—she took us all into her confidence with a sweeping smile of innocent yet half-mischievous artfulness—"I only know because I peeped over a letter he once got from his firm, telling him he must hustle up and be ready for the road the next day; but I think the name was Martinez—yes, Ramon Martinez."

In the dead silence that ensued—a silence so profound that we could hear the horses in the distant stable-yard rattling their harness—one of the younger "Excelsior" boys burst into a hysteric laugh, but the fierce eye of Yuba Bill was down upon him, and seemed to instantly stiffen him into a silent, grinning mask. The young girl, however, took no note of it. Following out, with lover-like diffusiveness, the reminiscences thus awakened, she went on:—

"Yes, it's mighty hard work, but he says it's all for me, and as soon as we're married he'll quit it. He might have quit it before, but he won't take no money of me, nor what I told him I could get out of dad! That ain't his style. He's mighty proud—if he is poor—is Charley. Why thar's all ma's money which she left me in the Savin's Bank that I wanted to draw out—for I had the right—and give it to him, but he wouldn't hear of it! Why, he wouldn't take one of the things I've got with me, if he knew it. And so he goes on ridin' and ridin', here and there and everywhere, and gettin' more and more played out and sad, and thin and pale as a spirit, and always so uneasy about his business, and startin' up at times when we're meetin' out in the South Woods or in the far clearin', and sayin'; 'I must be goin' now, Polly,' and yet always tryin' to be chiffle and chipper afore me. Why he must have rid miles and miles to have watched for me thar in the brush at the foot of Galloper's tonight, jest to see if all was safe; and Lordy! I'd have given him the signal and showed a light if I'd died for it the next minit. There! That's what I know of Charley—that's what I'm running away from home for—that's what I'm running to him for, and I don't care who knows it! And I only wish I'd done it afore—and I would—if—if—if—he'd only *asked me!* There now!" She stopped, panted, and choked. Then one of the sudden transitions of youthful emotion overtook the eager, laughing face; it clouded up with the swift change of childhood, a lightning quiver of expression broke over it, and—then came the rain!

I think this simple act completed our utter demoralization! We smiled feebly at each other with that assumption of masculine superiority which is miserably conscious of its own helplessness at such moments. We looked out of the window, blew our noses, said: "Eh—what?" and "I say," vaguely to each other, and were greatly relieved, and yet apparently astonished, when Yuba Bill, who had turned his back upon the fair speaker, and was kicking the logs in the fireplace, suddenly swept down upon us and bundled us all into the road, leaving Miss Mullins alone. Then he walked aside with Judge Thompson for a few moments; returned to us, autocratically demanded of the party a complete reticence towards Miss Mullins on the subject matter under discussion, reentered the station, reappeared with the young lady, suppressed a faint idiotic cheer which broke from us at the spectacle of her innocent face once more cleared and rosy, climbed the box, and in another moment we were under way.

"Then she don't know what her lover is yet?" asked the Expressman eagerly.

"No."

"Are *you* certain it's one of the gang?"

"Can't say *for sure*. It mout be a young chap from Yolo who bucked agin the tiger[3] at Sacramento, got regularly cleaned out and busted, and joined the gang for a flier. They say thar was a new hand in that job over at Keeley's,—and a mighty game one, too; and ez there was some buckshot onloaded that trip, he might hev got his share, and that would tally with what the girl said about his arm. See! Ef that's the man, I've heered he was the son of some big preacher in the States, and a college sharp to boot, who ran wild in 'Frisco, and played himself for all he was worth.

They're the wust kind to kick when they once get a foot over the traces. For stiddy, comf'ble kempany," added Bill reflectively, "give *me* the son of a man that was *hanged!*"

"But what are you going to do about this?"

"That depends upon the feller who comes to meet her."

"But you ain't going to try to take him? That would be playing it pretty low down on them both."

"Keep your hair on, Jimmy! The Judge and me are only going to rastle with the sperrit of that gay young galoot, when he drops down for his girl—and exhort him pow'ful! Ef he allows he's convicted of sin and will find the Lord, we'll marry him and the gal offhand at the next station, and the Judge will officiate himself for nothin'. We're goin' to have this yer elopement done on the square—and our waybill clean—you bet!"

"But you don't suppose he'll trust himself in your hands?"

"Polly will signal to him that it's all square."

"Ah!" said the Expressman. Nevertheless in those few moments the men seemed to have exchanged dispositions. The Expressman looked doubtfully, critically, and even cynically before him. Bill's face had relaxed, and something like a bland smile beamed across it, as he drove confidently and unhesitatingly forward.

Day, meantime, although full blown and radiant on the mountain summits around us, was yet nebulous and uncertain in the valleys into which we were plunging. Lights still glimmered in the cabins and few ranch buildings which began to indicate the thicker settlements. And the shadows were heaviest in a little copse, where a note from Judge Thompson in the coach was handed up to Yuba Bill, who at once slowly began to draw up his horses. The coach stopped finally near the junction of a small crossroad. At the same moment Miss Mullins slipped down from the vehicle, and, with a parting wave of her hand to the Judge, who had assisted her from the steps, tripped down the crossroad, and disappeared in its semi-obscurity. To our surprise the stage waited, Bill holding the reins listlessly in his hands. Five minutes passed—an eternity of expectation, and, as there was that in Yuba Bill's face which forbade idle questioning, an aching void of silence also! This was at last broken by a strange voice from the road:—

"Go on—we'll follow"

The coach started forward. Presently we heard the sound of other wheels behind us. We all craned our necks backward to get a view of the unknown, but by the growing light we could only see that we were followed at a distance by a buggy with two figures in it. Evidently Polly Mullins and her lover! We hoped that they would pass us. But the vehicle, although drawn by a fast horse, preserved its distance always, and it was plain that its driver had no desire to satisfy our curiosity. The Expressman had recourse to Bill.

"Is it the man you thought of?" he asked eagerly.

"I reckon," said Bill briefly.

"But," continued the Expressman, returning to his former skepticism, "what's to keep them both from levanting together now?"

Bill jerked his hand towards the boot with a grim smile.

"Their baggage."

"Oh!" said the Expressman.

"Yes," continued Bill. "We'll hang on to that gal's little frills and fixin's until this yer job's settled, and the ceremony's over, jest as ef we waz her own father. And, what's more, young man," he added, suddenly turning to the Expressman, "*you'll* express them trunks of hers *through to Sacramento* with your kempany's labels, and hand her the receipts and checks for them, so she *can get 'em there.* That'll keep *him* outer temptation and the reach o' the gang, until they get away among white men and civilization again. When your hoary-headed ole grandfather, or, to speak plainer, that partikler old whiskey-soaker known as Yuba Bill, wot sits on this box," he continued, with a diabolical wink at the Expressman, "waltzes in to pervide for a young couple jest startin' in life, thar's nothin' mean about his style, you bet. He fills the bill every time! Speshul Providences take a back seat when he's around."

When the station hotel and straggling settlement of Sugar Pine, now distinct and clear in the growing light, at last rose within rifleshot on the plateau, the buggy suddenly darted swiftly by us, so swiftly that the faces of the two occupants were barely distinguishable as they passed, and keeping the lead by a dozen lengths, reached the door of the hotel. The young girl and her companion leaped down and vanished within as we drew up. They had evidently determined to elude our curiosity, and were successful.

But the material appetites of the passengers, sharpened by the keen mountain air, were more potent than their curiosity, and, as the breakfast-bell rang out at the moment the stage stopped, a majority of them rushed into the dining-room and scrambled for places without giving much heed to the vanished couple or to the Judge and Yuba Bill, who had disappeared also. The through coach to Marysville and Sacramento was likewise waiting, for Sugar Pine was the limit of Bill's ministration, and the coach which we had just left went no farther. In the course of twenty minutes, however, there was a slight and somewhat ceremonious bustling in the hall and on the veranda, and Yuba Bill and the Judge reappeared. The latter was leading, with some elaboration of manner and detail, the shapely figure of Miss Mullins, and Yuba Bill was accompanying her companion to the buggy. We all rushed to the windows to get a good view of the mysterious stranger and probable ex-brigand whose life was now linked with our fair fellow-passenger. I am afraid, however, that we all participated in a certain impression of disappointment and doubt. Handsome and even cultivated-looking, he assuredly was—young and vigorous in appearance. But there was a certain half-shamed, half-defiant suggestion in his expression, yet coupled with a watchful lurking uneasiness which was not pleasant and hardly becoming in a bridegroom—and the possessor of such a bride. But the frank, joyous, innocent face of Polly Mullins, resplendent with a simple, happy confidence, melted our hearts again, and condoned the fellow's shortcomings. We waved our hands; I think we would have given three rousing cheers as they drove away if the omnipotent eye of Yuba Bill had not been upon us. It was well, for the next moment we were summoned to the presence of that soft-hearted autocrat.

We found him alone with the Judge in a private sitting-room, standing before a table on which there was a decanter and glasses. As we filed expectantly into the room and the door closed behind us, he cast a glance of hesitating tolerance over the group.

"Gentlemen," he said slowly, "you was all present at the beginnin' of a little game this mornin', and the Judge thar thinks that you oughter be let in at the finish. *I* don't see that it's any of *your* d—d business—so to speak; but ez the Judge here allows you're all in the secret, I've called you in to take a partin' drink to the

health of Mr. and Mrs. Charley Byng—ez is now comf'ably off on
their bridal tower. What *you* know or what *you* suspects of the
young galoot that's married the gal ain't worth shucks to anybody,
and I wouldn't give it to a yaller pup to play with, but the Judge
thinks you ought all to promise right here that you'll keep it dark.
That's his opinion. Ez far as my opinion goes, gen'l'men," continued Bill, with greater blandness and apparent cordiality, "I wanter
simply remark, in a keerless, offhand gin'ral way, that ef I ketch
any God-forsaken, lop-eared, chuckle-headed blatherin' idjet
airin' *his* opinion"—

"One moment, Bill," interposed Judge Thompson with a grave
smile; "let me explain. You understand, gentlemen," he said, turning to us, "the singular, and I may say affecting, situation which
our good-hearted friend here has done so much to bring to what
we hope will be a happy termination. I want to give here, as my
professional opinion, that there is nothing in his request which, in
your capacity as good citizens and law-abiding men, you may not
grant. I want to tell you, also, that you are condoning no offense
against the statutes; that there is not a particle of legal evidence before us of the criminal antecedents of Mr. Charles Byng, except
that which has been told you by the innocent lips of his betrothed,
which the law of the land has now sealed forever in the mouth of
his wife, and that our own actual experience of his acts have been
in the main exculpatory of any previous irregularity—if not in-
compatible with it. Briefly, no judge would charge, no jury convict, on such evidence. When I add that the young girl is of legal
age, that there is no evidence of any previous undue influence, but
rather of the reverse, on the part of the bridegroom, and that I was
content, as a magistrate, to perform the ceremony, I think you will
be satisfied to give your promise, for the sake of the bride, and
drink a happy life to them both."

I need not say that we did this cheerfully, and even extorted
from Bill a grunt of satisfaction. The majority of the company,
however, who were going with the through coach to Sacramento,
then took their leave, and, as we accompanied them to the veranda, we could see that Miss Polly Mullins's trunks were already
transferred to the other vehicle under the protecting seals and labels of the all-potent Express Company. Then the whip cracked,
the coach rolled away, and the last traces of the adventurous

young couple disappeared in the hanging red dust of its wheels.

But Yuba Bill's grim satisfaction at the happy issue of the episode seemed to suffer no abatement. He even exceeded his usual deliberately regulated potations, and, standing comfortably with his back to the center of the now deserted bar-room, was more than usually loquacious with the Expressman. "You see," he said, in bland reminiscence, "when your old Uncle Bill takes hold of a job like this, he puts it straight through without changin' hosses. Yet thar was a moment, young feller, when I thought I was stompt! It was when we'd made up our mind to make that chap tell the gal fust all what he was! Ef she'd rared or kicked in the traces, or hung back only ez much ez that, we'd hev given him jest five minits' law to get up and get and leave her, and we'd hev toted that gal and her fixin's back to her dad again! But she jest gave a little scream and start, and then went off inter hysterics, right on his buzzum, laughing and cryin' and sayin' that nothin' should part 'em. Gosh! if I didn't think *he* woz more cut up than she about it; a minit it looked as ef *he* didn't allow to marry her arter all, but that passed, and they was married hard and fast—you bet! I reckon he's had enough of stayin' out o' nights to last him, and ef the valley settlements hevn't got hold of a very shining member, at least the foothills hev got shut of one more of the Ramon Martinez gang."

"What's that about the Ramon Martinez gang?" said a quiet potential voice.

Bill turned quickly. It was the voice of the Divisional Superintendent of the Express Company,—a man of eccentric determination of character, and one of the few whom the autocratic Bill recognized as an equal,—who had just entered the barroom. His dusty pongee cloak and soft hat indicated that he had that morning arrived on a round of inspection.

"Don't care if I do, Bill," he continued, in response to Bill's invitatory gesture, walking to the bar. "It's a little raw out on the road. Well, what were you saying about Ramon Martinez gang? You haven't come across one of 'em, have you?"

"No," said Bill, with a slight blinking of his eye, as he ostentatiously lifted his glass to the light.

"And you *won't*," added the Superintendent, leisurely sipping his liquor. "For the fact is, the gang is about played out. Not from

want of a job now and then, but from the difficulty of disposing of
the results of their work. Since the new instructions to the agents
to identify and trace all dust and bullion offered to them went into
force, you see, they can't get rid of their swag. All the gang are
spotted at the offices, and it costs too much for them to pay a
fence or a middleman of any standing. Why, all that flaky river
gold they took from the Excelsior Company can be identified as
easy as if it was stamped with the company's mark. They can't
melt it down themselves; they can't get others to do it for them;
they can't ship it to the Mint or Assay Offices in Marysville and
'Frisco, for they won't take it without our certificate and seals;
and *we* don't take any undeclared freight *within* the lines that
we've drawn around their beat, except from people and agents
known. Why, *you* know that well enough, Jim," he said, suddenly
appealing to the Expressman, "don't you?"

Possibly the suddenness of the appeal caused the Expressman
to swallow his liquor the wrong way, for he was overtaken with a
fit of coughing, and stammered hastily as he laid down his glass,
"Yes—of course—certainly."

"No, sir," resumed the Superintendent cheerfully, "they're
pretty well played out. And the best proof of it is that they've
lately been robbing ordinary passengers' trunks. There was a
freight wagon 'held up' near Dow's Flat the other day, and a lot of
baggage gone through. I had to go down there to look into it.
Darned if they hadn't lifted a lot o' woman's wedding things from
that rich couple who got married the other day out at Marysville.
Looks as if they were playing it rather low down, don't it? Coming down to hardpan and the bed rock—eh?"

The Expressman's face was turned anxiously towards Bill, who,
after a hurried gulp of his remaining liquor, still stood staring at
the window. Then he slowly drew on one of his large gloves. "Ye
didn't," he said, with a slow, drawling, but perfectly distinct, ar-
ticulation, "happen to know old 'Skinner' Hemmings when you
were over there?"

"Yes."

"And his daughter?"

"He hasn't got any."

"A sort o' mild, innocent, guileless child of nature?" persisted
Bill, with a yellow face, a deadly calm and Satanic deliberation.

"No. I tell you he *hasn't* any daughter. Old man Hemmings is a confirmed old bachelor. He's too mean to support more than one."

"And you didn't happen to know any o' that gang, did ye?" continued Bill, with infinite protraction.

"Yes. Knew 'em all. There was French Pete, Cherokee Bob, Kanaka Joe, One-eyed Stillson, Softy Brown, Spanish Jack, and two or three Greasers."

"And ye didn't know a man by the name of Charley Byng?"

"No," returned the Superintendent, with a slight suggestion of weariness and a distraught glance towards the door.

"A dark, stylish chap, with shifty black eyes and a curled-up merstache?" continued Bill, with dry, colorless persistence.

"No. Look here, Bill, I'm in a little bit of a hurry—but I suppose you must have your little joke before we part. Now, what is your little game?"

"Wot you mean?" demanded Bill, with sudden brusqueness.

"Mean? Well, old man, you know as well as I do. You're giving me the very description of Ramon Martinez himself, ha! ha! No—Bill! you didn't play me this time. You're mighty spry and clever, but you didn't catch on just then."

He nodded and moved away with a light laugh. Bill turned a stony face to the Expressman. Suddenly a gleam of mirth came into his gloomy eyes. He bent over the young man, and said in a hoarse, chuckling whisper:—

"But I got even after all!"

"How?"

"He's tied up to that lying little she-devil, hard and fast!"

May 1893

Three Vagabonds of Trinidad

"OH! IT'S YOU, IS IT?" said the Editor.

The Chinese boy to whom the colloquialism was addressed answered literally, after his habit:—

"Allee same Li Tee; me no changee. Me no ollee China boy."

"That's so," said the Editor with an air of conviction. "I don't suppose there's another imp like you in all Trinidad County. Well, next time don't scratch outside there like a gopher, but come in."

"Lass time," suggested Li Tee blandly, "me tap tappee. You no like tap tappee. You say, alle same dam woodpeckel."

It was quite true—the highly sylvan surroundings of the Trinidad "Sentinel" office—a little clearing in a pine forest—and its attendant fauna, made these signals confusing. An accurate imitation of a woodpecker was also one of Li Tee's accomplishments.

The Editor without replying finished the note he was writing; at which Li Tee, as if struck by some coincident recollection, lifted up his long sleeve, which served him as a pocket, and carelessly shook out a letter on the table like a conjuring trick. The Editor, with a reproachful glance at him, opened it. It was only the ordinary request of an agricultural subscriber—one Johnson—that the Editor would "notice" a giant radish grown by the subscriber and sent by the bearer.

"Where's the radish, Li Tee?" said the Editor suspiciously.

"No hab got. Ask Mellikan boy."

"What?"

Here Li Tee condescended to explain that on passing the schoolhouse he had been set upon by the schoolboys, and that in the struggle the big radish—being, like most such monstrosities of the quick Californian soil, merely a mass of organized water—was "mashed" over the head of some of his assailants. The Editor, painfully aware of these regular persecutions of his errand boy, and perhaps realizing that a radish which could not be used as a bludgeon was not of a sustaining nature, forebore any reproof. "But I cannot notice what I haven't seen, Li Tee," he said good-humoredly.

"S'pose you lie—allee same as Johnson," suggested Li with equal cheerfulness. "He foolee you with lotten stuff—you foolee Mellikan man, allee same."

The Editor preserved a dignified silence until he had addressed his letter. "Take this to Mrs. Martin," he said, handing it to the boy; "and mind you keep clear of the schoolhouse. Don't go by the Flat either if the men are at work, and don't, if you value your skin, pass Flanigan's shanty, where you set off those firecrackers and nearly burnt him out the other day. Look out for Barker's dog at the crossing, and keep off the main road if the tunnel men are coming over the hill." Then remembering that he had virtually closed all the ordinary approaches to Mrs. Martin's house, he added, "Better go round by the woods, where you won't meet *any one.*"

The boy darted off through the open door, and the Editor stood for a moment looking regretfully after him. He liked his little *protégé* ever since that unfortunate child—a waif from a Chinese wash-house—was impounded by some indignant miners for bringing home a highly imperfect and insufficient washing, and kept as hostage for a more proper return of the garments. Unfortunately, another gang of miners, equally aggrieved, had at the same time looted the wash-house and driven off the occupants, so that Li Tee remained unclaimed. For a few weeks he became a sporting appendage of the miners' camp; the stolid butt of good-humored practical jokes, the victim alternately of careless indifference or of extravagant generosity. He received kicks and half-dollars intermittently, and pocketed both with stoical fortitude. But under this treatment he presently lost the docility and frugality which was part of his inheritance, and began to put his small wits against his tormentors, until they grew tired of their own mischief and his. But they knew not what to do with him. His pretty nankeen-yellow skin debarred him from the white "public school," while, although as a heathen he might have reasonably claimed attention from the Sabbath-school, the parents who cheerfully gave their contributions to the heathen *abroad,* objected to him as a companion of their children in the church at

home. At this juncture the Editor offered to take him into his
printing office as a "devil." For a while he seemed to be endeavoring, in his old literal way, to act up to that title. He inked everything but the press. He scratched Chinese characters of an abusive
import on "leads," printed them, and stuck them about the office;
he put "punk" in the foreman's pipe, and had been seen to swallow small type merely as a diabolical recreation. As a messenger he
was fleet of foot, but uncertain of delivery. Some time previously
the Editor had enlisted the sympathies of Mrs. Martin, the good-
natured wife of a farmer, to take him in her household on trial, but
on the third day Li Tee had run away. Yet the Editor had not de-
spaired, and it was to urge her to a second attempt that he dis-
patched that letter.

He was still gazing abstractedly into the depths of the wood
when he was conscious of a slight movement—but no sound—in a
clump of hazel near him, and a stealthy figure glided from it. He at
once recognized it as "Jim," a well-known drunken Indian vagrant
of the settlement—tied to its civilization by the single link of "fire
water," for which he forsook equally the Reservation where it was
forbidden and his own camps where it was unknown. Unconscious of his silent observer, he dropped upon all fours, with his
ear and nose alternately to the ground like some tracking animal.
Then having satisfied himself, he rose, and bending forward in a
dogged trot, made a straight line for the woods. He was followed
a few seconds later by his dog—a slinking, rough, wolf-like brute,
whose superior instinct, however, made him detect the silent presence of some alien humanity in the person of the Editor, and to
recognize it with a yelp of habit, anticipatory of the stone that he
knew was always thrown at him.

"That's cute," said a voice, "but it's just what I expected all
along."

The Editor turned quickly. His foreman was standing behind
him, and had evidently noticed the whole incident.

"It's what I allus said," continued the man. "That boy and that
Injin are thick as thieves. Ye can't see one without the other—and
they've got their little tricks and signals by which they follow each
other. T'other day when you was kalkilatin' Li Tee was doin' your
errands I tracked him out on the marsh, just by followin' that
ornery, pizenous dog o' Jim's. There was the whole caboodle of

'em—including Jim—campin' out, and eatin' raw fish that Jim had ketched, and green stuff they had both sneaked outer Johnson's garden. Mrs. Martin may *take* him, but she won't keep him long while Jim's round. What makes Li foller that blamed old Injin soaker, and what makes Jim, who, at least, is a 'Merican, take up with a furrin' heathen, just gets me."

The Editor did not reply. He had heard something of this before. Yet, after all, why should not these equal outcasts of civilization cling together!

*   *   *

Li Tee's stay with Mrs. Martin was brief. His departure was hastened by an untoward event—apparently ushered in, as in the case of other great calamities, by a mysterious portent in the sky. One morning an extraordinary bird of enormous dimensions was seen approaching from the horizon, and eventually began to hover over the devoted town. Careful scrutiny of this ominous fowl, however, revealed the fact that it was a monstrous Chinese kite, in the shape of a flying dragon. The spectacle imparted considerable liveliness to the community, which, however, presently changed to some concern and indignation. It appeared that the kite was secretly constructed by Li Tee in a secluded part of Mrs. Martin's clearing, but when it was first tried by him he found that through some error of design it required a tail of unusual proportions. This he hurriedly supplied by the first means he found—Mrs. Martin's clothes-line, with part of the weekly wash depending from it. This fact was not at first noticed by the ordinary sightseer, although the tail seemed peculiar—yet, perhaps, not more peculiar than a dragon's tail ought to be. But when the actual theft was discovered and reported through the town, a vivacious interest was created, and spy-glasses were used to identify the various articles of apparel still hanging on that ravished clothes-line. These garments, in the course of their slow disengagement from the clothes-pins through the gyrations of the kite, impartially distributed themselves over the town—one of Mrs. Martin's stockings falling upon the veranda of the Polka Saloon, and the other being afterwards discovered on the belfry of the First Methodist Church—to the scandal of the congregation. It would have been well if the re-

sult of Li Tee's invention had ended here. Alas! the kite-flyer and
his accomplice, "Injin Jim," were tracked by means of the kite's
tell-tale cord to a lonely part of the marsh and rudely dispossessed
of their charge by Deacon Hornblower and a constable. Unfortunately, the captors overlooked the fact that the kite-flyers had
taken the precaution of making a "half-turn" of the stout cord
around a log to ease the tremendous pull of the kite—whose
power the captors had not reckoned upon—and the Deacon incautiously substituted his own body for the log. A singular spectacle is said to have then presented itself to the on-lookers. The
Deacon was seen to be running wildly by leaps and bounds over
the marsh after the kite, closely followed by the constable in
equally wild efforts to restrain him by tugging at the end of the
line. The extraordinary race continued to the town until the constable fell, losing his hold of the line. This seemed to impart a singular specific levity to the Deacon, who, to the astonishment of
everybody, incontinently sailed up into a tree! When he was suc-
cored and cut down from the demoniac kite, he was found to have
sustained a dislocation of the shoulder, and the constable was severely shaken. By that one infelicitous stroke the two outcasts
made an enemy of the Law and the Gospel as represented in
Trinidad County. It is to be feared also that the ordinary emo-
tional instinct of a frontier community, to which they were now
simply abandoned, was as little to be trusted. In this dilemma they
disappeared from the town the next day—no one knew where. A
pale blue smoke rising from a lonely island in the bay for some
days afterwards suggested their possible refuge. But nobody
greatly cared. The sympathetic mediation of the Editor was
characteristically opposed by Mr. Parkin Skinner, a prominent
citizen:—

"It's all very well for you to talk sentiment about niggers, Chinamen, and Injins, and you fellers can laugh about the Deacon being snatched up to heaven like Elijah[1] in that blamed Chinese
chariot of a kite—but I kin tell you, gentlemen, that this is a white
man's country! Yes, sir, you can't get over it! The nigger of every
description—yeller, brown, or black, call him 'Chinese,' 'Injin,' or
'Kanaka,' or what you like—hez to clar off of God's footstool
when the Anglo-Saxon gets started! It stands to reason that they
can't live alongside o' printin' presses, M'Cormick's reapers,[2] and

the Bible! Yes, sir! the Bible; and Deacon Hornblower kin prove it
to you. It's our manifest destiny[3] to clar them out—that's what we
was put here for—and it's just the work we've got to do!"

I have ventured to quote Mr. Skinner's stirring remarks to show
that probably Jim and Li Tee ran away only in anticipation of a
possible lynching, and to prove that advanced sentiments of this
high and ennobling nature really obtained forty years ago in an
ordinary American frontier town which did not then dream of
Expansion and Empire!

Howbeit, Mr. Skinner did not make allowance for mere human
nature. One morning Master Bob Skinner, his son, aged twelve,
evaded the schoolhouse, and started in an old Indian "dug-out" to
invade the island of the miserable refugees. His purpose was not
clearly defined to himself, but was to be modified by circumstances. He would either capture Li Tee and Jim, or join them in
their lawless existence. He had prepared himself for either event
by surreptitiously borrowing his father's gun. He also carried vict-
uals, having heard that Jim ate grasshoppers and Li Tee rats, and
misdoubting his own capacity for either diet. He paddled slowly,
well in shore, to be secure from observation at home, and then
struck out boldly in his leaky canoe for the island—a tufted,
tussocky shred of the marshy promontory torn off in some tidal
storm. It was a lovely day, the bay being barely ruffled by the afternoon "trades"; but as he neared the island he came upon the swell
from the bar and the thunders of the distant Pacific, and grew a little frightened. The canoe, losing way, fell into the trough of the
swell, shipping salt water, still more alarming to the prairie-bred
boy. Forgetting his plan of a stealthy invasion, he shouted lustily
as the helpless and water-logged boat began to drift past the island;
at which a lithe figure emerged from the reeds, threw off a tattered
blanket, and slipped noiselessly, like some animal, into the water.
It was Jim, who, half wading, half swimming, brought the canoe
and boy ashore. Master Skinner at once gave up the idea of invasion, and concluded to join the refugees.

This was easy in his defenseless state, and his manifest delight
in their rude encampment and gypsy life, although he had been
one of Li Tee's oppressors in the past. But that stolid pagan had a
philosophical indifference which might have passed for Christian
forgiveness, and Jim's native reticence seemed like assent. And,

possibly, in the minds of these two vagabonds there might have been a natural sympathy for this other truant from civilization, and some delicate flattery in the fact that Master Skinner was not driven out, but came of his own accord. Howbeit, they fished together, gathered cranberries on the marsh, shot a wild duck and two plovers, and when Master Skinner assisted in the cooking of their fish in a conical basket sunk in the ground, filled with water, heated by rolling red-hot stones from their drift-wood fire into the buried basket, the boy's felicity was supreme. And what an afternoon! To lie, after this feast, on their bellies in the grass, replete like animals, hidden from everything but the sunshine above them; so quiet that gray clouds of sandpipers settled fearlessly around them, and a shining brown muskrat slipped from the ooze within a few feet of their faces—was to feel themselves a part of the wild life in earth and sky. Not that their own predatory instincts were hushed by this divine peace; that intermitting black spot upon the water, declared by the Indian to be a seal, the stealthy glide of a yellow fox in the ambush of a callow brood of mallards, the momentary straying of an elk from the upland upon the borders of the marsh, awoke their tingling nerves to the happy but fruitless chase. And when night came, too soon, and they pigged together around the warm ashes of their camp-fire, under the low lodge poles of their wigwam of dried mud, reeds, and drift-wood, with the combined odors of fish, wood-smoke, and the warm salt breath of the marsh in their nostrils, they slept contentedly. The distant lights of the settlement went out one by one, the stars came out, very large and very silent, to take their places. The barking of a dog on the nearest point was followed by another farther inland. But Jim's dog, curled at the feet of his master, did not reply. What had *he* to do with civilization?

The morning brought some fear of consequences to Master Skinner, but no abatement of his resolve not to return. But here he was oddly combated by Li Tee. "S'pose you go back allee same. You tellee fam'lee canoe go topside down—you plentee swimee to bush. Allee night in bush. Housee big way off—how can get? Sabe?"

"And I'll leave the gun, and tell Dad that when the canoe upset the gun got drowned," said the boy eagerly.

Li Tee nodded.

"And come again Saturday, and bring more powder and shot and a bottle for Jim," said Master Skinner excitedly.

"Good!" grunted the Indian.

Then they ferried the boy over to the peninsula, and set him on a trail across the marshes, known only to themselves, which would bring him home. And when the Editor the next morning chronicled among his news, "Adrift on the Bay—A Schoolboy's Miraculous Escape," he knew as little what part his missing Chinese errand boy had taken in it as the rest of his readers.

Meantime the two outcasts returned to their island camp. It may have occurred to them that a little of the sunlight had gone from it with Bob; for they were in a dull, stupid way fascinated by the little white tyrant who had broken bread with them. He had been delightfully selfish and frankly brutal to them, as only a schoolboy could be, with the addition of the consciousness of his superior race. Yet they each longed for his return, although he was seldom mentioned in their scanty conversation—carried on in monosyllables, each in his own language, or with some common English word, or more often restricted solely to signs. By a delicate flattery, when they did speak of him it was in what they considered to be his own language.

"Boston boy, plenty like catchee *him*," Jim would say, pointing to a distant swan. Or Li Tee, hunting a striped water snake from the reeds, would utter stolidly, "Melikan boy no likee snake." Yet the next two days brought some trouble and physical discomfort to them. Bob had consumed, or wasted, all their provisions—and, still more unfortunately, his righteous visit, his gun, and his superabundant animal spirits had frightened away the game, which their habitual quiet and taciturnity had beguiled into trustfulness. They were half starved, but they did not blame him. It would come all right when he returned. They counted the days, Jim with secret notches on the long pole, Li Tee with a string of copper "cash" he always kept with him. The eventful day came at last,—a warm autumn day, patched with inland fog like blue smoke and smooth, tranquil, open surfaces of wood and sea; but to their waiting, confident eyes the boy came not out of either. They kept a stolid silence all that day until night fell, when Jim said, "Mebbe Boston boy go dead." Li Tee nodded. It did not

seem possible to these two heathens that anything else could prevent the Christian child from keeping his word.

After that, by the aid of the canoe, they went much on the
marsh, hunting apart, but often meeting on the trail which Bob
had taken, with grunts of mutual surprise. These suppressed feelings, never made known by word or gesture, at last must have
found vicarious outlet in the taciturn dog, who so far forgot his
usual discretion as to once or twice seat himself on the water's
edge and indulge in a fit of howling. It had been a custom of
Jim's on certain days to retire to some secluded place, where,
folded in his blanket, with his back against a tree, he remained motionless for hours. In the settlement this had been usually referred
to the after effects of drink, known as the "horrors," but Jim had
explained it by saying it was "when his heart was bad." And now
it seemed, by these gloomy abstractions, that "his heart was bad"
very often. And then the long withheld rains came one night on
the wings of a fierce southwester, beating down their frail lodge
and scattering it abroad, quenching their camp-fire, and rolling up
the bay until it invaded their reedy island and hissed in their ears.
It drove the game from Jim's gun; it tore the net and scattered the
bait of Li Tee, the fisherman. Cold and half starved in heart and
body, but more dogged and silent than ever, they crept out in their
canoe into the stormtossed bay, barely escaping with their miserable lives to the marshy peninsula. Here, on their enemy's ground,
skulking in the rushes, or lying close behind tussocks, they at last
reached the fringe of forest below the settlement. Here, too, sorely
pressed by hunger, and doggedly reckless of consequences, they
forgot their caution, and a flight of teal fell to Jim's gun on the
very outskirts of the settlement.

It was a fatal shot, whose echoes awoke the forces of civilization against them. For it was heard by a logger in his hut near the
marsh, who, looking out, had seen Jim pass. A careless, good-
natured frontiersman, he might have kept the outcasts' mere presence to himself; but there was that damning shot! An Indian with
a gun! That weapon, contraband of law, with dire fines and penalties to whoso sold or gave it to him! A thing to be looked into—
some one to be punished! An Indian with a weapon that made him
the equal of the white! Who was safe? He hurried to town to lay

his information before the constable, but, meeting Mr. Skinner, imparted the news to him. The latter pooh-poohed the constable, who he alleged had not yet discovered the whereabouts of Jim, and suggested that a few armed citizens should make the chase themselves. The fact was that Mr. Skinner, never quite satisfied in his mind with his son's account of the loss of the gun, had put two and two together, and was by no means inclined to have his own gun possibly identified by the legal authority. Moreover, he went home and at once attacked Master Bob with such vigor and so highly colored a description of the crime he had committed, and the penalties attached to it, that Bob confessed. More than that, I grieve to say that Bob lied. The Indian had "stoled his gun," and threatened his life if he divulged the theft. He told how he was ruthlessly put ashore, and compelled to take a trail only known to them to reach his home. In two hours it was reported throughout the settlement that the infamous Jim had added robbery with violence to his illegal possession of the weapon. The secret of the island and the trail over the marsh was told only to a few.

Meantime it had fared hard with the fugitives. Their nearness to the settlement prevented them from lighting a fire, which might have revealed their hiding-place, and they crept together, shivering all night in a clump of hazel. Scared thence by passing but unsuspecting wayfarers wandering off the trail, they lay part of the next day and night amid some tussocks of salt grass, blown on by the cold sea-breeze; chilled, but securely hidden from sight. Indeed, thanks to some mysterious power they had of utter immobility, it was wonderful how they could efface themselves, through quiet and the simplest environment. The lee side of a straggling vine in the meadow, or even the thin ridge of cast-up drift on the shore, behind which they would lie for hours motionless, was a sufficient barrier against prying eyes. In this occupation they no longer talked together, but followed each other with the blind instinct of animals—yet always unerringly, as if conscious of each other's plans. Strangely enough, it was the *real* animal alone—their nameless dog—who now betrayed impatience and a certain human infirmity of temper. The concealment they were resigned to, the sufferings they mutely accepted, he alone resented! When certain scents or sounds, imperceptible to their senses, were blown across their path, he would, with bristling back, snarl himself into gut-

tural and strangulated fury. Yet, in their apathy, even this would
have passed them unnoticed, but that on the second night he disappeared suddenly, returning after two hours' absence with
bloody jaws—replete, but still slinking and snappish. It was only
in the morning that, creeping on their hands and knees through
the stubble, they came upon the torn and mangled carcass of a
sheep. The two men looked at each other without speaking—they
knew what this act of rapine meant to themselves. It meant a fresh
hue and cry after them—it meant that their starving companion
had helped to draw the net closer round them. The Indian
grunted, Li Tee smiled vacantly; but with their knives and fingers
they finished what the dog had begun, and became equally culpa-
ble. But that they were heathens, they could not have achieved a
delicate ethical responsibility in a more Christian-like way.

Yet the rice-fed Li Tee suffered most in their privations. His habitual apathy increased with a certain physical lethargy which Jim
could not understand. When they were apart he sometimes found
Li Tee stretched on his back with an odd stare in his eyes, and
once, at a distance, he thought he saw a vague thin vapor drift
from where the Chinese boy was lying and vanish as he approached. When he tried to arouse him there was a weak drawl in
his voice and a drug-like odor in his breath. Jim dragged him to a
more substantial shelter, a thicket of alder. It was dangerously near
the frequented road, but a vague idea had sprung up in Jim's now
troubled mind that, equal vagabonds though they were, Li Tee had
more claims upon civilization, through those of his own race who
were permitted to live among the white men, and were not hunted
to "reservations" and confined there like Jim's people. If Li Tee
was "heap sick," other Chinamen might find and nurse him. As
for Li Tee, he had lately said, in a more lucid interval: "Me go
dead—allee samee Mellikan boy. You go dead too—allee samee,"
and then lay down again with a glassy stare in his eyes. Far from
being frightened at this, Jim attributed his condition to some en-
chantment that Li Tee had evoked from one of his gods—just as he
himself had seen "medicine-men" of his own tribe fall into strange
trances, and was glad that the boy no longer suffered. The day advanced, and Li Tee still slept. Jim could hear the church bells ringing; he knew it was Sunday—the day on which he was hustled
from the main street by the constable; the day on which the shops

were closed, and the drinking saloons open only at the back door. The day whereon no man worked—and for that reason, though he knew it not, the day selected by the ingenious Mr. Skinner and a few friends as especially fitting and convenient for a chase of the fugitives. The bell brought no suggestion of this—though the dog snapped under his breath and stiffened his spine. And then he heard another sound, far off and vague, yet one that brought a flash into his murky eye, that lit up the heaviness of his Hebraic face,[4] and even showed a slight color in his high cheek-bones. He lay down on the ground, and listened with suspended breath. He heard it now distinctly. It was the Boston boy calling, and the word he was calling was "Jim."

Then the fire dropped out of his eyes as he turned with his usual stolidity to where Li Tee was lying. Him he shook, saying briefly: "Boston boy come back!" But there was no reply, the dead body rolled over inertly under his hand; the head fell back, and the jaw dropped under the pinched yellow face. The Indian gazed at him slowly, and then gravely turned again in the direction of the voice. Yet his dull mind was perplexed, for, blended with that voice were other sounds like the tread of clumsily stealthy feet. But again the voice called "Jim!" and raising his hands to his lips he gave a low whoop in reply. This was followed by silence, when suddenly he heard the voice—the boy's voice—once again, this time very near him, saying eagerly:—

"There he is!"

Then the Indian knew all. His face, however, did not change as he took up his gun, and a man stepped out of the thicket into the trail:—

"Drop that gun, you d—d Injin."

The Indian did not move.

"Drop it, I say!"

The Indian remained erect and motionless.

A rifle shot broke from the thicket. At first it seemed to have missed the Indian, and the man who had spoken cocked his own rifle. But the next moment the tall figure of Jim collapsed where he stood into a mere blanketed heap.

The man who had fired the shot walked towards the heap with the easy air of a conqueror. But suddenly there arose before him an awful phantom, the incarnation of savagery—a creature of blazing eyeballs, flashing tusks, and hot carnivorous breath. He had barely time to cry out "A wolf!" before its jaws met in his throat, and they rolled together on the ground.

But it was no wolf—as a second shot proved—only Jim's slinking dog; the only one of the outcasts who at that supreme moment had gone back to his original nature.

June 1900

A Pupil of Chestnut Ridge

THE SCHOOLMASTER of Chestnut Ridge was interrupted in his after-school solitude by the click of hoof and sound of voices on the little bridle path that led to the scant clearing in which his schoolhouse stood. He laid down his pen as the figures of a man and woman on horseback passed the windows and dismounted before the porch. He recognized the complacent, good-humored faces of Mr. and Mrs. Hoover, who owned a neighboring ranch of some importance and who were accounted well-to-do people by the community. Being a childless couple, however, while they generously contributed to the support of the little school, they had not added to its flock, and it was with some curiosity that the young schoolmaster greeted them and awaited the purport of their visit. This was protracted in delivery through a certain polite dalliance with the real subject characteristic of the Southwestern pioneer.

"Well, Almiry," said Mr. Hoover, turning to his wife after the first greeting with the schoolmaster was over, "this makes me feel like old times, you bet! Why, I ain't bin inside a schoolhouse since I was knee-high to a grasshopper. Thar's the benches, and the desks, and the books and all them 'a b, abs,' jest like the old days. Dear! Dear! But the teacher in those days was ez old and grizzled ez I be—and some o' the scholars—no offense to you, Mr. Brooks—was older and bigger nor you. But times is changed: yet look, Almiry, if thar ain't a hunk o' stale gingerbread in that desk jest as it uster be! Lord! how it all comes back! Ez I was sayin' only t'other day, we can't be too grateful to our parents for givin' us an eddication in our youth"; and Mr. Hoover, with the air of recalling an alma mater of sequestered gloom and cloistered erudition, gazed reverently around the new pine walls.

But Mrs. Hoover here intervened with a gracious appreciation of the schoolmaster's youth after her usual kindly fashion. "And don't you forget it, Hiram Hoover, that these young folks of to-day kin teach the old schoolmasters of 'way back more 'n you and I dream of. We've heard of your book larnin', Mr. Brooks, afore this, and we're proud to hev you here, even if the Lord has not pleased to give us the children to send to ye. But we've always paid our share in keeping up the school for others that was more favored, and now it looks as if He had not forgotten us, and ez if"—with a significant, half-shy glance at her husband and a cor-roborating nod from that gentleman—"ez if, reelly, we might be reckonin' to send you a scholar ourselves."

The young schoolmaster, sympathetic and sensitive, felt some-what embarrassed. The allusion to his extreme youth, mollified though it was by the salve of praise from the tactful Mrs. Hoover, had annoyed him, and perhaps added to his slight confusion over the information she vouchsafed. He had not heard of any late ad-dition to the Hoover family, he would not have been likely to, in his secluded habits; and although he was accustomed to the naïve and direct simplicity of the pioneer, he could scarcely believe that this good lady was announcing a maternal expectation. He smiled vaguely and begged them to be seated.

"Ye see," said Mr. Hoover, dropping upon a low bench, "the way the thing pans out is this. Almiry's brother is a pow'ful preacher down the coast at San Antonio and hez settled down thar with a big Free Will Baptist Church congregation and a heap o' land got from them Mexicans. Thar's a lot o' poor Spanish and In-jin trash that belong to the land, and Almiry's brother hez set about convertin' 'em, givin' 'em convickshion and religion, though the most of 'em is Papists and followers of the Scarlet Woman.[1] Thar was an orphan, a little girl that he got outer the hands o' them priests, kinder snatched as a brand from the burnin',[2] and he sent her to us to be brought up in the ways o' the Lord, knowin' that we had no children of our own. But we thought she oughter get the benefit o' schoolin' too, besides our own care, and we reckoned to bring her here reg'lar to school."

Relieved and pleased to help the good-natured couple in the care of the homeless waif, albeit somewhat doubtful of their reli-gious methods, the schoolmaster said he would be delighted to number her among his little flock. Had she already received any tuition?

"Only from them padres, ye know, things about saints, Virgin Marys, visions, and miracles," put in Mrs. Hoover; "and we kinder thought ez you know Spanish you might be able to get rid o' them in exchange for 'conviction o' sin' and 'justification by faith,' ye know."[3]

"I'm afraid," said Mr. Brooks, smiling at the thought of displacing the Church's "mysteries" for certain corybantic displays and thaumaturgical exhibitions he had witnessed at the Dissenters' camp meeting,[4] "that I must leave all that to you, and I must caution you to be careful what you do lest you also shake her faith in the alphabet and the multiplication table."

"Mebbee you're right," said Mrs. Hoover, mystified but good-natured; "but thar's one thing more we oughter tell ye. She's—she's a trifle dark complected."

The schoolmaster smiled. "Well?" he said patiently.

"She isn't a nigger nor an Injin, ye know, but she's kinder a half-Spanish, half-Mexican Injin, what they call 'mes—mes' "—

"Mestiza," suggested Mr. Brooks: "a half-breed or mongrel."

"I reckon. Now thar wouldn't be any objection to that, eh?" said Mr. Hoover a little uneasily.

"Not by me," returned the schoolmaster cheerfully. "And although this school is state-aided it's not a 'public school' in the eye of the law, so you have only the foolish prejudices of your neighbors to deal with." He had recognized the reason of their hesitation and knew the strong racial antagonism held towards the Negro and Indian by Mr. Hoover's Southwestern compatriots, and he could not refrain from "rubbing it in."

"They kin see," interposed Mrs. Hoover, "that she's not a nigger, for her hair don't 'kink,' and a furrin Injin, of course, is different from one o' our own."

"If they hear her speak Spanish, and you simply say she is a foreigner, as she is, it will be all right," said the schoolmaster smilingly. "Let her come, I'll look after her."

Much relieved, after a few more words the couple took their departure, the schoolmaster promising to call the next afternoon at the Hoovers' ranch and meet his new scholar. "Ye might give us a hint or two how she oughter be fixed up afore she joins the school."

The ranch was about four miles from the schoolhouse, and as

Mr. Brooks drew rein before the Hoovers' gate he appreciated the devotion of the couple who were willing to send the child that distance twice a day. The house, with its outbuildings, was on a more liberal scale than its neighbors, and showed few of the makeshifts and half-hearted advances towards permanent occupation common to the Southwestern pioneers, who were more or less nomads in instinct and circumstance. He was ushered into a well-furnished sitting room, whose glaring freshness was subdued and repressed by black-framed engravings of scriptural subjects. As Mr. Brooks glanced at them and recalled the schoolrooms of the old missions, with their monastic shadows which half hid the gaudy, tinseled saints and flaming or ensanguined hearts upon the walls, he feared that the little waif of Mother Church had not gained any cheerfulness in the exchange.

As she entered the room with Mrs. Hoover, her large dark eyes—the most notable feature in her small face—seemed to sustain the schoolmaster's fanciful fear in their half-frightened wonder. She was clinging closely to Mrs. Hoover's side, as if recognizing the good woman's maternal kindness even while doubtful of her purpose; but on the schoolmaster addressing her in Spanish, a singular change took place in their relative positions. A quick look of intelligence came into her melancholy eyes, and with it a slight consciousness of superiority to her protectors that was embarrassing to him. For the rest he observed merely that she was small and slightly built, although her figure was hidden in a long "check apron" or calico pinafore with sleeves—a local garment—which was utterly incongruous with her originality. Her skin was olive, inclining to yellow, or rather to that exquisite shade of buff to be seen in the new bark of the *madroño*. Her face was oval, and her mouth small and childlike, with little to suggest the aboriginal type in her other features.

The master's questions elicited from the child the fact that she could read and write, that she knew her "Hail Mary" and creed (happily the Protestant Mrs. Hoover was unable to follow this questioning), but he also elicited the more disturbing fact that her replies and confidences suggested a certain familiarity and equality of condition which he could only set down to his own youthfulness of appearance. He was apprehensive that she might even make some remark regarding Mrs. Hoover, and was not sorry that the latter did not understand Spanish. But before he left he managed to speak with Mrs. Hoover alone and suggested a change in the costume of the pupil when she came to school. "The better she is dressed," suggested the wily young diplomat, "the less likely is she to awaken any suspicion of her race."

"Now that's jest what's botherin' me, Mr. Brooks," returned Mrs. Hoover, with a troubled face, "for you see she is a growin' girl," and she concluded, with some embarrassment, "I can't quite make up my mind how to dress her."

"How old is she?" asked the master abruptly.

"Goin' on twelve, but,"—and Mrs. Hoover again hesitated.

"Why, two of my scholars, the Bromly girls, are over fourteen," said the master, "and you know how they are dressed"; but here he hesitated in his turn. It had just occurred to him that the little waif was from the extreme South, and the precocious maturity of the mixed races there was well known. He even remembered, to his alarm, to have seen brides of twelve and mothers of fourteen among the native villagers. This might also account for the suggestion of equality in her manner, and even for a slight coquettishness which he thought he had noticed in her when he had addressed her playfully as a muchacha.[5] "I should dress her in something Spanish," he said hurriedly, "something white, you know, with plenty of flounces and a little black lace, or a black silk skirt and a lace scarf, you know. She'll be all right if you don't make her look like a servant or a dependent," he added, with a show of confidence he was far from feeling. "But you haven't told me her name," he concluded.

"As we're reckonin' to adopt her," said Mrs. Hoover gravely, "you'll give her ours."

"But I can't call her 'Miss Hoover,' " suggested the master; "what's her first name?"

"We was thinkin' o' 'Serafina Ann,' " said Mrs. Hoover with more gravity.

"But what is her name?" persisted the master.

"Well," returned Mrs. Hoover, with a troubled look, "me and Hiram consider it's a heathenish sort of name for a young gal, but you'll find it in my brother's letter." She took a letter from under the lid of a large Bible on the table and pointed to a passage in it.

"The child was christened 'Concepcion,' " read the master. "Why, that's one of the Marys!"

"The which?" asked Mrs. Hoover severely.

"One of the titles of the Virgin Mary; 'Maria de la Concepcion,' " said Mr. Brooks glibly.

"It don't sound much like anythin' so Christian and decent as 'Maria' or 'Mary,' " returned Mrs. Hoover suspiciously.

"But the abbreviation, 'Concha,' is very pretty. In fact it's just the thing, it's so very Spanish," returned the master decisively. "And you know that the squaw who hangs about the mining camp is called 'Reservation Ann,' and old Mrs. Parkins's Negro cook is called 'Aunt Serafina,' so 'Serafina Ann' is too suggestive. 'Concha Hoover' 's the name."

"P'r'aps you're right," said Mrs. Hoover meditatively.

"And dress her so she'll look like her name and you'll be all right," said the master gayly as he took his departure.

Nevertheless, it was with some anxiety the next morning he heard the sound of hoofs on the rocky bridle path leading to the schoolhouse. He had already informed his little flock of the probable addition to their number, and their breathless curiosity now accented the appearance of Mr. Hoover riding past the window, followed by a little figure on horseback, half hidden in the graceful folds of a serape. The next moment they dismounted at the porch, the serape was cast aside, and the new scholar entered.

A little alarmed even in his admiration, the master nevertheless thought he had never seen a more dainty figure. Her heavily flounced white skirt stopped short just above her white-stockinged ankles and little feet, hidden in white satin, low-quartered slippers. Her black silk, shell-like jacket half clasped her stayless bust clad in an under-bodice of soft muslin that faintly outlined a contour which struck him as already womanly. A black lace veil which had protected her head, she had on entering slipped down to her shoulders with a graceful gesture, leaving one end of it pinned to her hair by a rose above her little yellow ear. The whole figure was so inconsistent with its present setting that the master inwardly resolved to suggest a modification of it to Mrs. Hoover as he, with great gravity, however, led the girl to the seat he had prepared for her. Mr. Hoover, who had been assisting disci-

pline as he conscientiously believed by gazing with hushed, rever-
ent reminiscence on the walls, here whispered behind his large
hand that he would call for her at "four o'clock" and tiptoed out
of the schoolroom. The master, who felt that everything would
depend upon his repressing the children's exuberant curiosity and
maintaining the discipline of the school for the next few minutes,
with supernatural gravity addressed the young girl in Spanish and
placed before her a few slight elementary tasks. Perhaps the
strangeness of the language, perhaps the unwonted seriousness of
the master, perhaps also the impassibility of the young stranger
herself, all contributed to arrest the expanding smiles on little
faces, to check their wandering eyes, and hush their eager whispers. By degrees heads were again lowered over their tasks, the
scratching of pencils on slates, and the far-off rapping of woodpeckers again indicated the normal quiet of the schoolroom, and
the master knew he had triumphed, and the ordeal was past.

But not as regarded himself, for although the new pupil had accepted his instructions with childlike submissiveness, and even as
it seemed to him with childlike comprehension, he could not help
noticing that she occasionally glanced at him with a demure suggestion of some understanding between them, or as if they were
playing at master and pupil. This naturally annoyed him and perhaps added a severer dignity to his manner, which did not appear
to be effective, however, and which he fancied secretly amused her.
Was she covertly laughing at him? Yet against this, once or twice,
as her big eyes wandered from her task over the room, they en-
countered the curious gaze of the other children, and he fancied he
saw an exchange of that freemasonry of intelligence common to
children in the presence of their elders even when strangers to
each other. He looked forward to recess to see how she would get
on with her companions; he knew that this would settle her status
in the school, and perhaps elsewhere. Even her limited English vocabulary would not in any way affect that instinctive, childlike test
of superiority, but he was surprised when the hour of recess came
and he had explained to her in Spanish and English its purpose, to
see her quietly put her arm around the waist of Matilda Bromly,
the tallest girl in the school, as the two whisked themselves off to
the playground. She was a mere child after all!

Other things seemed to confirm this opinion. Later, when the children returned from recess, the young stranger had instantly become a popular idol, and had evidently dispensed her favors and patronage generously. The elder Bromly girl was wearing her lace veil, another had possession of her handkerchief, and a third displayed the rose which had adorned her left ear, things of which the master was obliged to take note with a view of returning them to the prodigal little barbarian at the close of school. Later he was, however, much perplexed by the mysterious passage under the desks of some unknown object which apparently was making the circuit of the school. With the annoyed consciousness that he was perhaps unwittingly participating in some game, he finally "nailed it" in the possession of Demosthenes Walker, aged six, to the spontaneous outcry of "Cotched!" from the whole school. When produced from Master Walker's desk in company with a horned toad and a piece of gingerbread, it was found to be Concha's white satin slipper, the young girl herself, meanwhile, bending demurely over her task with the bereft foot tucked up like a bird's under her skirt. The master, reserving reproof of this and other enormities until later, contented himself with commanding the slipper to be brought to him, when he took it to her with the satirical remark in Spanish that the schoolroom was not a dressing room—*Camara para vestirse.*[6] To his surprise, however, she smilingly held out the tiny stockinged foot with a singular combination of the spoiled child and the coquettish señorita, and remained with it extended as if waiting for him to kneel and replace the slipper. But he laid it carefully on her desk.

"Put it on at once," he said in English.

There was no mistaking the tone of his voice, whatever his language. Concha darted a quick look at him like the momentary resentment of an animal, but almost as quickly her eyes became suffused, and with a hurried movement she put on the slipper.

"Please, sir, it dropped off and Jimmy Snyder passed it on," said a small explanatory voice among the benches.

"Silence!" said the master.

Nevertheless, he was glad to see that the school had not noticed the girl's familiarity even though they thought him "hard." He was not sure upon reflection but that he had magnified her offense and had been unnecessarily severe, and this feeling was augmented by his occasionally finding her looking at him with the melancholy, wondering eyes of a chidden animal. Later, as he was moving among the desks overlooking the tasks of the individual pupils, he observed from a distance that her head was bent over her desk while her lips were moving as if repeating to herself her lesson, and that afterwards, with a swift look around the room to assure herself that she was unobserved, she made a hurried sign of the cross. It occurred to him that this might have followed some penitential prayer of the child, and remembering her tuition by the padres it gave him an idea. He dismissed school a few moments earlier in order that he might speak to her alone before Mr. Hoover arrived.

Referring to the slipper incident and receiving her assurances that "she" (the slipper) was much too large and fell often "so," a fact really established by demonstration, he seized his opportunity. "But tell me, when you were with the padre and your slipper fell off, you did not expect him to put it on for you?"

Concha looked at him coyly and then said triumphantly, "Ah, no! but he was a priest, and you are a young caballero."

Yet even after this audacity Mr. Brooks found he could only recommend to Mr. Hoover a change in the young girl's slippers, the absence of the rose-pinned veil, and the substitution of a sunbonnet. For the rest he must trust to circumstances. As Mr. Hoover—who with large paternal optimism had professed to see already an improvement in her—helped her into the saddle, the schoolmaster could not help noticing that she had evidently expected him to perform that act of courtesy, and that she looked correspondingly reproachful.

"The holy fathers used sometimes to let me ride with them on their mules," said Concha, leaning over her saddle towards the schoolmaster.

"Eh, what, missy?" said the Protestant Mr. Hoover, pricking up his ears. "Now you just listen to Mr. Brooks's doctrines, and never mind them Papists," he added as he rode away, with the firm conviction that the master had already commenced the task of her spiritual conversion.

The next day the master awoke to find his little school famous. Whatever were the exaggerations or whatever the fancies carried home to their parents by the children, the result was an overwhelming interest in the proceedings and personnel of the school by the whole district. People had already called at the Hoover ranch to see Mrs. Hoover's pretty adopted daughter. The master, on his way to the schoolroom that morning, had found a few woodmen and charcoal burners lounging on the bridle path that led from the main road. Two or three parents accompanied their children to school, asserting they had just dropped in to see how "Aramanta" or "Tommy" were "gettin' on." As the school began to assemble, several unfamiliar faces passed the windows or were boldly flattened against the glass. The little schoolhouse had not seen such a gathering since it had been borrowed for a political meeting in the previous autumn. And the master noticed with some concern that many of the faces were the same which he had seen uplifted to the glittering periods of Colonel Starbottle, "the war horse of the Democracy."

For he could not shut his eyes to the fact that they came from no mere curiosity to see the novel and bizarre; no appreciation of mere picturesqueness or beauty; and alas! from no enthusiasm for the progression of education. He knew the people among whom he had lived, and he realized the fatal question of "color" had been raised in some mysterious way by those Southwestern emigrants who had carried into this "free state" their inherited prejudices. A few words convinced him that the unhappy children had variously described the complexion of their new fellow pupil, and it was believed that the "No'th'n" schoolmaster, aided and abetted by "capital" in the person of Hiram Hoover, had introduced either a "nigger wench," a "Chinese girl," or an "Injin baby" to the same educational privileges as the "pure whites," and so contaminated the sons of freemen in their very nests. He was able to reassure many that the child was of Spanish origin, but a majority preferred the evidence of their own senses, and lingered for that purpose. As the hour for her appearance drew near and passed, he was seized with a sudden fear that she might not come, that Mr. Hoover had been prevailed upon by his compatriots, in view of the excitement, to withdraw her from the school. But a faint cheer from the bridle path satisfied him, and the next moment a little retinue swept by the window, and he understood. The Hoovers had evidently determined to accent the Spanish character of their little charge. Concha, with a black riding skirt over her flounces, was now mounted on a handsome pinto mustang glittering with silver trappings, accompanied by a vaquero[7] in a velvet jacket, Mr. Hoover bringing up the rear. He, as he informed the master, had merely come to show the way to the vaquero, who hereafter would always accompany the child to and from school. Whether or not he had been induced to this display by the excitement did not transpire. Enough that the effect was a success. The riding skirt and her mustang's fripperies had added to Concha's piquancy, and if her origin was still doubted by some, the child herself was accepted with enthusiasm. The parents who were spectators were proud of this distinguished accession to their children's playmates, and when she dismounted amid the acclaim of her little companions, it was with the aplomb of a queen.

The master alone foresaw trouble in this encouragement of her precocious manner. He received her quietly, and when she had removed her riding skirt, glancing at her feet, said approvingly, "I am glad to see you have changed your slippers; I hope they fit you more firmly than the others."

The child shrugged her shoulders. "Quien sabe.[8] But Pedro (the vaquero) will help me now on my horse when he comes for me."

The master understood the characteristic *non sequitur*[9] as an allusion to his want of gallantry on the previous day, but took no notice of it. Nevertheless, he was pleased to see during the day that she was paying more attention to her studies, although they were generally rehearsed with the languid indifference to all mental accomplishment which belonged to her race. Once he thought to stimulate her activity through her personal vanity.

"Why can you not learn as quickly as Matilda Bromly? She is only two years older than you," he suggested.

"Ah! Mother of God!—why does she then try to wear roses like me? And with that hair. It becomes her not."

The master became thus aware for the first time that the elder Bromly girl, in "the sincerest form of flattery"[10] to her idol, was wearing a yellow rose in her tawny locks, and, further, that Master Bromly with exquisite humor had burlesqued his sister's imitation with a very small carrot stuck above his left ear. This the master promptly removed, adding an additional sum to the humorist's already overflowing slate by way of penance, and returned to Concha. "But wouldn't you like to be as clever as she?—you can if you will only learn."

"What for should I? Look you; she has a devotion for the tall one—the boy Brown! Ah! I want him not."

Yet, notwithstanding this lack of noble ambition, Concha seemed to have absorbed the "devotion" of the boys, big and little, and as the master presently discovered even that of many of the adult population. There were always loungers on the bridle-path at the opening and closing of school, and the vaquero, who now always accompanied her, became an object of envy. Possibly this caused the master to observe him closely. He was tall and thin, with a smooth complexionless face, but to the master's astonishment he had the blue gray eye of the higher or Castilian type of native Californian. Further inquiry proved that he was a son of one of the old impoverished Spanish grant holders whose leagues and cattle had been mortgaged to the Hoovers, who now retained the son to control the live stock "on shares." "It looks kinder ez ef he might hev an eye on that poorty little gal when she's an age to marry," suggested a jealous swain. For several days the girl submitted to her school tasks with her usual languid indifference and did not again transgress the ordinary rules. Nor did Mr. Brooks again refer to their hopeless conversation. But one afternoon he noticed that in the silence and preoccupation of the class she had substituted another volume for her text-book and was perusing it with the articulating lips of the unpracticed reader. He demanded it from her. With blazing eyes and both hands thrust into her desk she refused and defied him. Mr. Brooks slipped his arms around her waist, quietly lifted her from the bench—feeling her little teeth pierce the back of his hand as he did so, but secured the book. Two of the elder boys and girls had risen with excited faces.

"Sit down!" said the master sternly.

They resumed their places with awed looks. The master examined the book. It was a little Spanish prayer book. "You were reading this?" he said in her own tongue.

"Yes. You shall not prevent me!" she burst out. "Mother of God! *they* will not let me read it at the ranch. They would take it from me. And now *you*!"

"You may read it when and where you like, except when you should be studying your lessons," returned the master quietly. "You may keep it here in your desk and peruse it at recess. Come to me for it then. You are not fit to read it now."

The girl looked up with astounded eyes, which in the capriciousness of her passionate nature the next moment filled with tears. Then dropping on her knees she caught the master's bitten hand and covered it with tears and kisses. But he quietly disengaged it and lifted her to her seat. There was a sniffling sound among the benches, which, however, quickly subsided as he glanced around the room, and the incident ended.

Regularly thereafter she took her prayer book back at recess and disappeared with the children, finding, as he afterwards learned, a seat under a secluded buckeye tree, where she was not disturbed by them until her orisons were concluded. The children must have remained loyal to some command of hers, for the incident and this custom were never told out of school, and the master did not consider it his duty to inform Mr. or Mrs. Hoover. If the child could recognize some check—even if it were deemed by some a superstitious one—over her capricious and precocious nature, why should he interfere?

One day at recess he presently became conscious of the ceasing of those small voices in the woods around the schoolhouse, which were always as familiar and pleasant to him in his seclusion as the song of their playfellows—the birds themselves. The continued silence at last awakened his concern and curiosity. He had seldom intruded upon or participated in their games or amusements, remembering when a boy himself the heavy incompatibility of the best intentioned adult intruder to even the most hypocritically polite child at such a moment. A sense of duty, however, impelled him to step beyond the schoolhouse, where to his astonishment he found the adjacent woods empty and soundless. He was relieved, however, after penetrating its recesses, to hear the distant sound of small applause and the unmistakable choking gasps of Johnny Stidger's pocket accordion. Following the sound he came at last upon a little hollow among the sycamores, where the children were disposed in a ring, in the center of which, with a handkerchief in each hand, Concha the melancholy!—Concha the devout!—was dancing that most extravagant feat of the fandango—the audacious sembicuaca![11]

Yet, in spite of her rude and uncertain accompaniment, she was dancing it with a grace, precision, and lightness that was wonderful; in spite of its doubtful poses and seductive languors she was dancing it with the artless gaiety and innocence—perhaps from the suggestion of her tiny figure—of a mere child among an audience of children. Dancing it alone she assumed the parts of the man and woman; advancing, retreating, coquetting, rejecting, coyly be-witching, and at last yielding as lightly and as immaterially as the flickering shadows that fell upon them from the waving trees overhead. The master was fascinated yet troubled. What if there had been older spectators? Would the parents take the perfor-mance as innocently as the performer and her little audience? He thought it necessary later to suggest this delicately to the child. Her temper rose, her eyes flashed.

"Ah, the slipper, she is forbidden. The prayer book—she must not. The dance, it is not good. Truly, there is nothing."

For several days she sulked. One morning she did not come to school, nor the next. At the close of the third day the master called at the Hoovers' ranch.

Mrs. Hoover met him embarrassedly in the hall. "I was sayin' to Hiram he ought to tell ye, but he didn't like to till it was cer-tain. Concha's gone."

"Gone?" echoed the master.

"Yes. Run off with Pedro. Married to him yesterday by the Popish priest at the mission."

"Married! That child?"

"She wasn't no child, Mr. Brooks. We were deceived. My brother was a fool, and men don't understand these things. She was a grown woman—accordin' to these folks' ways and ages—when she kem here. And that's what bothered me."

There was a week's excitement at Chestnut Ridge, but it pleased the master to know that while the children grieved for the loss of Concha they never seemed to understand why she had gone.

Dec. 1901

CONDENSED NOVELS

Muck-a-Muck.

A MODERN INDIAN NOVEL.

After Cooper.[1]

———◆———

CHAPTER I.

IT WAS TOWARD the close of a bright October day. The last rays of the setting sun were reflected from one of those sylvan lakes peculiar to the Sierras of California. On the right the curling smoke of an Indian village rose between the columns of the lofty pines, while to the left the log cottage of Judge Tompkins, embowered in buckeyes, completed the enchanting picture.

Although the exterior of the cottage was humble and unpretentious, and in keeping with the wildness of the landscape, its interior gave evidence of the cultivation and refinement of its inmates. An aquarium, containing goldfishes, stood on a marble center-table at one end of the apartment, while a magnificent grand piano occupied the other. The floor was covered with a yielding tapestry carpet, and the walls were adorned with paintings from the pencils of Van Dyke, Rubens, Tintoretto, Michael Angelo, and the productions of the more modern Turner, Kensett, Church, and Bierstadt.[2] Although Judge Tompkins had chosen the frontiers of civilization as his home, it was impossible for him to entirely forego the habits and tastes of his former life. He was seated in a luxurious arm-chair, writing at a mahogany *écritoire*,[3] while his daughter, a lovely young girl of seventeen summers, plied her crochet-needle on an ottoman beside him. A bright fire of pine logs flickered and flamed on the ample hearth.

Genevra Octavia Tompkins was Judge Tompkins's only child. Her mother had long since died on the Plains. Reared in affluence, no pains had been spared with the daughter's education. She was a graduate of one of the principal seminaries, and spoke French with a perfect Benicia accent. Peerlessly beautiful, she was dressed in a white *moire antique* robe trimmed with *tulle*.[4] That simple rose-bud, with which most heroines exclusively decorate their hair, was all she wore in her raven locks.

The Judge was the first to break the silence.

"Genevra, the logs which compose yonder fire seem to have been incautiously chosen. The sibilation produced by the sap, which exudes copiously therefrom, is not conducive to composition."

"True, father, but I thought it would be preferable to the constant crepitation which is apt to attend the combustion of more seasoned ligneous fragments."

The Judge looked admiringly at the intellectual features of the graceful girl, and half forgot the slight annoyances of the green wood in the musical accents of his daughter. He was smoothing her hair tenderly, when the shadow of a tall figure, which suddenly darkened the doorway, caused him to look up.

———•———

CHAPTER II.

It needed but a glance at the new-comer to detect at once the form and features of the haughty aborigine,—the untaught and untrammelled son of the forest. Over one shoulder a blanket, negligently but gracefully thrown, disclosed a bare and powerful breast, decorated with a quantity of three-cent postage-stamps which he had despoiled from an Overland Mail stage a few weeks previous. A cast-off beaver of Judge Tompkins's, adorned by a simple feather, covered his erect head, from beneath which his straight locks descended. His right hand hung lightly by his side, while his left was engaged in holding on a pair of pantaloons, which the lawless grace and freedom of his lower limbs evidently could not brook.

"Why," said the Indian, in a low sweet tone,—"why does the Pale Face still follow the track of the Red Man? Why does he pursue him, even as *O-kee-chow,* the wild-cat, chases *Ka-ka,* the skunk? Why are the feet of *Sorrel-top,* the white chief, among the acorns of *Muck-a-Muck,* the mountain forest? Why," he repeated, quietly but firmly abstracting a silver spoon from the table,— "why do you seek to drive him from the wigwams of his fathers? His brothers are already gone to the happy hunting-grounds. Will the Pale Face seek him there?" And, averting his face from the Judge, he hastily slipped a silver cake-basket beneath his blanket, to conceal his emotion.

"*Muck-a-Muck* has spoken," said Genevra, softly. "Let him now listen. Are the acorns of the mountain sweeter than the esculent and nutritious bean of the Pale Face miner? Does my brother prize the edible qualities of the snail above that of the crisp and oleaginous bacon? Delicious are the grasshoppers that sport on the hillside,—are they better than the dried apples of the Pale Faces? Pleasant is the gurgle of the torrent, *Kish-Kish*, but is it better than the cluck-cluck of old Bourbon from the old stone bottle?"

"Ugh!" said the Indian,—"ugh! good. The White Rabbit is wise. Her words fall as the snow on Tootoonolo, and the rocky heart of Muck-a-Muck is hidden. What says my brother the Gray Gopher of Dutch Flat?"

"She has spoken, Muck-a-Muck," said the Judge, gazing fondly on his daughter. "It is well. Our treaty is concluded. No, thank you,—you need *not* dance the Dance of Snow Shoes, or the Moccasin Dance, the Dance of Green Corn, or the Treaty Dance. I would be alone. A strange sadness overpowers me."

"I go," said the Indian. "Tell your great chief in Washington, the Sachem Andy,[5] that the Red Man is retiring before the footsteps of the adventurous Pioneer. Inform him, if you please, that westward the star of empire takes its way,[6] that the chiefs of the Pi-Ute nation are for Reconstruction to a man, and that Klamath will poll a heavy Republican vote in the fall."

And folding his blanket more tightly around him, Muck-a-Muck withdrew.

CHAPTER III.

Genevra Tompkins stood at the door of the log-cabin, looking after the retreating Overland Mail stage which conveyed her father to Virginia City, "He may never return again," sighed the young girl as she glanced at the frightfully rolling vehicle and wildly careering horses,—"at least, with unbroken bones. Should he meet with an accident! I mind me now a fearful legend, familiar to my

childhood. Can it be that the drivers on this line are privately instructed to despatch all passengers maimed by accident, to prevent
tedious litigation? No, no. But why this weight upon my heart?"

She seated herself at the piano and lightly passed her hand over
the keys. Then, in a clear mezzo-soprano voice, she sang the first
verse of one of the most popular Irish ballads:—

> "O *Arrah, ma dheelish,* the distant *dudheen*
> Lies soft in the moonlight, *ma bouchal vourneon:*
> The springing *gossoons* on the heather are still,
> And the *caubeens* and *colleens* are heard on the hills."

But as the ravishing notes of her sweet voice died upon the air,
her hands sank listlessly to her side. Music could not chase away
the mysterious shadow from her heart. Again she rose. Putting on
a white crape bonnet, and carefully drawing a pair of lemon-
colored gloves over her taper fingers, she seized her parasol and
plunged into the depths of the pine forest.

————

CHAPTER IV.

Genevra had not proceeded many miles before a weariness seized
upon her fragile limbs, and she would fain seat herself upon the
trunk of a prostrate pine, which she previously dusted with her
handkerchief. The sun was just sinking below the horizon, and the
scene was one of gorgeous and sylvan beauty. "How beautiful is
Nature!" murmured the innocent girl, as, reclining gracefully
against the root of the tree, she gathered up her skirts and tied a
handkerchief around her throat. But a low growl interrupted her
meditation. Starting to her feet, her eyes met a sight which froze
her blood with terror.

The only outlet to the forest was the narrow path, barely wide
enough for a single person, hemmed in by trees and rocks, which
she had just traversed. Down this path, in Indian file, came a
monstrous grizzly, closely followed by a California lion, a wild-
cat, and a buffalo, the rear being brought up by a wild Spanish
bull. The mouths of the three first-animals were distended with
frightful significance; the horns of the last were lowered as omi-

nously. As Genevra was preparing to faint, she heard a low voice behind her.

"Eternally dog-gone my skin ef this ain't the puttiest chance yet."

At the same moment, a long, shining barrel dropped lightly from behind her, and rested over her shoulder.

Genevra shuddered.

"Dern ye—don't move!"

Genevra became motionless.

The crack of a rifle rang through the woods. Three frightful yells were heard, and two sullen roars. Five animals bounded into the air and five lifeless bodies lay upon the plain. The well-aimed bullet had done its work. Entering the open throat of the grizzly, it had traversed his body only to enter the throat of the California lion, and in like manner the catamount, until it passed through into the respective foreheads of the bull and the buffalo, and finally fell flattened from the rocky hillside.

Genevra turned quickly. "My preserver!" she shrieked, and fell into the arms of Natty Bumpo, the celebrated Pike Ranger of Donner Lake.

———·———

CHAPTER V.

The moon rose cheerfully above Donner Lake. On its placid bosom a dug-out canoe glided rapidly, containing Natty Bumpo and Genevra Tompkins.

Both were silent. The same thought possessed each, and perhaps there was sweet companionship even in the unbroken quiet. Genevra bit the handle of her parasol and blushed. Natty Bumpo took a fresh chew of tobacco. At length Genevra said, as if in half-spoken revery:—

"The soft shining of the moon and the peaceful ripple of the waves seem to say to us various things of an instructive and moral tendency."

"You may bet yer pile on that, Miss," said her companion, gravely. "It's all the preachin' and psalm-singin' I've heern since I was a boy."

"Noble being!" said Miss Tompkins to herself, glancing at the stately Pike as he bent over his paddle to conceal his emotion. "Reared in this wild seclusion, yet he has become penetrated with visible consciousness of a Great First Cause." Then, collecting herself, she said aloud: "Me-thinks 't were pleasant to glide ever thus down the stream of life, hand in hand with the one being whom the soul claims as its affinity. But what am I saying?"—and the delicate-minded girl hid her face in her hands.

A long silence ensued, which was at length broken by her companion.

"Ef you mean you're on the marry," he said, thoughtfully, "I ain't in no wise partikler!"

"My husband," faltered the blushing girl; and she fell into his arms.

In ten minutes more the loving couple had landed at Judge Tompkins's.

CHAPTER VI.

A year has passed away. Natty Bumpo was returning from Gold Hill, where he had been to purchase provisions. On his way to Donner Lake, rumors of an Indian uprising met his ears. "Dern their pesky skins, ef they dare to touch my Jenny," he muttered between his clenched teeth.

It was dark when he reached the borders of the lake. Around a glittering fire he dimly discerned dusky figures dancing. They were in war paint. Conspicuous among them was the renowned Muck-a-Muck. But why did the fingers of Natty Bumpo tighten convulsively around his rifle?

The chief held in his hand long tufts of raven hair. The heart of the pioneer sickened as he recognized the clustering curls of Genevra. In a moment his rifle was at his shoulder, and with a sharp "ping," Muck-a-Muck leaped into the air a corpse. To knock out the brains of the remaining savages, tear the tresses from the stiffening hand of Muck-a-Muck, and dash rapidly forward to the cottage of Judge Tompkins, was the work of a moment.

He burst open the door. Why did he stand transfixed with open mouth and distended eyeballs? Was the sight too horrible to be borne? On the contrary, before him, in her peerless beauty, stood Genevra Tompkins, leaning on her father's arm.

"Ye'r not scalped, then!" gasped her lover.

"No. I have no hesitation in saying that I am not; but why this abruptness?" responded Genevra.

Bumpo could not speak, but frantically produced the silken tresses. Genevra turned her face aside.

"Why, that's her waterfall!" said the Judge.

Bumpo sank fainting to the floor.

The famous Pike chieftain never recovered from the deceit, and refused to marry Genevra, who died, twenty years afterwards, of a broken heart. Judge Tompkins lost his fortune in Wild Cat. The stage passes twice a week the deserted cottage at Donner Lake. Thus was the death of Muck-a-Muck avenged.

Sept. 1865

The Haunted Man[1]

A CHRISTMAS STORY

By Ch—r—s D—ck—n—s.[2]

———◆———

PART I.

THE FIRST PHANTOM.

DON'T TELL ME that it wasn't a knocker. I had seen it often enough, and I ought to know. So ought the three-o'clock beer, in dirty high-lows, swinging himself over the railing, or executing a demoniacal jig upon the doorstep; so ought the butcher, although butchers as a general thing are scornful of such trifles; so ought the postman, to whom knockers of the most extravagant description were merely human weaknesses, that were to be pitied and used. And so ought, for the matter of that, etc., etc., etc.

But then it was *such* a knocker. A wild, extravagant, and utterly incomprehensible knocker. A knocker so mysterious and suspicious that Policeman X 37, first coming upon it, felt inclined to take it instantly in custody, but compromised with his professional instincts by sharply and sternly noting it with an eye that admitted of no nonsense, but confidently expected to detect its secret yet. An ugly knocker; a knocker with a hard, human face, that was a type of the harder human face within. A human face that held between its teeth a brazen rod. So hereafter, in the mysterious future should be held, etc., etc.

But if the knocker had a fierce human aspect in the glare of day, you should have seen it at night, when it peered out of the gathering shadows and suggested an ambushed figure; when the light of the street lamps fell upon it, and wrought a play of sinister expression in its hard outlines; when it seemed to wink meaningly at a shrouded figure who, as the night fell darkly, crept up the steps and passed into the mysterious house; when the swinging door disclosed a black passage into which the figure seemed to lose itself and become a part of the mysterious gloom; when the night grew boisterous and the fierce wind made furious charges at the knocker, as if to wrench it off and carry it away in triumph. Such a night as this.

It was a wild and pitiless wind. A wind that had commenced life as a gentle country zephyr, but wandering through manufacturing towns had become demoralized, and reaching the city had plunged into extravagant dissipation and wild excesses. A roistering wind that indulged in Bacchanalian shouts on the street corners, that knocked off the hats from the heads of helpless passengers, and then fulfilled its duties by speeding away, like all young prodigals,—to sea.

He sat alone in a gloomy library listening to the wind that roared in the chimney. Around him novels and story-books were strewn thickly; in his lap he held one with its pages freshly cut, and turned the leaves wearily until his eyes rested upon a portrait in its frontispiece. And as the wind howled the more fiercely, and the darkness without fell blacker, a strange and fateful likeness to that portrait appeared above his chair and leaned upon his shoulder. The Haunted Man gazed at the portrait and sighed. The figure gazed at the portrait and sighed too.

"Here again?" said the Haunted Man.

"Here again," it repeated in a low voice.

"Another novel?"

"Another novel."

"The old story?"

"The old story."

"I see a child," said the Haunted Man, gazing from the pages of the book into the fire,—"a most unnatural child, a model infant.[3] It is prematurely old and philosophic. It dies in poverty to slow music. It dies surrounded by luxury to slow music. It dies with an accompaniment of golden water and rattling carts to slow music. Previous to its decease it makes a will; it repeats the Lord's Prayer, it kisses the 'boofer lady.' That child—"

"Is mine," said the phantom.

"I see a good woman, undersized.[4] I see several charming women, but they are all undersized. They are more or less imbecile and idiotic, but always fascinating and undersized. They wear coquettish caps and aprons. I observe that feminine virtue is invariably below the medium height, and that it is always simple and infantine. These women—"

"Are mine."

"I see a haughty, proud, and wicked lady. She is tall and queenly. I remark that all proud and wicked women are tall and queenly. That woman—"

"Is mine," said the phantom, wringing his hands.

"I see several things continually impending. I observe that whenever an accident, a murder, or death is about to happen, there is something in the furniture, in the locality, in the atmosphere, that foreshadows and suggests it years in advance. I cannot say that in real life I have noticed it,—the perception of this surprising fact belongs—"

"To me!" said the phantom. The Haunted Man continued, in a despairing tone:—

"I see the influence of this in the magazines and daily papers; I see weak imitators rise up and enfeeble the world with senseless formula. I am getting tired of it. It won't do, Charles! it won't do!" and the Haunted Man buried his head in his hands and groaned. The figure looked down upon him sternly: the portrait in the frontispiece frowned as he gazed.

"Wretched man," said the phantom, "and how have these things affected you?"

"Once I laughed and cried, but then I was younger. Now, I would forget them if I could."

"Have then your wish. And take this with you, man whom I renounce. From this day henceforth you shall live with those whom I displace. Without forgetting me, 't will be your lot to walk through life as if we had not met. But first you shall survey these scenes that henceforth must be yours. At one to-night, prepare to meet the phantom I have raised. Farewell!"

The sound of its voice seemed to fade away with the dying wind, and the Haunted Man was alone. But the firelight flickered gaily, and the light danced on the walls, making grotesque figures of the furniture.

"Ha, ha!" said the Haunted Man, rubbing his hands gleefully; "now for a whiskey punch and a cigar."

BOOK II.

THE SECOND PHANTOM.

ONE! The stroke of the far-off bell had hardly died before the front door closed with a reverberating clang. Steps were heard along the passage; the library door swung open of itself, and the Knocker—yes, the Knocker—slowly strode into the room. The Haunted Man rubbed his eyes,—no! there could be no mistake about it,—it was the Knocker's face, mounted on a misty, almost imperceptible body. The brazen rod was transferred from its mouth to its right hand, where it was held like a ghostly truncheon.

"It's a cold evening," said the Haunted Man.

"It is," said the Goblin, in a hard, metallic voice.

"It must be pretty cold out there," said the Haunted Man, with vague politeness. "Do you ever—will you—take some hot water and brandy?"

"No," said the Goblin.

"Perhaps you'd like it cold, by way of change?" continued the Haunted Man, correcting himself, as he remembered the peculiar temperature with which the Goblin was probably familiar.

"Time flies," said the Goblin coldly. "We have no leisure for idle talk. Come!" He moved his ghostly truncheon toward the window, and laid his hand upon the other's arm. At his touch the body of the Haunted Man seemed to become as thin and incorporeal as that of the Goblin himself, and together they glided out of the window into the black and blowy night.

In the rapidity of their flight the senses of the Haunted Man seemed to leave him. At length they stopped suddenly.

"What do you see?" asked the Goblin.

"I see a battlemented mediaeval castle. Gallant men in mail ride over the drawbridge, and kiss their gauntleted fingers to fair ladies, who wave their lily hands in return. I see fight and fray and tournament. I hear roaring heralds bawling the charms of delicate women, and shamelessly proclaiming their lovers. Stay. I see a Jewess about to leap from a battlement. I see knightly deeds, violence, rapine, and a good deal of blood. I've seen pretty much the same at Astley's."[5]

"Look again."

"I see purple moors, glens, masculine women, bare-legged men, priggish book-worms, more violence, physical excellence, and blood. Always blood,—and the superiority of physical attainments."

"And how do you feel now?" said the Goblin.

The Haunted Man shrugged his shoulders. "None the better for being carried back and asked to sympathize with a barbarous age."

The Goblin smiled and clutched his arm; they again sped rapidly through the black night and again halted.

"What do you see?" said the Goblin.

"I see a barrack room, with a mess table, and a group of intoxicated Celtic officers telling funny stories, and giving challenges to duel. I see a young Irish gentleman capable of performing prodigies of valor. I learn incidentally that the acme of all heroism is the cornetcy of a dragoon regiment. I hear a good deal of French! No, thank you," said the Haunted Man hurriedly, as he stayed the waving hand of the Goblin; "I would rather *not* go to the Peninsula, and don't care to have a private interview with Napoleon."

Again the Goblin flew away with the unfortunate man, and from a strange roaring below them he judged they were above the ocean. A ship hove in sight, and the Goblin stayed its flight. "Look," he said, squeezing his companion's arm.

The Haunted Man yawned. "Don't you think, Charles, you're rather running this thing into the ground? Of course it's very moral and instructive, and all that. But ain't there a little too much pantomime about it? Come now!"

"Look!" repeated the Goblin, pinching his arm malevolently. The Haunted Man groaned.

"O, of course, I see her Majesty's ship Arethusa. Of course I am familiar with her stern First Lieutenant, her eccentric Captain, her one fascinating and several mischievous midshipmen. Of course I know it's a splendid thing to see all this, and not to be seasick. O, there the young gentlemen are going to play a trick on the purser. For God's sake, let us go," and the unhappy man absolutely dragged the Goblin away with him.

When they next halted, it was at the edge of a broad and boundless prairie, in the middle of an oak opening.

"I see," said the Haunted Man, without waiting for his cue, but mechanically, and as if he were repeating a lesson which the Goblin had taught him,— "I see the Noble Savage. He is very fine to look at! But I observe under his war-paint, feathers, and picturesque blanket, dirt, disease, and an unsymmetrical contour. I observe beneath his inflated rhetoric deceit and hypocrisy; beneath his physical hardihood, cruelty, malice, and revenge. The Noble Savage[6] is a humbug. I remarked the same to Mr. Catlin."[7]

"Come," said the phantom.

The Haunted Man sighed, and took out his watch. "Couldn't we do the rest of this another time?"

"My hour is almost spent, irreverent being, but there is yet a chance for your reformation. Come!"

Again they sped through the night, and again halted. The sound of delicious but melancholy music fell upon their ears.

"I see," said the Haunted Man, with something of interest in his manner,—"I see an old *moss-covered manse* beside a sluggish, flowing river. I see weird shapes: witches, Puritans, clergymen, little children, judges, mesmerized maidens, moving to the sound of melody that thrills me with its sweetness and purity. But, although carried along its calm and evenly flowing current, the shapes are strange and frightful: an eating lichen gnaws at the heart of each. Not only the clergymen, but witch, maiden, judge, and Puritan, all wear Scarlet Letters[8] of some kind burned upon their hearts. I am fascinated and thrilled, but I feel a morbid sensitiveness creeping over me. I—I beg your pardon." The Goblin was yawning frightfully. "Well, perhaps we had better go."

"One more, and the last," said the Goblin.

They were moving home. Streaks of red were beginning to appear in the eastern sky. Along the banks of the blackly flowing river by moorland and stagnant fens, by low houses, clustering close to the water's edge, like strange mollusks, crawled upon the beach to dry; by misty black barges, the more misty and indistinct seen through its mysterious veil, the river fog was slowly rising. So rolled away and rose from the heart of the Haunted Man, etc., etc.

They stopped before a quaint mansion of red brick. The Goblin waved his hand without speaking.

"I see," said the Haunted Man, "a gay drawing-room. I see my old friends of the club, of the college, of society, even as they lived and moved. I see the gallant and unselfish men, whom I have loved, and the snobs whom I have hated. I see strangely mingling with them, and now and then blending with their forms, our old friends Dick Steele, Addison, and Congreve.[9] I observe, though, that these gentlemen have a habit of getting too much in the way. The royal standard of Queen Anne, not in itself a beautiful ornament, is rather too prominent in the picture. The long galleries of black oak, the formal furniture, the old portraits, are picturesque, but depressing. The house is damp. I enjoy myself better here on the lawn, where they are getting up a Vanity Fair.[10] See, the bell rings, the curtain is rising, the puppets are brought out for a new play. Let me see."

The Haunted Man was pressing forward in his eagerness, but the hand of the Goblin stayed him, and pointing to his feet he saw, between him and the rising curtain, a new-made grave. And bending above the grave in passionate grief, the Haunted Man beheld the phantom of the previous night.

*   *   *

The Haunted Man started, and—woke. The bright sunshine streamed into the room. The air was sparkling with frost. He ran joyously to the window and opened it. A small boy saluted him with "Merry Christmas." The Haunted Man instantly gave him a Bank of England note. "How much like Tiny Tim,[11] Tom, and Bobby that boy looked,—bless my soul, what a genius this Dickens has!"

A knock at the door, and Boots entered.

"Consider your salary doubled instantly. Have you read *David Copperfield*?"[12]

"Yezzur."

"Your salary is quadrupled. What do you think of *The Old Curiosity Shop*?"[13]

The man instantly burst into a torrent of tears, and then into a roar of laughter.

"Enough! Here are five thousand pounds. Open a porterhouse, and call it, 'Our Mutual Friend.'[14] Huzza! I feel so happy!" And the Haunted Man danced about the room.

And so, bathed in the light of that blessed sun, and yet glowing with the warmth of a good action, the Haunted Man, haunted no longer, save by those shapes which make the dreams of children beautiful, reseated himself in his chair, and finished *Our Mutual Friend*.

Dec. 1865

The Stolen Cigar Case

I FOUND HEMLOCK JONES[1] in the old Brook Street lodgings, musing before the fire. With the freedom of an old friend I at once threw myself in my usual familiar attitude at his feet, and gently caressed his boot. I was induced to do this for two reasons: one, that it enabled me to get a good look at his bent, concentrated face; and the other, that it seemed to indicate my reverence for his superhuman insight. So absorbed was he even then, in tracking some mysterious clue, that he did not seem to notice me. But therein I was wrong—as I always was in my attempt to understand that powerful intellect.

"It is raining," he said, without lifting his head.

"You have been out, then?" I said quickly.

"No. But I see that your umbrella is wet, and that your overcoat has drops of water on it."

I sat aghast at his penetration. After a pause he said carelessly, as if dismissing the subject: "Besides, I hear the rain on the window. Listen."

I listened. I could scarcely credit my ears, but there was the soft pattering of drops on the panes. It was evident there was no deceiving this man!

"Have you been busy lately?" I asked, changing the subject. "What new problem—given up by Scotland Yard as inscrutable—has occupied that gigantic intellect?"

He drew back his foot slightly, and seemed to hesitate ere he returned it to its original position. Then he answered wearily: "Mere trifles—nothing to speak of. The Prince Kupoli has been here to get my advice regarding the disappearance of certain rubies from the Kremlin; the Rajah of Pootibad, after vainly beheading his entire bodyguard, has been obliged to seek my assistance to recover a jeweled sword. The Grand Duchess of Pretzel-Brauntswig is desirous of discovering where her husband was on the night of February 14; and last night"—he lowered his voice slightly—"a lodger in this very house, meeting me on the stairs, wanted to know why they didn't answer his bell."

I could not help smiling—until I saw a frown gathering on his inscrutable forehead.

"Pray remember," he said coldly, "that it was through such an apparently trivial question that I found out Why Paul Ferroll Killed His Wife,[2] and What Happened to Jones!"[3]

I became dumb at once. He paused for a moment, and then suddenly changing back to his usual pitiless, analytical style, he said: "When I say these are trifles, they are so in comparison to an affair that is now before me. A crime has been committed,—and, singularly enough, against myself. You start," he said. "You wonder who would have dared to attempt it. So did I; nevertheless, it has been done. *I* have been *robbed*!"

"*You* robbed! You, Hemlock Jones, the Terror of Peculators!" I gasped in amazement, arising and gripping the table as I faced him.

"Yes! Listen. I would confess it to no other. But *you* who have followed my career, who know my methods; you, for whom I have partly lifted the veil that conceals my plans from ordinary humanity,—you, who have for years rapturously accepted my confidences, passionately admired my inductions and inferences, placed yourself at my beck and call, become my slave, groveled at my feet, given up your practice except those few unremunerative and rapidly decreasing patients to whom, in moments of abstraction over *my* problems, you have administered strychnine for quinine and arsenic for Epsom salts; you, who have sacrificed anything and everybody to me,—*you* I make my confidant!"

I arose and embraced him warmly, yet he was already so engrossed in thought that at the same moment he mechanically placed his hand upon his watch chain as if to consult the time. "Sit down," he said. "Have a cigar?"

"I have given up cigar smoking," I said.

"Why?" he asked.

I hesitated, and perhaps colored. I had really given it up because, with my diminished practice, it was too expensive. I could afford only a pipe. "I prefer a pipe," I said laughingly. "But tell me of this robbery. What have you lost?"

He arose, and planting himself before the fire with his hands under his coattails, looked down upon me reflectively for a moment. "Do you remember the cigar case presented to me by the Turkish Ambassador for discovering the missing favorite of the Grand Vizier in the fifth chorus girl at the Hilarity Theatre? It was that one. I mean the cigar case. It was incrusted with diamonds."

"And the largest one had been supplanted by paste," I said.

"Ah," he said, with a reflective smile, "you know that?"

"You told me yourself. I remember considering it a proof of your extraordinary perception. But, by Jove, you don't mean to say you have lost it?"

He was silent for a moment. "No; it has been stolen, it is true, but I shall still find it. And by myself alone! In your profession, my dear fellow, when a member is seriously ill, he does not prescribe for himself, but calls in a brother doctor. Therein we differ. I shall take this matter in my own hands."

"And where could you find better?" I said enthusiastically. "I should say the cigar case is as good as recovered already."

"I shall remind you of that again," he said lightly. "And now, to show you my confidence in your judgment, in spite of my determination to pursue this alone, I am willing to listen to any suggestions from you."

He drew a memorandum book from his pocket and, with a grave smile, took up his pencil.

I could scarcely believe my senses. He, the great Hemlock Jones, accepting suggestions from a humble individual like myself! I kissed his hand reverently, and began in a joyous tone:

"First, I should advertise, offering a reward; I should give the same intimation in hand-bills, distributed at the 'pubs' and the pastry-cooks'. I should next visit the different pawnbrokers; I should give notice at the police station. I should examine the servants. I should thoroughly search the house and my own pockets. I speak relatively," I added, with a laugh. "Of course I mean *your* own."

He gravely made an entry of these details.

"Perhaps," I added, "you have already done this?"

"Perhaps," he returned enigmatically. "Now, my dear friend," he continued, putting the note-book in his pocket and rising, "would you excuse me for a few moments? Make yourself perfectly at home until I return; there may be some things," he added with a sweep of his hand toward his heterogeneously filled shelves, "that may interest you and while away the time. There are pipes and tobacco in that corner."

Then nodding to me with the same inscrutable face he left the room. I was too well accustomed to his methods to think much of his unceremonious withdrawal, and made no doubt he was off to investigate some clue which had suddenly occurred to his active intelligence.

Left to myself I cast a cursory glance over his shelves. There were a number of small glass jars containing earthy substances, labeled "Pavement and Road Sweepings," from the principal thoroughfares and suburbs of London, with the subdirections "for identifying foot-tracks." There were several other jars, labeled "Fluff from Omnibus and Road Car Seats," "Cocoanut Fibre and Rope Strands from Mattings in Public Places," "Cigarette Stumps and Match Ends from Floor of Palace Theatre, Row A, 1 to 50." Everywhere were evidences of this wonderful man's system and perspicacity.

I was thus engaged when I heard the slight creaking of a door, and I looked up as a stranger entered. He was a rough-looking man, with a shabby overcoat and a still more disreputable muffler around his throat and the lower part of his face. Considerably annoyed at his intrusion, I turned upon him rather sharply, when, with a mumbled, growling apology for mistaking the room, he shuffled out again and closed the door. I followed him quickly to the landing and saw that he disappeared down the stairs. With my mind full of the robbery, the incident made a singular impression upon me. I knew my friend's habit of hasty absences from his room in his moments of deep inspiration; it was only too probable that, with his powerful intellect and magnificent perceptive genius concentrated on one subject, he should be careless of his own belongings, and no doubt even forget to take the ordinary precaution of locking up his drawers. I tried one or two and found that I was right, although for some reason I was unable to open one to its fullest extent. The handles were sticky, as if some one had opened them with dirty fingers. Knowing Hemlock's fastidious cleanliness, I resolved to inform him of this circumstance, but I forgot it, alas! until—but I am anticipating my story.

His absence was strangely prolonged. I at last seated myself by the fire, and lulled by warmth and the patter of the rain on the window, I fell asleep. I may have dreamt, for during my sleep I had a vague semi-consciousness as of hands being softly pressed on my pockets—no doubt induced by the story of the robbery. When I came fully to my senses, I found Hemlock Jones sitting on the other side of the hearth, his deeply concentrated gaze fixed on the fire.

"I found you so comfortably asleep that I could not bear to awaken you," he said, with a smile.

I rubbed my eyes. "And what news?" I asked. "How have you succeeded?"

"Better than I expected," he said, "and I think," he added, tapping his note-book, "I owe much to *you*."

Deeply gratified, I awaited more. But in vain. I ought to have remembered that in his moods Hemlock Jones was reticence itself. I told him simply of the strange intrusion, but he only laughed.

Later, when I arose to go, he looked at me playfully. "If you were a married man," he said, "I would advise you not to go home until you had brushed your sleeve. There are a few short brown sealskin hairs on the inner side of your forearm, just where they would have adhered if your arm had encircled a sealskin coat with some pressure!"

"For once you are at fault," I said triumphantly; "the hair is my own, as you will perceive; I have just had it cut at the hairdresser's, and no doubt this arm projected beyond the apron."

He frowned slightly, yet, nevertheless, on my turning to go he embraced me warmly—a rare exhibition in that man of ice. He even helped me on with my overcoat and pulled out and smoothed down the flaps of my pockets. He was particular, too, in fitting my arm in my overcoat sleeve, shaking the sleeve down from the arm-hole to the cuff with his deft fingers. "Come again soon!" he said, clapping me on the back.

"At any and all times," I said enthusiastically; "I only ask ten minutes twice a day to eat a crust at my office, and four hours' sleep at night, and the rest of my time is devoted to you always, as you know."

"It is indeed," he said, with his impenetrable smile.

Nevertheless, I did not find him at home when I next called. One afternoon, when nearing my own home, I met him in one of his favorite disguises,—a long blue swallow-tailed coat, striped cotton trousers, large turn-over collar, blacked face, and white hat, carrying a tambourine. Of course to others the disguise was perfect, although it was known to myself, and I passed him—according to an old understanding between us—without the slightest recognition, trusting to a later explanation. At another time, as I was making a professional visit to the wife of a publican at the East End, I saw him, in the disguise of a broken-down artisan, looking into the window of an adjacent pawnshop. I was delighted to see that he was evidently following my suggestions, and in my joy I ventured to tip him a wink; it was abstractedly returned.

Two days later I received a note appointing a meeting at his lodgings that night. That meeting, alas! was the one memorable occurrence of my life, and the last meeting I ever had with Hemlock Jones! I will try to set it down calmly, though my pulses still throb with the recollection of it.

I found him standing before the fire, with that look upon his face which I had seen only once or twice in our acquaintance—a look which I may call an absolute concatenation of inductive and deductive ratiocination—from which all that was human, tender, or sympathetic was absolutely discharged. He was simply an icy algebraic symbol! Indeed, his whole being was concentrated to that extent that his clothes fitted loosely, and his head was absolutely so much reduced in size by his mental compression that his hat tipped back from his forehead and literally hung on his massive ears.

After I had entered he locked the doors, fastened the windows, and even placed a chair before the chimney. As I watched these significant precautions with absorbing interest, he suddenly drew a revolver and, presenting it to my temple, said in low, icy tones:

"Hand over that cigar case!"

Even in my bewilderment my reply was truthful, spontaneous, and involuntary. "I haven't got it," I said.

He smiled bitterly, and threw down his revolver. "I expected that reply! Then let me now confront you with something more awful, more deadly, more relentless and convincing than that mere lethal weapon,—the damning inductive and deductive proofs of your guilt!" He drew from his pocket a roll of paper and a notebook.

"But surely," I gasped, "you are joking! You could not for a moment believe"—

"Silence! Sit down!" I obeyed.

"You have condemned yourself," he went on pitilessly. "Condemned yourself on my processes,—processes familiar to you, applauded by you, accepted by you for years! We will go back to the time when you first saw the cigar case. Your expressions," he said in cold, deliberate tones, consulting his paper, were, 'How beautiful! I wish it were mine.' This was your first step in crime—and my first indication. From 'I *wish* it were mine' to 'I *will* have it mine,' and the mere detail, '*How can* I make it mine?' the advance was obvious. Silence! But as in my methods it was necessary that there should be an overwhelming inducement to the crime, that unholy admiration of yours for the mere trinket itself was not enough. You are a smoker of cigars."

"But," I burst out passionately, "I told you I had given up smoking cigars."

"Fool!" he said coldly, "that is the *second* time you have committed yourself. Of course you told me! What more natural than for you to blazon forth that prepared and unsolicited statement to *prevent* accusation. Yet, as I said before, even that wretched attempt to cover up your tracks was not enough. I still had to find that overwhelming, impelling motive necessary to affect a man like you. That motive I found in the strongest of all impulses— Love, I suppose you would call it," he added bitterly, "that night you called! You had brought the most conclusive proofs of it on your sleeve."

"But—" I almost screamed.

"Silence!" he thundered. "I know what you would say. You would say that even if you had embraced some Young Person in a sealskin coat, what had that to do with the robbery? Let me tell you, then, that that sealskin coat represented the quality and character of your fatal entanglement! You bartered your honor for it— that stolen cigar case was the purchaser of the sealskin coat!

"Silence! Having thoroughly established your motive, I now proceed to the commission of the crime itself. Ordinary people would have begun with that—with an attempt to discover the whereabouts of the missing object. These are not *my* methods."

So overpowering was his penetration that, although I knew

myself innocent, I licked my lips with avidity to hear the further details of this lucid exposition of my crime.

"You committed that theft the night I showed you the cigar case, and after I had carelessly thrown it in that drawer. You were sitting in that chair, and I had arisen to take something from that shelf. In that instant you secured your booty without rising. Silence! Do you remember when I helped you on with your overcoat the other night? I was particular about fitting your arm in. While doing so I measured your arm with a spring tape measure, from the shoulder to the cuff. A later visit to your tailor confirmed that measurement. It proved to be *the exact distance between your chair and that drawer*!"

I sat stunned.

"The rest are mere corroborative details! You were again tampering with the drawer when I discovered you doing so! Do not start! The stranger that blundered into the room with a muffler on—was myself! More, I had placed a little soap on the drawer handles when I purposely left you alone. The soap was on your hand when I shook it at parting. I softly felt your pockets, when you were asleep, for further developments. I embraced you when you left—that I might feel if you had the cigar case or any other articles hidden on your body. This confirmed me in the belief that you had already disposed of it in the manner and for the purpose I have shown you. As I still believed you capable of remorse and confession, I twice allowed you to see I was on your track: once in the garb of an itinerant Negro minstrel, and the second time as a workman looking in the window of the pawnshop where you pledged your booty."

"But," I burst out, "if you had asked the pawnbroker, you would have seen how unjust"—

"Fool!" he hissed, "that was one of *your* suggestions—to search the pawnshops! Do you suppose I followed any of your suggestions, the suggestions of the thief? On the contrary, they told me what to avoid."

"And I suppose," I said bitterly, "you have not even searched your drawer?"

"No," he said calmly.

I was for the first time really vexed. I went to the nearest drawer and pulled it out sharply. It stuck as it had before, leaving a part of the drawer unopened. By working it, however, I discovered that it was impeded by some obstacle that had slipped to the upper part of the drawer, and held it firmly fast. Inserting my hand, I pulled out the impeding object. It was the missing cigar case! I turned to him with a cry of joy.

But I was appalled at his expression. A look of contempt was now added to his acute, penetrating gaze. "I have been mistaken," he said slowly; "I had not allowed for your weakness and cowardice! I thought too highly of you even in your guilt! But I see now why you tampered with that drawer the other night. By some inexplicable means—possibly another theft—you took the cigar case out of pawn and, like a whipped hound, restored it to me in this feeble, clumsy fashion. You thought to deceive me, Hemlock Jones! More, you thought to destroy my infallibility. Go! I give you your liberty. I shall not summon the three policemen who wait in the adjoining room—but out of my sight forever!"

As I stood once more dazed and petrified, he took me firmly by the ear and led me into the hall, closing the door behind him. This reopened presently, wide enough to permit him to thrust out my hat, overcoat, umbrella, and overshoes, and then closed against me forever!

I never saw him again. I am bound to say, however, that thereafter my business increased, I recovered much of my old practice, and a few of my patients recovered also. I became rich. I had a brougham and a house in the West End. But I often wondered, pondering on that wonderful man's penetration and insight, if, in some lapse of consciousness, I had not really stolen his cigar case!

Nov. 1900

POETRY

To the Pliocene Skull[1]

(A GEOLOGICAL ADDRESS)

"Speak, O man, less recent! Fragmentary fossil!
　Primal pioneer of pliocene formation,
　Hid in lowest drifts below the earliest stratum
　　　Of volcanic tufa!

"Older than the beasts, the oldest Palaeotherium;
　Older than the trees, the oldest Cryptogami;
　Older than the hills, those infantile eruptions
　　　Of earth's epidermis!

"Eo—Mio—Plio—whatsoe'er the 'cene' was
　That those vacant sockets filled with awe and wonder,—
　Whether shores Devonian or Silurian beaches,—
　　　Tell us thy strange story!

"Or has the professor slightly antedated
　By some thousand years thy advent on this planet,
　Giving thee an air that's somewhat better fitted
　　　For cold-blooded creatures?

"Wert thou true spectator of that mighty forest
　When above thy head the stately Sigillaria
　Reared its columned trunks in that remote and distant
　　　Carboniferous epoch?

"Tell us of that scene,—the dim and watery woodland,
　Songless, silent, hushed, with never bird or insect,
　Veiled with spreading fronds and screened with tall club mosses,
　　　Lycopodiacea,—

"When beside thee walked the solemn Plesiosaurus,
 And around thee crept the festive Ichthyosaurus,
 While from time to time above thee flew and circled
   Cheerful Pterodactyls.

"Tell us of thy food,—those half-marine refections,
 Crinoids on the shell and Brachipods *au naturel*,—
 Cuttlefish to which the *pieuvre* of Victor Hugo[2]
   Seems a periwinkle.

"Speak, thou awful vestige of the earth's creation,
 Solitary fragment of remains organic!
 Tell the wondrous secret of thy past existence,—
   Speak! thou oldest primate!"

Even as I gazed, a thrill of the maxilla,
And a lateral movement of the condyloid process,
With post-pliocene sounds of healthy mastication,
   Ground the teeth together.

And from that imperfect dental exhibition,
Stained with express juices of the weed nicotian,
Came these hollow accents, blent with softer murmurs
   Of expectoration:

"Which my name is Bowers, and my crust was busted
 Falling down a shaft in Calaveras County;
 But I'd take it kindly if you'd send the pieces
   Home to old Missouri!"

July 1866

The Society Upon the Stanislaus[1]

I RESIDE at Table Mountain, and my name is Truthful James;
I am not up to small deceit or any sinful games;
And I'll tell in simple language what I know about the row
That broke up our Society upon the Stanislow.

But first I would remark, that it is not a proper plan
For any scientific gent to whale his fellow-man,
And, if a member don't agree with his peculiar whim,
To lay for that same member for to "put a head" on him.

Now nothing could be finer or more beautiful to see
Than the first six months' proceedings of that same Society,
Till Brown of Calaveras brought a lot of fossil bones
That he found within a tunnel near the tenement of Jones.

Then Brown he read a paper, and he reconstructed there,
From those same bones, an animal that was extremely rare;
And Jones then asked the Chair for a suspension of the rules,
Till he could prove that those same bones was one of his lost
      mules.

Then Brown he smiled a bitter smile, and said he was at fault,
It seemed he had been trespassing on Jones's family vault;
He was a most sarcastic man, this quiet Mr. Brown,
And on several occasions he had cleaned out the town.

Now I hold it is not decent for a scientific gent
To say another is an ass,—at least, to all intent;
Nor should the individual who happens to be meant
Reply by heaving rocks at him, to any great extent.

Then Abner Dean of Angel's raised a point of order, when
A chunk of old red sandstone took him in the abdomen,
And he smiled a kind of sickly smile, and curled up on the floor,
And the subsequent proceedings interested him no more.

For, in less time than I write it, every member did engage
In a warfare with the remnants of a palaeozoic age;
And the way they heaved those fossils in their anger was a sin,
Till the skull of an old mammoth caved the head of Thompson in.

And this is all I have to say of these improper games,
For I live at Table Mountain, and my name is Truthful James;
And I've told in simple language what I know about the row
That broke up our Society upon the Stanislow.

Sept. 1868

Plain Language from Truthful James

(TABLE MOUNTAIN, 1870)

WHICH I wish to remark,
    And my language is plain,
That for ways that are dark
    And for tricks that are vain,
The heathen Chinee is peculiar,
    Which the same I would rise to explain.

Ah Sin was his name;
    And I shall not deny,
In regard to the same,
    What that name might imply;
But his smile it was pensive and childlike,
    As I frequent remarked to Bill Nye.

It was August the third,
    And quite soft was the skies;
Which it might be inferred
    That Ah Sin was likewise;
Yet he played it that day upon William
    And me in a way I despise.

Which we had a small game,
    And Ah Sin took a hand:
It was Euchre. The same
    He did not understand;
But he smiled as he sat by the table,
    With the smile that was childlike and bland.

Yet the cards they were stocked
    In a way that I grieve,
And my feelings were shocked

At the state of Nye's sleeve,
Which was stuffed full of aces and bowers,
    And the same with intent to deceive.

But the hands that were played
    By that heathen Chinee,
And the points that he made,
    Were quite frightful to see,—
Till at last he put down a right bower,
    Which the same Nye had dealt unto me.

Then I looked up at Nye,
    And he gazed upon me;
And he rose with a sigh,
    And said, "Can this be?
We are ruined by Chinese cheap labor,"—
    And he went for that heathen Chinee.

In the scene that ensued
    I did not take a hand,
But the floor it was strewed
    Like the leaves on the strand
With the cards that Ah Sin had been hiding,
    In the game "he did not understand."

In his sleeves, which were long,
    He had twenty-four packs,[1]—
Which was coming it strong,
    Yet I state but the facts;
And we found on his nails, which were taper,
    What is frequent in tapers,—that's wax.

Which is why I remark,
    And my language is plain,
That for ways that are dark
    And for tricks that are vain,
The heathen Chinee is peculiar,—
    Which the same I am free to maintain.

Sept. 1870

Dickens in Camp

ABOVE the pines the moon was slowly drifting.
    The river sang below;
The dim Sierras, far beyond, uplifting
    Their minarets of snow.

The roaring camp-fire, with rude humor, painted
    The ruddy tints of health
On haggard face and form that drooped and fainted
    In the fierce race for wealth;

Till one arose, and from his pack's scant treasure
    A hoarded volume drew,
And cards were dropped from hands of listless leisure
    To hear the tale anew.

And then, while round them shadows gathered faster,
    And as the firelight fell,
He read aloud the book wherein the Master
    Had writ of "Little Nell."[1]

Perhaps 't was boyish fancy,—for the reader
    Was youngest of them all,—
But, as he read, from clustering pine and cedar
    A silence seemed to fall;

The fir-trees, gathering closer in the shadows,
    Listened in every spray,
While the whole camp with "Nell" on English meadows
    Wandered and lost their way.

And so in mountain solitudes—o'ertaken
    As by some spell divine—
Their cares dropped from them like the needles shaken
    From out the gusty pine.

Lost is that camp and wasted all its fire;
    And he who wrought that spell?
Ah! towering pine and stately Kentish spire,
    Ye have one tale to tell!

Lost is that camp, but let its fragrant story
    Blend with the breath that thrills
With hop-vine's incense all the pensive glory
    That fills the Kentish hills.

And on that grave where English oak and holly
    And laurel wreaths entwine,
Deem it not all a too presumptuous folly,
    This spray of Western pine!

July 1870

That Ebrew Jew

THERE once was a tradesman renowned as a screw
Who sold pins and needles and calicoes too,
Till he built up a fortune—the which as it grew
Just ruined small traders the whole city through—
    Yet one thing he knew,
    Between me and you,
    There was a distinction
    'Twixt Christian and Jew.

Till he died in his mansion—a great millionaire—
The owner of thousands; but nothing to spare
For the needy and poor who from hunger might drop,
And only a pittance to clerks in his shop.
    But left it all to
    A Lawyer, who knew
    A subtile distinction
    'Twixt Ebrew and Jew.

This man was no trader, but simply a friend
Of this Gent who kept shop and who, nearing his end,
Handed over a million—'t was only his due,
Who discovered this contrast 'twixt Ebrew and Jew.
    For he said, "If you view
    This case as I do,
    There *is* a distinction
    'Twixt Ebrew and Jew.

"For the Jew is a man who will make money through
His skill, his *finesse,* and his capital too,
And an Ebrew's a man that we Gentiles can 'do,'
So you see there's a contrast 'twixt Ebrew and Jew.

Ebrew and Jew,
Jew and Ebrew,
There's a subtile distinction
'Twixt Ebrew and Jew."

So he kept up his business of needles and pins,
But always one day he atoned for his sins,
But never the same day (for that wouldn't do),
That the Jew faced his God with the awful Ebrew.
For this man he knew,
Between me and you,
There was a distinction
'Twixt Ebrew and Jew.

So he sold soda-water and shut up the fount
Of a druggist whose creed was the Speech on the Mount;[1]
And he trafficked in gaiters and ruined the trade
Of a German whose creed was by great Luther made.[2]
But always he knew,
Between me and you,
A subtile distinction
'Twixt Ebrew and Jew.

Then he kept a hotel—here his trouble began—
In a fashion unknown to his primitive plan;
For the rule of this house to his manager ran,
"Don't give entertainment to Israelite man."
Yet the manager knew,
Between me and you,
No other distinction
'Twixt Ebrew and Jew.

"You may give to John Morrissey[3] supper and wine,
And Madame N.N.[4] to your care I'll resign;
You'll see that those Jenkins from Missouri Flat
Are properly cared for; but recollect that
Never a Jew
Who's not an Ebrew
Shall take up his lodgings
Here at the Grand U.

"You'll allow Miss McFlimsey[5] her diamonds to wear;
You'll permit the Van Dams[6] at the waiters to swear;
You'll allow Miss Décolleté[7] to flirt on the stair;
But as to an Israelite—pray have a care;
   For, between me and you,
   Though the doctrine is new,
   There's a business distinction
   'Twixt Ebrew and Jew."

Now, how shall we know?   Prophet, tell us, pray do,
Where the line of the Hebrew fades into the Jew?
Shall we keep out Disraeli and take Rothschild in?[8]
Or snub Meyerbeer and think Verdi a sin?[9]
   What shall we do?
   O, give us a few
   Points to distinguish
   'Twixt Ebrew and Jew.

There was One—Heaven help us!—who died in man's place,
With thorns on his forehead, but Love in his face:
And when "foxes had holes"[10] and birds in the air
Had their nests in the trees, there was no spot to spare
   For this "King of the Jews."
   Did the Romans refuse
   This right to the Ebrews
   Or only to Jews?

June 1877

Free Silver at Angel's

I RESIDE at Table Mountain, and my name is Truthful James,
I have told the tale of "William" and of "Ah Sin's" sinful games;
I have yarned of "Our Society," and certain gents I know,
Yet my words were plain and simple, and I never yet was low.

Thar is high-toned gents, ink-slingers; thar is folks as will allow
Ye can't reel off a story onless they've taught ye how;
Till they get the word *they're* wantin', *they're* allus cryin'
 "Whoa!"
All the while their mule is pullin' (that's their "Pegasus," you
 know).

We ain't built that way at Angel's—but why pursue this theme?
When things is whirling round us in a wild delusive dream;
When "fads" on "bikes" go scorchin' down—to t'other place you
 know
(for I speak in simple language—and I never yet was low.)

It was rainin' up at Angel's—we war sittin' round the bar,
Discussin' of "Free Silver" that was "going soon to par,"[1]
And Ah Sin stood thar a-listenin' like a simple guileless child,
That hears the Angels singin'—so dreamy like he smiled.

But we knew while he was standin' thar—of all that heathen
 heard
And saw—he never understood a single blessed word;
Till Brown of Calaveras, who had waltzed up on his bike,
Sez: "What is *your* opinion, John, that this Free Silver's like?"

But Ah Sin said, "No shabbee," in his childish, simple way,
And Brown he tipped a wink at us and then he had *his* say:

He demonstrated then and thar how silver was as good
As gold—if folks warn't blasted fools, and only understood!

He showed how we "were crucified upon a cross of gold"[2]
By millionaires, and banged his fist, until our blood ran cold.
He was a most convincin' man—was Brown in all his ways,
And his skill with a revolver, folks had oft remarked with praise.

He showed us how the ratio should be as "sixteen to one,"[3]
And he sorted out some dollars—while the boys enjoyed the
     fun—
And laid them on the counter—and heaped 'em in a pile,
While Ah Sin, *he* drew nearer with his happy, pensive smile.

"The heathen in his blindness bows down to wood and stone,"
Said Brown, "but this poor heathen won't bow to gold alone;
So speak, my poor Mongolian, and show us *your* idee
Of what we call 'Free Silver' and what is meant by 'Free.'"

Swift was the smile that stole across that heathen's face! I grieve
That swifter was the hand that swept those dollars up his sleeve.
"Me shabbee 'Silvel' allee same as Mellican man," says he;
"Me shabbee 'Flee' means 'B'longs to none,' so Chinaman catch
   he!"

Now, childlike as his logic was, it didn't justify
The way the whole crowd went for him without a reason why;
And the language Brown made use of I shall not attempt to show,
For my words are plain and simple—and I never yet was low.

Then Abner Dean called "Order!" and he said "that it would
     seem
The gentleman from China's deductions were extreme;
I move that we should teach him, in a manner that shall strike,
The 'bi-metallic balance' on Mr. Brown's new bike!"

Now Dean was scientific,—but was sinful, too, and gay,—
And I hold it most improper for a gent to act that way,
And having muddled Ah Sin's brains with that same silver craze,
To set him on a bicycle—and he not know its ways.

They set him on and set him off; it surely seemed a sin
To see him waltz from left to right, and wobble out and in,
Till his pig-tail caught within the wheel and wound up round its
    rim,
And that bicycle got up and reared—and then crawled over him.

"My poor Mongolian friend," said Dean, "it's plain that in your
    case
Your center point of gravity don't fall within your base.
We'll tie the silver in a bag and hang it from your queue,
And then—by scientific law—you'll keep your balance true!"

They tied that silver to his queue, and it hung down behind,
But always straight, no matter which the side Ah Sin inclined—
For though a sinful sort of man—and lightsome, too, I ween—
He was no slouch in *Science*—was Mister Abner Dean!

And here I would remark how vain are all deceitful tricks,—
The boomerang we throw comes back to give *us* its last licks,—
And that same weight on Ah Sin's queue set him up straight and
    plumb,
And he scooted past us down the grade and left us cold and
    dumb!

"Come back! Come back!" we called at last. We heard a shriek of
    glee,
And something sounding strangely like "All litee! Silvel's flee!"
And saw his feet tucked on the wheel—the bike go all alone!
And break the biggest record Angel's Camp had ever known!

He raised the hill without a spill, and still his speed maintained,
For why?—he traveled on the sheer momentum he had gained,
And vanished like a meteor—with his queue stretched in the gale,
Or I might say a Comet—takin' in that silver tail!

But not again we saw his face—nor Brown his "Silver Free"!
And I marvel in my simple mind howe'er these things can be!
But I do not reproduce the speech of Brown who saw him go,
For my words are pure and simple—and I never yet was low!

June 1898

ESSAYS

The Argonauts of '49

As so much of my writing has dealt with the Argonauts of '49, I propose, by way of introduction, to discourse briefly on an episode of American life as quaint and typical as that of the Greek adventurers whose name I have borrowed. It is a crusade without a cross, an exodus without a prophet. It is not a pretty story; I do not know that it is even instructive. It is of a life of which, perhaps, the best that can be said is that it exists no longer.

Let me first give an idea of the country which these people re-created, and the civilization they displaced. For more than three hundred years California was of all Christian countries the least known. The glow and glamour of Spanish tradition and discovery hung about it. There was an English map in which it was set down as an island. There was the Rio de Los Reyes[1]—a kind of gorgeous Mississippi—leading directly to the heart of the Continent, which De Fonte[2] claimed to have discovered. There was the Anian passage—a prophetic forecast of the Pacific Railroad—through which Maldonado[3] declared that he sailed to the North Atlantic. Another Spanish discoverer brought his mendacious personality directly from the Pacific, by way of Columbia River, to Lake Ontario;[4] on which, I am rejoiced to say, he found a Yankee vessel from Boston, whose captain informed him that *he* had come up from the Atlantic only a few days before him! Along the long line of iron-bound coast the old freebooters chased the timid Philippine galleons, and in its largest bay, beside the present gateway of the West,—San Francisco,—Sir Francis Drake lay for two weeks and scraped the barnacles from his adventurous keels.[5] It is only within the past twenty-five years, that a company of gold-diggers, turning up the ocean sands near Port Umpqua, came upon some large cakes of wax deeply imbedded in the broken and fire-scarred ribs of a wreck of ancient date. The Californian heart was at once fired at the discovery, and in a few weeks a hundred men or more were digging, burrowing, and scraping for the lost treasure of the Philippine galleon. At last they found—what think you?—a few cutlasses with an English stamp upon their blades. The enterprising and gallant—and slightly piratical—Sir Francis Drake had been there before them!

Yet they were peaceful, pastoral days for California. Through the great central valley the Sacramento poured an unstained current into a majestic bay, ruffled by no keels and fretted by no wharves. The Angelus bell rung at San Bernardino, and, taken up by every Mission tower along the darkening coast, called the good people to prayer and sleep before nine o'clock every night. Leagues of wild oats, progenitors of those great wheat fields that now drug the markets, hung their idle heads on the hillsides; vast herds of untamed cattle, whose hides and horns alone made the scant commerce of those days, wandered over the illimitable plains, knowing no human figure but that of the yearly riding vaquero on his unbroken mustang, which they regarded as the early aborigines did the Spanish cavalry, as one individual creation. Around the white walls of the Mission buildings were clustered the huts of the Indian neophytes, who dressed neatly, but not expensively, in mud. Presidios garrisomed by a dozen raw militiamen kept the secular order, and in the scattered pueblos rustic alcaldes dispensed, like Sancho Panza,[6] proverbial wisdom and practical equity to the bucolic litigants. In looking over some Spanish law papers, one day, I came upon a remarkable instance of the sagacity of Alcalde[7] Felipe Gomez of Santa Barbara. An injured wife accused her husband of serenading the wife of another. The faithless husband and his too seductive guitar were both produced in court. "Play," said the alcalde to the gay Lothario.[8] The unfortunate man was obliged to repeat his amorous performance of the preceding night. "I find nothing here," said the excellent alcalde after a moment's pause, "but an infamous voice and an execrable style. I dismiss the complaint of the Señora, but I shall hold the Señor on the charge of vilely disturbing the peace of Santa Barbara."

They were happy, tranquil days. The proprietors of the old ranchos ruled in a patriarchal style, and lived to a patriarchal age. On a soil half tropical in its character, in a climate wholly original in its practical conditions, a soft-handed Latin race slept and smoked the half year's sunshine away, and believed that they had discovered a new Spain! They awoke from their dream only to find themselves strangers on their own soil, foreigners in their own country, ignorant even of the treasure they had been sent to guard. A political and social earthquake, more powerful than any physical convulsions they had ever known, shook the foundation of the land, and in the disrupted strata and rent fissures the treasure suddenly glittered before their eyes.

Though the change came upon them suddenly, it had been prefigured by a chain of circumstances whose logical links future historians will not overlook. It was not the finding of a few grains of gold by a day laborer at Sutter's Mill,[9] but that for years before the way had been slowly opened and the doors unlocked to the people who were to profit by this discovery. The real pioneers of the lawless, irreligious band whose story I am repeating were the oldest and youngest religions known. Do Americans ever think that they owe their right to California to the Catholic Church and the Mormon brotherhood? Yet Father Junipero Serra ringing his bell in the heathen wilderness of Upper California, and Brigham Young leading his half famished legions from Nauvoo to Salt Lake,[10] were the two great commanders of the Argonauts of '49. All that western emigration which, prior to the gold discovery, penetrated the Oregon and California valleys and half Americanized the Coast, would have perished by the way, but for the providentially created oasis of Salt Lake City. The halting trains of alkali-poisoned oxen, the footsore and despairing teamsters, gathered rest and succor from the Mormon settlement. The British frigate that sailed into the port of Monterey a day or two late, saw the American flag that had, under this providence, crossed the continent, flying from the Cross of the Cathedral! A day sooner, and this story might have been an English record.

Were our friends, the Argonauts, at all affected by these coincidences? I think not. They had that lordly contempt for a southern, soft-tongued race which belonged to their Anglo-Saxon lineage. They were given to no superstitious romance, exalted by no special mission, stimulated by no high ambition; they were skeptical of even the existence of the golden fleece[11] until they saw it. Equal to their fate, they accepted with a kind of heathen philosophy whatever it might bring. "If there isn't any gold, what are you going to do with these sluice-boxes?" said a newly arrived emigrant to his friend. "They will make first-class coffins," answered the friend, with the simple directness of a man who has calculated all his chances. If they did not burn their vessels behind them, like Pizarro,[12] they at least left the good ship Argo dismantled and rotting at their Colchian wharf. Sailors were shipped only for the outward voyage; nobody expected to *return*, even those who anticipated failure. Fertile in expedients, they twisted their failures into a certain sort of success. Until recently, there stood in San Francisco a house of the early days whose foundations were built entirely of plug tobacco in boxes. The consignee had found a glut in the tobacco market, but lumber for foundations was at a tremendous premium![13] An Argonaut just arriving was amazed at recognizing in the boatman who pulled him ashore, and who charged him the modest sum of fifty dollars for the performance, a brother classmate of Oxford. "Were you not," he asked eagerly, "senior wrangler in '43?" "Yes," said the other significantly, "but I also pulled stroke oar against Cambridge." If the special training of years sometimes failed to procure pecuniary recognition, an idle accomplishment, sometimes even a physical peculiarity, succeeded. At my first breakfast in a restaurant on Long Wharf, I was haunted during the meal by a shadowy resemblance which the waiter who took my order bore to a gentleman to whom in my boyhood I had looked up as a mirror of elegance, urbanity, and social accomplishment. Fearful lest I should insult the waiter—who carried a revolver—by this reminiscence, I said nothing to him; but a later inquiry of the proprietor proved that my suspicions were correct. "He's mighty handy," said the man, "and kin talk elegant to a customer as is waiting for his cakes, and make him kinder forget he ain't sarved." With an earnest desire to restore my old friend to his former position, I asked if it would not be possible to fill his place. "I'm afraid not," said the proprietor with a sudden suspicion, and he added significantly, "I don't think you'd suit." It was this wonderful adaptability, perhaps influenced by a climate that produced fruit out of season, that helped the Argonauts to success, or mitigated their defeats. A now distinguished lawyer, remarkable for his Herculean build, found himself on landing without a cent—rather let me say without twenty dollars—to pay the porterage of his trunk to the hotel. Shouldering it, he was staggering from the landing, when a stranger stepped towards him, remarking he had not "half a load," quietly added his own valise to the lawyer's burden, and handing him ten dollars and his address, departed before the legal gentleman could recover from his astonishment. The valise, however, was punctually delivered, and the lawyer often congratulated himself on the comparative ease with which he won his first fee.

Much of the easy adaptability was due to the character of the people. What that character was, perhaps it would not be well to say. At least I should prefer to defer criticism until I could add to the calmness the safe distance of the historian. You will find some of their peculiarities described in the frank autobiographies of those two gentlemen who executed a little commission for Macbeth in which Banquo was concerned.[14] In distant parts of the continent they had left families, creditors, and in some instances even officers of justice, perplexed and lamenting. There were husbands who had deserted their own wives,—and in some extreme cases even the wives of others,—for this haven of refuge. Nor was it possible to tell from their superficial exterior, or even their daily walk and action, whether they were or were not named in the counts of this general indictment. Some of the best men had the worst antecedents, some of the worst rejoiced in a spotless puritan pedigree. "The boys seem to have taken a fresh deal all round," said Mr. John Oakhurst one day to me, with the easy confidence of a man who was conscious of his ability to win my money, "and there is no knowing whether a man will turn up knave or king." It is relevant to this anecdote that Mr. John Oakhurst himself came of a family whose ancestors regarded games of chance as sinful, because they were trifling and amusing, but who had never conceived they might be made the instruments of successful speculation and even tragic earnestness. "To think," said Mr. Oakhurst, as he rose from a ten minutes' sitting with a gain of five thousand dollars,—"to think there's folks as believes that keerds is a waste of time."

Such were the character and the antecedents of the men who gave the dominant and picturesque coloring to the life of that period. Doubtless the papers of the ancient Argo showed a cleaner bill of moral health, but doubtless no type of adventure more distinct or original. I would not have it inferred that there was not a class, respectable in numbers as in morals, among and yet distinct from these. But they have no place here save as a background to the salient outlines and deeply etched figures of the Argonauts. Character ruled, and the strongest was not always the best. Let me bring them a little nearer. Let me sketch two pictures of them: one in their gathered concourse in their city by the sea, one in their lonely scattered cabins in the camps of the Sierras.

It is the memorable winter of '52, a typical Californian winter—unlike anything known to most of my readers; a winter from whose snowy nest in the Sierras the fluttering, new-fledged Spring freed itself without a struggle. It is a season of falling rains and springing grasses, of long nights of shower, and days of cloud and sunshine. There are hours when the quickening earth seems to throb beneath one's feet, and the blue eyes of heaven to twinkle through its misty lashes. High up in the Sierras, unsunned depths of snow form the vast reservoirs that later will flood the plains, causing the homesick wanderers on the low-lands to look with awe upon a broad expanse of overflow, a lake that might have buried the State of Massachusetts in its yellow depths. The hillsides are gay with flowers, and, as in the old fairy story, every utterance of the kindly Spring falls from her lips to the ground in rubies and emeralds. And yet it is called "a hard season," and flour is fifty dollars a barrel. In San Francisco it has been raining steadily for two weeks. The streets are almost impassable with mud, and over some of the more dangerous depths planks are thrown. There are few street lamps, but the shops are still lighted, and the streets are full of long-bearded, long-booted men, eager for some new excitement, their only idea of recreation from the feverish struggle of the day. Perhaps it is a passing carriage—a phenomenal carriage, one of the half dozen known in the city—that becoming helplessly mired is instantly surrounded by a score of willing hands whose owners are only too happy to be rewarded by a glimpse of a female face through the window, even though that face be haggard, painted, or gratuitously plain. Perhaps it is in the little theater, where the cry of a baby in the audience brings down a tumultuous encore from the whole house. Perhaps it is in the gilded drinking saloon, into which some one rushes with arms extended at right angles, and conveys in that one pantomimic action the signal of the semaphore telegraph on Telegraph Hill[15] that a sidewheel steamer has arrived, and that there are "letters from home." Perhaps it is the long queue that afterwards winds and stretches from the Post Office half a mile away. Perhaps it is the eager men who, following it rapidly down, bid fifty, a hundred, two hundred, three hundred, and five hundred dollars for favored places in the line. Perhaps it is the haggard man who nervously tears open his letter and after a moment's breathless pause faints and falls senseless beside his comrades. Or perhaps it is a row and a shot in the streets, but in '52 this was hardly an excitement.

The gambling-saloon is always the central point of interest. There are four of them,—the largest public buildings in the city,— thronged and crowded all night. They are approached by no mysterious passage or guarded entrance, but are frankly open to the street, with the further invitation of gilding, lights, warmth, and music. Strange to say, there is a quaint decorum about them. They are the quietest halls in San Francisco. There is no drunkenness, no quarreling, scarcely any exultation or disappointment. Men who have already staked their health and fortune in this emigration are but little affected by the lesser stake on red or black, or the turn of a card. Business men who have gambled all day in their legitimate enterprise find nothing to excite them unduly here. In the intervals of music, a thoughtful calm pervades the vast assembly; people move around noiselessly from table to table, as if Fortune were nervous as well as fickle; a cane falling upon the floor causes every one to look up, a loud laugh or exclamation excites a stare of virtuous indignation. The most respectable citizens, though they might not play, are to be seen here of an evening. Old friends, who perhaps parted at the church door in the States, meet here without fear and without reproach. Even among the players are represented all classes and conditions of men. One night at a faro table a player suddenly slipped from his seat to the floor, a dead man. Three doctors, also players, after a brief examination, pronounced it disease of the heart. The coroner, sitting at the right of the dealer, instantly impaneled the rest of the players, who, laying down their cards, briefly gave a verdict in accordance with the facts, and went on with their game!

I do not mean to say that, under this surface calm, there was not often the intensest feeling. There was a Western man, who, having made a few thousands in the mines, came to San Francisco to take the Eastern steamer home. The night before he was to sail, he entered the Arcade saloon, and seating himself at a table in sheer listlessness, staked a twenty-dollar gold piece on the game. He won. He won again without removing his stake. It was, in short, that old story told so often—how in two hours he won a fortune, how an hour later he rose from the table a ruined man. Well—the steamer sailed without him. He was a simple man, knowing little of the world, and his sudden fortune and equally sudden reverse almost crazed him. He dared not write to the wife who awaited him; he had not pluck enough to return to the mines and build his fortune up anew. A fatal fascination held him to the spot. He took some humble occupation in the city, and regularly lost his scant earnings where his wealth had gone before. His ragged figure and haggard face appeared as regularly as the dealer at the table. So, a year passed. But if he had forgotten the waiting wife, she had not forgotten him. With infinite toil she at last pro-cured a passage to San Francisco, and was landed with her child penniless upon its wharf. In her sore extremity she told her story to a passing stranger—the last man, perhaps, to have met—Mr. John Oakhurst, a gambler! He took her to a hotel, and quietly provided for her immediate wants. Two or three evenings after this, the Western man, still playing at the same table, won some trifling stake three times in succession, as if Fortune were about to revisit him. At this moment, Mr. Oakhurst clapped him on the shoulder. "I will give you," he said, quietly, "three thousand dol-lars for your next play." The man hesitated. "Your wife is at the door," continued Mr. Oakhurst *sotto voce.* "Will you take it? Quick!" The man accepted. But the spirit of the gambler was strong within him, and as Mr. Oakhurst perhaps fully expected, he waited to see the result of the play. Mr. Oakhurst lost! With a look of gratitude the man turned to Oakhurst and seizing the three thousand dollars hurried away, as if fearful he might change his mind. "That was a bad spurt of yours, Jack," said a friend inno-cently, not observing the smile that had passed between the dealer and Jack. "Yes," said Jack coolly, "but I got tired of seein' that chap around." "But," said his friend in alarm, "you don't mean to say that you"—and he hesitated. "I mean to say, my dear boy," said Jack, "that this yer little deal was a put-up job betwixt the dealer and me. It's the first time," he added seriously, with an oath which I think the recording angel instantly passed to Jack's credit, "it's the first time as I ever played a game that wasn't *on the square.*"

The social life of that day was peculiar. Gentlemen made New Year's calls in long boots and red flannel shirts. In later days the wife of an old pioneer used to show a chair with a hole through its cushion made by a gentleman caller who, sitting down suddenly in bashful confusion, had exploded his revolver. The best-dressed men were gamblers; the best-dressed ladies had no right to that title. At balls and parties dancing was tabooed, owing to the unhappy complications which arose from the disproportionate number of partners to the few ladies that were present. The ingenious device of going through a quadrille with a different partner for each figure sprang from the fertile brain of a sorely beset San Francisco belle. The wife of an army officer told me that she never thought of returning home with the same escort, and not unfrequently was accompanied with what she called a "full platoon." "I never knew before," she said, "what they meant by 'the pleasure of *your company.*'" In the multiplicity of such attentions surely there was safety.

Such was the urban life of the Argonauts—its salient peculiarities softened and subdued by the constant accession of strangers from the East and the departure of its own citizens for the interior. As each succeeding ocean steamer brought fresh faces from the East, a corresponding change took place in the type and in the manners and morals. When fine clothes appeared upon the streets and men swore less frequently, people began to put locks on their doors and portable property was no longer out at night. As fine houses were built, real estate rose, and the dwellers in the old tents were pushed from the contiguity of their richer brothers. San Francisco saw herself naked, and was ashamed. The old Argonautic brotherhood, with its fierce sincerity, its terrible directness, its pathetic simplicity, was broken up. Some of the members were content to remain in a Circean palace of material and sensuous delight,[16] but the type was transferred to the mountains, and thither I propose to lead you.

It is a country unlike any other. Nature here is as rude, as inchoate, as unfinished, as the life. The people seem to have come here a thousand years too soon, and before the great hostess was ready to receive them. The forests, vast, silent, damp with their undergrowth of gigantic ferns, recall a remote carboniferous epoch. The trees are monstrous, somber, and monotonously alike. Everything is new, crude, and strange. The grass blades are enormous and far apart, there is no carpet to the soil; even the few Alpine flowers are odorless and bizarre. There is nothing soft, tender, or pastoral in the landscape. Nature affects the heroics rather than the bucolics. Theocritus himself could scarcely have given melody to the utterance of these Aetnean herdsmen, with their brierwood pipes, and their revolvers slung at their backs. There are vast spaces of rock and cliff, long intervals of ravine and cañon, and sudden and awful lapses of precipice. The lights and shadows are Rembrandtish, and against this background the faintest outline of a human figure stands out starkly.

They lived at first in tents, and then in cabins. The climate was gracious, and except for the rudest purposes of shelter from the winter rains, they could have slept out of doors the year round, as many preferred to do. As they grew more ambitious, perhaps a small plot of ground was enclosed and cultivated; but for the first few years they looked upon themselves as tenants at will, and were afraid of putting down anything they could not take away. Chimneys to their cabins were for a long time avoided as having this objectionable feature. Even at this day, deserted mining-camps are marked by the solitary adobe chimneys still left standing where the frame of the original cabin was moved to some newer location. Their housekeeping was of the rudest kind. For many months the frying-pan formed their only available cooking-utensil. It was lashed to the wandering miner's back, like the troubadour's guitar. He fried his bread, his beans, his bacon, and occasionally stewed his coffee, in this single vessel. But that Nature worked for him with a balsamic air and breezy tonics, he would have succumbed. Happily his meals were few and infrequent; happily the inventions of his mother East were equal to his needs. His progressive track through these mountain solitudes was marked with tin cans bearing the inscriptions: "Cove Oysters," "Shaker Sweet Corn," "Yeast Powder," "Boston Crackers," and the like. But in the hour of adversity and the moment of perplexity, his main reliance was beans! It was the sole legacy of the Spanish California. The conqueror and the conquered fraternized over their *frijoles*.

The Argonaut's dress was peculiar. He was ready if not skillful with his needle, and was fond of patching his clothes until the original material disappeared beneath a cloud of amendments. The flour-sack was his main dependence. When its contents had sustained and comforted the inner man, the husk clothed the outer one. Two gentlemen of respectability in earlier days lost their identity in the labels somewhat conspicuously borne on the seats of their trousers, and were known to the camp in all seriousness as "Genesee Mills" and "Eagle Brand." In the Southern mines a quantity of seamen's clothing, condemned by the Navy Department and sold at auction, was bought up, and for a year afterwards the somber woodland shades of Stanislaus and Merced were lightened by the white ducks and blue and white shirts of sailor landsmen. It was odd that the only picturesque bit of color in their dress was accidental, and owing to a careless, lazy custom. Their handkerchiefs of coarse blue, green, or yellow bandanna were for greater convenience in hot weather knotted at the ends and thrown shawlwise around the shoulders. Against a background of olive foliage, the effect was always striking and kaleidoscopic. The soft felt, broad-brimmed hat, since known as the California hat, was their only head-covering. A tall hat on anybody but a clergyman or a gambler would have justified a blow.

They were singularly handsome, to a man. Not solely in the muscular development and antique grace acquired through openair exercise and unrestrained freedom of limb, but often in color, expression, and even softness of outline. They were mainly young men, whose beards were virgin, soft, silken, and curling. They had not always time to cut their hair, and this often swept their shoulders with the lovelocks of Charles II.[17] There were faces that made one think of Delaroche's Savior.[18] There were dashing figures, bold-eyed, jauntily insolent, and cavalierly reckless, that would have delighted Meissonier.[19] Add to this the foreign element of Chilian and Mexican, and you have a combination of form and light and color unknown to any other modern English-speaking community. At sunset on the red mountain road, a Mexican packtrain perhaps slowly winds its way toward the plain. Each animal wears a gaily colored blanket beneath its pack saddle; the leading mule is musical with bells, and brightly caparisoned; the muleteers wear the national dress, with striped *serape* of red and black, deer-

skin trousers open from the knee, and fringes with bullion buttons, and have on each heel a silver spur with rowels three inches
in diameter. If they were thus picturesque in external magnifi-
cence, no less romantic were they in expression and character.
Their hospitality was barbaric, their generosity spontaneous.
Their appreciation of merit always took the form of pecuniary tes-
timonials, whether it was a church and parsonage given to a favorite preacher, or the Danaë-like shower of gold[20] they rained
upon the pretty person of a popular actress. No mendicant had to
beg; a sympathizing bystander took up a subscription in his hat.
Their generosity was emulative and cumulative. During the great
War of the Rebellion, the millions gathered in the Treasury of the
Sanitary Commission[21] had their source in a San Francisco bar-
room. "It's mighty rough on those chaps who are wounded," said
a casual drinker, "and I'm sorry for them." "How much are you
sorry?" asked a gambler. "Five hundred dollars," said the first
speaker aggressively. "I'll see that five hundred dollars, and go a
thousand better!" said the gambler, putting down the money. In
half an hour fifteen thousand dollars was telegraphed to Washington from San Francisco, and this great national charity—open to
North and South alike, afterwards reinforced by three millions of
California gold—sprang into life.

In their apparently thoughtless free-handedness there was often
a vein of practical sagacity. It is a well-known fact that after the
great fire in Sacramento,[22] the first subscription to the rebuilding
of the Methodist Church came from the hands of a noted gambler.
The good pastor, while accepting the gift, could not help asking the giver why he did not keep the money to build another
gambling-house. "It would be making things a little *monotonous*
out yer, ole man," responded the gambler gravely, "and it's variety
that's wanted for a big town."

They were splendidly loyal in their friendships. Perhaps the absence of female society and domestic ties turned the current of
their tenderness and sentiment towards each other. To be a man's
"partner" signified something more than a common pecuniary or
business interest; it was to be his friend through good or ill report,
in adversity or fortune, to cleave to him and none other—to be
ever jealous of him! There were Argonauts who were more faith-
ful to their partners than, I fear, they had ever been to their wives;

there were partners whom even the grave could not divide—who remained solitary and loyal to a dead man's memory. To insult a man's partner was to insult him; to step between two partners in a quarrel was attended with the same danger and uncertainty that involves the peacemaker in a conjugal dispute. The heroic possibilities of a Damon and a Pythias were always present;[23] there were men who had fulfilled all those conditions, and better still without a knowledge or belief that they were classical, with no mythology to lean their backs against, and hardly a conscious appreciation of a later faith that is symbolized by sacrifice. In these unions there were the same odd combinations often seen in the marital relations: a tall and a short man, a delicate sickly youth and a middle-aged man of powerful frame, a grave reticent nature and a spontaneous exuberant one. Yet in spite of these incongruities there was always the same blind unreasoning fidelity to each other. It is true that their zeal sometimes outran their discretion. There is a story extant that a San Francisco stranger, indulging in some free criticism of religious denominations, suddenly found himself sprawling upon the floor with an irate Kentuckian, revolver in hand, standing over him. When an explanation was demanded by the crowd, the Kentuckian pensively returned his revolver to his belt. "Well, *I* ain't got anythin' agin the stranger, but he said somethin' a minit ago agin Quakers, and I want him to understand that my *pardner* is a Quaker, and—a *peaceful man*!"

I should like to give some pictures of their domestic life, but the women were few and the family hearthstones and domestic altars still fewer. Of housewifely virtues the utmost was made; the model spouse invariably kept a boarding-house, and served her husband's guests. In rare cases, the woman who was a crown to her husband took in washing also.

There was a woman of this class who lived in a little mining-camp in the Sierras. Her husband was a Texan—a good-humored giant, who had won the respect of the camp probably quite as much by his amiable weakness as by his great physical power. She was an Eastern woman; had been, I think, a schoolmistress, and had lived in cities up to the time of her marriage and emigration. She was not, perhaps, personally attractive; she was plain and worn beyond her years, and her few personal accomplishments—a slight knowledge of French and Italian, music, the Latin classifi-

cation of plants, natural philosophy, and Blair's Rhetoric[24]—did
not tell upon the masculine inhabitants of Ringtail Cañon. Yet she
was universally loved, and Aunt Ruth, as she was called, or "Old
Ma'am Richards," was lifted into an idealization of the aunt,
mother, or sister of every miner in the camp. She reciprocated in a
thousand kindly ways, mending the clothes, ministering to the
sick, and even answering the long home letters of the men.

Presently she fell ill. Nobody knew exactly what was the matter with her, but she pined slowly away. When the burthen of her
household tasks was lifted from her shoulders, she took to long
walks, wandering over the hills, and was often seen upon the highest ridge at sunset, looking toward the east. Here at last she was
found senseless,—the result, it was said, of over exertion, and she
was warned to keep her house. So she kept her house, and even
went so far as to keep her bed. One day, to everybody's astonishment, she died. "Do you know what they say Ma'am Richards
died of?" said Yuba Bill to his partner. "The doctor says she died
of *nostalgia*," said Bill. "What blank thing is nostalgia?" asked the
other. "Well, it's a kind o' longin' to go to heaven!" Perhaps he
was right.

As a general thing the Argonauts were not burthened with
sentiment, and were utterly free from its more dangerous ally,
sentimentalism. They took a sardonic delight in stripping all
meretricious finery from their speech; they had a sarcastic fashion
of eliminating everything but the facts from poetic or imaginative
narrative. With all that terrible directness of statement which was
habitual to them, when they indulged in innuendo it was significantly cruel and striking. In the early days, Lynch law punished
horse-stealing with death. A man one day was arrested and
tried for this offense. After hearing the evidence, the jury duly retired to consult upon their verdict. For some reason—perhaps
from an insufficiency of proof, perhaps from motives of humanity,
perhaps because the census was already showing an alarming de-
crease in the male population—the jury showed signs of hesitation. The crowd outside became inpatient. After waiting an hour,
the ringleader put his head into the room and asked if the jury had
settled upon a verdict. "No," said the foreman. "Well," answered
the leader, "take your own time, gentlemen; only remember that
we're waitin' for this yer room to lay out the corpse in!"

Their humor was frequent, although never exuberant or spontaneous, and always contained a certain percentage of rude justice or morality under its sardonic exterior. The only ethical teaching of those days was through a joke or a sarcasm. While camps were moved by an epigram, the rude equity of Judge Lynch was swayed by a witticism. Even their pathos, which was more or less dramatic, partook of this quality. The odd expression, the quaint fancy, or even the grotesque gesture that rippled the surface consciousness with a smile, a moment later touched the depths of the heart with a sense of infinite sadness. They indulged sparingly in poetry and illustration, using only its rude, inchoate form of slang. Unlike the meaningless cues and catch-words of an older civilization, their slang was the condensed epigrammatic illustration of some fact, fancy, or perception. Generally it had some significant local derivation. The half-yearly drought brought forward the popular adjuration "dry up" to express the natural climax of evaporated fluency. "Played out" was a reminiscence of the gambling-table, and expressed that hopeless condition of affairs when even the operations of chance are suspended. To "take stock" in any statement, theory, or suggestion indicates a pecuniary degree of trustful credulity. One can hardly call that slang, even though it came from a gambler's lips, which gives such a vivid condensation of death and the reckoning hereafter as was conveyed in the expression, "handing in your checks." In those days the slang was universal; there was no occasion to which it seemed inconsistent. Thomas Starr King once told me that, after delivering a certain controversial sermon, he overheard the following dialogue between a parishioner and his friend. "Well," said the enthusiastic parishioner, referring to the sermon, "what do you think of King now?" "Think of him?" responded the friend, "why, he took every trick!"[25]

Sometimes, through the national habit of amusing exaggeration or equally grotesque understatement, certain words acquired a new significance. I remember the first night I spent in Virginia City was at a new hotel which had been but recently opened. After I had got comfortably to bed, I was aroused by the noise of scuffling and shouting below, punctuated by occasional pistol shots. In the morning I made my way to the bar-room, and found the landlord behind his counter with a bruised eye, a piece of court plaster extending from his cheek to his forehead, yet withal a pleasant smile upon his face. Taking my cue from this I said to him: "Well, landlord, you had rather a lively time here last night." "Yes," he replied, pleasantly. "It *was* rather a lively time!" "Do you often have such lively times in Virginia City?" I added, emboldened by his cheerfulness. "Well, no," he said, reflectively; "the fact is we've only just opened yer, and last night was about the first time that the boys seemed to be gettin' really *acquainted*!"

The man who objected to join in a bear hunt because "he hadn't lost any bears lately," and the man who replied to the tourist's question "if they grew any corn in that locality" by saying "not a d—d bit, in fact scarcely any," offered easy examples of this characteristic anti-climax and exaggeration. Often a flavor of gentle philosophy mingled with it. "In course I'd rather not drive a male team," said a teamster to me. "In course I'd rather run a bank or be President: but when you've lived as long as I have, stranger, you'll find that in this yer world a man don't always get his 'drathers.' " Often a man's trade or occupation lent a graphic power to his speech. On one occasion an engineer was relating to me the particulars of a fellow workman's death by consumption. "Poor Jim," he said, "he got to running slower and slower, until one day—he stopped on his center!" What a picture of the helpless hitch in this weary human machine! Sometimes the expression was borrowed from another's profession. At one time there was a difficulty in a surveyor's camp between the surveyor and a Chinaman. "If I was you," said a sympathizing teamster to the surveyor, "I'd jest take that chap and theodolite him out o' camp." Sometimes the slang was a mere echo of the formulas of some popular excitement or movement. During a camp-meeting in the mountains, a teamster who had been swearing at his cattle was rebuked for his impiety by a young woman who had just returned from the meeting. "Why, Miss," said the astonished teamster, "you don't call that swearing, do you? Why, you ought to hear Bill Jones exhort the impenitent mule!"

But can we entirely forgive the Argonaut for making his slang gratuitously permanent, for foisting upon posterity, who may forget these extenuating circumstances, such titles as "One Horse Gulch," "Poker Flat," "Greaser Cañon," "Fiddletown," "Murderer's Bar," and "Dead Broke"? The map of California is still

ghastly with this unhallowed christening. A tourist may well hesitate to write "Dead Broke" at the top of his letter, and any
stranger would be justified in declining an invitation to "Murderer's Bar." It seemed as if the early Californian took a sardonic
delight in the contrast which these names offered to the euphony
of the old Spanish titles. It is fortunate that with few exceptions
the counties of the State still bear the soft Castilian labials and
gentle vowels: Tuolumne, Tulare, Yolo, Calaveras, Sonoma,
Tehema, Siskyou, and Mendocino, to say nothing of the glorious
company of the Apostles who perpetually praise California
through the Spanish Catholic calendar. Yet wherever a saint
dropped a blessing, some sinner afterwards squatted with an epithet. Extremes often meet. The omnibuses in San Francisco used
to run from Happy Valley to the Mission Dolores.[26] You had to
go to Blaises first before you could get to Purissima. Yet I think
the ferocious directness of these titles was preferable to the pinch-
beck elegance of "Copperopolis," "Argentinia," the polyglot
monstrosities of "Oroville," of "Placerville," or the remarkable
sentiment of "Romeosburgh" and "Julietstown." Sometimes the
national tendency to abbreviation was singularly shown. "James-
town," near Sonora, was always known as "Jimtown,"[27] and "Mo-
quelumne Hill," after first suffering phonetic torture by being
spelt with a "k," was finally drawn and quartered and now appears
on the stage-coach as "Mok Hill." There were some names that
defied all conjecture. The Pioneer coaches changed horses at a
place called "Paradox." Why Paradox? No one could tell.

I wish I could say that the Spaniard fared any better than
his language at the hands of the Argonauts. He was called a
"Greaser," an unctuous reminiscence of the Mexican war, and applied erroneously to the Spanish Californian, who was *not* a Mexican. The pure blood of Castile ran in his veins. He held his lands
sometimes by royal patent of Charles V.[28] He was grave, simple,
and confiding. He accepted the Argonaut's irony as sincere, he
permitted him to squat on his lands, he allowed him to marry his
daughter. He found himself, in a few years, laughed at, landless,
and alone. In his sore extremity he entered into a defensive alliance
with some of his persecutors, and avenged himself after an extraordinary fashion. In all matters relating to early land grants he
was the evergreen witness; his was the only available memory, his

the only legal testimony, on the Coast. Perhaps strengthened by this repeated exercise, his memory became one of the most extraordinary, his testimony the most complete and corroborative, known to human experience. He recalled conversations, official orders, and precedents of fifty years ago as if they were matters of yesterday. He produced grants, *diseños*,[29] signatures, and letters with promptitude and despatch. He evolved evidence from his inner consciousness, and in less than three years Spanish land titles were lost in hopeless confusion and a cloud of witnesses. The wily Argonauts cursed the aptness of their pupil.

Socially he clung to his old customs. He had his regular *fandango*,[30] strummed his guitar, and danced the *sembicuaca*. He had his regular Sunday bull-fights after Mass. But the wily Argonaut introduced "breakdowns" in the *fandango*, substituted the banjo for the guitar, and Bourbon whiskey for *aquardiente*.[31] He even went so far as to interfere with the bull-fights, not so much from a sense of moral ethics as with a view to giving the bulls a show. On one or two occasions he substituted a grizzly bear, who not only instantly cleared the arena, but playfully wiped out the first two rows of benches beyond. He learned horsemanship from the Spaniard and—ran off his cattle.

Yet, before taking leave of the Spanish American, it is well to recall a single figure. It is that of the earliest pioneer known to Californian history. He comes to us toiling over a southern plain—an old man, weak, emaciated, friendless, and alone. He has left his weary muleteers and acolytes a league behind him, and has wandered on without scrip or wallet, bearing only a crucifix and a bell. It is a characteristic plain, one that tourists do not usually penetrate: scorched yet bleak, windswept, blasted and baked to its very foundations, and cracked into gaping chasms. As the pitiless sun goes down, the old man staggers forward and falls utterly exhausted. He lies there all night. Towards morning he is found by some Indians, a feeble, simple race, who in unconth kindness offer him food and drink. But before he accepts either, he rises to his knees, and there says matins and baptizes them in the Catholic faith. And then it occurs to him to ask them where he is, and he finds that he has penetrated into the unknown land. This was Padre Junipero Serra,[32] and the sun arose that morning on Christian California. Weighed by the usual estimates of success, his mission was a failure. The heathen stole his provisions and massacred his acolytes. It is said that the good fathers themselves sometimes confounded baptism and bondage, and laid the foundation of peonage; but in the bloodstained and tear-blotted chronicle of early California, there is no more heroic figure than the thin, travel-worn, self-centered, self-denying Franciscan friar.

If I have thus far refrained from eulogizing the virtues of another characteristic figure, it is because he came later. The Heathen Chinee was *not* an Argonaut. But he brought into the Argonaut's new life an odd conservatism. Quiet, calm, almost philosophic, but never obtrusive or aggressive, he never flaunted his three thousand years in the face of the men of to-day; he never obtruded his extensive mythology before men who were skeptical of even one God. He accepted at once a menial position with dignity and self-respect. He washed for the whole community, and made cleanliness an accessible virtue. He brought patience and novelty into the kitchen; he brought silence, obedience, and a certain degree of intelligence into the whole sphere of domestic service. He stood behind your chair, quiet, attentive, but uncommunicative. He waited upon you at table with the air of the man who, knowing himself superior, could not jeopardize his position. He worshipped the devil in your household with a frank sincerity and openness that shamed your own covert and feeble attempts in that direction. Although he wore your clothes, spoke your language, and imitated your vices, he was always involved in his own Celestial atmosphere. He consorted only with his fellows, consumed his own peculiar provisions, bought his goods of the Chinese companies, and when he died, his bones were sent to China! He left no track, trace, or imprint on the civilization. He claimed no civil right; he wanted no franchise. He took his regular beatings calmly; he submitted to scandalous extortion from state and individual with tranquility; he bore robbery and even murder with stoical fortitude. Perhaps it was well that he did. Christian civilization, which declared by statute that his testimony was valueless; which intimated by its practice that the same vices in a pagan were worse than in a Christian; which regarded the frailty of his women as being especially abominable and his own gambling propensities as something originally bad, taught him at least the Christian virtues of patience and resignation.

Did he ever get even with the Christian Argonauts? I am inclined to think that he did. Indeed, in some instances I may say that I know that he did. He had a universal, simple way of defrauding the customs. He filled the hollows of bamboo chairs with opium, and, sitting calmly on them, conversed with dignity with custom-house officials. He made the amplitude of his sleeve and trouser useful as well as ornamental on similar occasions. He evaded the state poll tax by taking the name and assuming the exact facial expression of some brother Celestial who had already paid. He turned his skill as a horticulturist to sinful account by investing rose bushes with imitations of that flower made out of carrots and turnips. He acquired Latin and Greek with peculative rather than scholastic intent, and borrowed fifty dollars from a Californian clergyman while he soothed his ear with the Homeric accents. But perhaps his most successful attempt at balancing his account with a Christian civilization was his career as a physician.

One day he opened a doctor's office in San Francisco. By the aid of clever confederates, miraculous cures were trumpeted through the land, until people began to flock to his healing ministration. His doorways were beset by an army of invalids. Two interpreters, like the angels in the old legend, listened night and day to the ills told by the people that crowded this Hygeian temple.[33] They translated into the common tongue the words of wisdom that fell from the oracular lips of this slant-eyed Apollo.[34] Doctor Lipotai was eminently successful. Presently, however, there were Chinese doctors on every corner. A sign with the proper monosyllables, a pig-tail and an interpreter, were the only stock in trade required. The pagan knew that no one would stop to reason. The ignorant heathen was aware that no one would stop to consider what superior opportunities the Chinese had for medical knowledge over the practitioners of his own land. This debased old idolater knew that these intelligent Christians would think that it might be *magic,* and so would come. And they did come. And he gave them green tea for tubercular consumption, ginger for aneurism, and made them smell punk for dropsy. The treatment was harmless, but wearisome. Suddenly, a well-known Oriental scholar published a list of the remedies ordinarily used in the Chinese medical practice. I regret to say that for obvious reasons I cannot repeat the unsavory list here. It was enough, however, to produce the ordinary symptoms of sea-sickness among the doctor's patients. The celestial star at once began to wane. The oracle ceased to be questioned. The sibyls got off their tripods. And Doctor Lipotai, with a half million in his pocket, returned to his native rice and the naïve simplicity of Chinese Camp.

And with this receding figure bringing up the rear of the procession, I close my review of the Argonauts of '49. In their rank and file there may be many who are personally known to some of my hearers. There may be gaps which the memory of others can supply. There are homes all over the world whose vacant places never can be filled; there are graves all over California on whose nameless mounds no one shall weep. I have said that it is not a pretty story. I should like to end it with a flourish of trumpets, but the band has gone on before, and the dust of the highway is beginning to hide them from my view. They are marching on to their city by the sea—to that great lodestone hill that Sindbad[35] saw, which they call "Lone Mountain." There, waiting at its base, one may fancy the Argo is still lying, and that when the last Argonaut shall have passed in, she too will spread her white wings and slip unnoticed through the Golden Gate that opens in the distance.

1882

The Rise of the 'Short Story'

As it has been the custom of good-natured reviewers to associate the present writer with the origin of the American 'short story,' he may have a reasonable excuse for offering the following reflections—partly the result of his own observations during the last thirty years, and partly from his experience in the introduction of this form of literature to the pages of the 'Western Magazine,' of which he was editor at the beginning of that period. But he is far from claiming the invention, or of even attributing its genesis to that particular occasion. The short story was familiar enough in form in America during the early half of the century; perhaps the proverbial haste of American life was some inducement to its brevity. It had been the medium through which some of the most characteristic work of the best American writers had won the approbation of the public. Poe[1]— a master of the art, as yet unsurpassed—had written; Longfellow and Hawthorne[2] had lent it the graces of the English classics. But it was not the American short story of to-day. It was not characteristic of American life, American habits, or American thought. It was not vital and instinct with the experience and observation of the average American; it made no attempt to follow his reasoning or to understand his peculiar form of expression—which it was apt to consider vulgar; it had no sympathy with those dramatic contrasts and surprises which are the wonders of American civilization; it took no account of the modifications of environment and of geographical limitations; indeed, it knew little of American geography. Of all that was distinctly American it was evasive—when it was not apologetic. And even when graced by the style of the best masters, it was distinctly provincial.

It would be easier to trace the causes which produced this than to assign any distinct occasion or period for the change. What was called American literature was still limited to English methods and upon English models. The best writers either wandered far afield for their inspiration, or, restricted to home material, were historical or legendary; artistically contemplative of their own country, but seldom observant. Literature abode on a scant fringe of the Atlantic seaboard, gathering the drift from other shores, and hearing the murmur of other lands rather than the voices of its own; it was either expressed in an artificial treatment of life in the cities, or, as with Irving,[3] was frankly satirical of provincial social ambition. There was much 'fine' writing; there were American Addisons, Steeles, and Lambs—there were provincial 'Spectators' and 'Tatlers.'[4] The sentiment was English. Even Irving in the pathetic sketch of 'The Wife,' echoed the style of 'Rosamund Gray.'[5] There were sketches of American life in the form of the English Essayists, with no attempt to understand the American character. The literary man had little sympathy with the rough and half-civilized masses who were making his country's history; if he used them at all it was as a foil to bring into greater relief his hero of the unmistakable English pattern. In his slavish imitation of the foreigner, he did not, however, succeed in retaining the foreigner's quick appreciation of novelty. It took an Englishman to first develop the humor and picturesqueness of American or 'Yankee' dialect, but Judge Haliburton succeeded better in reproducing 'Sam Slick's' speech than his character.[6] Dr. Judd's 'Margaret'[7]—one of the earlier American stories—although a vivid picture of New England farm life and strongly marked with local color, was in incident and treatment a mere imitation of English rural tragedy. It would, indeed, seem that while the American people had shaken off the English yoke in Government, politics, and national progression, while they had already startled the old world with invention and originality in practical ideas, they had never freed themselves from the trammels of English literary precedent. The old sneer 'Who reads an American book?'[8] might have been answered by another: 'There are no *American* books.'

But while the American literary imagination was still under the influence of English tradition, an unexpected factor was developing to diminish its power. It was *Humor*—of a quality as distinct and original as the country and civilization in which it was developed: It was at first noticeable in the anecdote or 'story,' and, after the fashion of such beginnings, was orally transmitted. It was common in the bar-rooms, the gatherings in the 'country store,' and finally at public meetings in the mouths of 'stump orators.' Arguments were clinched, and political principles illustrated, by 'a funny story.' It invaded even the camp meeting and pulpit. It at last received the currency of the public press. But wherever met it was so distinctly original and novel, so individual and characteristic, that it was at once known and appreciated abroad as 'an American story.' Crude at first, it received a literary polish in the press, but its dominant quality remained. It was concise and condensed, yet suggestive. It was delightfully extravagant—or a miracle of understatement. It voiced not only the dialect, but the habits of thought of a people or locality. It gave a new interest to slang. From a paragraph of a dozen lines it grew into a half column, but always retaining its conciseness and felicity of statement. It was a foe to prolixity of any kind, it admitted no fine writing nor affectation of style. It went directly to the point. It was burdened by no conscientiousness; it was often irreverent; it was devoid of all moral responsibility—but it was original! By degrees it developed character with its incident, often, in a few lines, gave a striking photograph of a community or a section, but always reached its conclusion without an unnecessary word. It became—and still exists—as an essential feature of newspaper literature. It was the parent of the American 'short story.'

But although these beginnings assumed more of a national character than American serious or polite literature, they were still purely comic, and their only immediate result was the development of a number of humorists in the columns of the daily press— all possessing the dominant national quality with a certain individuality of their own. For a while it seemed as if they were losing the faculty of story-telling in the elaboration of eccentric character—chiefly used as a vehicle for smart sayings, extravagant incident, or political satire. They were eagerly received by the public and in their day, were immensely popular, and probably were better known at home and abroad than the more academic but less national humorists of New York or Boston. The national note was always struck even in their individual variations, and the admirable portraiture of the shrewd and humorous showman in 'Artemus Ward'[9] survived his more mechanical bad spelling. Yet they did not invade the current narrative fiction; the short and long story-tellers went with their old-fashioned methods, their admirable morals, their well-worn sentiments, their colorless heroes and heroines of the first ranks of provincial society. Neither did social and political convulsions bring anything new in the way of Romance. The Mexican war gave us the delightful satires of Hosea Biglow,[10] but no dramatic narrative. The anti-slavery struggle before the War of the Rebellion produced a successful partisan political novel—on the old lines—with only the purely American characters of the Negro 'Topsy,' and the New England 'Miss Ophelia.'[11] The War itself, prolific as it was of poetry and eloquence—was barren of romance, except for Edward Everett Hale's artistic and sympathetic *The Man Without a Country*.[12] The tragedies enacted, the sacrifices offered, not only on the battlefield but in the division of families and households; the conflict of superb Quixotism and reckless gallantry against Reason and Duty fought out in quiet border farmhouses and plantations; the reincarnation of Puritan and Cavalier in a wild environment of trackless wastes, pestilential swamps, and rugged mountains; the patient endurance of both the conqueror and the conquered: all these found no echo in the romance of the period. Out of the battle smoke that covered half a continent drifted into the pages of magazines shadowy but correct figures of blameless virgins of the North—heroines or fashionable belles—habited as hospital nurses, bearing away the deeply wounded but more deeply misunderstood Harvard or Yale graduate lover who had rushed to bury his broken heart in the conflict. It seems almost incredible that, until the last few years, nothing worthy of that tremendous episode has been preserved by the pen of the romancer.

But if the war produced no characteristic American story it brought the literary man nearer his work. It opened to him distinct conditions of life in his own country, of which he had no previous conception; it revealed communities governed by customs and morals unlike his own, yet intensely human and American. The lighter side of some of these he had learned from the humorists before alluded to; the grim realities of war and the stress of circumstances had suddenly given them a pathetic or dramatic reality. Whether he had acquired this knowledge of them with a musket or a gilded strap on his shoulder, or whether he was later a peaceful 'carpet-bagger' into the desolate homes of the south and south-west, he knew something personally of their romantic and picturesque value in story. Many cultivated aspirants for literature, as well as many seasoned writers for the press, were among the volunteer soldiery. Again, the composition of the army was heterogeneous: regiments from the West rubbed shoulders with regiments from the East; spruce city clerks hobnobbed with back-woodsmen, and the student fresh from college shared his rations with the half-educated western farmer. The Union, for the first time, recognized its component parts; the natives knew each other. The literary man must have seen heroes and heroines where he had never looked for them, situations that he had never dreamt of. Yet it is a mortifying proof of the strength of inherited literary tra-ditions, that he never dared until quite recently to make a test of them. It is still more strange that he should have waited for the ini-tiative to be taken by a still more crude, wild, and more western civilization—that of California!

The gold discovery had drawn to the Pacific slope of the conti-nent a still more heterogeneous and remarkable population. The immigration of 1849 and 1850 had taken farmers from the plough, merchants from their desks, and students from their books, while every profession was represented in the motley crowd of gold-seekers. Europe and her colonies had contributed to swell these adventures—for adventures they were whatever their purpose; the risks were great, the journey long and difficult—the nearest came from a distance of over a thousand miles; that the men were necessarily pre-equipped with courage, faith, and endurance was a foregone conclusion. They were mainly young; a gray-haired man was a curiosity in the mines in the early days, and an object of rude respect and reverence. They were consequently free from the trammels of precedent or tradition in arranging their lives and making their rude homes. There was a singular fraternity in this ideal republic into which all men entered free and equal. Distinc-tion of previous position or advantages were unknown, even record and reputation for ill or good were of little benefit or em-barrassment to the possessor; men were accepted for what they ac-tually were, and what they could do in taking their part in the camp or settlement. The severest economy, the direst poverty, the most menial labor carried no shame nor disgrace with it; individ-ual success brought neither envy nor jealousy. What was one man's fortune to-day might be the luck of another to-morrow. Add to this Utopian simplicity of the people, the environment of magnificent scenery, a unique climate, and a vegetation that was marvellous in its proportions and spontaneity of growth; let it be further considered that the strongest relief was given to this picture by its setting among the crumbling ruins of early Spanish possession—whose monuments still existed in Mission and Presidio, and whose legitimate Castilian descendants still lived and moved in picturesque and dignified contrast to their energetic invaders—and it must be admitted that a condition of romantic and dramatic possibilities was created unrivalled in history.

But the earlier literature of the Pacific slope was, like that of the Atlantic seaboard, national and characteristic only in its humor. The local press sparkled with wit and satire, and, as in the East, developed its usual individual humorists. Of these should be mentioned the earliest pioneers of Californian humor—Lieut. Derby, a U.S. army engineer officer, author of a series of delightful extravagances known as the 'Squibob Papers,'[13] and the later and universally known 'Mark Twain,' who contributed 'The Jumping Frog of Calaveras' to the columns of the weekly press.[14] 'The San Francisco News Letter,' whose whilom contributor, Major Bierce, has since written some of the most graphic romances of the Civil War;[15] 'The Golden Era,' in which the present writer published his earlier sketches, and 'The Californian,' to which, as editor, in burlesque imitation of the enterprise of his journalistic betters, he contributed 'The Condensed Novels,' were the foremost literary weeklies.[16] These were all more or less characteristically American, but it was again remarkable that the more literary, romantic, and imaginative romances had no national flavor. The better remembered serious work in the pages of the only literary magazine 'The Pioneer,' was a romance of spiritualism and psychological study,[17] and a poem on the Chandos picture of Shakespeare![18]

With this singular experience before him, the present writer was called upon to take the editorial control of the 'Overland Monthly,' a much more ambitious magazine venture than had yet appeared in California.[19] The best writers had been invited to contribute to its pages. But in looking over his materials on preparing the first number, he was discouraged to find the same notable lack of characteristic fiction. There were good literary articles, sketches of foreign travel, and some essays in description of the natural resources of California—excellent from a commercial and advertising view-point. But he failed to discover anything of that wild and picturesque life which had impressed him, first as a truant schoolboy, and afterwards as a youthful schoolmaster among the mining population. In this perplexity he determined to attempt to make good the deficiency himself. He wrote 'The Luck of Roaring Camp.' However far short it fell of his ideal and his purpose, he conscientiously believed that he had painted much that 'he saw, and part of which he was,' that his subject and characters were distinctly Californian, as was equally his treatment of them. But an unexpected circumstance here intervened. The publication of the story was objected to by both printer and publisher, virtually for not being in the conventional line of subject, treatment, and morals! The introduction of the abandoned outcast mother of the foundling 'Luck,' and the language used by the characters, received a serious warning and protest. The writer was obliged to use his right as editor to save his unfortunate contribution from oblivion. When it appeared at last, he saw with consternation that the printer and publisher had really voiced the local opinion; that the press of California was still strongly dominated by the old conservatism and conventionalism of the East, and that when 'The Luck of Roaring Camp' was not denounced as 'improper' and 'corrupting,' it was coldly received as being 'singular' and 'strange.' A still more extraordinary instance of the 'provincial note' was struck in the criticism of a religious paper that the story was strongly 'unfavorable to immigration' and decidedly unprovocative of the 'investment of foreign capital.' However, its instantaneous and cordial acceptance as a new departure by the critics of the Eastern States and Europe enabled the writer to follow it with other stories of a like character. More than that, he was gratified to find a disposition on the part of his contributors to shake off their conservative trammels, and in an admirable and original sketch of a wandering circus attendant called 'Centrepole Bill,' he was delighted to recognize and welcome a convert.[20] The term 'imitators,' often used by the critics who, as previously stated, had claimed for the present writer the *invention* of this kind of literature, could not fairly apply to those who had cut loose from conventional methods, and sought to honestly describe the life around them, and he can only claim to have shown them that it could be done. How well it has since been done, what charm of individual flavor and style has been brought to it by such writers as Harris,[21] Cable,[22] Page,[23] Mark Twain in 'Huckleberry Finn,'[24] the author of the 'Prophet of the Great Smoky Mountains,'[25] and Miss Wilkins,[26] the average reader need not be told. It would seem evident, therefore, that the secret of the American short story was the treatment of characteristic American life, with absolute knowledge of its peculiarities and sympathy with its methods; with no fastidious ignoring of its habitual expression, or the inchoate poetry that may be found even hidden in its slang; with no moral determination except that which may be the legitimate outcome of the story itself; with no more elimination than may be necessary for the artistic conception, and never from the fear of the 'fetish' of conventionalism. Of such is the American short story of to-day—the germ of American literature to come.

July 1899

How I Went to the Mines

I HAD BEEN TWO YEARS in California before I ever thought of going to the mines, and my initiation into the vocation of gold digging was partly compulsory. The little pioneer settlement school,[1] of which I was the somewhat youthful and, I fear, the not over-competent master, was state-aided only to a limited extent; and as the bulk of its expense was borne by a few families in its vicinity, when two of them—representing perhaps a dozen children or pupils—one morning announced their intention of moving to a more prosperous and newer district, the school was incontinently closed.

In twenty-four hours I found myself destitute alike of my flock and my vocation. I am afraid I regretted the former the most. Some of the children I had made my companions and friends; and as I stood that bright May morning before the empty little bark-thatched schoolhouse in the wilderness, it was with an odd sensation that our little summer "play" at being schoolmaster and pupil was over. Indeed, I remember distinctly that a large hunk of gingerbread—a parting gift from a prize scholar a year older than myself—stood me in good stead in my future wanderings, for I was alone in the world at that moment and constitutionally improvident.

I had been frightfully extravagant even on my small income, spending much money on "boiled shirts," and giving as an excuse, which I since believe was untenable, that I ought to set an example in dress to my pupils. The result was that at this crucial moment I had only seven dollars in my pocket, five of which went to the purchase of a second-hand revolver, that I felt was necessary to signalize my abandonment of a peaceful vocation for one of greed and adventure.

For I had finally resolved to go to the mines and become a gold-digger. Other occupations and my few friends in San Francisco were expensively distant. The nearest mining district was forty miles away; the nearest prospect of aid was the hope of finding a miner whom I had casually met in San Francisco, and whom I shall call "Jim."[2] With only this name upon my lips I expected, like the deserted Eastern damsel in the ballad, to find my friend among the haunts of mining men. But my capital of two dollars would not allow the expense of stage-coach fare; I must walk to the mines, and I did.

I cannot clearly recall *how* I did it. The end of my first day's journey found me with blistered feet and the conviction that varnished leather shoes, however proper for the Master of Madrono Valley School in the exercise of his functions, were not suited to him when he was itinerant. Nevertheless, I clung to them as the last badge of my former life, carrying them in my hands when pain and pride made me at last forsake the frequented highway to travel barefooted in the trails.

I am afraid that my whole equipment was rather incongruous, and I remember that the few travelers I met on the road glanced at me with curiosity and some amusement. The odds and ends of my "pack"—a faded morocco dressing-case, an early gift from my mother, and a silver-handled riding-whip, also a gift—in juxtaposition with my badly rolled, coarse blue blanket and tin coffee-pot, were sufficiently provocative. My revolver, too, which would not swing properly in its holster from my hip, but worked around until it hung down in front like a Highlander's dirk, gave me considerable mortification.

A sense of pride, which kept me from arriving at my friend's cabin utterly penniless, forbade my seeking shelter and food at a wayside station. I ate the remainder of my gingerbread and camped out in the woods. To preclude any unnecessary sympathy, I may add that I was not at all hungry and had no sense of privation.

The loneliness that had once or twice come over me in meeting strangers on the traveled road, with whom I was too shy and proud to converse, vanished utterly in the sweet and silent companionship of the woods. I believe I should have felt my solitary vagabond condition greater in a strange hostelry or a crowded cabin. I heard the soft breathings of the lower life in the grass and ferns around me, saw the grave, sleepy stars above my head, and slept soundly, quite forgetting the pain of my blistered feet, or the handkerchiefs I had sacrificed for bandages.

In the morning, finding that I had emptied my water flask, I also found that I had utterly overlooked the first provision of camping—nearness to a water supply—and was fain to chew some unboiled coffee grains to flavor my scant breakfast, when I again took the trail.

I kept out of the main road as much as possible that day, although my detours cost me some extra walking, and by this time my bandaged feet had accumulated so much of the red dust that I suppose it would have been difficult to say what I wore on them. But in these excursions the balsamic air of the pines always revived me; the reassuring changes of scenery and distance viewed from those mountain ridges, the most wonderful I had ever seen, kept me in a state of excitement, and there was an occasional novelty of "outcrop" in the rocky trail that thrilled me with mysterious anticipation.

For this outcrop—a strange, white, porcelain-like rock, glinting like a tooth thrust through the red soil—was *quartz*, which I had been told indicated the vicinity of the gold-bearing district. Following these immaculate finger-posts, I came at about sunset upon a mile-long slope of pines still baking in the western glare, and beyond it, across an unfathomable abyss, a shelf in the opposite mountain-side, covered with white tents, looking not unlike the quartz outcrop I have spoken of. It was "the diggings"!

I do not know what I had expected, but I was conscious of some bitter disappointment. As I gazed, the sun sank below the serried summit of the slope on which I stood; a great shadow seemed to steal *up* rather than down the mountain, the tented shelf faded away, and a score of tiny diamond points of light, like stars, took its place. A cold wind rushed down the mountain-side, and I shivered in my thin clothes, drenched with the sweat of my day-long tramp.

It was nine o'clock when I reached the mining camp, itself only a fringe of the larger settlement beyond, and I had been on my feet since sunrise. Nevertheless, I halted at the outskirts, deposited my pack in the bushes, bathed my feet in a sluice of running water, so stained with the soil that it seemed to run blood, and, putting on my dreadful varnished shoes again, limped once more into respectability and the first cabin.

Here I found that my friend "Jim" was one of four partners on the "Gum Tree" claim, two miles on the other side of the settlement. There was nothing left for me but to push on to the "Magnolia Hotel," procure the cheapest refreshment and an hour's rest, and then limp as best I could to the "Gum Tree" claim.

I found the "Magnolia" a large wooden building, given over, in greater part, to an enormous drinking "saloon," filled with flashing mirrors and a mahogany bar. In the unimportant and stuffy little dining-room or restaurant, I selected some "fishballs and coffee," I think more with a view to cheapness and expedition than for their absolute sustaining power. The waiter informed me that it was possible that my friend "Jim" might be in the settlement, but that the barkeeper, who knew everything and everybody, could tell me or give me "the shortest cut to the claim."

From sheer fatigue I lingered at my meal, I fear, long past any decent limit, and then reentered the bar-room. It was crowded with miners and traders and a few smartly dressed professional-looking men. Here again my vanity led me into extravagance. I could not bear to address the important, white-shirt-sleeved and diamond-pinned barkeeper as a mere boyish suppliant for information. I was silly enough to demand a drink, and laid down, alas! another quarter.

I had asked my question, the barkeeper had handed me the decanter, and I had poured out the stuff with as much ease and grown-up confidence as I could assume, when a singular incident occurred. As it had some bearing upon my fortune, I may relate it here.

The ceiling of the saloon was supported by a half-dozen wooden columns, about eighteen inches square, standing in a line, parallel with the counter of the bar and about two feet from it. The front of the bar was crowded with customers, when suddenly, to my astonishment, they one and all put down their glasses and hurriedly backed into the spaces between the columns. At the same moment a shot was fired from the street through the large open doors that stood at right angles with the front of the counter and the columns.

The bullet raked and splintered the mouldings of the counter front, but with no other damage. The shot was returned from the upper end of the bar, and then for the first time I became aware that two men with leveled revolvers were shooting at each other through the saloon.

The bystanders in range were fully protected by the wooden columns; the barkeeper had "ducked" below the counter at the first shot. Six shots were exchanged by the duelists, but, as far as I could see, nobody was hurt. A mirror was smashed, and my glass had part of its rim carried cleanly away by the third shot and its contents spilt.

I had remained standing near the counter, and I presume I may have been protected by the columns. But the whole thing passed so quickly, and I was so utterly absorbed in its dramatic novelty, that I cannot recall having the slightest sensation of physical fear; indeed, I had been much more frightened in positions of less peril.

My only concern, and this was paramount, was that I might betray by any word or movement my youthfulness, astonishment, or unfamiliarity with such an experience. I think that any shy, vain schoolboy will understand this, and would probably feel as I did. So strong was this feeling, that while the sting of gunpowder was still in my nostrils I moved towards the bar, and, taking up my broken glass, said to the barkeeper, perhaps somewhat slowly and diffidently:

"Will you please fill me another glass? It's not my fault if this was broken."

The barkeeper, rising flushed and excited from behind the bar, looked at me with a queer smile, and then passed the decanter and a fresh glass. I heard a laugh and an oath behind me, and my cheeks flushed as I took a single gulp of the fiery spirit and hurried away.

But my blistered feet gave me a twinge of pain, and I limped on the threshold. I felt a hand on my shoulder, and a voice said quickly: "You ain't hurt, old man?" I recognized the voice of the man who had laughed, and responded quickly, growing more hot and scarlet, that my feet were blistered by a long walk, and that I was in a hurry to go to "Gum Tree" claim.

"Hold on," said the stranger. Preceding me to the street, he called to a man sitting in a buggy: "Drop him," pointing to me, "at

'Gum Tree' claim, and then come back here," helped me into the vehicle, clapped his hand on my shoulder, said to me enigmatically, "You'll do!" and quickly reentered the saloon.

It was only from the driver that I learned, during the drive, that the two combatants had quarreled a week before, had sworn to shoot each other "on sight," i.e., on their first accidental meeting, and that each "went armed." He added, disgustedly, that it was "mighty bad shooting," to which I, in my very innocence of these lethal weapons, and truthfulness to my youthful impressions, agreed!

I said nothing else of my own feelings, and, indeed, soon forgot them; for I was nearing the end of my journey, and *now,* for the first time, although I believe it a common experience of youth, I began to feel a doubt of the wisdom of my intentions. During my long tramp, and in the midst of my privations, I had never doubted it; but now, as I neared "Jim's" cabin, my youthfulness and inefficiency and the extravagance of my quest of a mere acquaintance for aid and counsel came to me like a shock. But it was followed by a greater one. When at last I took leave of my driver and entered the humble little log cabin of the "Gum Tree Company," I was informed that "Jim" only a few days before had given up his partnership and gone to San Francisco.

Perhaps there was something in my appearance that showed my weariness and disappointment, for one of the partners dragged out the only chair in the cabin—he and the other partners had been sitting on boxes tilted on end—and offered it to me, with the inevitable drink. With this encouragement, I stammered out my story. I think I told the exact truth. I was too weary to even magnify my acquaintance with the absent "Jim."

They listened without comment. I dare say they had heard the story before. I am quite convinced they had each gone through a harder experience than mine. Then occurred what I believe could have occurred only in California in that age of simplicity and confidence. Without a word of discussion among themselves, without a word of inquiry as to myself, my character or prospects, they offered me the vacant partnership "to try."

In any event I was to stay there until I could make up my mind. As I was scarcely able to stand, one of them volunteered to fetch my pack from its "cache" in the bushes four miles away; and then,

to my astonishment, conversation instantly turned upon other
topics—literature, science, philosophy, everything but business
and practical concerns. Two of the partners were graduates of a
Southern college and the other a bright young farmer.

I went to bed that night in the absent Jim's bunk, one-fourth
owner of a cabin and a claim I knew nothing of. As I looked about
me at the bearded faces of my new partners, although they were
all apparently only a few years older than myself, I wondered if
we were not "playing" at being partners in "Gum Tree" claim, as I
had played at being schoolmaster in Madrono Valley.

When I awoke late the next morning and stared around the
empty cabin, I could scarcely believe that the events of the preceding night were not a dream. My pack, which I had left four miles
away, lay at my feet. By the truthful light of day I could see that
I was lying apparently in a parallelogram of untrimmed logs,
between whose interstices, here and there, the glittering sunlight
streamed.

A roof of bark thatch, on which a woodpecker was foolishly
experimenting, was above my head; four wooden "bunks," like a
ship's berth, were around the two sides of the room; a table, a
chair, and three stools, fashioned from old packing-boxes, were
the only furniture. The cabin was lighted by a window of two
panes let into one gable, by the open door, and by a chimney of
adobe, that entirely filled the other gable, and projected scarcely a
foot above the apex of the roof.

I was wondering whether I had not strayed into a deserted
cabin, a dreadful suspicion of the potency of the single drink I had
taken in the saloon coming over me, when my three partners entered. Their explanation was brief. I had needed rest, they had delicately forborne to awaken me before. It was twelve o'clock! My
breakfast was ready. They had something "funny" to tell me! I
was a hero!

My conduct during the shooting affray at the "Magnolia" had
been discussed, elaborately exaggerated, and interpreted by eye-
witnesses; the latest version being that I had calmly stood at the
bar, coolly demanding to be served by the crouching barkeeper,
while the shots were being fired! I am afraid even my new friends
put down my indignant disclaimer to youthful bashfulness, but,
seeing that I was distressed, they changed the subject.

Yes! I might, if I wanted, do some "prospecting" that day. Where? Oh, anywhere on ground not already claimed; there were hundreds of square miles to choose from. What was I to do? What! was it possible I had never prospected before? No! Nor dug gold at all? Never!

I saw them glance hurriedly at each other; my heart sank, until I noticed that their eyes were eager and sparkling! Then I learned that my ignorance was blessed! Gold miners were very superstitious; it was one of their firm beliefs that "luck" would inevitably follow the *first* essay of the neophyte or "greenhorn." This was called "nigger luck"; i.e., the inexplicable good fortune of the inferior and incompetent. It was not very complimentary to myself, but in my eagerness to show my gratitude to my new partners I accepted it.

I dressed hastily, and swallowed my breakfast of coffee, salt pork, and "flapjacks." A pair of old deerskin moccasins, borrowed from a squaw who did the camp washing, was a luxury to my blistered feet; and, equipped with a pick, a long-handled shovel, and a prospecting-pan, I demanded to be led at once to my field of exploit. But I was told that this was impossible; I must find it myself, alone, or the charm would be broken!

I fixed upon a grassy slope, about two hundred yards from the cabin, and limped thither. The slope faced the magnificent *cañon* and the prospect I had seen the day before from the further summit. In my vivid recollection of that eventful morning I quite distinctly remember that I was, nevertheless, so entranced with the exterior "prospect" that for some moments I forgot the one in the ground at my feet. Then I began to dig.

My instructions were to fill my pan with the dirt taken from as large an area as possible near the surface. In doing this I was sorely tempted to dig lower in search of more hidden treasure, and in one or two deeper strokes of my pick I unearthed a bit of quartz with little seams or veins that glittered promisingly. I put them hopefully in my pocket, but duly filled my pan. This I took, not without some difficulty, owing to its absurd weight, to the nearest sluice-box, and, as instructed, tilted my pan in the running water.

As I rocked it from side to side, in a surprisingly short time the lighter soil of deep red color was completely washed away, leaving a glutinous clayey pudding mixed with small stones, like plums.

Indeed, there was a fascinating reminiscence of "dirt pies" in this boyish performance. The mud, however, soon yielded to the flowing water, and left only the stones and "black sand." I removed the former with my fingers, retaining only a small, flat, pretty, disk-like stone, heavier than the others—it looked like a blackened coin—and this I put in my pocket with the quartz. Then I proceeded to wash away the black sand.

I must leave my youthful readers to imagine my sensations when at last I saw a dozen tiny star-points of gold adhering to the bottom of the pan! They were so small that I was fearful of washing further, lest they should wash away. It was not until later that I found that their specific gravity made that almost impossible. I ran joyfully to where my partners were at work, holding out my pan.

"Yes, he's got the color," said one blandly. "I knew it."

I was disappointed. "Then I haven't struck it?" I said hesitatingly.

"Not in *this* pan. You've got about a quarter of a dollar here."

My face fell. "But," he continued smilingly, "you've only to get that amount in four pans, and you've made your daily 'grub.' "

"And that's all," added the other, "that we, or indeed *any one* on this hill, have made for the last six months!"

This was another shock to me. But I do not know whether I was as much impressed by it as by the perfect good humor and youthful unconcern with which it was uttered. Still, I was disappointed in my first effort. I hesitatingly drew the two bits of quartz from my pocket.

"I found them," I said. "They look as if they had some metal in them. See how it sparkles."

My partner smiled. "Iron pyrites," he said; "but what's that?" he added quickly, taking the little disk-like stone from my hand. "Where did you get this?"

"In the same hole. Is it good for anything?"

He did not reply to me, but turned to his two other partners, who had eagerly pressed around him. "Look!"

He laid the fragment on another stone, and gave it a smart blow with the point of his pick. To my astonishment it did not crumble or break, but showed a little dent from the pick point that was bright yellow!

I had no time, nor indeed need, to ask another question. "Run for your barrow!" he said to one. "Write out a 'Notice,' and bring the stakes," to the other; and the next moment, forgetful of my blistered feet, we were flying over to the slope. A claim was staked out, the "Notice" put up, and we all fell to work to load up our wheelbarrow. We carried four loads to the sluice-boxes before we began to wash.

The nugget I had picked up was worth about twelve dollars. We carried many loads; we worked that day and the next, hopefully, cheerfully, and without weariness. Then we worked at the claim daily, dutifully, and regularly for three weeks. We sometimes got "the color," we sometimes didn't, but we nearly always got enough for our daily "grub." We laughed, joked, told stories, "spouted poetry," and enjoyed ourselves as in a perpetual picnic. But that twelve-dollar nugget was the first and last "strike" we made on the new "Tenderfoot" claim.

Nov. 1899

Bohemian Days in San Francisco

IT IS BUT JUST to the respectable memory of San Francisco that in these vagrant recollections I should deprecate at once any suggestion that the levity of my title described its dominant tone at any period of my early experiences. On the contrary, it was a singular fact that while the rest of California was swayed by an easy, careless unconventionalism, or swept over by waves of emotion and sentiment, San Francisco preserved an intensely material and practical attitude, and even a certain austere morality. I do not, of course, allude to the brief days of '49, when it was a straggling beach of huts and stranded hulks, but to the earlier stages of its development into the metropolis of California. Its first tottering steps in that direction were marked by a distinct gravity and decorum. Even during the period when the revolver settled small private difficulties, and Vigilance Committees adjudicated larger public ones, an unmistakable seriousness and respectability was the ruling sign of its governing class. It was not improbable that under the reign of the Committee the lawless and vicious class were more appalled by the moral spectacle of several thousand blackcoated, serious-minded business men in embattled procession than by mere force of arms, and one "suspect"—a prizefighter—is known to have committed suicide in his cell after confrontation with his grave and passionless shopkeeping judges. Even that peculiar quality of Californian humor which was apt to mitigate the extravagances of the revolver and the uncertainties of poker had no place in the decorous and responsible utterance of San Francisco. The press was sober, materialistic, practical—when it was not severely admonitory of existing evil; the few smaller papers that indulged in levity were considered libelous and improper. Fancy was displaced by heavy articles on the revenues of the State and inducements to the investment of capital. Local news was under an implied censorship which suppressed anything that

might tend to discourage timid or cautious capital. Episodes of romantic lawlessness or pathetic incidents of mining life were carefully edited—with the comment that these things belonged to the
past, and that life and property were now "as safe in San Francisco
as in New York or London."

Wonder-loving visitors in quest of scenes characteristic of the
civilization were coldly snubbed with this assurance. Fires, floods,
and even seismic convulsions were subjected to a like grimly materialistic optimism. I have a vivid recollection of a ponderous editorial[1] on one of the severer earthquakes, in which it was asserted
that only the *unexpectedness* of the onset prevented San Francisco
from meeting it in a way that would be deterrent of all future at-
tacks. The unconsciousness of the humor was only equaled by the
gravity with which it was received by the whole business community. Strangely enough, this grave materialism flourished side by
side with—and was even sustained by—a narrow religious strict-
ness more characteristic of the Pilgrim Fathers of a past century
than the Western pioneers of the present. San Francisco was early
a city of churches and church organizations to which the leading
men and merchants belonged. The lax Sundays of the dying Spanish race seemed only to provoke a revival of the rigors of the Puritan Sabbath. With the Spaniard and his Sunday afternoon bullfight
scarcely an hour distant, the San Francisco pulpit thundered
against Sunday picnics. One of the popular preachers,[2] declaiming
upon the practice of Sunday dinner-giving, averred that when he
saw a guest in his best Sunday clothes standing shamelessly upon
the doorstep of his host, he felt like seizing him by the shoulder
and dragging him from that threshold of perdition.

Against the actual heathen the feeling was even stronger, and
reached its climax one Sunday when a Chinaman was stoned to
death[3] by a crowd of children returning from Sunday-school. I am
offering these examples with no ethical purpose, but merely to indicate a singular contradictory condition which I do not think
writers of early Californian history have fairly recorded. It is not
my province to suggest any theory for these appalling exceptions
to the usual good-humored lawlessness and extravagance of the
rest of the State. They may have been essential agencies to the
growth and evolution of the city. They were undoubtedly sincere.
The impressions I propose to give of certain scenes and incidents

of my early experience must, therefore, be taken as purely personal and Bohemian, and their selection as equally individual and vagrant. I am writing of what interested me at the time, though not perhaps of what was more generally characteristic of San Francisco.

I had been there a week—an idle week, spent in listless outlook for employment; a full week in my eager absorption of the strange life around me and a photographic sensitiveness to certain scenes and incidents of those days, which start out of my memory today as freshly as the day they impressed me.

One of these recollections is of "steamer night," as it was called,—the night of "steamer day,"—preceding the departure of the mail steamship with the mails for "home." Indeed, at that time San Francisco may be said to have lived from steamer day to steamer day; bills were made due on that day, interest computed to that period, and accounts settled. The next day was the turning of a new leaf: another essay to fortune, another inspiration of energy. So recognized was the fact that even ordinary changes of condition, social and domestic, were put aside until *after* steamer day. "I'll see what I can do after next steamer day" was the common cautious or hopeful formula. It was the "Saturday night" of many a wage-earner—and to him a night of festivity. The thoroughfares were animated and crowded; the saloons and theaters full. I can recall myself at such times wandering along the City Front, as the business part of San Francisco was then known. Here the lights were burning all night, the first streaks of dawn finding the merchants still at their counting-house desks. I remember the dim lines of warehouses lining the insecure wharves of rotten piles, half filled in—that had ceased to be wharves, but had not yet become streets,—their treacherous yawning depths, with the uncertain gleam of tarlike mud below, at times still vocal with the lap and gurgle of the tide. I remember the weird stories of disappearing men found afterward imbedded in the ooze in which they had fallen and gasped their life away. I remember the two or three ships, still left standing where they were beached a year or two before, built in between warehouses, their bows projecting into the roadway. There was the dignity of the sea and its boundless freedom in their beautiful curves, which the abutting houses could not destroy, and even something of the sea's loneliness in the far-spaced ports and cabin windows lit up by the lamps of the prosaic landsmen who plied their trades behind them. One of these ships, transformed into, a hotel, retained its name, the Niantic,[4] and part of its characteristic interior unchanged. I remember these ships' old tenants—the rats—who had increased and multiplied to such an extent that at night they fearlessly crossed the wayfarer's path at every turn, and even invaded the gilded saloons of Montgomery Street. In the Niantic their pit-a-pat was met on every staircase, and it was said that sometimes in an excess of sociability they accompanied the traveler to his room. In the early "cloth-and-papered" houses—so called because the ceilings were not plastered, but simply covered by stretched and whitewashed cloth—their scamperings were plainly indicated in zigzag movements of the sagging cloth, or they became actually visible by finally dropping through the holes they had worn in it! I remember the house whose foundations were made of boxes of plug tobacco[5]—part of a jettisoned cargo—used instead of more expensive lumber; and the adjacent warehouse where the trunks of the early and forgotten "forty-niners" were stored, and—never claimed by their dead or missing owners—were finally sold at auction. I remember the strong breath of the sea over all, and the constant onset of the trade winds which helped to disinfect the deposit of dirt and grime, decay and wreckage, which were stirred up in the later evolutions of the city.

Or I recall, with the same sense of youthful satisfaction and unabated wonder, my wanderings through the Spanish Quarter, where three centuries of quaint customs, speech, and dress were still preserved; where the proverbs of Sancho Panza were still spoken in the language of Cervantes,[6] and the high-flown illusions of the La Manchian knight still a part of the Spanish Californian hidalgo's dream. I recall the more modern "Greaser," or Mexican—his index finger steeped in cigarette stains; his velvet jacket and his crimson sash; the many-flounced skirt and lace manta of his women, and their caressing intonations—the one musical utterance of the whole hard-voiced city. I suppose I had a boy's digestion and bluntness of taste in those days, for the combined odor of tobacco, burned paper, and garlic, which marked that melodious breath, did not affect me.

Perhaps from my Puritan training I experienced a more fearful

joy in the gambling saloons. They were the largest and most com-
fortable, even as they were the most expensively decorated rooms
in San Francisco. Here again the gravity and decorum which I
have already alluded to were present at that earlier period—
though perhaps from concentration of another kind. People
staked and lost their last dollar with a calm solemnity and a resignation that was almost Christian. The oaths, exclamations, and
feverish interruptions which often characterized more dignified
assemblies were absent here. There was no room for the lesser
vices; there was little or no drunkenness; the gaudily dressed and
painted women who presided over the wheels of fortune or performed on the harp and piano attracted no attention from those
ascetic players. The man who had won ten thousand dollars and
the man who had lost everything rose from the table with equal silence and imperturbability. *I* never witnessed any tragic sequel to
those losses; *I* never heard of any suicide on account of them. Neither can I recall any quarrel or murder directly attributable to this
kind of gambling. It must be remembered that these public games
were chiefly rouge et noir, monté, faro, or roulette, in which the
antagonist was Fate, Chance, Method, or the impersonal "bank,"
which was supposed to represent them all; there was no individual
opposition or rivalry; nobody challenged the decision of the
"croupier," or dealer.

I remember a conversation at the door of one saloon which was
as characteristic for its brevity as it was a type of the prevailing
stoicism. "Hello!" said a departing miner, as he recognized a
brother miner coming in, "when did you come down?" "This
morning," was the reply. "Made a strike on the bar?" suggested
the first speaker. "You bet!" said the other, and passed in. I
chanced an hour later to be at the same place as they met again—
their relative positions changed. "Hello! Whar now?" said the in-
comer. "Back to the bar." "Cleaned out?" "You bet!" Not a word
more explained a common situation.

My first youthful experience at those tables was an accidental
one. I was watching roulette one evening, intensely absorbed in
the mere movement of the players. Either they were so preoccupied with the game, or I was really older looking than my actual
years, but a bystander laid his hand familiarly on my shoulder, and
said, as to an ordinary *habitué*,[7] "Ef you're not chippin' in your-

self, pardner, s'pose you give *me* a show." Now I honestly believe
that up to that moment I had no intention, nor even a desire, to
try my own fortune. But in the embarrassment of the sudden address I put my hand in my pocket, drew out a coin, and laid it,
with an attempt at carelessness, but a vivid consciousness that I
was blushing, upon a vacant number. To my horror I saw that I
had put down a large coin—the bulk of my possessions! I did not
flinch, however; I think any boy who reads this will understand
my feeling; it was not only my coin but my manhood at stake. I
gazed with a miserable show of indifference at the players, at the
chandelier—anywhere but at the dreadful ball spinning round the
wheel. There was a pause; the game was declared, the rake rattled
up and down, but still I did not look at the table. Indeed, in my inexperience of the game and my embarrassment, I doubt if I should
have known if I had won or not. I had made up my mind that I
should lose, but I must do so like a man, and, above all, without
giving the least suspicion that I was a greenhorn. I even affected to
be listening to the music. The wheel spun again; the game was declared, the rake was busy, but I did not move. At last the man I
had displaced touched me on the arm and whispered, "Better
make a straddle and divide your stake this time." I did not understand him, but as I saw he was looking at the board, I was obliged
to look, too. I drew back dazed and bewildered! Where my coin
had lain a moment before was a glittering heap of gold.

My stake had doubled, quadrupled, and doubled again. I did
not know how much then—I do not know now—it may have
been not more than three or four hundred dollars—but it dazzled
and frightened me. "Make your game, gentlemen," said the
croupier monotonously. I thought he looked at me—indeed,
everybody seemed to be looking at me—and my companion repeated his warning. But here I must again appeal to the boyish
reader in defense of my idiotic obstinacy. To have taken advice
would have shown my youth. I shook my head—I could not trust
my voice. I smiled, but with a sinking heart, and let my stake remain. The ball again sped round the wheel, and stopped. There
was a pause. The croupier indolently advanced his rake and swept
my whole pile with others into the bank! I had lost it all. Perhaps
it may be difficult for me to explain why I actually felt relieved,
and even to some extent triumphant, but I seemed to have asserted

my grown-up independence—possibly at the cost of reducing the number of my meals for days; but what of that! I was a man! I wish I could say that it was a lesson to me. I am afraid it was not. It was true that I did not gamble again, but then I had no especial desire to—and there was no temptation. I am afraid it was an incident without a moral. Yet it had one touch characteristic of the period which I like to remember. The man who had spoken to me, I think, suddenly realized, at the moment of my disastrous *coup,* the fact of my extreme youth. He moved toward the banker, and leaning over him whispered a few words. The banker looked up, half impatiently, half kindly—his hand straying tentatively toward the pile of coin. I instinctively knew what he meant, and, summoning my determination, met his eyes with all the indifference I could assume, and walked away.

I had at that period a small room at the top of a house owned by a distant relation—a second or third cousin, I think. He was a man of independent and original character, had a Ulyssean experience of men and cities, and an old English name of which he was proud. While in London he had procured from the Heralds' College his family arms, whose crest was stamped upon a quantity of plate he had brought with him to California. The plate, together with an exceptionally good cook, which he had also brought, and his own epicurean tastes, he utilized in the usual practical Californian fashion by starting a rather expensive half-club, half-restaurant in the lower part of the building—which he ruled somewhat autocratically, as became his crest. The restaurant was too expensive for me to patronize, but I saw many of its frequenters as well as those who had rooms at the club. They were men of very distinct personality; a few celebrated, and nearly all notorious. They represented a Bohemianism—if such it could be called—less innocent than my later experiences. I remember, however, one handsome young fellow whom I used to meet occasionally on the staircase, who captured my youthful fancy. I met him only at midday, as he did not rise till late, and this fact, with a certain scrupulous elegance and neatness in his dress, ought to have made me suspect that he was a gambler. In my inexperience it only invested him with a certain romantic mystery.

One morning as I was going out to my very early breakfast at a cheap Italian café on Long Wharf, I was surprised to find him also descending the staircase. He was scrupulously dressed even at that early hour, but I was struck by the fact that he was all in black, and his slight figure, buttoned to the throat in a tightly fitting frock coat, gave, I fancied, a singular melancholy to his pale Southern face. Nevertheless, he greeted me with more than his usual serene cordiality, and I remembered that he looked up with a half-puzzled, half-amused expression at the rosy morning sky as he walked a few steps with me down the deserted street. I could not help saying that I was astonished to see him up so early, and he admitted that it was a break in his usual habits, but added with a smiling significance I afterwards remembered that it was "an even chance if he did it again." As we neared the street corner a man in a buggy drove up impatiently. In spite of the driver's evident haste, my handsome acquaintance got in leisurely, and, lifting his glossy hat to me with a pleasant smile, was driven away. I have a very lasting recollection of his face and figure as the buggy disappeared down the empty street. I never saw him again. It was not until a week later that I knew that an hour after he left me that morning he was lying dead in a little hollow behind the Mission Dolores—shot through the heart in a duel for which he had risen so early.

I recall another incident of that period, equally characteristic, but happily less tragic in sequel. I was in the restaurant one morning talking to my cousin when a man entered hastily and said something to him in a hurried whisper. My cousin contracted his eyebrows and uttered a suppressed oath. Then with a gesture of warning to the man he crossed the room quietly to a table where a regular *habitué* of the restaurant was lazily finishing his breakfast. A large silver coffee-pot with a stiff wooden handle stood on the table before him. My cousin leaned over the guest familiarly and apparently made some hospitable inquiry as to his wants, with his hand resting lightly on the coffee-pot handle. Then—possibly because, my curiosity having been excited, I was watching him more intently than the others—*I* saw what probably no one else saw— that he deliberately upset the coffee-pot and its contents over the guest's shirt and waistcoat. As the victim sprang up with an exclamation, my cousin overwhelmed him with apologies for his carelessness, and, with protestations of sorrow for the accident, actually insisted upon dragging the man upstairs into his own private room, where he furnished him with a shirt and waistcoat of his own. The side door had scarcely closed upon them, and I was still lost in wonder at what I had seen, when a man entered from the street. He was one of the desperate set I have already spoken of, and thoroughly well known to those present. He cast a glance around the room, nodded to one or two of the guests, and then walked to a side table and took up a newspaper. I was conscious at once that a singular constraint had come over the other guests—a nervous awkwardness that at last seemed to make itself known to the man himself, who, after an affected yawn or two, laid down the paper and walked out.

"That was a mighty close call," said one of the guests with a sigh of relief.

"You bet! And that coffee-pot spill was the luckiest kind of accident for Peters," returned another.

"For both," added the first speaker, "for Peters was armed too, and would have seen him come in!"

A word or two explained all. Peters and the last comer had quarreled a day or two before, and had separated with the intention to "shoot on sight," that is, wherever they met,—a form of duel common to those days. The accidental meeting in the restaurant would have been the occasion, with the usual sanguinary consequence, but for the word of warning given to my cousin by a passer-by who knew that Peters' antagonist was coming to the restaurant to look at the papers. Had my cousin repeated the warning to Peters himself he would only have prepared him for the conflict—which he would not have shirked—and so precipitated the affray.

The ruse of upsetting the coffee-pot, which everybody but myself thought an accident, was to get him out of the room before the other entered. I was too young then to venture to intrude upon my cousin's secrets, but two or three years afterwards I taxed him with the trick and he admitted it regretfully. I believe that a strict interpretation of the "code" would have condemned his act as unsportsmanlike, if not *unfair!*

I recall another incident connected with the building equally characteristic of the period. The United States Branch Mint stood very near it, and its tall, factory-like chimneys overshadowed my cousin's roof. Some scandal had arisen from an alleged leakage of gold in the manipulation of that metal during the various processes of smelting and refining. One of the excuses offered was the volatilization of the precious metal and its escape through the draft of the tall chimneys. All San Francisco laughed at this explanation until it learned that a corroboration of the theory had been established by an assay of the dust and grime of the roofs in the vicinity of the Mint. These had yielded distinct traces of gold. San Francisco stopped laughing, and that portion of it which had roofs in the neighborhood at once began prospecting. Claims were staked out on these airy placers, and my cousin's roof, being the very next one to the chimney, and presumably "in the lead," was disposed of to a speculative company for a considerable sum. I remember my cousin telling me the story—for the occurrence was quite recent—and taking me with him to the roof to explain it, but I am afraid I was more attracted by the mystery of the closely guarded building, and the strangely tinted smoke which arose from this temple where money was actually being "made," than by anything else. Nor did I dream as I stood there—a very lanky, open-mouthed youth—that only three or four years later I should be the secretary of its superintendent.[8] In my more adventurous ambition I am afraid I would have accepted the suggestion halfheartedly. Merely to have helped to stamp the gold which other people had adventurously found was by no means a part of my youthful dreams.

At the time of these earlier impressions the Chinese had not yet become the recognized factors in the domestic and business economy of the city which they had come to be when I returned from the mines three years later. Yet they were even then a more remarkable and picturesque contrast to the bustling, breathless, and brand-new life of San Francisco than the Spaniard. The latter seldom flaunted his faded dignity in the principal thoroughfares. "John" was to be met everywhere. It was a common thing to see a long file of sampan coolies carrying their baskets slung between them, on poles, jostling a modern, well-dressed crowd in Montgomery Street, or to get a whiff of their burned punk in the side streets; while the road leading to their temporary burial-ground at Lone Mountain was littered with slips of colored paper scattered from their funerals. They brought an atmosphere of the Arabian Nights into the hard, modern civilization; their shops—not always confined at that time to a Chinese quarter—were replicas of the bazaars of Canton and Peking, with their quaint display of little dishes on which tidbits of food delicacies were exposed for sale, all of the dimensions and unreality of a doll's kitchen or a child's housekeeping.

They were a revelation to the Eastern immigrant, whose preconceived ideas of them were borrowed from the ballet or pantomime; they did not wear scalloped drawers and hats with jingling bells on their points, nor did I ever see them dance with their forefingers vertically extended. They were always neatly dressed, even the commonest of coolies, and their festive dresses were marvels. As traders they were grave and patient; as servants they were sad and civil,[9] a and all were singularly infantine in their natural simplicity. The living representatives of the oldest civilization in the world, they seemed like children. Yet they kept their beliefs and sympathies to themselves, never fraternizing with the *fanqui*, or foreign devil, or losing their singular racial qualities. They indulged in their own peculiar habits; of their social and inner life, San Francisco knew but little and cared less. Even at this early period, and before I came to know them more intimately, I remember an incident of their daring fidelity to their own customs that was accidentally revealed to me. I had become acquainted with a Chinese youth of about my own age, as I imagined,—although from mere outward appearance it was generally impossible to judge of a Chinaman's age between the limits of seventeen and forty years,—and he had, in a burst of confidence, taken me to see some characteristic sights in a Chinese warehouse within a stone's throw of the Plaza. I was struck by the singular circumstance that while the warehouse was an erection of wood in the ordinary hasty Californian style, there were certain brick and stone divisions in its interior, like small rooms or closets, evidently added by the Chinamen tenants. My companion stopped before a long, very narrow entrance, a mere longitudinal slit in the brick wall, and with a wink of infantine deviltry motioned me to look inside. I did so, and saw a room, really a cell, of fair height but scarcely six feet square, and barely able to contain a rude, slanting couch of stone covered with matting, on which lay, at a painful angle, a richly dressed Chinaman. A single glance at his dull, staring, abstracted eyes and half-opened mouth showed me he was in an opium trance. This was not in itself a novel sight, and I was moving away when I was suddenly startled by the appearance of his hands, which were stretched helplessly before him on his body, and at first sight seemed to be in a kind of wicker cage.

I then saw that his finger-nails were seven or eight inches long, and were supported by bamboo splints. Indeed, they were no longer human nails, but twisted and distorted quills, giving him the appearance of having gigantic claws. "Velly big Chinaman," whispered my cheerful friend; "first-chop man—high classee—no can washee—no can eat—no dlinke, no catchee him own glub allee same nothee man—China boy must catchee glub for him, allee time! Oh, him first-chop man—you bettee!"

I had heard of this singular custom of indicating caste before, and was amazed and disgusted, but I was not prepared for what followed. My companion, evidently thinking he had impressed me, grew more reckless as showman, and saying to me, "Now me showee you one funny thing—heap makee you laugh," led me hurriedly across a little courtyard swarming with chickens and rabbits, when he stopped before another inclosure. Suddenly brushing past an astonished Chinaman who seemed to be standing guard, he thrust me into the inclosure in front of a most extraordinary object. It was a Chinaman, wearing a huge, square, wooden frame fastened around his neck like a collar, and fitting so tightly and rigidly that the flesh rose in puffy weals around his cheeks. He was chained to a post, although it was as impossible for him to have escaped with his wooden cage through the narrow doorway as it was for him to lie down and rest in it. Yet I am bound to say that his eyes and face expressed nothing but apathy, and there was no appeal to the sympathy of the stranger. My companion said hurriedly,—

"Velly bad man; stealee heap from Chinamen," and then, apparently alarmed at his own indiscreet intrusion, hustled me away as quickly as possible amid a shrill cackling of protestation from a few of his own countrymen who had joined the one who was keeping guard. In another moment we were in the street again— scarce a step from the Plaza, in the full light of Western civilization—not a stone's throw from the courts of justice.

My companion took to his heels and left me standing there bewildered and indignant. I could not rest until I had told my story, but without betraying my companion, to an elder acquaintance, who laid the facts before the police authorities. I had expected to be closely cross-examined—to be doubted—to be disbelieved. To my surprise, I was told that the police had already cognizance of similar cases of illegal and barbarous punishments, but that the victims themselves refused to testify against their countrymen—and it was impossible to convict or even to identify them. "A white man can't tell one Chinese from another, and there are always a dozen of 'em ready to swear that the man you've got isn't the one." I was startled to reflect that I, too, could not have conscientiously sworn to either jailor or the tortured prisoner—or perhaps even to my cheerful companion. The police, on some pretext, made a raid upon the premises a day or two afterwards, but without result. I wondered if they had caught sight of the high-class, first-chop individual, with the helplessly outstretched fingers, as that story I had kept to myself.

But these barbaric vestiges in John Chinaman's habits did not affect his relations with the San Franciscans. He was singularly peaceful, docile, and harmless as a servant, and, with rare exceptions, honest and temperate. If he sometimes matched cunning with cunning, it was the flattery of imitation. He did most of the menial work of San Francisco, and did it cleanly. Except that he exhaled a peculiar druglike odor, he was not personally offensive in domestic contact, and by virtue of being the recognized laundryman of the whole community his own blouses were always freshly washed and ironed. His conversational reserve arose, not from his having to deal with an unfamiliar language,—for he had picked up a picturesque and varied vocabulary with ease,—but from his natural temperament. He was devoid of curiosity, and utterly unimpressed by anything but the purely business concerns of those he served. Domestic secrets were safe with him; his indifference to your thoughts, actions, and feelings had all the contempt which his three thousand years of history and his innate belief in your inferiority seemed to justify. He was blind and deaf in your household because you didn't interest him in the least. It was said that a gentleman, who wished to test his impassiveness, arranged with his wife to come home one day and, in the hearing of his Chinese waiter—who was more than usually intelligent—to disclose with well-simulated emotion the details of a murder he had just committed. He did so. The Chinaman heard it without a sign of horror or attention even to the lifting of an eyelid, but continued his duties unconcerned. Unfortunately, the gentleman, in order to increase the horror of the situation, added that now there was nothing left for him but to cut his throat. At this John quietly left the room. The gentleman was delighted at the success of his ruse until the door reopened and John reappeared with his master's razor, which he quietly slipped—as if it had been a forgotten fork—beside his master's plate, and calmly resumed his serving. I have always considered this story to be quite as improbable as it was inartistic, from its tacit admission of a certain interest on the part of the Chinaman. *I* never knew one who would have been sufficiently concerned to go for the razor.

His taciturnity and reticence may have been confounded with rudeness of address, although he was always civil enough. "I see you have listened to me and done exactly what I told you," said a lady, commending some performance of her servant after a previous lengthy lecture; "that's very nice." "Yes," said John calmly, "you talkee allee time; talkee allee too much." "I always find Ling very polite," said another lady, speaking of her cook, "but I wish he did not always say to me, 'Good-night, John,' in a high falsetto voice." She had not recognized the fact that he was simply repeating her own salutation with his marvelous instinct of relentless imitation, even as to voice. I hesitate to record the endless stories of his misapplication of that faculty which were then current, from the one of the laundryman who removed the buttons from the shirts that were sent to him to wash that they might agree with the condition of the one offered him as a pattern for "doing up," to that of the unfortunate employer who, while showing John how to handle valuable china carefully, had the misfortune to drop a plate himself—an accident which was followed by the prompt breaking of another by the neophyte, with the addition of "Oh, hellee!" in humble imitation of his master.

I have spoken of his general cleanliness; I am reminded of one or two exceptions, which I think, however, were errors of zeal. His manner of sprinkling clothes in preparing them for ironing was peculiar. He would fill his mouth with perfectly pure water from a glass beside him, and then, by one dexterous movement of his lips in a prolonged expiration, squirt the water in an almost invisible misty shower on the article before him. Shocking as this was at first to the sensibilities of many American employers, it was finally accepted, and even commended. It was some time after this that the mistress of a household, admiring the deft way in which her cook had spread a white sauce on certain dishes, was cheerfully informed that the method was "allee same."

His recreations at that time were chiefly gambling, for the Chinese theater wherein the latter produced his plays (which lasted for several months and comprised the events of a whole dynasty) was not yet built. But he had one or two companies of jugglers who occasionally performed also at American theaters. I remember a singular incident which attended the début of a newly arrived company. It seemed that the company had been taken on their Chinese reputation solely, and there had been no previous rehearsal before the American stage manager. The theater was filled with an audience of decorous and respectable San Franciscans of both sexes. It was suddenly emptied in the middle of the performance; the curtain came down with an alarmed and blushing manager apologizing to deserted benches, and the show abruptly terminated. Exactly *what* had happened never appeared in the public papers, nor in the published apology of the manager. It afforded a few days' mirth for wicked San Francisco, and it was epigrammatically summed up in the remark that "no woman could be found in San Francisco who was at that performance, and no man who was not."[10] Yet it was alleged even by John's worst detractors that he was innocent of any intended offense. Equally innocent, but perhaps more morally instructive, was an incident that brought his career as a singularly successful physician to a disastrous close. An ordinary native Chinese doctor, practicing entirely among his own countrymen, was reputed to have made extraordinary cures with two or three American patients. With no other advertising than this, and apparently no other inducement offered to the public than what their curiosity suggested, he was presently besieged by hopeful and eager sufferers. Hundreds of patients were turned away from his crowded doors. Two interpreters sat, day and night, translating the ills of ailing San Francisco to this medical oracle, and dispensing his prescriptions—usually small powders—in exchange for current coin. In vain the regular practitioners pointed out that the Chinese possessed no superior med-

ical knowledge, and that their religion, which proscribed dissec-
tion and autopsies, naturally limited their understanding of the
body into which they put their drugs. Finally they prevailed upon
an eminent Chinese authority to give them a list of the remedies
generally used in the Chinese pharmacopoeia, and this was privately circulated. For obvious reasons I may not repeat it here.
But it was summed up—again after the usual Californian epigrammatic style—by the remark that "whatever were the comparative
merits of Chinese and American practice, a simple perusal of
the list would prove that the Chinese were capable of producing
the most powerful emetic known." The craze subsided in a single
day; the interpreters and their oracle vanished; the Chinese doctors' signs, which had multiplied, disappeared, and San Francisco
awoke cured of its madness, at the cost of some thousand dollars.

My Bohemian wanderings were confined to the limits of the
city, for the very good reason that there was little elsewhere to go.
San Francisco was then bounded on one side by the monotonously restless waters of the bay, and on the other by a stretch of
equally restless and monotonously shifting sand dunes as far as
the Pacific shore. Two roads penetrated this waste: one to Lone
Mountain—the cemetery; the other to the Cliff House—happily
described as "an eight-mile drive with a cocktail at the end of it."
Nor was the humor entirely confined to this felicitous description.
The Cliff House itself, half restaurant, half drinking saloon,
fronting the ocean and the Seal Rock, where disporting seals were
the chief object of interest, had its own peculiar symbol. The de-
canters, wine-glasses, and tumblers at the bar were all engraved in
old English script with the legal initials "L.S." (*Locus Sigilli*),—
"the place of the seal."

On the other hand, Lone Mountain, a dreary promontory giving upon the Golden Gate and its striking sunsets, had little to
soften its weird suggestiveness. As the common goal of the successful and unsuccessful, the carved and lettered shaft of the man
who had made a name, and the staring blank headboard of the
man who had none, climbed the sandy slopes together. I have seen
the funerals of the respectable citizen who had died peacefully in
his bed, and the notorious desperado who had died "with his
boots on," followed by an equally impressive cortége of sorrow-
ing friends, and often the self-same priest. But more awful than its

barren loneliness was the utter absence of peacefulness and rest in this dismal promontory. By some wicked irony of its situation and climate it was the personification of unrest and change. The incessant trade winds carried its loose sands hither and thither, uncovering the decaying coffins of early pioneers, to bury the wreaths and flowers, laid on a grave of to-day, under their obliterating waves. No tree to shade them from the glaring sky above could live in those winds, no turf would lie there to resist the encroaching sand below. The dead were harried and hustled even in their graves by the persistent sun, the unremitting wind, and the unceasing sea. The departing mourner saw the contour of the very mountain itself change with the shifting dunes as he passed, and his last look beyond rested on the hurrying, eager waves forever hastening to the Golden Gate.

If I were asked to say what one thing impressed me as the dominant and characteristic note of San Francisco, I should say it was this untiring presence of sun and wind and sea. They typified, even if they were not, as I sometimes fancied, the actual incentive to the fierce, restless life of the city. I could not think of San Francisco without the trade winds; I could not imagine its strange, incongruous, multigenerous procession marching to any other music. They were always there in my youthful recollections; they were there in my more youthful dreams of the past as the mysterious *vientes generales*[11] that blew the Philippine galleons home.

For six months they blew from the northwest, for six months from the southwest, with unvarying persistency. They were there every morning, glittering in the equally persistent sunlight, to chase the San Franciscan from his slumber; they were there at midday, to stir his pulses with their beat; they were there again at night, to hurry him through the bleak and flaring gas-lit streets to bed. They left their mark on every windward street or fence or gable, on the outlying sand dunes; they lashed the slow coasters home, and hurried them to sea again; they whipped the bay into turbulence on their way to Contra Costa, whose level shoreland oaks they had trimmed to windward as cleanly and sharply as with a pruning-shears. Untiring themselves, they allowed no laggards; they drove the San Franciscan from the wall against which he would have leaned, from the scant shade in which at noontide he might have rested. They turned his smallest fires into conflagrations, and kept him ever alert, watchful, and eager. In return, they scavenged his city and held it clean and wholesome; in summer they brought him the soft sea-fog for a few hours to soothe his abraded surfaces; in winter they brought the rains and dashed the whole coast-line with flowers, and the staring sky above it with soft, unwonted clouds. They were always there—strong, vigilant, relentless, material, unyielding, triumphant.

Jan. 1900

EXPLANATORY NOTES

"The Legend of Monte del Diablo"

1. *ayuntamientos* and *juntas*: Councils and meetings.
2. Serra: Father Junipero Serra (1713–1784), Spanish Jesuit monk and founder of the California missions after his arrival in the New World in 1767.
3. one zealous Padre: Probably Fermín Francisco de Lasuén (1720?–1803), Serra's successor as governor of the California missions.
4. Salamanca: An ancient university town northwest of Madrid.
5. Las Casas and Balboa: Bartolomé de Las Casas (1474–1566), Spanish missionary in New Spain. Vasco Núñez de Balboa (c. 1475–1519), Spanish conquistador and the first European to gaze upon the Pacific Ocean.
6. Ophir of Solomon: A gold-producing region often mentioned in the Old Testament (e.g., I Kings 9:28; I Kings 22:48; II Chronicles 8:18; II Chronicles 9:10).
7. protection of St. Ignatius: Ignatius of Loyola (1491–1556), Spanish monk, founder of the Society of Jesus.
8. *madroño*: Arbutus.
9. arquebuse: An early portable gun, fired by a matchlock and trigger.
10. *ave*: Ave Maria or Hail Mary.
11. *Diablo*: Devil or fiend.
12. *chimisal* bushes: Sometimes known as "chimisa grass," a type of desert shrub.
13. bosky *cañada* or bosque *cañada*: A narrow, wooded canyon.
14. *Angelus*: Prayer bell.
15. *hidalgo*: Nobleman.
16. "the heathen": This quotation attributed to St. Ignatius is so "discreet" Harte apparently invented it.
17. the likeness of a comely damsel: According to St. Athanasius' life of St. Anthony the Abbot (250–355), Satan once masqueraded as a woman to tempt the founder of monasticism.
18. paternoster: The Lord's Prayer.
19. cross of Santiago: A red cross in the form of a sword, an emblem on the coat of arms of the Knights of Santiago, founded in the 12th cen-

tury as a military-religious order. Santiago was the shortened Spanish form of St. James, patron saint of Spain.

20. Castile and Aragon: Regions of Spain united in 1516 during the reign of Charles I of Spain and V of the Holy Roman Empire (1500–1558).

21. thrust the Moor from Granada: Mohammedan Spain consisted of several small Arab states in the early Middle Ages, among them Granada. After a series of military defeats, the Moors were expelled from Spain in the 13th century.

22. Alonzo de Ojeda: (1468?–1515), Spanish explorer who accompanied Columbus on his second voyage (1493) and explored the northern coast of South America in 1499. As Governor of New Andalucía (modern Colombia), he was infamous as an oppressor of natives.

23. Ishmaelites: Outcasts and wanderers.

24. Styx: The river encircling Hell.

25. Sathanas: Satan.

26. *varas*: Rods.

27. *caballero*: Gentleman.

"The Luck of Roaring Camp"

1. *ab initio*: From the first.

2. "city of refuge": Such a sanctuary was the subject of a long biblical tradition. See Numbers 35:26–27; Deuteronomy 19:1–12; Joshua 20:2; and Hebrews 11:10–16.

3. Raphael: (1483–1520), Master painter of the Italian Renaissance.

4. Hamlet: The indecisive hero of Shakespeare's tragedy *Hamlet* (1602).

5. Romulus and Remus: Twin brothers who founded Rome, according to Roman legend, and who had been raised by wolves.

6. *ex officio*: By virtue of office.

7. derringer: A short-barreled, high-caliber pistol, one of which was famously used by John Wilkes Booth to assassinate Abraham Lincoln in 1865. Named for its American inventor Henry Derringer (1806–1868).

8. Arethusa: A Greek nymph.

"The Outcasts of Poker Flat"

1. Mother Shipton: A legendary medieval English prophetess best known in the 1860s for having predicted the Second Coming of Christ and the end of the world in 1881.

2. Parthian volley: The Parthians of first-century Asia pretended flight before turning on their enemies.

3. Piney Woods: Harte invokes the title of *Piney Woods Tavern; or, Sam*

Slick in Texas (1858) by the southwestern humorist Samuel Adams Hammett (1816–1865), aka "Philip Paxton."

4. *sotto voce*: Under the voice or in an undertone.

5. *cachéd*: Stored or hidden in a cache.

6. Covenanter's swing: The militant 17th-century Scottish Covenanters demanded separation from the Church of England.

7. "I'm proud to live in the service of the Lord,/And I'm bound to die in His army": The refrain to "Service of the Lord," an early American spiritual.

8. Pope's translation of Iliad: The neo-classical translation of Homer's *Iliad* by the English poet Alexander Pope (1688–1744) appeared in six installments between 1715 and 1720.

9. Peleus: In Greek myth, the father of Achilles.

10. Achilles: Greek hero of the Trojan War.

"Miggles"

1. Washoe: Silver mining region in western Nevada.

2. "rock of refuge": Psalm 31:1–16.

3. "sere and yellow leaf": "My way of life / Is fall'n into the sear, the yellow leaf" (*Macbeth* V, iii, 22–23).

4. Caliban bearing logs for this Miranda: The deformed slave Caliban is pardoned by the magician Prospero, father of Miranda, at the close of Shakespeare's *The Tempest* (1611). A more likely source for Harte's allusion is Robert Browning's poem "Caliban Upon Setebos" (1864): while "Prosper and Miranda sleep / In confidence he drudges at their task" (lines 20–21).

5. *Ursa Minor*: The "lesser bear" constellation, also the Little Dipper with the star at the end of the handle marking the north celestial pole.

6. Una and her lion: The heroine and her protector in the first book of the allegorical epic *The Faerie Queen* (1590) by Edmund Spenser (1552?–1599).

7. Memnon: The king of Ethiopia, according to Greek mythology, who though killed by Achilles during the Trojan War, is immortalized by Zeus.

8. "the feet of him she loved": Mary Magdelene anoints the feet of Jesus (John 12:3).

"Tennessee's Partner"

1. saleratus: Baking soda.

2. *chaparral*: A thicket of shrubs.

"The Idyl of Red Gulch"

1. Samson and Delilah: Delilah caused Samson to "shave off the seven locks of his head; and she began to afflict him, and his strength went from him" (Judges 16:19).
2. rescuer Adolphus: Probably Gustavus II Adolphus (1594–1632), king of Sweden who resisted the imperial designs of Germany during the Thirty Years War.

"Brown of Calavaras"

1. "Nelly's grave": In George F. Root's sentimental ballad "The Hazel Dell" (1853), a grieving lover observes that "the silent stars are nightly weeping, / O'er poor Nelly's grave."
2. Sister Anne's "flock of sheep": In the popular nursery tale "Blue Beard," the character of Sister Anne mistakenly believes a cloud of dust on the horizon has been raised by a flock of sheep.

"Mr. Thompson's Prodigal"

1. "Enter ye the narrer gate": Christ's words in Matthew 7:13.
2. hic jacets: Hic jacet or "here lies," an inscription on a tombstone.
3. "eat, drink, and be merry": In Christ's parable of the prodigal son, the father orders his servants to "bring hither the fatted calf, and kill it; and let us eat, and be merry; for this my son was dead, and is alive again, and is found" (Luke 15:2–24).
4. house on the sand-hills: An apparent allusion to Christ's words in Matthew 7:26–27 about the "foolish man" who "built his house upon the sand: And the rain descended, and the floods came, and the winds blew, and beat upon the house; and it fell."
5. Doxology: A hymn of praise to God.
6. "peace that passeth understanding": "And the peace of God, which passeth all understanding, shall keep your hearts and minds through Christ" (Philippians 4:7).
7. "Knock, and it shall be opened to you": Christ's words in Matthew 7:7.
8. "By their works shall ye know them": Christ's words in Matthew 7:16.

"The Iliad of Sandy Bar"

1. sabe: Know or understand.
2. Arcadia: A region of rustic simplicity and pastoral ease.

3. Pactolian resources: That is, gold. According to Greek myth, the river Pactolus contained the gold King Midas washed away. The river was also the source of King Croesus' wealth.
4. fatal quicksands: See note 4 to "Mr. Thompson's Prodigal."
5. Hector arose from the ditch: In Homer's *Iliad*, the hero of the siege of Troy who, after he is hurled to the ground by Ajax, is revived by Apollo.

"The Poet of Sierra Flat"

1. *protégé*: Literally, "under the protection," hence a student or follower.
2. Byron, Moore, Tennyson: George Gordon, Lord Byron (1788–1824), English romantic poet; Thomas Moore (1779–1852), Irish poet and Byron's biographer; Alfred Lord Tennyson (1809–1892), English poet and poet laureate from 1850 until his death.
3. John Milton: (1608–1674), English Puritan, author of *Paradise Lost* (1667).
4. *ennui*: Boredom.
5. Longfellow: Henry Wadsworth Longfellow (1807–1882), American poet. Longfellow was "the man I most revered," Harte allowed in his memoir of the poet ("Longfellow," *Good Words*, 23 [June 1882], 385–387).
6. Browning: Robert Browning (1812–1889), English poet. See also Scharnhorst, "Browning and Bret Harte," *ANQ*, ns 12 (Summer 1999), 41–43.
7. *gamin*: A street urchin.

"How Santa Claus Came to Simpson's Bar"

1. *tules*: Large bulrushes found in southwestern lakes and marshes.
2. Jim Smiley: Also the name of the victim whose frog is filled with quailshot in Mark Twain's "Jim Smiley and His Jumping Frog" (1865).
3. "red herons": Red herrings.
4. childblains: Chilblains; that is, sores or festers.
5. *pasear*: Walk or hike.
6. *riata*: Lariat.
7. "Excelsior": In Longfellow's poem (1841), a young man of genius resists an invitation as he runs through an Alpine village: "Oh, stay," the maiden said, "and rest / Thy weary head upon this breast!" He is afterwards found dead from an avalanche.

"Wan Lee, the Pagan"

1. devil: Printer's assistant.
2. Confucius and Mencius: Ancient Chinese teachers. In 1867 Harte had reviewed *Confucius and the Chinese Classics*, edited by A.W. Loomis and published by Anton Roman of San Francisco, for the *Springfield Republican*: "Here are the Chinese classics comprising Mencius, Confucius, Buddhist tracts and poetry—the profound wisdom of the ancient East, composed, stereotyped, printed and bound in this modern city of the West" (*Bret Harte's California: Letters to the Springfield Republican and Christian Register, 1866–67,* ed. Gary Scharnhorst [Albuquerque: Univ. of New Mexico Press, 1990], p. 141).
3. *tour de force*: An exceptional feat.
4. "godlike Webster": Daniel Webster (1782–1852), American politician and statesman.
5. "sad and civil": Olivia's description of Malvolio in Shakespeare's *Twelfth Night* (III, iv, 5).
6. "eminent statesmen": Harte refers ironically to local politicians who advocated restricted Chinese immigration, such as Henry H. Haight (1825–1878), who was elected California governor in 1867; and Eugene Casserly (1820–1883), U.S. senator from California between 1869 and 1873. See also *Bret Harte's California*, pp. 122, 126, 128–129, 137.
7. "stoned to death": In a letter to the *Springfield Republican* in February 1867, Harte reported in detail on the "late riots and outrages on the Chinese. . . . To throw stones at a Chinaman was a youthful pastime of great popularity, and was to a certain extent recognized and encouraged by parents and guardians, as long as the stones went to their mark with accuracy, and did not come in contact with a superior civilization" (*Bret Harte's California*, p. 113). Similarly, Harte wrote over a year later that the "youth of the metropolis, early taught his social status, throw stones at [the Chinese] in the street" ("From California," *Springfield Republican*, 8 April 1868, 2:5).

"An Ingénue of the Sierras"

1. "Lethean stream": In Greek myth, the river of forgetfulness or oblivion that flows through Hades.
2. Pike Country girl: A character-type in American humor, an ignorant Western immigrant from Pike County (wherever that may be) who speaks in dialect and is often the target of jokes.
3. "bucked agin the tiger": "Gambled at faro" (Harte's note).

"Three Vagabonds of Trinidad"

1. Elijah: Hebrew prophet who ascends from earth in a chariot of fire (II Kings 2:11).
2. M'Cormick's reapers: Cyrus H. McCormick (1809–1884) perfected the grain reaper in 1831, patented it in 1834, and moved his company to Chicago in 1847 to manufacture it.
3. manifest destiny: Jingoistic phrase suggesting the U.S. should occupy the whole of the North American continent.
4. "Hebraic face": Harte, whose paternal grandfather Henry Hart was an orthodox Jew, often associated Indians and Jews in his fiction. See also Margaret Duckett, "Bret Harte's Portrayal of Half-Breeds," *American Literature*, 25 (May 1953), 59–83.

"A Pupil of Chestnut Ridge"

1. Papists and followers of the Scarlet Woman: Roman Catholics and adulterers. According to Revelation 17:4–5, the Scarlet Woman was the "mother of harlots and abominations of the earth."
2. "a brand from the burnin'": "ye were as a firebrand plucked out of the burning" (Amos 4:11).
3. " 'conviction o' sin' and 'justification by faith' ": Cardinal Protestant doctrines.
4. "Dissenters' camp meeting": An evangelical Protestant, probably Methodist, revival.
5. muchacha: Girl.
6. "*Camara para vestirse*": Dressing room.
7. vaquero: Cowboy.
8. "Quien sabe": Who knows.
9. *non sequitur*: An illogical conclusion.
10. "sincerest form of flattery": That is, imitation.
11. sembicuaca: An erotic dance.

"Muck-a-Muck"

1. Cooper: James Fenimore Cooper (1789–1851), author of the Leatherstocking Tales featuring the pioneer scout Natty Bumppo.
2. Van Dyke, Rubens, Tintoretto, Michael Angelo, Turner, Kensett, Church, Bierstadt: Sir Anthony Van Dyke (1599–1641), Flemish religious and portrait painter; Peter Paul Rubens (1577–1640), the most prominent member of the Flemish school; Tintoretto (1518–1594), one of the masters of the Venetian Renaissance; Michelangelo Buonarroti (1475–1564), the master of the Italian Renaissance;

J.M.W. Turner (1775–1851), English landscape painter; John Frederick Kensett (1818–1872), American landscape painter of the Hudson River School; Frederick Edwin Church (1826–1900), American landscape painter of the Hudson River School; Albert Bierstadt (1830–1902), American landscape painter. Harte had known Bierstadt in California in the 1860s. See *Bret Harte's California*, p. 133.

3. *écritoire*: Writing case or desk.

4. *moire antique* robe trimmed with *tulle*: An old-fashioned, patterned robe trimmed with fine netting.

5. Sachem Andy: Andrew Johnson (1808–1875), seventeenth President of the United States (1865–1869).

6. "Westward the Star": Quotation from the "Oration at Plymouth" (1802), by John Quincy Adams (1767–1848), sixth President of the United States.

"The Haunted Man"

1. title: Both the title of this "condensed novel" and its situation mimic Charles Dickens's final Christmas tale, "The Haunted Man and the Ghost's Bargain" (1848). Harte also parodies Dickens's most popular Christmas story, *A Christmas Carol* (1843).

2. Ch—r—s D—ck—n—s: Charles Dickens (1812–1870), English novelist. See also Joseph H. Gardner, "Bret Harte and the Dickensian Mode in America," *Canadian Review of American Studies*, 2 (Fall 1971), 89–101.

3. "model infant": Harte alludes to the death of young Paul Dombey in Dickens's novel *Dombey and Son* (1846–1848).

4. "good woman, undersized": Harte alludes to the death of old Betty Higden in Dickens's novel *Our Mutual Friend* (1863).

5. Astley's: Astley's Royal Amphitheatre, opened as a riding school in 1768.

6. Noble Savage: A tenet of primitivism, which held that human nature is essentially good in a state of nature. During the 18th and early 19th centuries, the American Indian epitomized for many European and American intellectuals all that the "noble savage" ought to be—honorable, graceful, vigorous, brave, dignified.

7. Catlin: George Catlin (1796–1872) made several excursions to the West between 1830–1836 and executed over a hundred paintings on Indian subjects. He also published *Letters and Notes on the Manners, Customs, and Conditions of North American Indians* (1844).

8. Scarlet Letters: Harte alludes to *Mosses from an Old Manse* (1846) and *The Scarlet Letter* (1850) by the American romancer Nathaniel

Hawthorne (1804–1864), about the consequences of sin in 17th-century Boston.

9. Steele, Addison, and Congreve: Joseph Addison (1672–1719), English essayist, poet, and playwright; Richard Steele (1672–1729), English editor, essayist, and playwright; William Congreve (1670–1729), English playwright. Addison was a frequent contributor to literary journals edited by his friend Steele, including the twice-weekly *Tatler* (1709–1711) and the daily *Spectator* (1711–1712, 1714).

10. Vanity Fair: Satirical novel by William Makepeace Thackeray (1811–1863), English novelist.

11. Tiny Tim: A crippled young boy in Dickens's *A Christmas Carol*.

12. *David Copperfield*: Dickens's 1850 novel.

13. *The Old Curiosity Shop*: Dickens's 1840–1841 novel.

14. "Our Mutual Friend": See note 4 above.

"The Stolen Cigar Case"

1. Hemlock Jones: A parodic type of Sherlock Holmes, the detective-hero of a series of stories by Sir Arthur Conan Doyle (1859–1930). After Harte's death in 1902, Doyle contributed to a fund to support his widow Anna (1832–1920) and younger daughter Ethel (1875–1964).

2. Paul Ferroll: The Victorian mystery novel *Why Paul Ferroll Killed His Wife* (1860) by Caroline Wigley Clive (1801–1873).

3. Jones: The Victorian play *What Happened to Jones: An Original Farce in Three Acts* (1897) by George H. Broadhurst (1866–1952).

"To the Pliocene Skull"

1. "This extraordinary fossil is in the possession of Prof. Josiah D. Whitney, of the State Geological Survey of California. The poem was based on the following paragraph from the daily press of 1866: 'A human skull has been found in California, in the pliocene formation. This skull is the remnant not only of the earliest pioneer of this State, but the oldest known human being. . . . The skull was found in a shaft 150 feet deep, two miles from Angels in Calaveras County, by a miner named James Watson, who gave it to Mr. Scribner, a merchant, who gave it to Dr. Jones, who sent it to the State Geological Survey. . . . ' The published volume of the State Survey of the Geology of California states that man existed here contemporaneously with the mastodon, but this fossil proves that he was here before the mastodon was known to exist" (Harte's note). See also *Bret Harte's California*, pp. 62–63.

2. "*pieuvre* of Victor Hugo": Pew-oeuvre, a pun on "oeuvre," or body of work. Harte refers to the ostensible stench of Hugo's stories.

"The Society Upon the Stanislaus"

1. Harte's original title for this poem was "Proceedings of the Academy of Natural Sciences at Smith's Crossing/Tuolumne County."

"Plain Language from Truthful James"

1. "twenty-four packs": Sometimes misprinted "twenty-four jacks."

"Dickens in Camp"

1. "Little Nell": A young character who dies toward the close of Dickens's *The Old Curiosity Shop* (1840–1841).

"That Ebrew Jew"

1. "Speech on the Mount": Christ's Sermon on the Mount (Matthew 5–7).
2. "great Luther": Martin Luther (1483–1546), German leader of the Protestant Reformation.
3. John Morrissey: (1831–1878), prizefighter and popular Irish politician, congressman from New York, and the subject of a satirical essay signed "B.H." in the San Francisco *Alta California*, 11 November 1866, 2:2.
4. Madame N.N.: Perhaps the character of Madame Nathan, who appears in at least ten of Balzac's stories. A promiscuous woman who was nevertheless "respectable."
5. Miss McFlimsey: The popular poem "Nothing to Wear" (1857) by William Allen Butler (1825–1902) satirized the pretensions of the socialite Flora M'Flimsy.
6. Van Dams: An old Dutch patroon family in New York.
7. Miss Décolleté: Literally, Miss Bare Shoulders. The term refers to a style of gown that leaves the neck and shoulders bare.
8. Disraeli and Rothschild: Prominent Jewish political and financial leaders. Benjamin Disraeli (1804–1881), novelist and British prime minister. Baron Lionel Nathan de Rothschild (1808–1879).
9. Meyerbeer and Verdi: Prominent composers. While Giacomo Meyerbeer (1791–1864) was Jewish, Harte errs in implying that Giuseppe Verdi (1813–1901) was also Jewish.

10. "foxes had holes": "And Jesus said to him, 'Foxes have holes and birds of the air have nests, but the Son of Man has nowhere to lay his head' " (Matthew 8:20).

"Free Silver at Angel's"

1. "going soon to par": Reaching its assigned value.
2. "crucified upon a cross of gold": In a speech at the Democratic National Convention in 1896, William Jennings Byran appealed for "free silver" or bimetallism, concluding that "You shall not press down upon the brow of labor this crown of thorns, you shall not crucify mankind upon a cross of gold."
3. sixteen to one: The ratio of silver to gold favored by the advocates of "free silver" or bimetallism.

"The Argonauts of '49"

1. Rio de Los Reyes: River of the kings.
2. De Fonte: Harte confuses Bartholomew de Fonte with Juan de Fuca (see note 4 below). De Fuca claimed in 1596 that he had sailed up the Pacific coast in 1592 and discovered the Strait of Anian, a passage through North America.
3. Maldonado: In 1609, Lorenzo Maldonado claimed that in 1588 he had entered the strait near Labrador and sailed to Acapulco.
4. Another Spanish discoverer: According to Charles Chapman (*A History of California: The Spanish Period* [New York: Macmillan, 1925], pp. 75–76), Bartholomew de Fonte "is supposed to have made his voyage in 1640, though both Fonte and the story were invented in 1708. . . . These reputed voyages are entirely discredited now, but they had a tremendous influence on explorations."
5. Sir Francis Drake: (1540?–1596), English explorer and buccaneer who sailed up the west coast of North America in the *Golden Hind* in 1579.
6. Sancho Panza: The peasant squire in Cervantes's satirical romance *Don Quixote* (1605, 1615).
7. alcalde: Mayor.
8. gay Lothario: A rake or seducer of women.
9. Sutter's Mill: Named for John Sutter (1803–1880), the site of the discovery of gold near Sacramento, California, in 1848.
10. Brigham Young: (1801–1877), Mormon leader who led their migration to Nauvoo, Illinois, and then to the Great Basin of Utah in 1846–47.

11. golden fleece: According to Greek mythology, Jason and the sailors aboard the ship *Argo* sought the fleece of the ram that carried Phrixus and Helle from Boeotia.

12. Pizarro: Francisco Pizarro (c. 1476–1541), Spanish conquistador, conquerer of Peru.

13. foundations: Harte had mentioned this detail twice earlier in his career, first in a letter to the *Springfield Republican* in August 1866: "I remember, several years ago, to have been shown the foundations of a house near one of the wharves built up on boxes of plug tobacco, which, at the time it was laid, was worth less than the necessary, though scarcer, timber. It had been of course ruined by salt water" (*Bret Harte's California*, p. 64). Soon after his arrival in Boston in the spring of 1871, he again told Annie Fields, the wife of his publisher, the story of the block of early San Francisco houses "laid on boxes of tobacco" (M.A. DeWolfe Howe, *Memories of a Hostess* [Boston: Atlantic Monthly Press, 1922], p. 234).

14. commission for Macbeth in which Banquo was concerned: In Shakespeare's tragedy *Macbeth*, witches prophesize that the hero will become King of Scotland but that Banquo's heirs would eventually hold the throne. In an attempt to prevent the realization of the prophecy, Macbeth commissions two murderers to kill Banquo in Act III, scene 1.

15. semaphore telegraph: The signal-telegraph that utilized flags atop what came to be known as Telegraph Hill in San Francisco.

16. Circean palace: In Greek myth, Circe was an enchantress who turned Odysseus' men into swine.

17. lovelocks of Charles II: The "Merry Monarch" (1630–1685), King of England after the death of Cromwell and the Restoration of 1660 until his death.

18. Delaroche's Savior: A painting by the artist Hippolyte Delaroche (1797–1856).

19. Meissonier: Juste Aurèle Meissonier (1695–1750), a French goldsmith and rococo designer.

20. Danaë-like shower of gold: In Greek myth, the imprisoned Danaë, daughter of Acrisius, is visited by Zeus in a shower of gold and impregnated.

21. Sanitary Commission: A forerunner of the American Red Cross. Mark Twain recounts a similar story in chapter XLV of *Roughing It* (1872).

22. great fire in Sacramento: In fact, there had been two conflagrations. In November 1852 a fire had destroyed two-thirds of the buildings in Sacramento, and in July 1854 a second fire had destroyed some 200 buildings.

23. Damon and Pythias: Two young Syracusan men whose loyalty epitomizes genuine friendship.
24. Blair's Rhetoric: Hugh Blair's *Lectures on Rhetoric and Belles Lettres* (1783) or *Essays on Rhetoric* (1784).
25. "took every trick": Harte's friend and mentor Thomas Starr King (1824–1864), minister of the First Unitarian Church in San Francisco, arrived in California in April 1860. Harte recounted the same anecdote in a letter to the Boston *Christian Register* dated 14 July 1866 (*Bret Harte's California*, p. 66).
26. Mission Dolores: The first church in San Francisco, founded in June 1776.
27. "Jimtown": Mary Austin realistically rewrites Harte in her essay "Jimville: A Bret Harte Town," *Atlantic Monthly*, 90 (November 1902), 690–694.
28. Charles V of Spain: (1500–1558). Actually king of Spain as Charles I after 1516 and emperor Charles V of the Holy Roman Empire after 1519, who inherited all Spanish lands and all the hereditary lands of the Hapsburgs.
29. *diseños*: Sketches or designs.
30. *fandango*: A lively Spanish dance.
31. *aguardiente*: Liquor.
32. Serra: See note 2 to "The Legend of Monte del Diablo."
33. Hygeian temple: Hygeia, the Greek goddess of health.
34. Apollo: The Greek god of medicine.
35. Sindbad: The legendary sailor in *One Thousand and One Nights* or the *Arabian Nights' Entertainments*.

"The Rise of the 'Short Story'"

1. Edgar Allan Poe: (1809–1849), American writer.
2. Hawthorne: See note 8 to "The Haunted Man" above.
3. Washington Irving: (1783–1859), American writer, author of *The Sketch-Book* (1819).
4. Addison, Steele, Lamb: Charles Lamb (1775–1834), English essayist, poet, and critic. See also note 9 to "The Haunted Man."
5. "Rosamund Gray": Lamb's *A Tale of Rosamund Gray and Old Blind Margaret* (1798).
6. Sam Slick: A comic Yankee peddler, a character created by the Canadian author Thomas Chandler Haliburton (1796–1865).
7. Judd's Margaret: *Margaret: a Tale of the Real and the Ideal* (1845) by the Unitarian minister Sylvester Judd (1813–1853).
8. "Who reads an American book?": The English aphorist Sidney Smith posed the derisive question in 1820: "And who, the wide world over, reads an American book?"

9. Artemus Ward: Pseudonym of the Down East dialect humorist Charles Farrar Browne (1834–1867).

10. Hosea Biglow: The narrator of James Russell Lowell's satirical verses "The Biglow Papers" (1846, 1867), the first series written to oppose the Mexican War and the second to support the Union during the Civil War.

11. Topsy and Miss Ophelia: Characters in Harriet Beecher Stowe's anti-slavery novel *Uncle Tom's Cabin* (1851–52).

12. *The Man Without a Country*: A patriotic story by Edward Everett Hale published in the *Atlantic Monthly* in December 1863.

13. Squibob Papers: A collection of Western humor writings (1865) by George H. Derby (1823–1861), aka "John Phoenix."

14. Mark Twain: Pseudonym of Samuel L. Clemens (1835–1910). Harte and Clemens met in California in 1864. Harte reminisced later that Clemens told him the story of "Jim Smiley and His Jumping Frog" before he submitted it for publication (Henry J.W. Dam, "A Morning with Bret Harte," *McClure's*, 4 [December 1894], 47–48). After publication of the sketch in the New York *Saturday Press*, Harte reprinted it in the *Californian* in December 1865. See especially Margaret Duckett's *Mark Twain and Bret Harte* (Norman: University of Oklahoma Press, 1964).

15. Major Bierce: The satirist Ambrose Bierce (1842–1914?), a Union officer and occasional contributor to the *Overland Monthly* during Harte's editorship. See also Stanley T. Williams, "Ambrose Bierce and Bret Harte," *American Literature*, 17 (May 1945), 179–180.

16. "foremost literary weeklies": Harte first contributed to the *Golden Era* in 1857 and joined the staff of the paper as a compositor in 1860. With C.H. Webb (1834–1905), he was a founding editor of the weekly *Californian* in 1864.

17. "The Pioneer": The first San Francisco literary magazine, established in 1854.

18. "Chandos picture of Shakespeare": Once owned by the Duke of Chandos, this portrait hangs in the National Portrait Gallery, London.

19. *Overland Monthly*: Magazine established in San Francisco in 1868 with Harte as founding editor to which he contributed several of his best-known works, including "The Luck of Roaring Camp," "The Outcasts of Poker Flat," "Tennessee's Partner," and "Plain Language from Truthful James."

20. "Centrepole Bill": George F. Emery's tale "Centrepole Bill" appeared in the *Overland Monthly*, 4 (January 1870), 83–88.

21. Harris: Joel Chandler Harris (1848–1908), author of the "Uncle Remus" stories.

22. Cable: George Washington Cable (1844–1925), author of *Old Creole Days* (1879).
23. Page: Thomas Nelson Page (1853–1922), author of *In Ole Virginia* (1887).
24. "Huckleberry Finn": Mark Twain's picaresque novel set in the antebellum South, published in England in 1884.
25. "Prophet of the Great Smoky Mountains": An 1885 novel by Mary Noailles Murfree (1850–1922), aka "Charles Egbert Craddock."
26. Miss Wilkins: Mary E. Wilkins (1852–1930), aka Mary E. Wilkins Freeman, author of such New England local color writings as *A Humble Romance and Other Stories* (1887), *A New England Nun and Other Stories* (1891), and *Pembroke* (1894).

"How I Went to the Mines"

1. "the little pioneer settlement school": Harte opened a "little bark-thatched" school on Dry Creek near the town of Sonora, California, in spring 1857 which he soon closed for lack of students. See "Francis Bret Harte," *Chicago Tribune*, 20 November 1870, p. 6.
2. "Jim": Jim Gillis (1830–1907). His brother Steve Gillis (1838–1918) offered an entirely different perspective on the events described in Harte's essay. He remembered that Harte appeared on foot one day at the Gillis brothers' claim on Jackass Hill near Tuttletown in Tuolumne County. "He came upon my brother Jim" just as he was "taking out a rich pocket of gold. Poor little Bret stood in the trail, dusty and tired and hungry and dead broke and looked down into my brother's pan which contained a good pile of free gold. Well, Jim took him in and kept him for four days" ("Gillis on Bret Harte," San Francisco *Town Talk*, 8 January 1915).

"Bohemian Days in San Francisco"

1. "ponderous editorial": After an earthquake rocked San Francisco on October 21, 1868, the local daily papers minimized the damage lest the news offend business leaders. Harte ridiculed such timidity in the next issue of the *Overland Monthly*: "Judging from the daily journals, [the earthquake] seems to have been complimentary to San Francisco. In fact, it has been suggested that, with a little more care and preparation on our part, the earthquake would have been very badly damaged in the encounter" ("Etc.," 1 [November 1868], 480).
2. "popular preachers": In a letter to the Boston *Christian Register* in late June 1866, Harte criticized the Reverend Andrew L. Stone (1815–1892) of the First Congregational Church of San Francisco for

politicizing the issue of Sunday worship: "the Doctor's remarks have only provoked raillery and opposition" (*Bret Harte's California*, pp. 47–49).

3. "stoned to death": See note 7 to "Wan Lee, the Pagan."

4. Niantic: The ship *Niantic*, after delivering 248 miners to San Francisco in July 1849, was run aground near the foot of Clay Street and converted into a storeship. The San Francisco fire of May 1851 left it little more than a charred hull. The Niantic Hotel was then erected upon its ruins. Harte appropriated such banalities in some of his late fiction. In the first chapter of "Trent's Trust" (1901), the hero upon his arrival in the city sees "the hull of a stranded ship already built into a block of rude tenements," and in "A Ship of '49" (1885) he embellished the legend of a lost treasure secreted somewhere aboard the ship/hotel.

5. boxes of plug tobacco: See note 13 to "The Argonauts of '49."

6. language of Cervantes: That is, Spanish. The novelist Miguel de Cervantes Saavedra (1547–1616) was the author of *Don Quixote*.

7. *habitué*: A person with a particular habit.

8. secretary of its superintendent: Harte was hired by the superintendent of the U.S. Mint in San Francisco, Robert B. Swain (1822–1872), in summer 1863 to serve as his assistant at a salary of $180 a month. He held the job for six years. In 1868 the sinecure paid him $270 a month and he directed a staff of twelve. The joke went around that he was paid a salary merely to sign his name twice a day.

9. See note 5 to "Wan Lee, the Pagan."

10. the performance: Harte misremembers a couple of points. In late September 1867, a troupe of Japanese, not Chinese, jugglers performed at the Metropolitan Theatre in San Francisco. As Harte reported at the time to the *Springfield Republican*, "One of the tricks—and a very ingenious one—was the spinning of two large tops which ascended an inclined plane, and then opened, disclosing, the one, a rabbit . . . and the other—but here I must seek safety in periphrasis. . . . Well, the other top disclosed what a prudish Neapolitan government to-day takes such pains to conceal" in Pompeii (that is, a phallus). "The petrified audience could not dodge the fact. Some few rose to leave the house, some audibly expressed their disgust, but a majority were astonished to silence" (*Bret Harte's California*, pp. 146–47). The episode was widely reported in the local press the next day, September 25, 1867: "an unpardonable vulgarity" (*Alta California*), an "indescribable vulgarity" (*Dramatic Chronicle*), "an indecency perhaps unparalleled on any stage" (*Evening Bulletin*).

11. *vientes generales*: Prevailing winds.

FOR THE BEST IN PAPERBACKS, LOOK FOR THE

In every corner of the world, on every subject under the sun, Penguin represents quality and variety—the very best in publishing today.

For complete information about books available from Penguin—including Puffins, Penguin Classics, and Compass—and how to order them, write to us at the appropriate address below. Please note that for copyright reasons the selection of books varies from country to country.

In the United Kingdom: Please write to *Dept. EP, Penguin Books Ltd, Bath Road, Harmondsworth, West Drayton, Middlesex UB7 0DA.*

In the United States: Please write to *Penguin Putnam Inc., P.O. Box 12289 Dept. B, Newark, New Jersey 07101-5289* or call 1-800-788-6262.

In Canada: Please write to *Penguin Books Canada Ltd, 10 Alcorn Avenue, Suite 300, Toronto, Ontario M4V 3B2.*

In Australia: Please write to *Penguin Books Australia Ltd, P.O. Box 257, Ringwood, Victoria 3134.*

In New Zealand: Please write to *Penguin Books (NZ) Ltd, Private Bag 102902, North Shore Mail Centre, Auckland 10.*

In India: Please write to *Penguin Books India Pvt Ltd, 11 Panchsheel Shopping Centre, Panchsheel Park, New Delhi 110 017.*

In the Netherlands: Please write to *Penguin Books Netherlands bv, Postbus 3507, NL-1001 AH Amsterdam.*

In Germany: Please write to *Penguin Books Deutschland GmbH, Metzlerstrasse 26, 60594 Frankfurt am Main.*

In Spain: Please write to *Penguin Books S. A., Bravo Murillo 19, 1° B, 28015 Madrid.*

In Italy: Please write to *Penguin Italia s.r.l., Via Benedetto Croce 2, 20094 Corsico, Milano.*

In France: Please write to *Penguin France, Le Carré Wilson, 62 rue Benjamin Baillaud, 31500 Toulouse.*

In Japan: Please write to *Penguin Books Japan Ltd, Kaneko Building, 2-3-25 Koraku, Bunkyo-Ku, Tokyo 112.*

In South Africa: Please write to *Penguin Books South Africa (Pty) Ltd, Private Bag X14, Parkview, 2122 Johannesburg.*